new moon

STEPHENIE MEYER

Megan Tingley Books
LITTLE, BROWN AND COMPANY
New York ❧ Boston

Little, Brown and Company

Hachette Book Group USA
1271 Avenue of the Americas, New York, NY 10020
Visit our Web site at www.lb-teens.com

First Edition: September 2006

Meyer, Stephenie, 1973–
New Moon : a novel / by Stephenie Meyer. — 1st ed.
p.   cm.
Summary: When the Cullens, including her beloved Edward,
leave Forks rather than risk revealing that they are vampires,
it is almost too much for eighteen-year-old Bella to bear,
but she finds solace in her friend Jacob until he is drawn
into a "cult" and changes in terrible ways.

ISBN-13: 978-0-316-16019-3
ISBN-10: 0-316-16019-9
[1. Vampires — Fiction. 2. Werewolves — Fiction. 3. High schools — Fiction.
4. Schools — Fiction. 5. Washington (State) — Fiction.] 1. Title.
PZ7.M57188New 2006
[Fic]—dc22   2006012309

20 19 18 17 16 15

Q-FF

Printed in the United States of America

For my dad, Stephen Morgan—
No one has ever been given more loving and unconditional
support than I have been given by you.
I love you, too.

◄◄ ►►

CONTENTS

*These violent delights have violent ends
And in their triumph die, like fire and powder,
Which, as they kiss, consume.*

Romeo and Juliet, *Act II, Scene VI*

PREFACE

I FELT LIKE I WAS TRAPPED IN ONE OF THOSE TERRIFYING nightmares, the one where you have to run, run till your lungs burst, but you can't make your body move fast enough. My legs seemed to move slower and slower as I fought my way through the callous crowd, but the hands on the huge clock tower didn't slow. With relentless, uncaring force, they turned inexorably toward the end—the end of everything.

But this was no dream, and, unlike the nightmare, I wasn't running for *my* life; I was racing to save something infinitely more precious. My own life meant little to me today.

Alice had said there was a good chance we would both

die here. Perhaps the outcome would be different if she weren't trapped by the brilliant sunlight; only I was free to run across this bright, crowded square.

And I couldn't run fast enough.

So it didn't matter to me that we were surrounded by our extraordinarily dangerous enemies. As the clock began to toll out the hour, vibrating under the soles of my sluggish feet, I knew I was too late—and I was glad something bloodthirsty waited in the wings. For in failing at this, I forfeited any desire to live.

The clock tolled again, and the sun beat down from the exact center point of the sky.

1. PARTY

I WAS NINETY-NINE POINT NINE PERCENT SURE I WAS dreaming.

The reasons I was so certain were that, first, I was standing in a bright shaft of sunlight—the kind of blinding clear sun that never shone on my drizzly new hometown in Forks, Washington—and second, I was looking at my Grandma Marie. Gran had been dead for six years now, so that was solid evidence toward the dream theory.

Gran hadn't changed much; her face looked just the same as I remembered it. The skin was soft and withered, bent into a thousand tiny creases that clung gently to the bone underneath. Like a dried apricot, but with a puff of thick white hair standing out in a cloud around it.

Our mouths—hers a wizened pucker—spread into the same surprised half-smile at just the same time. Apparently, she hadn't been expecting to see me, either.

I was about to ask her a question; I had so many— What was she doing here in my dream? What had she been up to in the past six years? Was Pop okay, and had they found each other, wherever they were?—but she opened her mouth when I did, so I stopped to let her go first. She paused, too, and then we both smiled at the little awkwardness.

"Bella?"

It wasn't Gran who called my name, and we both turned to see the addition to our small reunion. I didn't have to look to know who it was; this was a voice I would know anywhere—know, and respond to, whether I was awake or asleep . . . or even dead, I'd bet. The voice I'd walk through fire for—or, less dramatically, slosh every day through the cold and endless rain for.

Edward.

Even though I was always thrilled to see him—conscious or otherwise—and even though I was *almost* positive that I was dreaming, I panicked as Edward walked toward us through the glaring sunlight.

I panicked because Gran didn't know that I was in love with a vampire—nobody knew that—so how was I supposed to explain the fact that the brilliant sunbeams were shattering off his skin into a thousand rainbow shards like he was made of crystal or diamond?

Well, Gran, you might have noticed that my boyfriend glitters. It's just something he does in the sun. Don't worry about it. . . .

What was he *doing?* The whole reason he lived in Forks, the rainiest place in the world, was so that he could be outside in the daytime without exposing his family's secret. Yet here he was, strolling gracefully toward me—with the most beautiful smile on his angel's face—as if I were the only one here.

In that second, I wished that I was not the one exception to his mysterious talent; I usually felt grateful that I was the only person whose thoughts he couldn't hear just as clearly as if they were spoken aloud. But now I wished he could hear me, too, so that he could hear the warning I was screaming in my head.

I shot a panicked glance back at Gran, and saw that it was too late. She was just turning to stare back at me, her eyes as alarmed as mine.

Edward—still smiling so beautifully that my heart felt like it was going to swell up and burst through my chest—put his arm around my shoulder and turned to face my grandmother.

Gran's expression surprised me. Instead of looking horrified, she was staring at me sheepishly, as if waiting for a scolding. And she was standing in such a strange position—one arm held awkwardly away from her body, stretched out and then curled around the air. Like she had her arm around someone I couldn't see, someone invisible . . .

Only then, as I looked at the bigger picture, did I notice the huge gilt frame that enclosed my grandmother's form. Uncomprehending, I raised the hand that wasn't wrapped around Edward's waist and reached out to touch her. She mimicked the movement exactly, mirrored it. But where our fingers should have met, there was nothing but cold glass . . .

With a dizzying jolt, my dream abruptly became a nightmare.

There was no Gran.

That was *me.* Me in a mirror. Me—ancient, creased, and withered.

Edward stood beside me, casting no reflection, excruciatingly lovely and forever seventeen.

He pressed his icy, perfect lips against my wasted cheek. "Happy birthday," he whispered.

I woke with a start—my eyelids popping open wide—and gasped. Dull gray light, the familiar light of an overcast morning, took the place of the blinding sun in my dream.

Just a dream, I told myself. *It was only a dream.* I took a deep breath, and then jumped again when my alarm went off. The little calendar in the corner of the clock's display informed me that today was September thirteenth.

Only a dream, but prophetic enough in one way, at least. Today was my birthday. I was officially eighteen years old.

I'd been dreading this day for months.

All through the perfect summer—the happiest summer I had ever had, the happiest summer *anyone anywhere* had ever had, and the rainiest summer in the history of the Olympic Peninsula—this bleak date had lurked in ambush, waiting to spring.

And now that it had hit, it was even worse than I'd feared it would be. I could feel it—I was older. Every day

I got older, but this was different, worse, quantifiable. I was eighteen.

And Edward never would be.

When I went to brush my teeth, I was almost surprised that the face in the mirror hadn't changed. I stared at myself, looking for some sign of impending wrinkles in my ivory skin. The only creases were the ones on my forehead, though, and I knew that if I could manage to relax, they would disappear. I couldn't. My eyebrows stayed lodged in a worried line over my anxious brown eyes.

It was just a dream, I reminded myself again. Just a dream . . . but also my worst nightmare.

I skipped breakfast, in a hurry to get out of the house as quickly as possible. I wasn't entirely able to avoid my dad, and so I had to spend a few minutes acting cheerful. I honestly tried to be excited about the gifts I'd asked him not to get me, but every time I had to smile, it felt like I might start crying.

I struggled to get a grip on myself as I drove to school. The vision of Gran—I would *not* think of it as me—was hard to get out of my head. I couldn't feel anything but despair until I pulled into the familiar parking lot behind Forks High School and spotted Edward leaning motionlessly against his polished silver Volvo, like a marble tribute to some forgotten pagan god of beauty. The dream had not done him justice. And he was waiting there for *me,* just the same as every other day.

Despair momentarily vanished; wonder took its place. Even after half a year with him, I still couldn't believe that I deserved this degree of good fortune.

His sister Alice was standing by his side, waiting for me, too.

Of course Edward and Alice weren't really related (in Forks the story was that all the Cullen siblings were adopted by Dr. Carlisle Cullen and his wife, Esme, both plainly too young to have teenage children), but their skin was precisely the same pale shade, their eyes had the same strange golden tint, with the same deep, bruise-like shadows beneath them. Her face, like his, was also startlingly beautiful. To someone in the know—someone like me—these similarities marked them for what they were.

The sight of Alice waiting there—her tawny eyes brilliant with excitement, and a small silver-wrapped square in her hands—made me frown. I'd told Alice I didn't want anything, *anything,* not gifts or even attention, for my birthday. Obviously, my wishes were being ignored.

I slammed the door of my '53 Chevy truck—a shower of rust specks fluttered down to the wet blacktop—and walked slowly toward where they waited. Alice skipped forward to meet me, her pixie face glowing under her spiky black hair.

"Happy birthday, Bella!"

"Shh!" I hissed, glancing around the lot to make sure no one had heard her. The last thing I wanted was some kind of celebration of the black event.

She ignored me. "Do you want to open your present now or later?" she asked eagerly as we made our way to where Edward still waited.

"No presents," I protested in a mumble.

She finally seemed to process my mood. "Okay . . .

later, then. Did you like the scrapbook your mom sent you? And the camera from Charlie?"

I sighed. Of course she would know what my birthday presents were. Edward wasn't the only member of his family with unusual skills. Alice would have "seen" what my parents were planning as soon as they'd decided that themselves.

"Yeah. They're great."

"*I* think it's a nice idea. You're only a senior once. Might as well document the experience."

"How many times have *you* been a senior?"

"That's different."

We reached Edward then, and he held out his hand for mine. I took it eagerly, forgetting, for a moment, my glum mood. His skin was, as always, smooth, hard, and very cold. He gave my fingers a gentle squeeze. I looked into his liquid topaz eyes, and my heart gave a not-quite-so-gentle squeeze of its own. Hearing the stutter in my heart-beats, he smiled again.

He lifted his free hand and traced one cool fingertip around the outside of my lips as he spoke. "So, as discussed, I am not allowed to wish you a happy birthday, is that correct?"

"Yes. That is correct." I could never quite mimic the flow of his perfect, formal articulation. It was something that could only be picked up in an earlier century.

"Just checking." He ran his hand through his tousled bronze hair. "You *might* have changed your mind. Most people seem to enjoy things like birthdays and gifts."

Alice laughed, and the sound was all silver, a wind

chime. "Of course you'll enjoy it. Everyone is supposed to be nice to you today and give you your way, Bella. What's the worst that could happen?" She meant it as a rhetorical question.

"Getting older," I answered anyway, and my voice was not as steady as I wanted it to be.

Beside me, Edward's smile tightened into a hard line.

"Eighteen isn't very old," Alice said. "Don't women usually wait till they're twenty-nine to get upset over birthdays?"

"It's older than Edward," I mumbled.

He sighed.

"Technically," she said, keeping her tone light. "Just by one little year, though."

And I supposed . . . if I could be *sure* of the future I wanted, sure that I would get to spend forever with Edward, and Alice and the rest of the Cullens (preferably not as a wrinkled little old lady) . . . then a year or two one direction or the other wouldn't matter to me so much. But Edward was dead set against any future that changed me. Any future that made me like him—that made me immortal, too.

An impasse, he called it.

I couldn't really see Edward's point, to be honest. What was so great about mortality? Being a vampire didn't look like such a terrible thing—not the way the Cullens did it, anyway.

"What time will you be at the house?" Alice continued, changing the subject. From her expression, she was up to exactly the kind of thing I'd been hoping to avoid.

"I didn't know I had plans to be there."

"Oh, be fair, Bella!" she complained. "You aren't going to ruin all our fun like that, are you?"

"I thought my birthday was about what *I* want."

"I'll get her from Charlie's right after school," Edward told her, ignoring me altogether.

"I have to work," I protested.

"You don't, actually," Alice told me smugly. "I already spoke to Mrs. Newton about it. She's trading your shifts. She said to tell you 'Happy Birthday.'"

"I—I still can't come over," I stammered, scrambling for an excuse. "I, well, I haven't watched *Romeo and Juliet* yet for English."

Alice snorted. "You have *Romeo and Juliet* memorized."

"But Mr. Berty said we needed to see it performed to fully appreciate it—that's how Shakespeare intended it to be presented."

Edward rolled his eyes.

"You've already seen the movie," Alice accused.

"But not the nineteen-sixties version. Mr. Berty said it was the best."

Finally, Alice lost the smug smile and glared at me. "This can be easy, or this can be hard, Bella, but one way or the other—"

Edward interrupted her threat. "Relax, Alice. If Bella wants to watch a movie, then she can. It's her birthday."

"So there," I added.

"I'll bring her over around seven," he continued. "That will give you more time to set up."

Alice's laughter chimed again. "Sounds good. See you tonight, Bella! It'll be fun, you'll see." She grinned—the wide smile exposed all her perfect, glistening teeth—then pecked me on the cheek and danced off toward her first class before I could respond.

"Edward, please—" I started to beg, but he pressed one cool finger to my lips.

"Let's discuss it later. We're going to be late for class."

No one bothered to stare at us as we took our usual seats in the back of the classroom (we had almost every class together now—it was amazing the favors Edward could get the female administrators to do for him). Edward and I had been together too long now to be an object of gossip anymore. Even Mike Newton didn't bother to give me the glum stare that used to make me feel a little guilty. He smiled now instead, and I was glad he seemed to have accepted that we could only be friends. Mike had changed over the summer—his face had lost some of the roundness, making his cheekbones more prominent, and he was wearing his pale blond hair a new way; instead of bristly, it was longer and gelled into a carefully casual disarray. It was easy to see where his inspiration came from—but Edward's look wasn't something that could be achieved through imitation.

As the day progressed, I considered ways to get out of whatever was going down at the Cullen house tonight. It would be bad enough to have to celebrate when I was in the mood to mourn. But, worse than that, this was sure to involve attention and gifts.

Attention is never a good thing, as any other accident-prone klutz would agree. No one wants a spotlight when they're likely to fall on their face.

And I'd very pointedly asked—well, ordered really—

that no one give me any presents this year. It looked like Charlie and Renée weren't the only ones who had decided to overlook that.

I'd never had much money, and that had never bothered me. Renée had raised me on a kindergarten teacher's salary. Charlie wasn't getting rich at his job, either—he was the police chief here in the tiny town of Forks. My only personal income came from the three days a week I worked at the local sporting goods store. In a town this small, I was lucky to have a job. Every penny I made went into my microscopic college fund. (College was Plan B. I was still hoping for Plan A, but Edward was just so stubborn about leaving me human. . . .)

Edward had a *lot* of money—I didn't even want to think about how much. Money meant next to nothing to Edward or the rest of the Cullens. It was just something that accumulated when you had unlimited time on your hands and a sister who had an uncanny ability to predict trends in the stock market. Edward didn't seem to understand why I objected to him spending money on me— why it made me uncomfortable if he took me to an expensive restaurant in Seattle, why he wasn't allowed to buy me a car that could reach speeds over fifty-five miles an hour, or why I wouldn't let him pay my college tuition (he was ridiculously enthusiastic about Plan B). Edward thought I was being unnecessarily difficult.

But how could I let him give me things when I had nothing to reciprocate with? He, for some unfathomable reason, wanted to be with me. Anything he gave me on top of that just threw us more out of balance.

As the day went on, neither Edward nor Alice brought my birthday up again, and I began to relax a little.

We sat at our usual table for lunch.

A strange kind of truce existed at that table. The three of us—Edward, Alice, and I—sat on the extreme southern end of the table. Now that the "older" and somewhat scarier (in Emmett's case, certainly) Cullen siblings had graduated, Alice and Edward did not seem quite so intimidating, and we did not sit here alone. My other friends, Mike and Jessica (who were in the awkward post-breakup friendship phase), Angela and Ben (whose relationship had survived the summer), Eric, Conner, Tyler, and Lauren (though that last one didn't really count in the friend category) all sat at the same table, on the other side of an invisible line. That line dissolved on sunny days when Edward and Alice always skipped school, and then the conversation would swell out effortlessly to include me.

Edward and Alice didn't find this minor ostracism odd or hurtful the way I would have. They barely noticed it. People always felt strangely ill at ease with the Cullens, almost afraid for some reason they couldn't explain to themselves. I was a rare exception to that rule. Sometimes it bothered Edward how very comfortable I was with being close to him. He thought he was hazardous to my health—an opinion I rejected vehemently whenever he voiced it.

The afternoon passed quickly. School ended, and Edward walked me to my truck as he usually did. But this time, he held the passenger door open for me. Alice must have been taking his car home so that he could keep me from making a run for it.

I folded my arms and made no move to get out of the rain. "It's my birthday, don't I get to drive?"

"I'm pretending it's not your birthday, just as you wished."

"If it's not my birthday, then I don't have to go to your house tonight . . ."

"All right." He shut the passenger door and walked past me to open the driver's side. "Happy birthday."

"Shh," I shushed him halfheartedly. I climbed in the opened door, wishing he'd taken the other offer.

Edward played with the radio while I drove, shaking his head in disapproval.

"Your radio has horrible reception."

I frowned. I didn't like it when he picked on my truck. The truck was great—it had personality.

"You want a nice stereo? Drive your own car." I was so nervous about Alice's plans, on top of my already gloomy mood, that the words came out sharper than I'd meant them. I was hardly ever bad-tempered with Edward, and my tone made him press his lips together to keep from smiling.

When I parked in front of Charlie's house, he reached over to take my face in his hands. He handled me very carefully, pressing just the tips of his fingers softly against my temples, my cheekbones, my jawline. Like I was especially breakable. Which was exactly the case—compared with him, at least.

"You should be in a good mood, today of all days," he whispered. His sweet breath fanned across my face.

"And if I don't want to be in a good mood?" I asked, my breathing uneven.

His golden eyes smoldered. "Too bad."

My head was already spinning by the time he leaned closer and pressed his icy lips against mine. As he intended, no doubt, I forgot all about my worries, and concentrated on remembering how to inhale and exhale.

His mouth lingered on mine, cold and smooth and gentle, until I wrapped my arms around his neck and threw myself into the kiss with a little too much enthusiasm. I could feel his lips curve upward as he let go of my face and reached back to unlock my grip on him.

Edward had drawn many careful lines for our physical relationship, with the intent being to keep me alive. Though I respected the need for maintaining a safe distance between my skin and his razor-sharp, venom-coated teeth, I tended to forget about trivial things like that when he was kissing me.

"Be good, please," he breathed against my cheek. He pressed his lips gently to mine one more time and then pulled away, folding my arms across my stomach.

My pulse was thudding in my ears. I put one hand over my heart. It drummed hyperactively under my palm.

"Do you think I'll ever get better at this?" I wondered, mostly to myself. "That my heart might someday stop trying to jump out of my chest whenever you touch me?"

"I really hope not," he said, a bit smug.

I rolled my eyes. "Let's go watch the Capulets and Montagues hack each other up, all right?"

"Your wish, my command."

Edward sprawled across the couch while I started the movie, fast-forwarding through the opening credits.

When I perched on the edge of the sofa in front of him, he wrapped his arms around my waist and pulled me against his chest. It wasn't exactly as comfortable as a sofa cushion would be, what with his chest being hard and cold—and perfect—as an ice sculpture, but it was definitely preferable. He pulled the old afghan off the back of the couch and draped it over me so I wouldn't freeze beside his body.

"You know, I've never had much patience with Romeo," he commented as the movie started.

"What's wrong with Romeo?" I asked, a little offended. Romeo was one of my favorite fictional characters. Until I'd met Edward, I'd sort of had a thing for him.

"Well, first of all, he's in love with this Rosaline—don't you think it makes him seem a little fickle? And then, a few minutes after their wedding, he kills Juliet's cousin. That's not very brilliant. Mistake after mistake. Could he have destroyed his own happiness any more thoroughly?"

I sighed. "Do you want me to watch this alone?"

"No, I'll mostly be watching you, anyway." His fingers traced patterns across the skin of my arm, raising goose bumps. "Will you cry?"

"Probably," I admitted, "if I'm paying attention."

"I won't distract you then." But I felt his lips on my hair, and it was very distracting.

The movie eventually captured my interest, thanks in large part to Edward whispering Romeo's lines in my ear—his irresistible, velvet voice made the actor's voice sound weak and coarse by comparison. And I did cry, to his amusement, when Juliet woke and found her new husband dead.

"I'll admit, I do sort of envy him here," Edward said, drying the tears with a lock of my hair.

"She's very pretty."

He made a disgusted sound. "I don't envy him the *girl*—just the ease of the suicide," he clarified in a teasing tone. "You humans have it so easy! All you have to do is throw down one tiny vial of plant extracts. . . ."

"What?" I gasped.

"It's something I had to think about once, and I knew from Carlisle's experience that it wouldn't be simple. I'm not even sure how many ways Carlisle tried to kill himself in the beginning . . . after he realized what he'd become. . . ." His voice, which had grown serious, turned light again. "And he's clearly still in excellent health."

I twisted around so that I could read his face. "What are you talking about?" I demanded. "What do you mean, this something you had to think about once?"

"Last spring, when you were . . . nearly killed . . ." He paused to take a deep breath, struggling to return to his teasing tone. "Of course I was trying to focus on finding you alive, but part of my mind was making contingency plans. Like I said, it's not as easy for me as it is for a human."

For one second, the memory of my last trip to Phoenix washed through my head and made me feel dizzy. I could see it all so clearly—the blinding sun, the heat waves coming off the concrete as I ran with desperate haste to find the sadistic vampire who wanted to torture me to death. James, waiting in the mirrored room with my mother as his hostage—or so I'd thought. I hadn't known it was all a ruse. Just as James hadn't known that Edward was racing to save me; Edward made it in time, but it had been a close one. Unthinkingly, my fingers traced the crescent-shaped scar on my hand that was always just a few degrees cooler than the rest of my skin.

I shook my head—as if I could shake away the bad memories—and tried to grasp what Edward meant. My stomach plunged uncomfortably. "Contingency plans?" I repeated.

"Well, I wasn't going to live without you." He rolled his eyes as if that fact were childishly obvious. "But I wasn't sure how to *do* it—I knew Emmett and Jasper would never help . . . so I was thinking maybe I would go to Italy and do something to provoke the Volturi."

I didn't want to believe he was serious, but his golden eyes were brooding, focused on something far away in the distance as he contemplated ways to end his own life. Abruptly, I was furious.

"What is a *Volturi*?" I demanded.

"The Volturi are a family," he explained, his eyes still remote. "A very old, very powerful family of our kind. They are the closest thing our world has to a royal family, I suppose. Carlisle lived with them briefly in his early years, in Italy, before he settled in America—do you remember the story?"

"Of course I remember."

I would never forget the first time I'd gone to his home, the huge white mansion buried deep in the forest beside the river, or the room where Carlisle—Edward's father in so many real ways—kept a wall of paintings that illustrated his personal history. The most vivid, most wildly colorful canvas there, the largest, was from Carlisle's time in Italy. Of course I remembered the calm quartet of men, each with the exquisite face of a seraph, painted into the highest balcony overlooking the swirling mayhem of color. Though the painting was centuries old, Carlisle—the blond angel—remained unchanged. And I remembered the three others, Carlisle's early acquaintances. Edward had never used the name *Volturi* for the beautiful trio, two black-haired, one snow white. He'd called them Aro, Caius, and Marcus, nighttime patrons of the arts. . . .

"Anyway, you don't irritate the Volturi," Edward went on, interrupting my reverie. "Not unless you want to die—or whatever it is we do." His voice was so calm, it made him sound almost bored by the prospect.

My anger turned to horror. I took his marble face between my hands and held it very tightly.

"You must never, never, never think of anything like that again!" I said. "No matter what might ever happen to me, you are *not allowed* to hurt yourself!"

"I'll never put you in danger again, so it's a moot point."

"*Put* me in danger! I thought we'd established that all the bad luck is my fault?" I was getting angrier. "How dare you even think like that?" The idea of Edward ceasing to exist, even if I were dead, was impossibly painful.

"What would you do, if the situation were reversed?" he asked.

"That's not the same thing."

He didn't seem to understand the difference. He chuckled.

"What if something did happen to you?" I blanched at the thought. "Would you want me to go *off* myself?"

A trace of pain touched his perfect features.

"I guess I see your point . . . a little," he admitted. "But what would I do without you?"

"Whatever you were doing before I came along and complicated your existence."

He sighed. "You make that sound so easy."

"It should be. I'm not really that interesting."

He was about to argue, but then he let it go. "Moot point," he reminded me. Abruptly, he pulled himself up into a more formal posture, shifting me to the side so that we were no longer touching.

"Charlie?" I guessed.

Edward smiled. After a moment, I heard the sound of the police cruiser pulling into the driveway. I reached out and took his hand firmly. My dad could deal with that much.

Charlie came in with a pizza box in his hands.

"Hey, kids." He grinned at me. "I thought you'd like a break from cooking and washing dishes for your birthday. Hungry?"

"Sure. Thanks, Dad."

Charlie didn't comment on Edward's apparent lack of appetite. He was used to Edward passing on dinner.

"Do you mind if I borrow Bella for the evening?" Edward asked when Charlie and I were done.

I looked at Charlie hopefully. Maybe he had some concept of birthdays as stay-at-home, family affairs—this was my first birthday with him, the first birthday since my mom, Renée, had remarried and gone to live in Florida, so I didn't know what he would expect.

"That's fine—the Mariners are playing the Sox tonight," Charlie explained, and my hope disappeared. "So I won't be any kind of company. . . . Here." He scooped up the camera he'd gotten me on Renée's suggestion (because I would need pictures to fill up my scrapbook), and threw it to me.

He ought to know better than that—I'd always been coordinationally challenged. The camera glanced off the tip of my finger, and tumbled toward the floor. Edward snagged it before it could crash onto the linoleum.

"Nice save," Charlie noted. "If they're doing something fun at the Cullens' tonight, Bella, you should take some pictures. You know how your mother gets—she'll be wanting to see the pictures faster than you can take them."

"Good idea, Charlie," Edward said, handing me the camera.

I turned the camera on Edward, and snapped the first picture. "It works."

"That's good. Hey, say hi to Alice for me. She hasn't been over in a while." Charlie's mouth pulled down at one corner.

"It's been three days, Dad," I reminded him. Charlie was crazy about Alice. He'd become attached last spring when she'd helped me through my awkward convalescence; Charlie would be forever grateful to her for saving him from the horror of an almost-adult daughter who needed help showering. "I'll tell her."

"Okay. You kids have fun tonight." It was clearly a dismissal. Charlie was already edging toward the living room and the TV.

Edward smiled, triumphant, and took my hand to pull me from the kitchen.

When we got to the truck, he opened the passenger door for me again, and this time I didn't argue. I still had a hard time finding the obscure turnoff to his house in the dark.

Edward drove north through Forks, visibly chafing at the speed limit enforced by my prehistoric Chevy. The engine groaned even louder than usual as he pushed it over fifty.

"Take it easy," I warned him.

"You know what you would love? A nice little Audi coupe. Very quiet, lots of power . . ."

"There's nothing wrong with my truck. And speaking of expensive nonessentials, if you know what's good for you, you didn't spend any money on birthday presents."

"Not a dime," he said virtuously.

"Good."

"Can you do me a favor?"

"That depends on what it is."

He sighed, his lovely face serious. "Bella, the last real birthday any of us had was Emmett in 1935. Cut us a little slack, and don't be too difficult tonight. They're all very excited."

It always startled me a little when he brought up things like that. "Fine, I'll behave."

"I probably should warn you . . ."

"Please do."

"When I say they're all excited . . . I do mean *all* of them."

"Everyone?" I choked. "I thought Emmett and Rosalie were in Africa." The rest of Forks was under the impression that the older Cullens had gone off to college this year, to Dartmouth, but I knew better.

"Emmett wanted to be here."

"But . . . Rosalie?"

"I know, Bella. Don't worry, she'll be on her best behavior."

I didn't answer. Like I could just *not* worry, that easy. Unlike Alice, Edward's other "adopted" sister, the golden blond and exquisite Rosalie, didn't like me much. Actually, the feeling was a little bit stronger than just dislike. As far as Rosalie was concerned, I was an unwelcome intruder into her family's secret life.

I felt horribly guilty about the present situation, guessing that Rosalie and Emmett's prolonged absence was my fault, even as I furtively enjoyed not having to see her. Emmett, Edward's playful bear of a brother, I *did* miss. He was in many ways just like the big brother I'd always wanted . . . only much, much more terrifying.

Edward decided to change the subject. "So, if you won't let me get you the Audi, isn't there anything that you'd like for your birthday?"

The words came out in a whisper. "You know what I want."

A deep frown carved creases into his marble forehead. He obviously wished he'd stuck to the subject of Rosalie.

It felt like we'd had this argument a lot today.

"Not tonight, Bella. Please."

"Well, maybe Alice will give me what I want."

Edward growled—a deep, menacing sound. "This isn't going to be your last birthday, Bella," he vowed.

"That's not fair!"

I thought I heard his teeth clench together.

We were pulling up to the house now. Bright light shined from every window on the first two floors. A long line of glowing Japanese lanterns hung from the porch eaves, reflecting a soft radiance on the huge cedars that surrounded the house. Big bowls of flowers—pink roses—lined the wide stairs up to the front doors.

I moaned.

Edward took a few deep breaths to calm himself. "This is a party," he reminded me. "Try to be a good sport."

"Sure," I muttered.

He came around to get my door, and offered me his hand.

"I have a question."

He waited warily.

"If I develop this film," I said, toying with the camera in my hands, "will you show up in the picture?"

Edward started laughing. He helped me out of the car, pulled me up the stairs, and was still laughing as he opened the door for me.

They were all waiting in the huge white living room; when I walked through the door, they greeted me with a loud chorus of "Happy birthday, Bella!" while I blushed and looked down. Alice, I assumed, had covered every flat surface with pink candles and dozens of crystal bowls filled with hundreds of roses. There was a table with a white cloth draped over it next to Edward's grand piano, holding a pink birthday cake, more roses, a stack of glass plates, and a small pile of silver-wrapped presents.

It was a hundred times worse than I'd imagined.

Edward, sensing my distress, wrapped an encouraging arm around my waist and kissed the top of my head.

Edward's parents, Carlisle and Esme—impossibly youthful and lovely as ever—were the closest to the door. Esme hugged me carefully, her soft, caramel-colored hair brushing against my cheek as she kissed my forehead, and then Carlisle put his arm around my shoulders.

"Sorry about this, Bella," he stage-whispered. "We couldn't rein Alice in."

Rosalie and Emmett stood behind them. Rosalie didn't smile, but at least she didn't glare. Emmett's face was stretched into a huge grin. It had been months since I'd seen them; I'd forgotten how gloriously beautiful Rosalie was—it almost hurt to look at her. And had Emmett always been so . . . *big*?

"You haven't changed at all," Emmett said with mock disappointment. "I expected a perceptible difference, but here you are, red-faced just like always."

"Thanks a lot, Emmett," I said, blushing deeper.

He laughed, "I have to step out for a second"—he paused to wink conspicuously at Alice—"Don't do anything funny while I'm gone."

"I'll try."

Alice let go of Jasper's hand and skipped forward, all her teeth sparkling in the bright light. Jasper smiled, too, but kept his distance. He leaned, long and blond, against the post at the foot of the stairs. During the days we'd had to spend cooped up together in Phoenix, I'd thought he'd gotten over his aversion to me. But he'd gone back to exactly how he'd acted before—avoiding me as much as possible—

the moment he was free from that temporary obligation to protect me. I knew it wasn't personal, just a precaution, and I tried not to be overly sensitive about it. Jasper had more trouble sticking to the Cullens' diet than the rest of them; the scent of human blood was much harder for him to resist than the others—he hadn't been trying as long.

"Time to open presents," Alice declared. She put her cool hand under my elbow and towed me to the table with the cake and the shiny packages.

I put on my best martyr face. "Alice, I know I told you I didn't want anything—"

"But I didn't listen," she interrupted, smug. "Open it." She took the camera from my hands and replaced it with a big, square silver box.

The box was so light that it felt empty. The tag on top said that it was from Emmett, Rosalie, and Jasper. Self-consciously, I tore the paper off and then stared at the box it concealed.

It was something electrical, with lots of numbers in the name. I opened the box, hoping for further illumination. But the box *was* empty.

"Um . . . thanks."

Rosalie actually cracked a smile. Jasper laughed. "It's a stereo for your truck," he explained. "Emmett's installing it right now so that you can't return it."

Alice was always one step ahead of me.

"Thanks, Jasper, Rosalie," I told them, grinning as I remembered Edward's complaints about my radio this afternoon—all a setup, apparently. "Thanks, Emmett!" I called more loudly.

I heard his booming laugh from my truck, and I couldn't help laughing, too.

"Open mine and Edward's next," Alice said, so excited her voice was a high-pitched trill. She held a small, flat square in her hand.

I turned to give Edward a basilisk glare. "You promised."

Before he could answer, Emmett bounded through the door. "Just in time!" he crowed. He pushed in behind Jasper, who had also drifted closer than usual to get a good look.

"I didn't spend a dime," Edward assured me. He brushed a strand of hair from my face, leaving my skin tingling from his touch.

I inhaled deeply and turned to Alice. "Give it to me," I sighed.

Emmett chuckled with delight.

I took the little package, rolling my eyes at Edward while I stuck my finger under the edge of the paper and jerked it under the tape.

"Shoot," I muttered when the paper sliced my finger; I pulled it out to examine the damage. A single drop of blood oozed from the tiny cut.

It all happened very quickly then.

"No!" Edward roared.

He threw himself at me, flinging me back across the table. It fell, as I did, scattering the cake and the presents, the flowers and the plates. I landed in the mess of shattered crystal.

Jasper slammed into Edward, and the sound was like the crash of boulders in a rock slide.

There was another noise, a grisly snarling that seemed to be coming from deep in Jasper's chest. Jasper tried to shove past Edward, snapping his teeth just inches from Edward's face.

Emmett grabbed Jasper from behind in the next second, locking him into his massive steel grip, but Jasper struggled on, his wild, empty eyes focused only on me.

Beyond the shock, there was also pain. I'd tumbled down to the floor by the piano, with my arms thrown out instinctively to catch my fall, into the jagged shards of glass. Only now did I feel the searing, stinging pain that ran from my wrist to the crease inside my elbow.

Dazed and disoriented, I looked up from the bright red blood pulsing out of my arm—into the fevered eyes of the six suddenly ravenous vampires.

2. STITCHES

CARLISLE WAS THE ONLY ONE WHO STAYED CALM. Centuries of experience in the emergency room were evident in his quiet, authoritative voice.

"Emmett, Rose, get Jasper outside."

Unsmiling for once, Emmett nodded. "Come on, Jasper."

Jasper struggled against Emmett's unbreakable grasp, twisting around, reaching toward his brother with his bared teeth, his eyes still past reason.

Edward's face was whiter than bone as he wheeled to crouch over me, taking a clearly defensive position. A low warning growl slid from between his clenched teeth. I could tell that he wasn't breathing.

Rosalie, her divine face strangely smug, stepped in front of Jasper—keeping a careful distance from his teeth—and helped Emmett wrestle him through the glass door that Esme held open, one hand pressed over her mouth and nose.

Esme's heart-shaped face was ashamed. "I'm so sorry, Bella," she cried as she followed the others into the yard.

"Let me by, Edward," Carlisle murmured.

A second passed, and then Edward nodded slowly and relaxed his stance.

Carlisle knelt beside me, leaning close to examine my arm. I could feel the shock frozen on my face, and I tried to compose it.

"Here, Carlisle," Alice said, handing him a towel.

He shook his head. "Too much glass in the wound." He reached over and ripped a long, thin scrap from the bottom of the white tablecloth. He twisted it around my arm above the elbow to form a tourniquet. The smell of the blood was making me dizzy. My ears rang.

"Bella," Carlisle said softly. "Do you want me to drive you to the hospital, or would you like me to take care of it here?"

"Here, please," I whispered. If he took me to the hospital, there would be no way to keep this from Charlie.

"I'll get your bag," Alice said.

"Let's take her to the kitchen table," Carlisle said to Edward.

Edward lifted me effortlessly, while Carlisle kept the pressure steady on my arm.

"How are you doing, Bella?" Carlisle asked.

"I'm fine." My voice was reasonably steady, which pleased me.

Edward's face was like stone.

Alice was there. Carlisle's black bag was already on the table, a small but brilliant desk light plugged into the wall. Edward sat me gently into a chair, and Carlisle pulled up another. He went to work at once.

Edward stood over me, still protective, still not breathing.

"Just go, Edward," I sighed.

"I can handle it," he insisted. But his jaw was rigid; his eyes burned with the intensity of the thirst he fought, so much worse for him than it was for the others.

"You don't need to be a hero," I said. "Carlisle can fix me up without your help. Get some fresh air."

I winced as Carlisle did something to my arm that stung.

"I'll stay," he said.

"Why are you so masochistic?" I mumbled.

Carlisle decided to intercede. "Edward, you may as well go find Jasper before he gets too far. I'm sure he's upset with himself, and I doubt he'll listen to anyone but you right now."

"Yes," I eagerly agreed. "Go find Jasper."

"You might as well do something useful," Alice added.

Edward's eyes narrowed as we ganged up on him, but, finally, he nodded once and sprinted smoothly through the kitchen's back door. I was sure he hadn't taken a breath since I'd sliced my finger.

A numb, dead feeling was spreading through my arm.

Though it erased the sting, it reminded me of the gash, and I watched Carlisle's face carefully to distract me from what his hands were doing. His hair gleamed gold in the bright light as he bent over my arm. I could feel the faint stirrings of unease in the pit of my stomach, but I was determined not to let my usual squeamishness get the best of me. There was no pain now, just a gentle tugging sensation that I tried to ignore. No reason to get sick like a baby.

If she hadn't been in my line of sight, I wouldn't have noticed Alice give up and steal out of the room. With a tiny, apologetic smile on her lips, she disappeared through the kitchen doorway.

"Well, that's everyone," I sighed. "I can clear a room, at least."

"It's not your fault," Carlisle comforted me with a chuckle. "It could happen to anyone."

"*Could,*" I repeated. "But it usually just happens to me."

He laughed again.

His relaxed calm was only more amazing set in direct contrast with everyone else's reaction. I couldn't find any trace of anxiety in his face. He worked with quick, sure movements. The only sound besides our quiet breathing was the soft *plink, plink* as the tiny fragments of glass dropped one by one to the table.

"How can you do this?" I demanded. "Even Alice and Esme . . ." I trailed off, shaking my head in wonder. Though the rest of them had given up the traditional diet of vampires just as absolutely as Carlisle had, he was the only one who could bear the smell of my blood without suffering from the intense temptation. Clearly, this was much more difficult than he made it seem.

"Years and years of practice," he told me. "I barely notice the scent anymore."

"Do you think it would be harder if you took a vacation from the hospital for a long time? And weren't around any blood?"

"Maybe." He shrugged his shoulders, but his hands remained steady. "I've never felt the need for an extended holiday." He flashed a brilliant smile in my direction. "I enjoy my work too much."

Plink, plink, plink. I was surprised at how much glass there seemed to be in my arm. I was tempted to glance at the growing pile, just to check the size, but I knew that idea would not be helpful to my no-vomiting strategy.

"What is it that you enjoy?" I wondered. It didn't make sense to me—the years of struggle and self-denial he must have spent to get to the point where he could endure this so easily. Besides, I wanted to keep him talking; the conversation kept my mind off the queasy feeling in my stomach.

His dark eyes were calm and thoughtful as he answered. "Hmm. What I enjoy the very most is when my . . . enhanced abilities let me save someone who would otherwise have been lost. It's pleasant knowing that, thanks to what I can do, some people's lives are better because I exist. Even the sense of smell is a useful diagnostic tool at times." One side of his mouth pulled up in half a smile.

I mulled that over while he poked around, making sure all the glass splinters were gone. Then he rummaged in his bag for new tools, and I tried not to picture a needle and thread.

"You try very hard to make up for something that was never your fault," I suggested while a new kind of tugging started at the edges of my skin. "What I mean is, it's not like you asked for this. You didn't choose this kind of life, and yet you have to work so *hard* to be good."

"I don't know that I'm making up for anything," he disagreed lightly. "Like everything in life, I just had to decide what to do with what I was given."

"That makes it sound too easy."

He examined my arm again. "There," he said, snipping a thread. "All done." He wiped an oversized Q-tip, dripping with some syrup-colored liquid, thoroughly across the operation site. The smell was strange; it made my head spin. The syrup stained my skin.

"In the beginning, though," I pressed while he taped another long piece of gauze securely in place, sealing it to my skin. "Why did you even think to try a different way than the obvious one?"

His lips turned up in a private smile. "Hasn't Edward told you this story?"

"Yes. But I'm trying to understand what you were thinking. . . ."

His face was suddenly serious again, and I wondered if his thoughts had gone to the same place that mine had. Wondering what I would be thinking when—I refused to think *if*—it was me.

"You know my father was a clergyman," he mused as he cleaned the table carefully, rubbing everything down with wet gauze, and then doing it again. The smell of alcohol burned in my nose. "He had a rather harsh view of the world, which I was already beginning to question before the time that I changed." Carlisle put all the dirty gauze and the glass slivers into an empty crystal bowl. I didn't understand what he was doing, even when he lit the match. Then he threw it onto the alcohol-soaked fibers, and the sudden blaze made me jump.

"Sorry," he apologized. "That ought to do it. . . . So I didn't agree with my father's particular brand of faith. But never, in the nearly four hundred years now since I was born, have I ever seen anything to make me doubt whether God exists in some form or the other. Not even the reflection in the mirror."

I pretended to examine the dressing on my arm to hide my surprise at the direction our conversation had taken. Religion was the last thing I expected, all things considered. My own life was fairly devoid of belief. Charlie considered himself a Lutheran, because that's what his parents had been, but Sundays he worshipped by the river with a fishing pole in his hand. Renée tried out a church now and then, but, much like her brief affairs with tennis, pottery, yoga, and French classes, she moved on by the time I was aware of her newest fad.

"I'm sure all this sounds a little bizarre, coming from a vampire." He grinned, knowing how their casual use of that word never failed to shock me. "But I'm hoping that there is still a point to this life, even for us. It's a long shot, I'll admit," he continued in an offhand voice. "By all accounts, we're damned regardless. But I hope, maybe foolishly, that we'll get some measure of credit for trying."

"I don't think that's foolish," I mumbled. I couldn't imagine anyone, deity included, who wouldn't be impressed by Carlisle. Besides, the only kind of heaven *I* could appreciate would have to include Edward. "And I don't think anyone else would, either."

"Actually, you're the very first one to agree with me."

"The rest of them don't feel the same?" I asked, surprised, thinking of only one person in particular.

Carlisle guessed the direction of my thoughts again. "Edward's with me up to a point. God and heaven exist . . . and so does hell. But he doesn't believe there is an afterlife for our kind." Carlisle's voice was very soft; he stared out the big window over the sink, into the darkness. "You see, he thinks we've lost our souls."

I immediately thought of Edward's words this afternoon: *unless you want to die—or whatever it is that we do.* The lightbulb flicked on over my head.

"That's the real problem, isn't it?" I guessed. "That's why he's being so difficult about me."

Carlisle spoke slowly. "I look at my . . . *son.* His strength, his goodness, the brightness that shines out of him—and it only fuels that hope, that faith, more than ever. How could there not be more for one such as Edward?"

I nodded in fervent agreement.

"But if I believed as he does . . ." He looked down at me with unfathomable eyes. "If you believed as he did. Could you take away *his* soul?"

The way he phrased the question thwarted my answer.

If he'd asked me whether I would risk my soul for Edward, the reply would be obvious. But would I risk Edward's soul? I pursed my lips unhappily. That wasn't a fair exchange.

"You see the problem."

I shook my head, aware of the stubborn set of my chin. Carlisle sighed.

"It's my choice," I insisted.

"It's his, too." He held up his hand when he could see that I was about to argue. "Whether he is responsible for doing that to you."

"He's not the only one able to do it." I eyed Carlisle speculatively.

He laughed, abruptly lightening the mood. "Oh, no! You're going to have to work this out with *him*." But then he sighed. "That's the one part I can never be sure of. I *think*, in most other ways, that I've done the best I could with what I had to work with. But was it right to doom the others to this life? I can't decide."

I didn't answer. I imagined what my life would be like if Carlisle had resisted the temptation to change his lonely existence . . . and shuddered.

"It was Edward's mother who made up my mind." Carlisle's voice was almost a whisper. He stared unseeingly out the black windows.

"His mother?" Whenever I'd asked Edward about his parents, he would merely say that they had died long ago, and his memories were vague. I realized Carlisle's memory of them, despite the brevity of their contact, would be perfectly clear.

"Yes. Her name was Elizabeth. Elizabeth Masen. His father, Edward Senior, never regained consciousness in the hospital. He died in the first wave of the influenza. But Elizabeth was alert until almost the very end. Edward looks a great deal like her—she had that same strange bronze shade to her hair, and her eyes were exactly the same color green."

"His eyes were green?" I murmured, trying to picture it.

"Yes. . . ." Carlisle's ocher eyes were a hundred years away now. "Elizabeth worried obsessively over her son. She hurt her own chances of survival trying to nurse him from her sickbed. I expected that he would go first, he was so much worse off than she was. When the end came for her, it was very quick. It was just after sunset, and I'd arrived to relieve the doctors who'd been working all day. That was a hard time to pretend—there was so much work to be done, and I had no need of rest. How I hated to go back to my house, to hide in the dark and pretend to sleep while so many were dying.

"I went to check Elizabeth and her son first. I'd grown attached—always a dangerous thing to do considering the fragile nature of humans. I could see at once that she'd taken a bad turn. The fever was raging out of control, and her body was too weak to fight anymore.

"She didn't look weak, though, when she glared up at me from her cot.

"'Save him!' she commanded me in the hoarse voice that was all her throat could manage.

"'I'll do everything in my power,' I promised her, taking her hand. The fever was so high, she probably couldn't even tell how unnaturally cold mine felt. Everything felt cold to her skin.

"'You must,' she insisted, clutching at my hand with enough strength that I wondered if she wouldn't pull through the crisis after all. Her eyes were hard, like stones, like emeralds. 'You must do everything in *your* power. What others cannot do, that is what you must do for my Edward.'

"It frightened me. She looked at me with those piercing eyes, and, for one instant, I felt certain that she knew my secret. Then the fever overwhelmed her, and she never regained consciousness. She died within an hour of making her demand.

"I'd spent decades considering the idea of creating a companion for myself. Just one other creature who could really know me, rather than what I pretended to be. But I could never justify it to myself—doing what had been done to me.

"There Edward lay, dying. It was clear that he had only hours left. Beside him, his mother, her face somehow not yet peaceful, not even in death."

Carlisle saw it all again, his memory unblurred by the intervening century. I could see it clearly, too, as he spoke—the despair of the hospital, the overwhelming atmosphere of death. Edward burning with fever, his life slipping away with each tick of the clock . . . I shuddered again, and forced the picture from my mind.

"Elizabeth's words echoed in my head. How could she guess what I could do? Could anyone really want that for her son?

"I looked at Edward. Sick as he was, he was still beautiful. There was something pure and good about his face. The kind of face I would have wanted my son to have.

"After all those years of indecision, I simply acted on a whim. I wheeled his mother to the morgue first, and then I came back for him. No one noticed that he was still breathing. There weren't enough hands, enough eyes, to keep track of half of what the patients needed. The morgue was empty—of the living, at least. I stole him out the back door, and carried him across the rooftops back to my home.

"I wasn't sure what had to be done. I settled for recreating the wounds I'd received myself, so many centuries earlier in London. I felt bad about that later. It was more painful and lingering than necessary.

"I wasn't sorry, though. I've never been sorry that I saved Edward." He shook his head, coming back to the present. He smiled at me. "I suppose I should take you home now."

"I'll do that," Edward said. He came through the shadowy dining room, walking slowly for him. His face was smooth, unreadable, but there was something wrong with his eyes—something he was trying very hard to hide. I felt a spasm of unease in my stomach.

"Carlisle can take me," I said. I looked down at my shirt; the light blue cotton was soaked and spotted with my blood. My right shoulder was covered in thick pink frosting.

"I'm fine." Edward's voice was unemotional. "You'll need to change anyway. You'd give Charlie a heart attack the way you look. I'll have Alice get you something." He strode out the kitchen door again.

I looked at Carlisle anxiously. "He's very upset."

"Yes," Carlisle agreed. "Tonight is exactly the kind of thing that he fears the most. You being put in danger, because of what we are."

"It's not his fault."

"It's not yours, either."

I looked away from his wise, beautiful eyes. I couldn't agree with that.

Carlisle offered me his hand and helped me up from the table. I followed him out into the main room. Esme had come back; she was mopping the floor where I'd fallen—with straight bleach from the smell of it.

"Esme, let me do that." I could feel that my face was bright red again.

"I'm already done." She smiled up at me. "How do you feel?"

"I'm fine," I assured her. "Carlisle sews faster than any other doctor I've had."

They both chuckled.

Alice and Edward came in the back doors. Alice hurried to my side, but Edward hung back, his face indecipherable.

"C'mon," Alice said. "I'll get you something less macabre to wear."

She found me a shirt of Esme's that was close to the same color mine had been. Charlie wouldn't notice, I was sure. The long white bandage on my arm didn't look nearly as serious when I was no longer spattered in gore. Charlie was never surprised to see me bandaged.

"Alice," I whispered as she headed back to the door.

"Yes?" She kept her voice low, too, and looked at me curiously, her head cocked to the side.

"How bad is it?" I couldn't be sure if my whispering was a wasted effort. Even though we were upstairs, with the door closed, perhaps he could hear me.

Her face tensed. "I'm not sure yet."

"How's Jasper?"

She sighed. "He's very unhappy with himself. It's all so much more of challenge for him, and he hates feeling weak."

"It's not his fault. You'll tell him that I'm not mad at him, not at all, won't you?"

"Of course."

Edward was waiting for me by the front door. As I got to the bottom of the staircase, he held it open without a word.

"Take your things!" Alice cried as I walked warily toward Edward. She scooped up the two packages, one half-opened, and my camera from under the piano, and pressed them into my good arm. "You can thank me later, when you've opened them."

Esme and Carlisle both said a quiet goodnight. I could see them stealing quick glances at their impassive son, much like I was.

It was a relief to be outside; I hurried past the lanterns and the roses, now unwelcome reminders. Edward kept pace with me silently. He opened the passenger side for me, and I climbed in without complaint.

On the dashboard was a big red ribbon, stuck to the new stereo. I pulled it off, throwing it to the floor. As Edward slid into the other side, I kicked the ribbon under my seat.

He didn't look at me or the stereo. Neither of us switched it on, and the silence was somehow intensified by the sudden thunder of the engine. He drove too fast down the dark, serpentine lane.

The silence was making me insane.

"Say something," I finally begged as he turned onto the freeway.

"What do you want me to say?" he asked in a detached voice.

I cringed at his remoteness. "Tell me you forgive me."

That brought a flicker of life to his face—a flicker of anger. "Forgive *you*? For what?"

"If I'd been more careful, nothing would have happened."

"Bella, you gave yourself a paper cut—that hardly deserves the death penalty."

"It's still my fault."

My words opened up the floodgate.

"Your fault? If you'd cut yourself at Mike Newton's house, with Jessica there and Angela and your other normal friends, the worst that could possibly have happened would be what? Maybe they couldn't find you a bandage? If you'd tripped and knocked over a pile of glass plates on your own—without someone throwing you into them—

even then, what's the worst? You'd get blood on the seats when they drove you to the emergency room? Mike Newton could have held your hand while they stitched you up—and he wouldn't be fighting the urge to kill you the whole time he was there. Don't try to take any of this on yourself, Bella. It will only make me more disgusted with myself."

"How the hell did Mike Newton end up in this conversation?" I demanded.

"Mike Newton ended up in this conversation because Mike Newton would be a hell of a lot healthier for you to be with," he growled.

"I'd rather die than be with Mike Newton," I protested. "I'd rather die than be with anyone but you."

"Don't be melodramatic, please."

"Well then, don't you be ridiculous."

He didn't answer. He glared through the windshield, his expression black.

I racked my brain for some way to salvage the evening. When we pulled up in front of my house, I still hadn't come up with anything.

He killed the engine, but his hands stayed clenched around the steering wheel.

"Will you stay tonight?" I asked.

"I should go home."

The last thing I wanted was for him to go wallow in remorse.

"For my birthday," I pressed.

"You can't have it both ways—either you want people to ignore your birthday or you don't. One or the other."

His voice was stern, but not as serious as before. I breathed a silent sigh of relief.

"Okay. I've decided that I don't want you to ignore my birthday. I'll see you upstairs."

I hopped out, reaching back in for my packages. He frowned.

"You don't have to take those."

"I want them," I responded automatically, and then wondered if he was using reverse psychology.

"No, you don't. Carlisle and Esme spent money on you."

"I'll live." I tucked the presents awkwardly under my good arm and slammed the door behind me. He was out of the truck and by my side in less than a second.

"Let me carry them, at least," he said as he took them away. "I'll be in your room."

I smiled. "Thanks."

"Happy birthday," he sighed, and leaned down to touch his lips to mine.

I reached up on my toes to make the kiss last longer when he pulled away. He smiled my favorite crooked smile, and then he disappeared into the darkness.

The game was still on; as soon as I walked through the front door I could hear the announcer rambling over the babble of the crowd.

"Bell?" Charlie called.

"Hey, Dad," I said as I came around the corner. I held my arm close to my side. The slight pressure burned, and I wrinkled my nose. The anesthetic was apparently losing its effectiveness.

"How was it?" Charlie lounged across the sofa with his bare feet propped up on the arm. What was left of his curly brown hair was crushed flat on one side.

"Alice went overboard. Flowers, cake, candles, presents—the whole bit."

"What did they get you?"

"A stereo for my truck." And various unknowns.

"Wow."

"Yeah," I agreed. "Well, I'm calling it a night."

"I'll see you in the morning."

I waved. "See ya."

"What happened to your arm?"

I flushed and cursed silently. "I tripped. It's nothing."

"Bella," he sighed, shaking his head.

"Goodnight, Dad."

I hurried up to the bathroom, where I kept my pajamas for just such nights as these. I shrugged into the matching tank top and cotton pants that I'd gotten to replace the holey sweats I used to wear to bed, wincing as the movement pulled at the stitches. I washed my face one-handed, brushed my teeth, and then skipped to my room.

He was sitting in the center of my bed, toying idly with one of the silver boxes.

"Hi," he said. His voice was sad. He was wallowing.

I went to the bed, pushed the presents out of his hands, and climbed into his lap.

"Hi." I snuggled into his stone chest. "Can I open my presents now?"

"Where did the enthusiasm come from?" he wondered.

"You made me curious."

I picked up the long flat rectangle that must have been from Carlisle and Esme.

"Allow me," he suggested. He took the gift from my hand and tore the silver paper off with one fluid movement. He handed the rectangular white box back to me.

"Are you sure I can handle lifting the lid?" I muttered, but he ignored me.

Inside the box was a long thick piece of paper with an overwhelming amount of fine print. It took me a minute to get the gist of the information.

"We're going to Jacksonville?" And I was excited, in spite of myself. It was a voucher for plane tickets, for both me and Edward.

"That's the idea."

"I can't believe it. Renée is going to flip! You don't mind, though, do you? It's sunny, you'll have to stay inside all day."

"I think I can handle it," he said, and then frowned. "If I'd had any idea that you could respond to a gift this appropriately, I would have made you open it in front of Carlisle and Esme. I thought you'd complain."

"Well, of course it's too much. But I get to take you with me!"

He chuckled. "Now I wish I'd spent money on your present. I didn't realize that you were capable of being reasonable."

I set the tickets aside and reached for his present, my curiosity rekindled. He took it from me and unwrapped it like the first one.

He handed back a clear CD jewel case, with a blank silver CD inside.

"What is it?" I asked, perplexed.

He didn't say anything; he took the CD and reached around me to put it in the CD player on the bedside table. He hit play, and we waited in silence. Then the music began.

I listened, speechless and wide-eyed. I knew he was waiting for my reaction, but I couldn't talk. Tears welled up, and I reached up to wipe them away before they could spill over.

"Does your arm hurt?" he asked anxiously.

"No, it's not my arm. It's beautiful, Edward. You couldn't have given me anything I would love more. I can't believe it." I shut up, so I could listen.

It was his music, his compositions. The first piece on the CD was my lullaby.

"I didn't think you would let me get a piano so I could play for you here," he explained.

"You're right."

"How does your arm feel?"

"Just fine." Actually, it was starting to blaze under the bandage. I wanted ice. I would have settled for his hand, but that would have given me away.

"I'll get you some Tylenol."

"I don't need anything," I protested, but he slid me off his lap and headed for the door.

"Charlie," I hissed. Charlie wasn't exactly aware that Edward frequently stayed over. In fact, he would have a stroke if that fact were brought to his attention. But I didn't feel too guilty for deceiving him. It wasn't as if we were up to anything he wouldn't want me to be up to. Edward and his rules . . .

"He won't catch me," Edward promised as he disappeared silently out the door . . . and returned, catching the door before it had swung back to touch the frame. He had the glass from the bathroom and the bottle of pills in one hand.

I took the pills he handed me without arguing—I knew I would lose the argument. And my arm really was starting to bother me.

My lullaby continued, soft and lovely, in the background.

"It's late," Edward noted. He scooped me up off the bed with one arm, and pulled the cover back with the other. He put me down with my head on my pillow and tucked the quilt around me. He lay down next to me—on top of the blanket so I wouldn't get chilled—and put his arm over me.

I leaned my head against his shoulder and sighed happily.

"Thanks again," I whispered.

"You're welcome."

It was quiet for a long moment as I listened to my lullaby drift to a close. Another song began. I recognized Esme's favorite.

"What are you thinking about?" I wondered in a whisper.

He hesitated for a second before he told me. "I was thinking about right and wrong, actually."

I felt a chill tingle along my spine.

"Remember how I decided that I wanted you to *not* ignore my birthday?" I asked quickly, hoping it wasn't too clear that I was trying to distract him.

"Yes," he agreed, wary.

"Well, I was thinking, since it's still my birthday, that I'd like you to kiss me again."

"You're greedy tonight."

"Yes, I am—but please, don't do anything you don't want to do," I added, piqued.

He laughed, and then sighed. "Heaven forbid that I should do anything I don't want to do," he said in a strangely desperate tone as he put his hand under my chin and pulled my face up to his.

The kiss began much the same as usual—Edward was as careful as ever, and my heart began to overreact like it always did. And then something seemed to change. Suddenly his lips became much more urgent, his free hand twisted into my hair and held my face securely to his. And, though my hands tangled in his hair, too, and though I was clearly beginning to cross his cautious lines, for once he didn't stop me. His body was cold through the thin quilt, but I crushed myself against him eagerly.

When he stopped it was abrupt; he pushed me away with gentle, firm hands.

I collapsed back onto my pillow, gasping, my head spinning. Something tugged at my memory, elusive, on the edges.

"Sorry," he said, and he was breathless, too. "That was out of line."

"*I* don't mind," I panted.

He frowned at me in the darkness. "Try to sleep, Bella."

"No, I want you to kiss me again."

"You're overestimating my self-control."

"Which is tempting you more, my blood or my body?" I challenged.

"It's a tie." He grinned briefly in spite of himself, and then was serious again. "Now, why don't you stop pushing your luck and go to sleep?"

"Fine," I agreed, snuggling closer to him. I really did feel exhausted. It had been a long day in so many ways, yet I felt no sense of relief at its end. Almost as if something worse was coming tomorrow. It was a silly premonition— what could be worse than today? Just the shock catching up with me, no doubt.

Trying to be sneaky about it, I pressed my injured arm against his shoulder, so his cool skin would sooth the burning. It felt better at once.

I was halfway asleep, maybe more, when I realized what his kiss had reminded me of: last spring, when he'd had to leave me to throw James off my trail, Edward had kissed me goodbye, not knowing when—or if—we would see each other again. This kiss had the same almost painful edge for some reason I couldn't imagine. I shuddered into unconsciousness, as if I were already having a nightmare.

3. THE END

I felt absolutely hideous in the morning. I hadn't slept well; my arm burned and my head ached. It didn't help my outlook that Edward's face was smooth and remote as he kissed my forehead quickly and ducked out my window. I was afraid of the time I'd spent unconscious, afraid that he might have been thinking about right and wrong again while he watched me sleep. The anxiety seemed to ratchet up the intensity of the pounding in my head.

Edward was waiting for me at school, as usual, but his face was still wrong. There was something buried in his eyes that I couldn't be sure of—and it scared me. I didn't want to bring up last night, but I wasn't sure if avoiding the subject would be worse.

He opened my door for me.

"How do you feel?"

"Perfect," I lied, cringing as the sound of the slamming door echoed in my head.

We walked in silence, he shortening his stride to match mine. There were so many questions I wanted to ask, but most of those questions would have to wait, because they were for Alice: How was Jasper this morning? What had they said when I was gone? What had Rosalie said? And most importantly, what could she see happening now in her strange, imperfect visions of the future? Could she guess what Edward was thinking, why he was so gloomy? Was there a foundation for the tenuous, instinctive fears that I couldn't seem to shake?

The morning passed slowly. I was impatient to see Alice, though I wouldn't be able to really talk to her with Edward there. Edward remained aloof. Occasionally he would ask about my arm, and I would lie.

Alice usually beat us to lunch; she didn't have to keep pace with a sloth like me. But she wasn't at the table, waiting with a tray of food she wouldn't eat.

Edward didn't say anything about her absence. I wondered to myself if her class was running late—until I saw Conner and Ben, who were in her fourth hour French class.

"Where's Alice?" I asked Edward anxiously.

He looked at the granola bar he was slowly pulverizing between his fingertips while he answered. "She's with Jasper."

"Is he okay?"

"He's gone away for a while."

"What? Where?"

Edward shrugged. "Nowhere in particular."

"And Alice, too," I said with quiet desperation. Of course, if Jasper needed her, she would go.

"Yes. She'll be gone for a while. She was trying to convince him to go to Denali."

Denali was where the one other band of unique vampires—good ones like the Cullens—lived. Tanya and her family. I'd heard of them now and again. Edward had run to them last winter when my arrival had made Forks difficult for him. Laurent, the most civilized member of James's little coven, had gone there rather than siding with James against the Cullens. It made sense for Alice to encourage Jasper to go there.

I swallowed, trying to dislodge the sudden lump in my throat. The guilt made my head bow and my shoulders slump. I'd run them out of their home, just like Rosalie and Emmett. I was a plague.

"Is your arm bothering you?" he asked solicitously.

"Who cares about my stupid arm?" I muttered in disgust.

He didn't answer, and I put my head down on the table.

By the end of the day, the silence was becoming ridiculous. I didn't want to be the one to break it, but apparently that was my only choice if I ever wanted him to talk to me again.

"You'll come over later tonight?" I asked as he walked me—silently—to my truck. He always came over.

"Later?"

It pleased me that he seemed surprised. "I have to work. I had to trade with Mrs. Newton to get yesterday off."

"Oh," he murmured.

"So you'll come over when I'm home, though, right?" I hated that I felt suddenly unsure about this.

"If you want me to."

"I always want you," I reminded him, with perhaps a little more intensity than the conversation required.

I expected he would laugh, or smile, or react somehow to my words.

"All right, then," he said indifferently.

He kissed my forehead again before he shut the door on me. Then he turned his back and loped gracefully toward his car.

I was able to drive out of the parking lot before the panic really hit, but I was hyperventilating by the time I got to Newton's.

He just needed time, I told myself. He would get over this. Maybe he was sad because his family was disappearing. But Alice and Jasper would come back soon, and Rosalie and Emmett, too. If it would help, I would stay away from the big white house on the river—I'd never set foot there again. That didn't matter. I'd still see Alice at school. She would have to come back for school, right? And she was at my place all the time anyway. She wouldn't want to hurt Charlie's feelings by staying away.

No doubt I would also run into Carlisle with regularity—in the emergency room.

After all, what had happened last night was nothing. Nothing *had* happened. So I fell down—that was the story of my life. Compared to last spring, it seemed especially unimportant. James had left me broken and nearly dead from loss of blood—and yet Edward had handled the interminable weeks in the hospital *much* better than this. Was it because, this time, it wasn't an enemy he'd had to protect me from? Because it was his brother?

Maybe it would be better if he took me away, rather than his family being scattered. I grew slightly less depressed as I considered all the uninterrupted alone time. If he could just last through the school year, Charlie wouldn't be able to object. We could go away to college, or pretend that's what we were doing, like Rosalie and Emmett this year. Surely Edward could wait a year. What was a year to an immortal? It didn't even seem like that much to me.

I was able to talk myself into enough composure to handle getting out of the truck and walking to the store. Mike Newton had beaten me here today, and he smiled and waved when I came in. I grabbed my vest, nodding vaguely in his direction. I was still imagining pleasant scenarios that consisted of me running away with Edward to various exotic locales.

Mike interrupted my fantasy. "How was your birthday?"

"Ugh," I mumbled. "I'm glad it's over."

Mike looked at me from the corners of his eyes like I was crazy.

Work dragged. I wanted to see Edward again, praying that he would be past the worst of this, whatever it was exactly, by the time I saw him again. It's nothing, I told myself over and over again. Everything will go back to normal.

The relief I felt when I turned onto my street and saw

Edward's silver car parked in front of my house was an overwhelming, heady thing. And it bothered me deeply that it should be that way.

I hurried through the front door, calling out before I was completely inside.

"Dad? Edward?"

As I spoke, I could hear the distinctive theme music from ESPN's SportsCenter coming from the living room.

"In here," Charlie called.

I hung my raincoat on its peg and hurried around the corner.

Edward was in the armchair, my father on the sofa. Both had their eyes trained on the TV. The focus was normal for my father. Not so much for Edward.

"Hi," I said weakly.

"Hey, Bella," my father answered, eyes never moving. "We just had cold pizza. I think it's still on the table."

"Okay."

I waited in the doorway. Finally, Edward looked over at me with a polite smile. "I'll be right behind you," he promised. His eyes strayed back to the TV.

I stared for another minute, shocked. Neither one seemed to notice. I could feel something, panic maybe, building up in my chest. I escaped to the kitchen.

The pizza held no interest for me. I sat in my chair, pulled my knees up, and wrapped my arms around them. Something was very wrong, maybe more wrong than I'd realized. The sounds of male bonding and banter continued from the TV set.

I tried to get control of myself, to reason with myself.

What's the worst that can happen? I flinched. That was definitely the wrong question to ask. I was having a hard time breathing right.

Okay, I thought again, *what's the worst I can live through?* I didn't like that question so much, either. But I thought through the possibilities I'd considered today.

Staying away from Edward's family. Of course, he wouldn't expect Alice to be part of that. But if Jasper was off limits, that would lessen the time I could have with her. I nodded to myself—I could live with that.

Or going away. Maybe he wouldn't want to wait till the end of the school year, maybe it would have to be now.

In front of me, on the table, my presents from Charlie and Renée were where I had left them, the camera I hadn't had the chance to use at the Cullens' sitting beside the album. I touched the pretty cover of the scrapbook my mother had given me, and sighed, thinking of Renée. Somehow, living without her for as long as I had did not make the idea of a more permanent separation easier. And Charlie would be left all alone here, abandoned. They would both be so hurt . . .

But we'd come back, right? We'd visit, of course, wouldn't we?

I couldn't be certain about the answer to that.

I leaned my cheek against my knee, staring at the physical tokens of my parents' love. I'd known this path I'd chosen was going to be hard. And, after all, I was thinking about the worst-case scenario—the very worst I could live through.

I touched the scrapbook again, flipping the front cover

over. Little metal corners were already in place to hold the first picture. It wasn't a half-bad idea, to make some record of my life here. I felt a strange urge to get started. Maybe I didn't have that long left in Forks.

I toyed with the wrist strap on the camera, wondering about the first picture on the roll. Could it possibly turn out anything close to the original? I doubted it. But he didn't seem worried that it would be blank. I chuckled to myself, thinking of his carefree laughter last night. The chuckle died away. So much had changed, and so abruptly. It made me feel a little bit dizzy, like I was standing on an edge, a precipice somewhere much too high.

I didn't want to think about that anymore. I grabbed the camera and headed up the stairs.

My room hadn't really changed all that much in the seventeen years since my mother had been here. The walls were still light blue, the same yellowed lace curtains hung in front of the window. There was a bed, rather than a crib, but she would recognize the quilt draped untidily over the top—it had been a gift from Gran.

Regardless, I snapped a picture of my room. There wasn't much else I could do tonight—it was too dark outside—and the feeling was growing stronger, it was almost a compulsion now. I would record everything about Forks before I had to leave it.

Change was coming. I could feel it. It wasn't a pleasant prospect, not when life was perfect the way it was.

I took my time coming back down the stairs, camera in hand, trying to ignore the butterflies in my stomach as I thought of the strange distance I didn't want to see in

Edward's eyes. He would get over this. Probably he was worried that I would be upset when he asked me to leave. I would let him work through it without meddling. And I would be prepared when he asked.

I had the camera ready as I leaned around the corner, being sneaky. I was sure there was no chance that I had caught Edward by surprise, but he didn't look up. I felt a brief shiver as something icy twisted in my stomach; I ignored that and took the picture.

They both looked at me then. Charlie frowned. Edward's face was empty, expressionless.

"What are you doing, Bella?" Charlie complained.

"Oh, come on." I pretended to smile as I went to sit on the floor in front of the sofa where Charlie lounged. "You know Mom will be calling soon to ask if I'm using my presents. I have to get to work before she can get her feelings hurt."

"Why are you taking pictures of me, though?" he grumbled.

"Because you're so handsome," I replied, keeping it light. "And because, since you bought the camera, you're obligated to be one of my subjects."

He mumbled something unintelligible.

"Hey, Edward," I said with admirable indifference. "Take one of me and my dad together."

I threw the camera toward him, carefully avoiding his eyes, and knelt beside the arm of the sofa where Charlie's face was. Charlie sighed.

"You need to smile, Bella," Edward murmured.

I did my best, and the camera flashed.

"Let me take one of you kids," Charlie suggested. I knew he was just trying to shift the camera's focus from himself.

Edward stood and lightly tossed him the camera.

I went to stand beside Edward, and the arrangement felt formal and strange to me. He put one hand lightly on my shoulder, and I wrapped my arm more securely around his waist. I wanted to look at his face, but I was afraid to.

"Smile, Bella," Charlie reminded me again.

I took a deep breath and smiled. The flash blinded me.

"Enough pictures for tonight," Charlie said then, shoving the camera into a crevice of the sofa cushions and rolling over it. "You don't have to use the whole roll now."

Edward dropped his hand from my shoulder and twisted casually out of my arm. He sat back down in the armchair.

I hesitated, and then went to sit against the sofa again. I was suddenly so frightened that my hands were shaking. I pressed them into my stomach to hide them, put my chin on my knees and stared at the TV screen in front of me, seeing nothing.

When the show ended, I hadn't moved an inch. Out of the corner of my eye, I saw Edward stand.

"I'd better get home," he said.

Charlie didn't look up from the commercial. "See ya."

I got awkwardly to my feet—I was stiff from sitting so still—and followed Edward out the front door. He went straight to his car.

"Will you stay?" I asked, no hope in my voice.

I expected his answer, so it didn't hurt as much.

"Not tonight."

I didn't ask for a reason.

He got in his car and drove away while I stood there, unmoving. I barely noticed that it was raining. I waited, without knowing what I waited for, until the door opened behind me.

"Bella, what are you doing?" Charlie asked, surprised to see me standing there alone and dripping.

"Nothing." I turned and trudged back to the house.

It was a long night, with little in the way of rest.

I got up as soon as there was a faint light outside my window. I dressed for school mechanically, waiting for the clouds to brighten. When I had eaten a bowl of cereal, I decided that it was light enough for pictures. I took one of my truck, and then the front of the house. I turned and snapped a few of the forest by Charlie's house. Funny how it didn't seem sinister like it used to. I realized I would miss this—the green, the timelessness, the mystery of the woods. All of it.

I put the camera in my school bag before I left. I tried to concentrate on my new project rather than the fact that Edward apparently hadn't gotten over things during the night.

Along with the fear, I was beginning to feel impatience. How long could this last?

It lasted through the morning. He walked silently beside me, never seeming to actually look at me. I tried to concentrate on my classes, but not even English could hold my attention. Mr. Berty had to repeat his question about Lady Capulet twice before I realized he was talking to me. Edward whispered the correct answer under his breath and then went back to ignoring me.

At lunch, the silence continued. I felt like I was going to start screaming at any moment, so, to distract myself, I leaned across the table's invisible line and spoke to Jessica.

"Hey, Jess?"

"What's up, Bella?"

"Could you do me a favor?" I asked, reaching into my bag. "My mom wants me to get some pictures of my friends for a scrapbook. So, take some pictures of everybody, okay?"

I handed her the camera.

"Sure," she said, grinning, and turned to snap a candid shot of Mike with his mouth full.

A predictable picture war ensued. I watched them hand the camera around the table, giggling and flirting and complaining about being on film. It seemed strangely childish. Maybe I just wasn't in the mood for normal human behavior today.

"Uh-oh," Jessica said apologetically as she returned the camera. "I think we used all your film."

"That's okay. I think I already got pictures of everything else I needed."

After school, Edward walked me back to the parking lot in silence. I had to work again, and for once, I was glad. Time with me obviously wasn't helping things. Maybe time alone would be better.

I dropped my film off at the Thriftway on my way to Newton's, and then picked up the developed pictures after work. At home, I said a brief hi to Charlie, grabbed a granola bar from the kitchen, and hurried up to my room with the envelope of photographs tucked under my arm.

I sat in the middle of my bed and opened the envelope with wary curiosity. Ridiculously, I still half expected the first print to be a blank.

When I pulled it out, I gasped aloud. Edward looked just as beautiful as he did in real life, staring at me out of the picture with the warm eyes I'd missed for the past few days. It was almost uncanny that anyone could look so . . . so . . . beyond description. No thousand words could equal this picture.

I flipped through the rest of the stack quickly once, and then laid three of them out on the bed side by side.

The first was the picture of Edward in the kitchen, his warm eyes touched with tolerant amusement. The second was Edward and Charlie, watching ESPN. The difference in Edward's expression was severe. His eyes were careful here, reserved. Still breathtakingly beautiful, but his face was colder, more like a sculpture, less alive.

The last was the picture of Edward and me standing awkwardly side by side. Edward's face was the same as the last, cold and statue-like. But that wasn't the most troubling part of this photograph. The contrast between the two of us was painful. He looked like a god. I looked very average, even for a human, almost shamefully plain. I flipped the picture over with a feeling of disgust.

Instead of doing my homework, I stayed up to put my pictures into the album. With a ballpoint pen I scrawled captions under all the pictures, the names and the dates. I got to the picture of Edward and me, and, without looking at it too long, I folded it in half and stuck it under the metal tab, Edward-side up.

When I was done, I stuffed the second set of prints in a fresh envelope and penned a long thank-you letter to Renée.

Edward still hadn't come over. I didn't want to admit that he was the reason I'd stayed up so late, but of course he was. I tried to remember the last time he'd stayed away like this, without an excuse, a phone call . . . He never had.

Again, I didn't sleep well.

School followed the silent, frustrating, terrifying pattern of the last two days. I felt relief when I saw Edward waiting for me in the parking lot, but it faded quickly. He was no different, unless maybe more remote.

It was hard to even remember the reason for all this mess. My birthday already felt like the distant past. If only Alice would come back. Soon. Before this got any more out of hand.

But I couldn't count on that. I decided that, if I couldn't talk to him today, really talk, then I was going to see Carlisle tomorrow. I had to do something.

After school, Edward and I were going to talk it out, I promised myself. I wasn't accepting any excuses.

He walked me to my truck, and I steeled myself to make my demands.

"Do you mind if I come over today?" he asked before we got to the truck, beating me to the punch.

"Of course not."

"Now?" he asked again, opening my door for me.

"Sure," I kept my voice even, though I didn't like the

urgency in his tone. "I was just going to drop a letter for Renée in the mailbox on the way. I'll meet you there."

He looked at the fat envelope on the passenger seat. Suddenly, he reached over me and snagged it.

"I'll do it," he said quietly. "And I'll still beat you there." He smiled my favorite crooked smile, but it was wrong. It didn't reach his eyes.

"Okay," I agreed, unable to smile back. He shut the door, and headed toward his car.

He did beat me home. He was parked in Charlie's spot when I pulled up in front of the house. That was a bad sign. He didn't plan to stay, then. I shook my head and took a deep breath, trying to locate some courage.

He got out of his car when I stepped out of the truck, and came to meet me. He reached to take my book bag from me. That was normal. But he shoved it back onto the seat. That was not normal.

"Come for a walk with me," he suggested in an unemotional voice, taking my hand.

I didn't answer. I couldn't think of a way to protest, but I instantly knew that I wanted to. I didn't like this. *This is bad, this is very bad,* the voice in my head repeated again and again.

But he didn't wait for an answer. He pulled me along toward the east side of the yard, where the forest encroached. I followed unwillingly, trying to think through the panic. It was what I wanted, I reminded myself. The chance to talk it all through. So why was the panic choking me?

We'd gone only a few steps into the trees when he

stopped. We were barely on the trail—I could still see the house.

Some walk.

Edward leaned against a tree and stared at me, his expression unreadable.

"Okay, let's talk," I said. It sounded braver than it felt.

He took a deep breath.

"Bella, we're leaving."

I took a deep breath, too. This was an acceptable option. I thought I was prepared. But I still had to ask.

"Why now? Another year—"

"Bella, it's time. How much longer could we stay in Forks, after all? Carlisle can barely pass for thirty, and he's claiming thirty-three now. We'd have to start over soon regardless."

His answer confused me. I thought the point of leaving was to let his family live in peace. Why did we have to leave if they were going? I stared at him, trying to understand what he meant.

He stared back coldly.

With a roll of nausea, I realized I'd misunderstood.

"When you say *we*—," I whispered.

"I mean my family and myself." Each word separate and distinct.

I shook my head back and forth mechanically, trying to clear it. He waited without any sign of impatience. It took a few minutes before I could speak.

"Okay," I said. "I'll come with you."

"You can't, Bella. Where we're going . . . It's not the right place for you."

"Where you are is the right place for me."

"I'm no good for you, Bella."

"Don't be ridiculous." I wanted to sound angry, but it just sounded like I was begging. "You're the very best part of my life."

"My world is not for you," he said grimly.

"What happened with Jasper—that was nothing, Edward! Nothing!"

"You're right," he agreed. "It was exactly what was to be expected."

"You promised! In Phoenix, you promised that you would stay—"

"As long as that was best for you," he interrupted to correct me.

"*No!* This is about my soul, isn't it?" I shouted, furious, the words exploding out of me—somehow it still sounded like a plea. "Carlisle told me about that, and I don't care, Edward. I don't care! You can have my soul. I don't want it without you—it's yours already!"

He took a deep breath and stared, unseeingly, at the ground for a long moment. His mouth twisted the tiniest bit. When he finally looked up, his eyes were different, harder—like the liquid gold had frozen solid.

"Bella, I don't want you to come with me." He spoke the words slowly and precisely, his cold eyes on my face, watching as I absorbed what he was really saying.

There was a pause as I repeated the words in my head a few times, sifting through them for their real intent.

"You . . . don't . . . want me?" I tried out the words, confused by the way they sounded, placed in that order.

"No."

I stared, uncomprehending, into his eyes. He stared back without apology. His eyes were like topaz—hard and clear and very deep. I felt like I could see into them for miles and miles, yet nowhere in their bottomless depths could I see a contradiction to the word he'd spoken.

"Well, that changes things." I was surprised by how calm and reasonable my voice sounded. It must be because I was so numb. I couldn't realize what he was telling me. It still didn't make any sense.

He looked away into the trees as he spoke again. "Of course, I'll always love you . . . in a way. But what happened the other night made me realize that it's time for a change. Because I'm . . . *tired* of pretending to be something I'm not, Bella. I am not human." He looked back, and the icy planes of his perfect face were *not* human. "I've let this go on much too long, and I'm sorry for that."

"Don't." My voice was just a whisper now; awareness was beginning to seep through me, trickling like acid through my veins. "Don't do this."

He just stared at me, and I could see from his eyes that my words were far too late. He already had.

"You're not good for me, Bella." He turned his earlier words around, and so I had no argument. How well I knew that I wasn't good enough for him.

I opened my mouth to say something, and then closed it again. He waited patiently, his face wiped clean of all emotion. I tried again.

"If . . . that's what you want."

He nodded once.

My whole body went numb. I couldn't feel anything below the neck.

"I would like to ask one favor, though, if that's not too much," he said.

I wonder what he saw on my face, because something flickered across his own face in response. But, before I could identify it, he'd composed his features into the same serene mask.

"Anything," I vowed, my voice faintly stronger.

As I watched, his frozen eyes melted. The gold became liquid again, molten, burning down into mine with an intensity that was overwhelming.

"Don't do anything reckless or stupid," he ordered, no longer detached. "Do you understand what I'm saying?"

I nodded helplessly.

His eyes cooled, the distance returned. "I'm thinking of Charlie, of course. He needs you. Take care of yourself—for him."

I nodded again. "I will," I whispered.

He seemed to relax just a little.

"And I'll make you a promise in return," he said. "I promise that this will be the last time you'll see me. I won't come back. I won't put you through anything like this again. You can go on with your life without any more interference from me. It will be as if I'd never existed."

My knees must have started to shake, because the trees were suddenly wobbling. I could hear the blood pounding faster than normal behind my ears. His voice sounded farther away.

He smiled gently. "Don't worry. You're human—your

memory is no more than a sieve. Time heals all wounds for your kind."

"And your memories?" I asked. It sounded like there was something stuck in my throat, like I was choking.

"Well"—he hesitated for a short second—"I won't forget. But *my* kind . . . we're very easily distracted." He smiled; the smile was tranquil and it did not touch his eyes.

He took a step away from me. "That's everything, I suppose. We won't bother you again."

The plural caught my attention. That surprised me; I would have thought I was beyond noticing anything.

"Alice isn't coming back," I realized. I don't know how he heard me—the words made no sound—but he seemed to understand.

He shook his head slowly, always watching my face.

"No. They're all gone. I stayed behind to tell you goodbye."

"Alice is gone?" My voice was blank with disbelief.

"She wanted to say goodbye, but I convinced her that a clean break would be better for you."

I was dizzy; it was hard to concentrate. His words swirled around in my head, and I heard the doctor at the hospital in Phoenix, last spring, as he showed me the X-rays. *You can see it's a clean break*, his finger traced along the picture of my severed bone. *That's good. It will heal more easily, more quickly.*

I tried to breathe normally. I needed to concentrate, to find a way out of this nightmare.

"Goodbye, Bella," he said in the same quiet, peaceful voice.

"Wait!" I choked out the word, reaching for him, willing my deadened legs to carry me forward.

I thought he was reaching for me, too. But his cold hands locked around my wrists and pinned them to my sides. He leaned down, and pressed his lips very lightly to my forehead for the briefest instant. My eyes closed.

"Take care of yourself," he breathed, cool against my skin.

There was a light, unnatural breeze. My eyes flashed open. The leaves on a small vine maple shuddered with the gentle wind of his passage.

He was gone.

With shaky legs, ignoring the fact that my action was useless, I followed him into the forest. The evidence of his path had disappeared instantly. There were no footprints, the leaves were still again, but I walked forward without thinking. I could not do anything else. I had to keep moving. If I stopped looking for him, it was over.

Love, life, meaning . . . over.

I walked and walked. Time made no sense as I pushed slowly through the thick undergrowth. It was hours passing, but also only seconds. Maybe it felt like time had frozen because the forest looked the same no matter how far I went. I started to worry that I was traveling in a circle, a very small circle at that, but I kept going. I stumbled often, and, as it grew darker and darker, I fell often, too.

Finally, I tripped over something—it was black now, I had no idea what caught my foot—and I stayed down. I rolled onto my side, so that I could breathe, and curled up on the wet bracken.

As I lay there, I had a feeling that more time was passing than I realized. I couldn't remember how long it had been since nightfall. Was it always so dark here at night? Surely, as a rule, some little bit of moonlight would filter down through the clouds, through the chinks in the canopy of trees, and find the ground.

Not tonight. Tonight the sky was utterly black. Perhaps there was no moon tonight—a lunar eclipse, a new moon.

A new moon. I shivered, though I wasn't cold.

It was black for a long time before I heard them calling.

Someone was shouting my name. It was muted, muffled by the wet growth that surrounded me, but it was definitely my name. I didn't recognize the voice. I thought about answering, but I was dazed, and it took a long time to come to the conclusion that I *should* answer. By then, the calling had stopped.

Sometime later, the rain woke me up. I don't think I'd really fallen asleep; I was just lost in an unthinking stupor, holding with all my strength to the numbness that kept me from realizing what I didn't want to know.

The rain bothered me a little. It was cold. I unwrapped my arms from around my legs to cover my face.

It was then that I heard the calling again. It was farther away this time, and sometimes it sounded like several voices were calling at once. I tried to breathe deeply. I remembered that I should answer, but I didn't think they would be able to hear me. Would I be able to shout loud enough?

Suddenly, there was another sound, startlingly close. A kind of snuffling, an animal sound. It sounded big. I wondered if I should feel afraid. I didn't—just numb. It didn't matter. The snuffling went away.

The rain continued, and I could feel the water pooling up against my cheek. I was trying to gather the strength to turn my head when I saw the light.

At first it was just a dim glow reflecting off the bushes in the distance. It grew brighter and brighter, illuminating a large space unlike the focused beam of a flashlight. The light broke through the closest brush, and I could see that it was a propane lantern, but that was all I could see—the brightness blinded me for a moment.

"Bella."

The voice was deep and unfamiliar, but full of recognition. He wasn't calling my name to search, he was acknowledging that I was found.

I stared up—impossibly high it seemed—at the dark face that I could now see above me. I was vaguely aware that the stranger probably only looked so tall because my head was still on the ground.

"Have you been hurt?"

I knew the words meant something, but I could only stare, bewildered. How could the meaning matter at this point?

"Bella, my name is Sam Uley."

There was nothing familiar about his name.

"Charlie sent me to look for you."

Charlie? That struck a chord, and I tried to pay more attention to what he was saying. Charlie mattered, if nothing else did.

The tall man held out a hand. I gazed at it, not sure what I was supposed to do.

His black eyes appraised me for a second, and then he shrugged. In a quick and supple motion, he pulled me up from the ground and into his arms.

I hung there, limp, as he loped swiftly through the wet forest. Some part of me knew this should upset me—being carried away by a stranger. But there was nothing left in me to upset.

It didn't seem like too much time passed before there were lights and the deep babble of many male voices. Sam Uley slowed as he approached the commotion.

"I've got her!" he called in a booming voice.

The babble ceased, and then picked up again with more intensity. A confusing swirl of faces moved over me. Sam's voice was the only one that made sense in the chaos, perhaps because my ear was against his chest.

"No, I don't think she's hurt," he told someone. "She just keeps saying 'He's gone.'"

Was I saying that out loud? I bit down on my lip.

"Bella, honey, are you all right?"

That was one voice I would know anywhere—even distorted, as it was now, with worry.

"Charlie?" My voice sounded strange and small.

"I'm right here, baby."

There was a shifting under me, followed by the leathery smell of my dad's sheriff jacket. Charlie staggered under my weight.

"Maybe I should hold on to her," Sam Uley suggested.

"I've got her," Charlie said, a little breathless.

He walked slowly, struggling. I wished I could tell him to put me down and let me walk, but I couldn't find my voice.

There were lights everywhere, held by the crowd walking with him. It felt like a parade. Or a funeral procession. I closed my eyes.

"We're almost home now, honey," Charlie mumbled now and then.

I opened my eyes again when I heard the door unlock. We were on the porch of our house, and the tall dark man named Sam was holding the door for Charlie, one arm extended toward us, as if he was preparing to catch me when Charlie's arms failed.

But Charlie managed to get me through the door and to the couch in the living room.

"Dad, I'm all wet," I objected feebly.

"That doesn't matter." His voice was gruff. And then he was talking to someone else. "Blankets are in the cupboard at the top of the stairs."

"Bella?" a new voice asked. I looked at the gray-haired man leaning over me, and recognition came after a few slow seconds.

"Dr. Gerandy?" I mumbled.

"That's right, dear," he said. "Are you hurt, Bella?"

It took me a minute to think that through. I was confused by the memory of Sam Uley's similar question in the woods. Only Sam had asked something else: *Have you been hurt?* he'd said. The difference seemed significant somehow.

Dr. Gerandy was waiting. One grizzled eyebrow rose, and the wrinkles on his forehead deepened.

"I'm not hurt," I lied. The words were true enough for what he'd asked.

His warm hand touched my forehead, and his fingers pressed against the inside of my wrist. I watched his lips as he counted to himself, his eyes on his watch.

"What happened to you?" he asked casually.

I froze under his hand, tasting panic in the back of my throat.

"Did you get lost in the woods?" he prodded. I was aware of several other people listening. Three tall men with dark faces—from La Push, the Quileute Indian reservation down on the coastline, I guessed—Sam Uley among them, were standing very close together and staring at me. Mr. Newton was there with Mike and Mr. Weber, Angela's father; they all were watching me more surreptitiously than the strangers. Other deep voices rumbled from the kitchen and outside the front door. Half the town must have been looking for me.

Charlie was the closest. He leaned in to hear my answer.

"Yes," I whispered. "I got lost."

The doctor nodded, thoughtful, his fingers probing gently against the glands under my jaw. Charlie's face hardened.

"Do you feel tired?" Dr. Gerandy asked.

I nodded and closed my eyes obediently.

"I don't think there's anything wrong with her," I heard the doctor mutter to Charlie after a moment. "Just exhaustion. Let her sleep it off, and I'll come check on her tomorrow," he paused. He must have looked at his watch, because he added, "Well, later today actually."

There was a creaking sound as they both pushed off from the couch to get to their feet.

"Is it true?" Charlie whispered. Their voices were farther away now. I strained to hear. "Did they leave?"

"Dr. Cullen asked us not to say anything," Dr. Gerandy answered. "The offer was very sudden; they had to choose immediately. Carlisle didn't want to make a big production out of leaving."

"A little warning might have been nice," Charlie grumbled.

Dr. Gerandy sounded uncomfortable when he replied. "Yes, well, in this situation, some warning might have been called for."

I didn't want to listen anymore. I felt around for the edge of the quilt someone had laid on top of me, and pulled it over my ear.

I drifted in and out of alertness. I heard Charlie whisper thanks to the volunteers as, one by one, they left. I felt his fingers on my forehead, and then the weight of another blanket. The phone rang a few times, and he hurried to catch it before it could wake me. He muttered reassurances in a low voice to the callers.

"Yeah, we found her. She's okay. She got lost. She's fine now," he said again and again.

I heard the springs in the armchair groan when he settled himself in for the night.

A few minutes later, the phone rang again.

Charlie moaned as he struggled to his feet, and then he rushed, stumbling, to the kitchen. I pulled my head deeper under the blankets, not wanting to listen to the same conversation again.

"Yeah," Charlie said, and yawned.

His voice changed, it was much more alert when he spoke again. "Where?" There was a pause. "You're sure it's outside the reservation?" Another short pause. "But what could be burning out *there?*" He sounded both worried and mystified. "Look, I'll call down there and check it out."

I listened with more interest as he punched in a number.

"Hey, Billy, it's Charlie—sorry I'm calling so early . . . no, she's fine. She's sleeping. . . . Thanks, but that's not why I called. I just got a call from Mrs. Stanley, and she says that from her second-story window she can see fires out on the sea cliffs, but I didn't really. . . . Oh!" Suddenly there was an edge in his voice—irritation . . . or anger. "And why are they doing that? Uh huh. Really?" He said it sarcastically. "Well, don't apologize to *me*. Yeah, yeah. Just make sure the flames don't spread. . . . I know, I know, I'm surprised they got them lit at all in this weather."

Charlie hesitated, and then added grudgingly. "Thanks for sending Sam and the other boys up. You were right— they do know the forest better than we do. It was Sam who found her, so I owe you one. . . . Yeah, I'll talk to you later," he agreed, still sour, before hanging up.

Charlie muttered something incoherent as he shuffled back to the living room.

"What's wrong?" I asked.

He hurried to my side.

"I'm sorry I woke you, honey."

"Is something burning?"

"It's nothing," he assured me. "Just some bonfires out on the cliffs."

"Bonfires?" I asked. My voice didn't sound curious. It sounded dead.

Charlie frowned. "Some of the kids from the reservation being rowdy," he explained.

"Why?" I wondered dully.

I could tell he didn't want to answer. He looked at the floor under his knees. "They're celebrating the news." His tone was bitter.

There was only one piece of news I could think of, try as I might not to. And then the pieces snapped together. "Because the Cullens left," I whispered. "They don't like the Cullens in La Push—I'd forgotten about that."

The Quileutes had their superstitions about the "cold ones," the blood-drinkers that were enemies to their tribe, just like they had their legends of the great flood and wolf-men ancestors. Just stories, folklore, to most of them. Then there were the few that believed. Charlie's good friend Billy Black believed, though even Jacob, his own son, thought he was full of stupid superstitions. Billy had warned me to stay away from the Cullens. . . .

The name stirred something inside me, something that began to claw its way toward the surface, something I knew I didn't want to face.

"It's ridiculous," Charlie spluttered.

We sat in silence for a moment. The sky was no longer black outside the window. Somewhere behind the rain, the sun was beginning to rise.

"Bella?" Charlie asked.

I looked at him uneasily.

"He left you alone in the woods?" Charlie guessed.

I deflected his question. "How did you know where to find me?" My mind shied away from the inevitable awareness that was coming, coming quickly now.

"Your note," Charlie answered, surprised. He reached into the back pocket of his jeans and pulled out a much-abused piece of paper. It was dirty and damp, with multiple creases from being opened and refolded many times. He unfolded it again, and held it up as evidence. The messy handwriting was remarkably close to my own.

Going for a walk with Edward, up the path, it said. *Back soon, B.*

"When you didn't come back, I called the Cullens, and no one answered," Charlie said in a low voice. "Then I called the hospital, and Dr. Gerandy told me that Carlisle was gone."

"Where did they go?" I mumbled.

He stared at me. "Didn't Edward tell you?"

I shook my head, recoiling. The sound of his name unleashed the thing that was clawing inside of me—a pain that knocked me breathless, astonished me with its force.

Charlie eyed me doubtfully as he answered. "Carlisle took a job with a big hospital in Los Angeles. I guess they threw a lot of money at him."

Sunny L.A. The last place they would really go. I remembered my nightmare with the mirror . . . the bright sunlight shimmering off of his skin—

Agony ripped through me with the memory of his face.

"I want to know if Edward left you alone out there in the middle of the woods," Charlie insisted.

His name sent another wave of torture through me. I shook my head, frantic, desperate to escape the pain. "It was my fault. He left me right here on the trail, in sight of the house . . . but I tried to follow him."

Charlie started to say something; childishly, I covered my ears. "I can't talk about this anymore, Dad. I want to go to my room."

Before he could answer, I scrambled up from the couch and lurched my way up the stairs.

Someone had been in the house to leave a note for Charlie, a note that would lead him to find me. From the minute that I'd realized this, a horrible suspicion began to grow in my head. I rushed to my room, shutting and locking the door behind me before I ran to the CD player by my bed.

Everything looked exactly the same as I'd left it. I pressed down on the top of the CD player. The latch unhooked, and the lid slowly swung open.

It was empty.

The album Renée had given me sat on the floor beside the bed, just where I'd put it last. I lifted the cover with a shaking hand.

I didn't have to flip any farther than the first page. The little metal corners no longer held a picture in place. The page was blank except for my own handwriting scrawled across the bottom: *Edward Cullen, Charlie's kitchen, Sept. 13th.*

I stopped there. I was sure that he would have been very thorough.

It will be as if I'd never existed, he'd promised me.

I felt the smooth wooden floor beneath my knees, and then the palms of my hands, and then it was pressed against the skin of my cheek. I hoped that I was fainting, but, to my disappointment, I didn't lose consciousness. The waves of pain that had only lapped at me before now reared high up and washed over my head, pulling me under.

I did not resurface.

OCTOBER

NOVEMBER

DECEMBER

JANUARY

4. WAKING UP

TIME PASSES. EVEN WHEN IT SEEMS IMPOSSIBLE. EVEN when each tick of the second hand aches like the pulse of blood behind a bruise. It passes unevenly, in strange lurches and dragging lulls, but pass it does. Even for me.

CHARLIE'S FIST CAME DOWN ON THE TABLE. "THAT'S IT, Bella! I'm sending you home."

I looked up from my cereal, which I was pondering rather than eating, and stared at Charlie in shock. I hadn't been following the conversation—actually, I hadn't been aware that we were having a conversation—and I wasn't sure what he meant.

"I *am* home," I mumbled, confused.

"I'm sending you to Renée, to Jacksonville," he clarified.

Charlie watched with exasperation as I slowly grasped the meaning of his words.

"What did I do?" I felt my face crumple. It was so

unfair. My behavior had been above reproach for the past four months. After that first week, which neither of us ever mentioned, I hadn't missed a day of school or work. My grades were perfect. I never broke curfew—I never went anywhere from which to break curfew in the first place. I only very rarely served leftovers.

Charlie was scowling.

"You didn't *do* anything. That's the problem. You never do anything."

"You want me to get into trouble?" I wondered, my eyebrows pulling together in mystification. I made an effort to pay attention. It wasn't easy. I was so used to tuning everything out, my ears felt stopped up.

"Trouble would be better than this . . . this moping around all the time!"

That stung a bit. I'd been careful to avoid all forms of moroseness, moping included.

"I am not moping around."

"Wrong word," he grudgingly conceded. "Moping would be better—that would be doing *something*. You're just . . . lifeless, Bella. I think that's the word I want."

This accusation struck home. I sighed and tried to put some animation into my response.

"I'm sorry, Dad." My apology sounded a little flat, even to me. I'd thought I'd been fooling him. Keeping Charlie from suffering was the whole point of all this effort. How depressing to think that the effort had been wasted.

"I don't want you to apologize."

I sighed. "Then tell me what you do want me to do."

"Bella," he hesitated, scrutinizing my reaction to his

next words. "Honey, you're not the first person to go through this kind of thing, you know."

"I know that." My accompanying grimace was limp and unimpressive.

"Listen, honey. I think that—that maybe you need some help."

"Help?"

He paused, searching for the words again. "When your mother left," he began, frowning, "and took you with her." He inhaled deeply. "Well, that was a really bad time for me."

"I know, Dad," I mumbled.

"But I handled it," he pointed out. "Honey, you're not handling it. I waited, I hoped it would get better." He stared at me and I looked down quickly. "I think we both know it's not getting better."

"I'm fine."

He ignored me. "Maybe, well, maybe if you talked to someone about it. A professional."

"You want me to see a shrink?" My voice was a shade sharper as I realized what he was getting at.

"Maybe it would help."

"And maybe it wouldn't help one little bit."

I didn't know much about psychoanalysis, but I was pretty sure that it didn't work unless the subject was relatively honest. Sure, I could tell the truth—if I wanted to spend the rest of my life in a padded cell.

He examined my obstinate expression, and switched to another line of attack.

"It's beyond me, Bella. Maybe your mother—"

"Look," I said in a flat voice. "I'll go out tonight, if you want. I'll call Jess or Angela."

"That's not what I want," he argued, frustrated. "I don't think I can live through seeing you try *harder*. I've never seen anyone trying so hard. It hurts to watch."

I pretended to be dense, looking down at the table. "I don't understand, Dad. First you're mad because I'm not doing anything, and then you say you don't want me to go out."

"I want you to be happy—no, not even that much. I just want you not to be miserable. I think you'll have a better chance if you get out of Forks."

My eyes flashed up with the first small spark of feeling I'd had in too long to contemplate.

"I'm not leaving," I said.

"Why not?" he demanded.

"I'm in my last semester of school—it would screw everything up."

"You're a good student—you'll figure it out."

"I don't want to crowd Mom and Phil."

"Your mother's been dying to have you back."

"Florida is too hot."

His fist came down on the table again. "We both know what's really going on here, Bella, and it's not good for you." He took a deep breath. "It's been months. No calls, no letters, no contact. You can't keep waiting for him."

I glowered at him. The heat almost, but not quite, reached my face. It had been a long time since I'd blushed with any emotion.

This whole subject was utterly forbidden, as he was well aware.

"I'm not waiting for anything. I don't expect anything," I said in a low monotone.

"Bella—," Charlie began, his voice thick.

"I have to get to school," I interrupted, standing up and yanking my untouched breakfast from the table. I dumped my bowl in the sink without pausing to wash it out. I couldn't deal with any more conversation.

"I'll make plans with Jessica," I called over my shoulder as I strapped on my school bag, not meeting his eyes. "Maybe I won't be home for dinner. We'll go to Port Angeles and watch a movie."

I was out the front door before he could react.

In my haste to get away from Charlie, I ended up being one of the first ones to school. The plus side was that I got a really good parking spot. The downside was that I had free time on my hands, and I tried to avoid free time at all costs.

Quickly, before I could start thinking about Charlie's accusations, I pulled out my Calculus book. I flipped it open to the section we should be starting today, and tried to make sense of it. Reading math was even worse than listening to it, but I was getting better at it. In the last several months, I'd spent ten times the amount of time on Calculus than I'd ever spent on math before. As a result, I was managing to keep in the range of a low A. I knew Mr. Varner felt my improvement was all due to his superior teaching methods. And if that made him happy, I wasn't going to burst his bubble.

I forced myself to keep at it until the parking lot was full, and I ended up rushing to English. We were working on *Animal Farm*, an easy subject matter. I didn't mind communism; it was a welcome change from the exhausting romances that made up most of the curriculum. I settled into my seat, pleased by the distraction of Mr. Berty's lecture.

Time moved easily while I was in school. The bell rang all too soon. I started repacking my bag.

"Bella?"

I recognized Mike's voice, and I knew what his next words would be before he said them.

"Are you working tomorrow?"

I looked up. He was leaning across the aisle with an anxious expression. Every Friday he asked me the same question. Never mind that I hadn't taken so much as a sick day. Well, with one exception, months ago. But he had no reason to look at me with such concern. I was a model employee.

"Tomorrow is Saturday, isn't it?" I said. Having just had it pointed out to me by Charlie, I realized how lifeless my voice really sounded.

"Yeah, it is," he agreed. "See you in Spanish." He waved once before turning his back. He didn't bother walking me to class anymore.

I trudged off to Calculus with a grim expression. This was the class where I sat next to Jessica.

It had been weeks, maybe months, since Jess had even greeted me when I passed her in the hall. I knew I had offended her with my antisocial behavior, and she was sulking. It wasn't going to be easy to talk to her now—especially to ask her to do me a favor. I weighed my options carefully as I loitered outside the classroom, procrastinating.

I wasn't about to face Charlie again without some kind of social interaction to report. I knew I couldn't lie, though the thought of driving to Port Angeles and back alone—being sure my odometer reflected the correct mileage, just in case he checked—was very tempting. Jessica's mom was the biggest gossip in town, and Charlie was bound to run into Mrs. Stanley sooner rather than later. When he did, he would no doubt mention the trip. Lying was out.

With a sigh, I shoved the door open.

Mr. Varner gave me a dark look—he'd already started the lecture. I hurried to my seat. Jessica didn't look up as I sat next to her. I was glad that I had fifty minutes to mentally prepare myself.

This class flew by even faster than English. A small part of that speed was due to my goody-goody preparation this morning in the truck—but mostly it stemmed from the fact that time always sped up when I was looking forward to something unpleasant.

I grimaced when Mr. Varner dismissed the class five minutes early. He smiled like he was being nice.

"Jess?" My nose wrinkled as I cringed, waiting for her to turn on me.

She twisted in her seat to face me, eyeing me incredulously. "Are you talking to *me*, Bella?"

"Of course." I widened my eyes to suggest innocence.

"What? Do you need help with Calculus?" Her tone was a tad sour.

"No." I shook my head. "Actually, I wanted to know if you would . . . go to the movies with me tonight? I really need a girls' night out." The words sounded stiff, like badly delivered lines, and she looked suspicious.

"Why are you asking *me?*" she asked, still unfriendly.

"You're the first person I think of when I want girl time." I smiled, and I hoped the smile looked genuine. It was probably true. She was at least the first person I thought of when I wanted to avoid Charlie. It amounted to the same thing.

She seemed a little mollified. "Well, I don't know."

"Do you have plans?"

"No . . . I guess I can go with you. What do you want to see?"

"I'm not sure what's playing," I hedged. This was the tricky part. I racked my brain for a clue—hadn't I heard someone talk about a movie recently? Seen a poster? "How about that one with the female president?"

She looked at me oddly. "Bella, that one's been out of the theater *forever.*"

"Oh." I frowned. "Is there anything you'd like to see?"

Jessica's natural bubbliness started to leak out in spite of herself as she thought out loud. "Well, there's that new romantic comedy that's getting great reviews. I want to see that one. And my dad just saw *Dead End* and he really liked it."

I grasped at the promising title. "What's that one about?"

"Zombies or something. He said it was the scariest thing he'd seen in years."

"That sounds perfect." I'd rather deal with real zombies than watch a romance.

"Okay." She seemed surprised by my response. I tried to remember if I liked scary movies, but I wasn't sure. "Do you want me to pick you up after school?" she offered.

"Sure."

Jessica smiled at me with tentative friendliness before she left. My answering smile was just a little late, but I thought that she saw it.

The rest of the day passed quickly, my thoughts focused on planning for tonight. I knew from experience that once I got Jessica talking, I would be able to get away with a few mumbled responses at the appropriate moments. Only minimal interaction would be required.

The thick haze that blurred my days now was sometimes confusing. I was surprised when I found myself in my room, not clearly remembering the drive home from school or even opening the front door. But that didn't matter. Losing track of time was the most I asked from life.

I didn't fight the haze as I turned to my closet. The numbness was more essential in some places than in others. I barely registered what I was looking at as I slid the door aside to reveal the pile of rubbish on the left side of my closet, under the clothes I never wore.

My eyes did not stray toward the black garbage bag that held my present from that last birthday, did not see the shape of the stereo where it strained against the black plastic; I didn't think of the bloody mess my nails had been when I'd finished clawing it out of the dashboard.

I yanked the old purse I rarely used off the nail it hung from, and shoved the door shut.

Just then I heard a horn honking. I swiftly traded my wallet from my schoolbag into the purse. I was in a hurry, as if rushing would somehow make the night pass more quickly.

I glanced at myself in the hall mirror before I opened the door, arranging my features carefully into a smile and trying to hold them there.

"Thanks for coming with me tonight," I told Jess as I climbed into the passenger seat, trying to infuse my tone with gratitude. It had been a while since I'd really thought about what I was saying to anyone besides Charlie. Jess was harder. I wasn't sure which were the right emotions to fake.

"Sure. So, what brought this on?" Jess wondered as she drove down my street.

"Brought what on?"

"Why did you suddenly decide . . . to go out?" It sounded like she changed her question halfway through.

I shrugged. "Just needed a change."

I recognized the song on the radio then, and quickly reached for the dial. "Do you mind?" I asked.

"No, go ahead."

I scanned through the stations until I found one that was harmless. I peeked at Jess's expression as the new music filled the car.

Her eyes squinted. "Since when do you listen to rap?"

"I don't know," I said. "A while."

"You like this?" she asked doubtfully.

"Sure."

It would be much too hard to interact with Jessica normally if I had to work to tune out the music, too. I nodded my head, hoping I was in time with the beat.

"Okay. . . ." She stared out the windshield with wide eyes.

"So what's up with you and Mike these days?" I asked quickly.

"You see him more than I do."

The question hadn't started her talking like I'd hoped it would.

"It's hard to talk at work," I mumbled, and then I tried again. "Have you been out with anyone lately?"

"Not really. I go out with Conner sometimes. I went out with Eric two weeks ago." She rolled her eyes, and I sensed a long story. I clutched at the opportunity.

"Eric *Yorkie*? Who asked who?"

She groaned, getting more animated. "He did, of course! I couldn't think of a nice way to say no."

"Where did he take you?" I demanded, knowing she would interpret my eagerness as interest. "Tell me all about it."

She launched into her tale, and I settled into my seat, more comfortable now. I paid strict attention, murmuring in sympathy and gasping in horror as called for. When she was finished with her Eric story, she continued into a Conner comparison without any prodding.

The movie was playing early, so Jess thought we should

hit the twilight showing and eat later. I was happy to go along with whatever she wanted; after all, I was getting what I wanted—Charlie off my back.

I kept Jess talking through the previews, so I could ignore them more easily. But I got nervous when the movie started. A young couple was walking along a beach, swinging hands and discussing their mutual affection with gooey falseness. I resisted the urge to cover my ears and start humming. I had not bargained for a romance.

"I thought we picked the zombie movie," I hissed to Jessica.

"This *is* the zombie movie."

"Then why isn't anyone getting eaten?" I asked desperately.

She looked at me with wide eyes that were almost alarmed. "I'm sure that part's coming," she whispered.

"I'm getting popcorn. Do you want any?"

"No, thanks."

Someone shushed us from behind.

I took my time at the concession counter, watching the clock and debating what percentage of a ninety-minute movie could be spent on romantic exposition. I decided ten minutes was more than enough, but I paused just inside the theater doors to be sure. I could hear horrified screams blaring from the speakers, so I knew I'd waited long enough.

"You missed everything," Jess murmured when I slid back into my seat. "Almost everyone is a zombie now."

"Long line." I offered her some popcorn. She took a handful.

The rest of the movie was comprised of gruesome zombie attacks and endless screaming from the handful of people left alive, their numbers dwindling quickly. I would have thought there was nothing in that to disturb me. But I felt uneasy, and I wasn't sure why at first.

It wasn't until almost the very end, as I watched a haggard zombie shambling after the last shrieking survivor, that I realized what the problem was. The scene kept cutting between the horrified face of the heroine, and the dead, emotionless face of her pursuer, back and forth as it closed the distance.

And I realized which one resembled me the most.

I stood up.

"Where are you going? There's, like, two minutes left," Jess hissed.

"I need a drink," I muttered as I raced for the exit.

I sat down on the bench outside the theater door and tried very hard not to think of the irony. But it was ironic, all things considered, that, in the end, I would wind up as a *zombie*. I hadn't seen that one coming.

Not that I hadn't dreamed of becoming a mythical monster once—just never a grotesque, animated corpse. I shook my head to dislodge that train of thought, feeling panicky. I couldn't afford to think about what I'd once dreamed of.

It was depressing to realize that I wasn't the heroine anymore, that my story was over.

Jessica came out of the theater doors and hesitated, probably wondering where the best place was to search for me. When she saw me, she looked relieved, but only for a moment. Then she looked irritated.

"Was the movie too scary for you?" she wondered.

"Yeah," I agreed. "I guess I'm just a coward."

"That's funny." She frowned. "I didn't think you *were* scared—I was screaming all the time, but I didn't hear you scream once. So I didn't know why you left."

I shrugged. "Just scared."

She relaxed a little. "That was the scariest movie I think I've ever seen. I'll bet we're going to have nightmares tonight."

"No doubt about that," I said, trying to keep my voice normal. It was inevitable that I would have nightmares, but they wouldn't be about zombies. Her eyes flashed to my face and away. Maybe I hadn't succeeded with the normal voice.

"Where do you want to eat?" Jess asked.

"I don't care."

"Okay."

Jess started talking about the male lead in the movie as we walked. I nodded as she gushed over his hotness, unable to remember seeing a non-zombie man at all.

I didn't watch where Jessica was leading me. I was only vaguely aware that it was dark and quieter now. It took me longer than it should have to realize why it was quiet. Jessica had stopped babbling. I looked at her apologetically, hoping I hadn't hurt her feelings.

Jessica wasn't looking at me. Her face was tense; she stared straight ahead and walked fast. As I watched, her eyes darted quickly to the right, across the road, and back again.

I glanced around myself for the first time.

We were on a short stretch of unlit sidewalk. The little shops lining the street were all locked up for the night, windows black. Half a block ahead, the streetlights started up again, and I could see, farther down, the bright golden arches of the McDonald's she was heading for.

Across the street there was one open business. The windows were covered from inside and there were neon signs, advertisements for different brands of beer, glowing in front of them. The biggest sign, in brilliant green, was the name of the bar—One-Eyed Pete's. I wondered if there was some pirate theme not visible from outside. The metal door was propped open; it was dimly lit inside, and the low murmur of many voices and the sound of ice clinking in glasses floated across the street. Lounging against the wall beside the door were four men.

I glanced back at Jessica. Her eyes were fixed on the path ahead and she moved briskly. She didn't look frightened—just wary, trying to not attract attention to herself.

I paused without thinking, looking back at the four men with a strong sense of déjà vu. This was a different road, a different night, but the scene was so much the same. One of them was even short and dark. As I stopped and turned toward them, that one looked up in interest.

I stared back at him, frozen on the sidewalk.

"Bella?" Jess whispered. "What are you doing?"

I shook my head, not sure myself. "I think I know them . . . ," I muttered.

What was I doing? I should be running from this memory as fast as I could, blocking the image of the four lounging men from my mind, protecting myself with the numbness I couldn't function without. Why was I stepping, dazed, into the street?

It seemed too coincidental that I should be in Port Angeles with Jessica, on a dark street even. My eyes focused on the short one, trying to match the features to my memory of the man who had threatened me that night almost a year ago. I wondered if there was any way I would recognize the man, if it was really him. That particular part of that particular evening was just a blur. My body remembered it better than my mind did; the tension in my legs as I tried to decide whether to run or to stand my ground, the dryness in my throat as I struggled to build a decent scream, the tight stretch of skin across my knuckles as I clenched my hands into fists, the chills on the back of my neck when the dark-haired man called me "sugar." . . .

There was an indefinite, implied kind of menace to these men that had nothing to do with that other night. It sprung from the fact that they were strangers, and it was dark here, and they outnumbered us—nothing more specific than that. But it was enough that Jessica's voice cracked in panic as she called after me.

"Bella, come *on*!"

I ignored her, walking slowly forward without ever making the conscious decision to move my feet. I didn't understand why, but the nebulous threat the men presented drew me toward them. It was a senseless impulse, but I hadn't felt *any* kind of impulse in so long. . . . I followed it.

Something unfamiliar beat through my veins. Adrenaline, I realized, long absent from my system, drumming my pulse faster and fighting against the lack of sensation. It was strange—why the adrenaline when there was no fear? It was almost as if it were an echo of the last time I'd stood like this, on a dark street in Port Angeles with strangers.

I saw no reason for fear. I couldn't imagine anything in the world that there was left to be afraid of, not physically at least. One of the few advantages of losing everything.

I was halfway across the street when Jess caught up to me and grabbed my arm.

"Bella! You can't go in a bar!" she hissed.

"I'm not going in," I said absently, shaking her hand off. "I just want to see something. . . ."

"Are you crazy?" she whispered. "Are you suicidal?"

That question caught my attention, and my eyes focused on her.

"No, I'm not." My voice sounded defensive, but it was true. I wasn't suicidal. Even in the beginning, when death unquestionably would have been a relief, I didn't consider it. I owed too much to Charlie. I felt too responsible for Renée. I had to think of them.

And I'd made a promise not to do anything stupid or reckless. For all those reasons, I was still breathing.

Remembering that promise, I felt a twinge of guilt,

but what I was doing right now didn't really count. It wasn't like I was taking a blade to my wrists.

Jess's eyes were round, her mouth hung open. Her question about suicide had been rhetorical, I realized too late.

"Go eat," I encouraged her, waving toward the fast food. I didn't like the way she looked at me. "I'll catch up in a minute."

I turned away from her, back to the men who were watching us with amused, curious eyes.

"Bella, stop this right now!"

My muscles locked into place, froze me where I stood. Because it wasn't Jessica's voice that rebuked me now. It was a furious voice, a familiar voice, a beautiful voice—soft like velvet even though it was irate.

It was *his* voice—I was exceptionally careful not to think his name—and I was surprised that the sound of it did not knock me to my knees, did not curl me onto the pavement in a torture of loss. But there was no pain, none at all.

In the instant that I heard his voice, everything was very clear. Like my head had suddenly surfaced out of some dark pool. I was more aware of everything—sight, sound, the feel of the cold air that I hadn't noticed was blowing sharply against my face, the smells coming from the open bar door.

I looked around myself in shock.

"Go back to Jessica," the lovely voice ordered, still angry. "You promised—nothing stupid."

I was alone. Jessica stood a few feet from me, staring at

me with frightened eyes. Against the wall, the strangers watched, confused, wondering what I was doing, standing there motionless in the middle of the street.

I shook my head, trying to understand. I knew he wasn't there, and yet, he felt improbably close, close for the first time since . . . since the end. The anger in his voice was concern, the same anger that was once very familiar—something I hadn't heard in what felt like a lifetime.

"Keep your promise." The voice was slipping away, as if the volume was being turned down on a radio.

I began to suspect that I was having some kind of hallucination. Triggered, no doubt, by the memory—the déjà vu, the strange familiarity of the situation.

I ran through the possibilities quickly in my head.

Option one: I was crazy. That was the layman's term for people who heard voices in their heads.

Possible.

Option two: My subconscious mind was giving me what it thought I wanted. This was wish fulfillment—a momentary relief from pain by embracing the incorrect idea that *he* cared whether I lived or died. Projecting what he would have said if A) he were here, and B) he would be in any way bothered by something bad happening to me.

Probable.

I could see no option three, so I hoped it was the second option and this was just my subconscious running amuck, rather than something I would need to be hospitalized for.

My reaction was hardly sane, though—I was *grateful*. The sound of his voice was something that I'd feared I was losing, and so, more than anything else, I felt overwhelming gratitude that my unconscious mind had held onto that sound better than my conscious one had.

I was not allowed to think of him. That was something I tried to be very strict about. Of course I slipped; I was only human. But I was getting better, and so the pain was something I could avoid for days at a time now. The trade-off was the never-ending numbness. Between pain and nothing, I'd chosen nothing.

I waited for the pain now. I was not numb—my senses felt unusually intense after so many months of the haze—but the normal pain held off. The only ache was the disappointment that his voice was fading.

There was a second of choice.

The wise thing would be to run away from this potentially destructive—and certainly mentally unstable—development. It would be stupid to encourage hallucinations.

But his voice was fading.

I took another step forward, testing.

"Bella, turn around," he growled.

I sighed in relief. The anger was what I wanted to hear—false, fabricated evidence that he cared, a dubious gift from my subconscious.

Very few seconds had passed while I sorted this all out. My little audience watched, curious. It probably looked like I was just dithering over whether or not I was going to approach them. How could they guess that I was standing there enjoying an unexpected moment of insanity?

"Hi," one of the men called, his tone both confident and a bit sarcastic. He was fair-skinned and fair-haired, and he stood with the assurance of someone who thought of himself as quite good-looking. I couldn't tell whether he was or not. I was prejudiced.

The voice in my head answered with an exquisite snarl. I smiled, and the confident man seemed to take that as encouragement.

"Can I help you with something? You look lost." He grinned and winked.

I stepped carefully over the gutter, running with water that was black in the darkness.

"No. I'm not lost."

Now that I was closer—and my eyes felt oddly in focus—I analyzed the short, dark man's face. It was not familiar in any way. I suffered a curious sensation of disappointment that this was not the terrible man who had tried to hurt me almost a year ago.

The voice in my head was quiet now.

The short man noticed my stare. "Can I buy you a drink?" he offered, nervous, seeming flattered that I'd singled him out to stare at.

"I'm too young," I answered automatically.

He was baffled—wondering why I had approached them. I felt compelled to explain.

"From across the street, you looked like someone I knew. Sorry, my mistake."

The threat that had pulled me across the street had evaporated. These were not the dangerous men I remembered. They were probably nice guys. Safe. I lost interest.

"That's okay," the confident blonde said. "Stay and hang out with us."

"Thanks, but I can't." Jessica was hesitating in the

middle of the street, her eyes wide with outrage and betrayal.

"Oh, just a few minutes."

I shook my head, and turned to rejoin Jessica.

"Let's go eat," I suggested, barely glancing at her. Though I appeared to be, for the moment, freed of the zombie abstraction, I was just as distant. My mind was preoccupied. The safe, numb deadness did not come back, and I got more anxious with every minute that passed without its return.

"What were you thinking?" Jessica snapped. "You don't know them—they could have been psychopaths!"

I shrugged, wishing she would let it go. "I just thought I knew the one guy."

"You are so odd, Bella Swan. I feel like I don't know who you are."

"Sorry." I didn't know what else to say to that.

We walked to McDonald's in silence. I'd bet that she was wishing we'd taken her car instead of walking the short distance from the theater, so that she could use the drive-through. She was just as anxious now for this evening to be over as I had been from the beginning.

I tried to start a conversation a few times while we ate, but Jessica was not cooperative. I must have really offended her.

When we go back in the car, she tuned the stereo back to her favorite station and turned the volume too loud to allow easy conversation.

I didn't have to struggle as hard as usual to ignore the music. Even though my mind, for once, was not carefully numb and empty, I had too much to think about to hear the lyrics.

I waited for the numbness to return, or the pain. Because the pain must be coming. I'd broken my personal rules. Instead of shying away from the memories, I'd walked forward and greeted them. I'd heard his voice, so clearly, in my head. That was going to cost me, I was sure of it. Especially if I couldn't reclaim the haze to protect myself. I felt too alert, and that frightened me.

But relief was still the strongest emotion in my body—relief that came from the very core of my being.

As much as I struggled not to think of him, I did not struggle to *forget*. I worried—late in the night, when the exhaustion of sleep deprivation broke down my defenses—that it *was* all slipping away. That my mind was a sieve, and I would someday not be able to remember the precise color of his eyes, the feel of his cool skin, or the texture of his voice. I could not *think* of them, but I must *remember* them.

Because there was just one thing that I had to believe to be able to live—I had to know that he existed. That was all. Everything else I could endure. So long as he existed.

That's why I was more trapped in Forks than I ever had been before, why I'd fought with Charlie when he suggested a change. Honestly, it shouldn't matter; no one was ever coming back here.

But if I were to go to Jacksonville, or anywhere else bright and unfamiliar, how could I be sure he was real? In a place where I could never imagine him, the conviction might fade . . . and that I could not live through.

Forbidden to remember, terrified to forget; it was a hard line to walk.

I was surprised when Jessica stopped the car in front of my house. The ride had not taken long, but, short as it seemed, I wouldn't have thought that Jessica could go that long without speaking.

"Thanks for going out with me, Jess," I said as I opened my door. "That was...fun." I hoped that *fun* was the appropriate word.

"Sure," she muttered.

"I'm sorry about . . . after the movie."

"Whatever, Bella." She glared out the windshield instead of looking at me. She seemed to be growing angrier rather than getting over it.

"See you Monday?"

"Yeah. Bye."

I gave up and shut the door. She drove away, still without looking at me.

I'd forgotten her by the time I was inside.

Charlie was waiting for me in the middle of the hall, his arms folded tight over his chest with his hands balled into fists.

"Hey, Dad," I said absentmindedly as I ducked around Charlie, heading for the stairs. I'd been thinking about *him* for too long, and I wanted to be upstairs before it caught up with me.

"Where have you been?" Charlie demanded.

I looked at my dad, surprised. "I went to a movie in Port Angeles with Jessica. Like I told you this morning."

"Humph," he grunted.

"Is that okay?"

He studied my face, his eyes widening as if he saw something unexpected. "Yeah, that's fine. Did you have fun?"

"Sure," I said. "We watched zombies eat people. It was great."

His eyes narrowed.

"'Night, Dad."

He let me pass. I hurried to my room.

I lay in my bed a few minutes later, resigned as the pain finally made its appearance.

It was a crippling thing, this sensation that a huge hole had been punched through my chest, excising my most vital organs and leaving ragged, unhealed gashes around the edges that continued to throb and bleed despite the passage of time. Rationally, I knew my lungs must still be intact, yet I gasped for air and my head spun like my efforts yielded me nothing. My heart must have been beating, too, but I couldn't hear the sound of my pulse in my ears; my hands felt blue with cold. I curled inward, hugging my ribs to hold myself together. I scrambled for my numbness, my denial, but it evaded me.

And yet, I found I could survive. I was alert, I felt the pain—the aching loss that radiated out from my chest, sending wracking waves of hurt through my limbs and head—but it was manageable. I could live through it. It didn't feel like the pain had weakened over time, rather that I'd grown strong enough to bear it.

Whatever it was that had happened tonight—and whether it was the zombies, the adrenaline, or the hallucinations that were responsible—it had woken me up.

For the first time in a long time, I didn't know what to expect in the morning.

5. CHEATER

"BELLA, WHY DON'T YOU TAKE OFF," MIKE SUGGESTED, his eyes focused off to the side, not really looking at me. I wondered how long that had been going on without me noticing.

It was a slow afternoon at Newton's. At the moment there were only two patrons in the store, dedicated backpackers from the sound of their conversation. Mike had spent the last hour going through the pros and cons of two brands of lightweight packs with them. But they'd taken a break from serious pricing to indulge in trying to one-up each other with their latest tales from the trail. Their distraction had given Mike a chance to escape.

"I don't mind staying," I said. I still hadn't been able to

sink back into my protective shell of numbness, and everything seemed oddly close and loud today, like I'd taken cotton out of my ears. I tried to tune out the laughing hikers without success.

"I'm telling you," said the thickset man with the orange beard that didn't match his dark brown hair. "I've seen grizzlies pretty close up in Yellowstone, but they had nothing on this brute." His hair was matted, and his clothes looked like they'd been on his back for more than a few days. Fresh from the mountains.

"Not a chance. Black bears don't get that big. The grizzlies you saw were probably cubs." The second man was tall and lean, his face tanned and wind-whipped into an impressive leathery crust.

"Seriously, Bella, as soon as these two give up, I'm closing the place down," Mike murmured.

"If you want me to go…" I shrugged.

"On all fours it was taller than you," the bearded man insisted while I gathered my things together. "Big as a house and pitch-black. I'm going to report it to the ranger here. People ought to be warned—this wasn't up on the mountain, mind you—this was only a few miles from the trailhead."

Leather-face laughed and rolled his eyes. "Let me guess—you were on your way in? Hadn't eaten real food or slept off the ground in a week, right?"

"Hey, uh, Mike, right?" the bearded man called, looking toward us.

"See you Monday," I mumbled.

"Yes, sir," Mike replied, turning away.

"Say, have there been any warnings around here recently—about black bears?"

"No, sir. But it's always good to keep your distance and store your food correctly. Have you seen the new bear-safe canisters? They only weigh two pounds . . ."

The doors slid open to let me out into the rain. I hunched over inside my jacket as I dashed for my truck. The rain hammering against my hood sounded unusually loud, too, but soon the roar of the engine drowned out everything else.

I didn't want to go back to Charlie's empty house. Last night had been particularly brutal, and I had no desire to revisit the scene of the suffering. Even after the pain had subsided enough for me to sleep, it wasn't over. Like I'd told Jessica after the movie, there was never any doubt that I would have nightmares.

I always had nightmares now, every night. Not nightmares really, not in the plural, because it was always the *same* nightmare. You'd think I'd get bored after so many months, grow immune to it. But the dream never failed to horrify me, and only ended when I woke myself with screaming. Charlie didn't come in to see what was wrong anymore, to make sure there was no intruder strangling me or something like that—he was used to it now.

My nightmare probably wouldn't even frighten someone else. Nothing jumped out and screamed, "Boo!" There were no zombies, no ghosts, no psychopaths. There was nothing, really. Only nothing. Just the endless maze of moss-covered trees, so quiet that the silence was an uncomfortable pressure against my eardrums. It was dark, like dusk on a cloudy day, with only enough light to see that there was nothing to see. I hurried through the gloom without a path, always searching, searching, searching, getting more frantic as the time stretched on, trying to move faster, though the speed made me clumsy. . . . Then there would come the point in my dream— and I could feel it coming now, but could never seem to wake myself up before it hit—when I couldn't remember what it was that I was searching for. When I realized that there *was* nothing to search for, and nothing to find. That there never had been anything more than just this empty, dreary wood, and there never would be anything more for me . . . nothing but nothing. . . .

That was usually about when the screaming started.

I wasn't paying attention to where I was driving—just wandering through empty, wet side roads as I avoided the ways that would take me home—because I didn't have anywhere to go.

I wished I could feel numb again, but I couldn't remember how I'd managed it before. The nightmare was nagging at my mind and making me think about things that would cause me pain. I didn't want to remember the forest. Even as I shuddered away from the images, I felt my eyes fill with tears and the aching begin around the edges of the hole in my chest. I took one hand from the steering wheel and wrapped it around my torso to hold it in one piece.

It will be as if I'd never existed. The words ran through my head, lacking the perfect clarity of my hallucination last night. They were just words, soundless, like print on a page. Just words, but they ripped the hole wide open, and I stomped on the brake, knowing I should not drive while this incapacitated.

I curled over, pressing my face against the steering wheel and trying to breathe without lungs.

I wondered how long this could last. Maybe someday, years from now—if the pain would just decrease to the point where I could bear it—I would be able to look back on those few short months that would always be the best of my life. And, if it were possible that the pain would ever soften enough to allow me to do that, I was sure that I would feel grateful for as much time as he'd given me. More than I'd asked for, more than I'd deserved. Maybe someday I'd be able to see it that way.

But what if this hole never got any better? If the raw edges never healed? If the damage was permanent and irreversible?

I held myself tightly together. *As if he'd never existed*, I thought in despair. What a stupid and impossible promise to make! He could steal my pictures and reclaim his gifts, but that didn't put things back the way they'd been before I'd met him. The physical evidence was the most insignificant part of the equation. *I* was changed, my insides altered almost past the point of recognition. Even my outsides looked different—my face sallow, white except for the purple circles the nightmares had left under my eyes. My eyes were dark enough against my pallid skin that—if I were beautiful, and seen from a distance—I might even pass for a vampire now. But I was not beautiful, and I probably looked closer to a zombie.

As if he'd never existed? That was insanity. It was a promise that he could never keep, a promise that was broken as soon as he'd made it.

I thumped my head against the steering wheel, trying to distract myself from the sharper pain.

It made me feel silly for ever worrying about keeping *my* promise. Where was the logic in sticking to an agreement that had already been violated by the other party? Who cared if I was reckless and stupid? There was no reason to avoid recklessness, no reason why I shouldn't get to be stupid.

I laughed humorlessly to myself, still gasping for air. Reckless in Forks—now there was a hopeless proposition.

The dark humor distracted me, and the distraction eased the pain. My breath came easier, and I was able to lean back against the seat. Though it was cold today, my forehead was damp with sweat.

I concentrated on my hopeless proposition to keep from sliding back into the excruciating memories. To be reckless in Forks would take a lot of creativity—maybe more than I had. But I wished I could find some way. . . . I might feel better if I weren't holding fast, all alone, to a broken pact. If I were an oath-breaker, too. But how could I cheat on my side of the deal, here in this harmless little town? Of course, Forks hadn't *always* been so harmless, but now it was exactly what it had always appeared to be. It was dull, it was safe.

I stared out the windshield for a long moment, my thoughts moving sluggishly—I couldn't seem to make those thoughts go anywhere. I cut the engine, which was groaning in a pitiful way after idling for so long, and stepped out into the drizzle.

The cold rain dripped through my hair and then trickled across my cheeks like freshwater tears. It helped to clear my head. I blinked the water from my eyes, staring blankly across the road.

After a minute of staring, I recognized where I was. I'd parked in the middle of the north lane of Russell Avenue. I was standing in front of the Cheneys' house—my truck was blocking their driveway—and across the road lived the Markses. I knew I needed to move my truck, and that I ought to go home. It was wrong to wander the way I had, distracted and impaired, a menace on the roads of Forks. Besides, someone would notice me soon enough, and report me to Charlie.

As I took a deep breath in preparation to move, a sign in the Markses' yard caught my eye—it was just a big piece of cardboard leaning against their mailbox post, with black letters scrawled in caps across it.

Sometimes, kismet happens.

Coincidence? Or was it meant to be? I didn't know, but it seemed kind of silly to think that it was somehow fated, that the dilapidated motorcycles rusting in the Markses' front yard beside the hand-printed FOR SALE, AS IS sign were serving some higher purpose by existing there, right where I needed them to be.

So maybe it wasn't kismet. Maybe there were just all kinds of ways to be reckless, and I only now had my eyes open to them.

Reckless and stupid. Those were Charlie's two very favorite words to apply to motorcycles.

Charlie's job didn't get a lot of action compared to cops in bigger towns, but he did get called in on traffic accidents. With the long, wet stretches of freeway twisting and turning through the forest, blind corner after blind corner, there was no shortage of *that* kind of action. But even with all the huge log-haulers barreling around the turns, mostly people walked away. The exceptions to that rule were often on motorcycles, and Charlie had seen one too many victims, almost always kids, smeared on the highway. He'd made me promise before I was ten that I would never accept a ride on a motorcycle. Even at that age, I didn't have to think twice before promising. Who would want to ride a motorcycle *here*? It would be like taking a sixty-mile-per-hour bath.

So many promises I kept . . .

It clicked together for me then. I wanted to be stupid and reckless, and I wanted to break promises. Why stop at one?

That's as far as I thought it through. I sloshed through the rain to the Markses' front door and rang the bell.

One of the Marks boys opened the door, the younger one, the freshman. I couldn't remember his name. His sandy hair only came up to my shoulder.

He had no trouble remembering my name. "Bella Swan?" he asked in surprise.

"How much do you want for the bike?" I panted, jerking my thumb over my shoulder toward the sales display.

"Are you serious?" he demanded.

"Of course I am."

"They don't work."

I sighed impatiently—this was something I'd already inferred from the sign. "How much?"

"If you really want one, just take it. My mom made my dad move them down to the road so they'd get picked up with the garbage."

I glanced at the bikes again and saw that they were resting on a pile of yard clippings and dead branches. "Are you positive about that?"

"Sure, you want to ask her?"

It was probably better not to involve adults who might mention this to Charlie.

"No, I believe you."

"You want me to help you?" he offered. "They're not light."

"Okay, thanks. I only need one, though."

"Might as well take both," the boy said. "Maybe you could scavenge some parts."

He followed me out into the downpour and helped me load both of the heavy bikes into the back of my truck. He seemed eager to be rid of them, so I didn't argue.

"What are you going to do with them, anyway?" he asked. "They haven't worked in years."

"I kind of guessed that," I said, shrugging. My spur-of-the-moment whim hadn't come with a plan intact. "Maybe I'll take them to Dowling's."

He snorted. "Dowling would charge more to fix them than they'd be worth running."

I couldn't argue with that. John Dowling had earned a reputation for his pricing; no one went to him except in an emergency. Most people preferred to make the drive up to Port Angeles, if their car was able. I'd been very lucky on that front—I'd been worried, when Charlie first gifted me my ancient truck, that I wouldn't be able to afford to keep it running. But I'd never had a single problem with it, other than the screaming-loud engine and the fifty-five-mile-per-hour maximum speed limit. Jacob Black had kept it in great shape when it had belonged to his father, Billy. . . .

Inspiration hit like a bolt of lightning—not unreasonable, considering the storm. "You know what? That's okay. I know someone who builds cars."

"Oh. That's good." He smiled in relief.

He waved as I pulled away, still smiling. Friendly kid.

I drove quickly and purposefully now, in a hurry to get home before there was the slightest chance of Charlie appearing, even in the highly unlikely event that he might knock off early. I dashed through the house to the phone, keys still in hand.

"Chief Swan, please," I said when the deputy answered. "It's Bella."

"Oh, hey, Bella," Deputy Steve said affably. "I'll go get him."

I waited.

"What's wrong, Bella?" Charlie demanded as soon as he picked up the phone.

"Can't I call you at work without there being an emergency?"

He was quiet for a minute. "You never have before. *Is* there an emergency?"

"No. I just wanted directions to the Blacks' place—I'm not sure I can remember the way. I want to visit Jacob. I haven't seen him in months."

When Charlie spoke again, his voice was much happier. "That's a great idea, Bells. Do you have a pen?"

The directions he gave me were very simple. I assured him that I would be back for dinner, though he tried to tell me not to hurry. He wanted to join me in La Push, and I wasn't having that.

So it was with a deadline that I drove too quickly through the storm-darkened streets out of town. I hoped I could get Jacob alone. Billy would probably tell on me if he knew what I was up to.

While I drove, I worried a little bit about Billy's reaction to seeing me. He would be *too* pleased. In Billy's mind, no doubt, this had all worked out better than he had dared to hope. His pleasure and relief would only remind me of the one I couldn't bear to be reminded of. *Not again today*, I pleaded silently. I was spent.

The Blacks' house was vaguely familiar, a small wooden place with narrow windows, the dull red paint making it resemble a tiny barn. Jacob's head peered out of the window before I could even get out of the truck. No doubt the familiar roar of the engine had tipped him off to my approach. Jacob had been very grateful when Charlie bought Billy's truck for me, saving Jacob from having to drive it when he came of age. I liked my truck very much, but Jacob seemed to consider the speed restrictions a shortcoming.

He met me halfway to the house.

"Bella!" His excited grin stretched wide across his face, the bright teeth standing in vivid contrast to the deep russet color of his skin. I'd never seen his hair out of its usual ponytail before. It fell like black satin curtains on either side of his broad face.

Jacob had grown into some of his potential in the last eight months. He'd passed that point where the soft muscles of childhood hardened into the solid, lanky build of a teenager; the tendons and veins had become prominent under the red-brown skin of his arms, his hands. His face was still sweet like I remembered it, though it had hardened, too—the planes of his cheekbones sharper, his jaw squared off, all childish roundness gone.

"Hey, Jacob!" I felt an unfamiliar surge of enthusiasm at his smile. I realized that I was pleased to see him. This knowledge surprised me.

I smiled back, and something clicked silently into place, like two corresponding puzzle pieces. I'd forgotten how much I really liked Jacob Black.

He stopped a few feet away from me, and I stared up at him in surprise, leaning my head back though the rain pelted my face.

"You grew again!" I accused in amazement.

He laughed, his smile widening impossibly. "Six five," he announced with self-satisfaction. His voice was deeper, but it had the husky tone I remembered.

"Is it ever going to stop?" I shook my head in disbelief. "You're huge."

"Still a beanpole, though." He grimaced. "Come inside! You're getting all wet."

He led the way, twisting his hair in his big hands as he walked. He pulled a rubber band from his hip pocket and wound it around the bundle.

"Hey, Dad," he called as he ducked to get through the front door. "Look who stopped by."

Billy was in the tiny square living room, a book in his hands. He set the book in his lap and wheeled himself forward when he saw me.

"Well, what do you know! It's good to see you, Bella."

We shook hands. Mine was lost in his wide grasp.

"What brings you out here? Everything okay with Charlie?"

"Yes, absolutely. I just wanted to see Jacob—I haven't seen him in forever."

Jacob's eyes brightened at my words. He was smiling so big it looked like it would hurt his cheeks.

"Can you stay for dinner?" Billy was eager, too.

"No, I've got to feed Charlie, you know."

"I'll call him now," Billy suggested. "He's always invited."

I laughed to hide my discomfort. "It's not like you'll never see me again. I promise I'll be back again soon—so much you'll get sick of me." After all, if Jacob could fix the bike, someone had to teach me how to ride it.

Billy chuckled in response. "Okay, maybe next time."

"So, Bella, what do you want to do?" Jacob asked.

"Whatever. What were you doing before I interrupted?" I was strangely comfortable here. It was familiar, but only distantly. There were no painful reminders of the recent past.

Jacob hesitated. "I was just heading out to work on my car, but we can do something else . . ."

"No, that's perfect!" I interrupted. "I'd love to see your car."

"Okay," he said, not convinced. "It's out back, in the garage."

Even better, I thought to myself. I waved at Billy. "See you later."

A thick stand of trees and shrubbery concealed his garage from the house. The garage was no more than a couple of big preformed sheds that had been bolted together with their interior walls knocked out. Under this shelter, raised on cinder blocks, was what looked to me like a completed automobile. I recognized the symbol on the grille, at least.

"What kind of Volkswagen is that?" I asked.

"It's an old Rabbit—1986, a classic."

"How's it going?"

"Almost finished," he said cheerfully. And then his voice dropped into a lower key. "My dad made good on his promise last spring."

"Ah," I said.

He seemed to understand my reluctance to open the subject. I tried not to remember last May at the prom. Jacob had been bribed by his father with money and car parts to deliver a message there. Billy wanted me to stay a safe distance from the most important person in my life. It turned out that his concern was, in the end, unnecessary. I was all too safe now.

But I was going to see what I could do to change that.

"Jacob, what do you know about motorcycles?" I asked.

He shrugged. "Some. My friend Embry has a dirt bike. We work on it together sometimes. Why?"

"Well . . . ," I pursed my lips as I considered. I wasn't sure if he could keep his mouth shut, but I didn't have many other options. "I recently acquired a couple of bikes, and they're not in the greatest condition. I wonder if you could get them running?"

"Cool." He seemed truly pleased by the challenge. His face glowed. "I'll give it a try."

I held up one finger in warning. "The thing is," I explained, "Charlie doesn't approve of motorcycles. Honestly, he'd probably bust a vein in his forehead if he knew about this. So you can't tell Billy."

"Sure, sure." Jacob smiled. "I understand."

"I'll pay you," I continued.

This offended him. "No. I want to help. You can't pay me."

"Well . . . how about a trade, then?" I was making this up as I went, but it seemed reasonable enough. "I only need one bike—and I'll need lessons, too. So how about this? I'll give you the other bike, and then you can teach me."

"Swee-eet." He made the word into two syllables.

"Wait a sec—are you legal yet? When's your birthday?"

"You missed it," he teased, narrowing his eyes in mock resentment. "I'm sixteen."

"Not that your age ever stopped you before," I muttered. "Sorry about your birthday."

"Don't worry about it. I missed yours. What are you, forty?"

I sniffed. "Close."

"We'll have a joint party to make up for it."

"Sounds like a date."

His eyes sparkled at the word.

I needed to reign in the enthusiasm before I gave him the wrong idea—it was just that it had been a long time since I'd felt so light and buoyant. The rarity of the feeling made it more difficult to manage.

"Maybe when the bikes are finished—our present to ourselves," I added.

"Deal. When will you bring them down?"

I bit my lip, embarrassed. "They're in my truck now," I admitted.

"Great." He seemed to mean it.

"Will Billy see if we bring them around?"

He winked at me. "We'll be sneaky."

We eased around from the east, sticking to the trees when we were in view of the windows, affecting a casual-looking stroll, just in case. Jacob unloaded the bikes swiftly from the truck bed, wheeling them one by one into the shrubbery where I hid. It looked too easy for him—I'd remembered the bikes being much, much heavier than that.

"These aren't half bad," Jacob appraised as we pushed

them through the cover of the trees. "This one here will actually be worth something when I'm done—it's an old Harley Sprint."

"That one's yours, then."

"Are you sure?"

"Absolutely."

"These are going to take some cash, though," he said, frowning down at the blackened metal. "We'll have to save up for parts first."

"*We* nothing," I disagreed. "If you're doing this for free, I'll pay for the parts."

"I don't know . . . ," he muttered.

"I've got some money saved. College fund, you know." *College, schmollege*, I thought to myself. It wasn't like I'd saved up enough to go anywhere special—and besides, I had no desire to leave Forks anyway. What difference would it make if I skimmed a little bit off the top?

Jacob just nodded. This all made perfect sense to him.

As we skulked back to the makeshift garage, I contemplated my luck. Only a teenage boy would agree to this: deceiving both our parents while repairing dangerous vehicles using money meant for my college education. He didn't see anything wrong with that picture. Jacob was a gift from the gods.

6. FRIENDS

THE MOTORCYCLES DIDN'T NEED TO BE HIDDEN ANY further than simply placing them in Jacob's shed. Billy's wheelchair couldn't maneuver the uneven ground separating it from the house.

Jacob started pulling the first bike—the red one, which was destined for me—to pieces immediately. He opened up the passenger door of the Rabbit so I could sit on the seat instead of the ground. While he worked, Jacob chattered happily, needing only the lightest of nudges from me to keep the conversation rolling. He updated me on the progress of his sophomore year of school, running on about his classes and his two best friends.

"Quil and Embry?" I interrupted. "Those are unusual names."

Jacob chuckled. "Quil's is a hand-me-down, and I think Embry got named after a soap opera star. I can't say anything, though. They fight dirty if you start on their names—they'll tag team you."

"Good friends." I raised one eyebrow.

"No, they are. Just don't mess with their names."

Just then a call echoed in the distance. "Jacob?" someone shouted.

"Is that Billy?" I asked.

"No." Jacob ducked his head, and it looked like he was blushing under his brown skin. "Speak of the devil," he mumbled, "and the devil shall appear."

"Jake? Are you out here?" The shouting voice was closer now.

"Yeah!" Jacob shouted back, and sighed.

We waited through the short silence until two tall, dark-skinned boys strolled around the corner into the shed.

One was slender, and almost as tall as Jacob. His black hair was chin-length and parted down the middle, one side tucked behind his left ear while the right side swung free. The shorter boy was more burly. His white T-shirt strained over his well-developed chest, and he seemed gleefully conscious of that fact. His hair was so short it was almost a buzz.

Both boys stopped short when they saw me. The thin boy glanced swiftly back and forth between Jacob and me, while the brawny boy kept his eyes on me, a slow smile spreading across his face.

"Hey, guys," Jacob greeted them halfheartedly.

"Hey, Jake," the short one said without looking away from me. I had to smile in response, his grin was so impish. When I did, he winked at me. "Hi, there."

"Quil, Embry—this is my friend, Bella."

Quil and Embry, I still didn't know which was which, exchanged a loaded look.

"Charlie's kid, right?" the brawny boy asked me, holding out his hand.

"That's right," I confirmed, shaking hands with him. His grasp was firm; it looked like he was flexing his bicep.

"I'm Quil Ateara," he announced grandly before releasing my hand.

"Nice to meet you, Quil."

"Hey, Bella. I'm Embry, Embry Call—you probably already figured that out, though." Embry smiled a shy smile and waved with one hand, which he then shoved in the pocket of his jeans.

I nodded. "Nice to meet you, too."

"So what are you guys doing?" Quil asked, still looking at me.

"Bella and I are going to fix up these bikes," Jacob explained inaccurately. But *bikes* seemed to be the magic word. Both boys went to examine Jacob's project, drilling him with educated questions. Many of the words they used were unfamiliar to me, and I figured I'd have to have a Y chromosome to really understand the excitement.

They were still immersed in talk of parts and pieces when I decided that I needed to head back home before Charlie showed up here. With a sigh, I slid out of the Rabbit.

Jacob looked up, apologetic. "We're boring you, aren't we?"

"Naw." And it wasn't a lie. I was *enjoying* myself—how strange. "I just have to go cook dinner for Charlie."

"Oh . . . well, I'll finish taking these apart tonight and figure out what more we'll need to get started rebuilding them. When do you want to work on them again?"

"Could I come back tomorrow?" Sundays were the bane of my existence. There was never enough homework to keep me busy.

Quil nudged Embry's arm and they exchanged grins.

Jacob smiled in delight. "That would be great!"

"If you make a list, we can go shop for parts," I suggested.

Jacob's face fell a little. "I'm still not sure I should let you pay for everything."

I shook my head. "No way. I'm bankrolling this party. You just have to supply the labor and expertise."

Embry rolled his eyes at Quil.

"That doesn't seem right," Jacob shook his head.

"Jake, if I took these to a mechanic, how much would he charge me?" I pointed out.

He smiled. "Okay, you're getting a deal."

"Not to mention the riding lessons," I added.

Quil grinned widely at Embry and whispered something I didn't catch. Jacob's hand flashed out to smack the back of Quil's head. "That's it, get out," he muttered.

"No, really, I have to go," I protested, heading for the door. "I'll see you tomorrow, Jacob."

As soon as I was out of sight, I heard Quil and Embry chorus, "Wooooo!"

The sound of a brief scuffle followed, interspersed with an "ouch" and a "hey!"

"If either of you set so much as one toe on my land to-morrow . . ." I heard Jacob threaten. His voice was lost as I walked through the trees.

I giggled quietly. The sound made my eyes widen in wonder. I was laughing, actually laughing, and there wasn't even anyone watching. I felt so weightless that I laughed again, just make the feeling last longer.

I beat Charlie home. When he walked in I was just tak-ing the fried chicken out of the pan and laying it on a pile of paper towels.

"Hey, Dad." I flashed him a grin.

Shock flitted across his face before he pulled his expres-sion together. "Hey, honey," he said, his voice uncertain. "Did you have fun with Jacob?"

I started moving the food to the table. "Yeah, I did."

"Well, that's good." He was still cautious. "What did you two do?"

Now it was my turn to be cautious. "I hung out in his garage and watched him work. Did you know he's re-building a Volkswagen?"

"Yeah, I think Billy mentioned that."

The interrogation had to stop when Charlie began chewing, but he continued to study my face as he ate.

After dinner, I dithered around, cleaning the kitchen twice, and then did my homework slowly in the front room while Charlie watched a hockey game. I waited as long as I could, but finally Charlie mentioned the late hour. When I didn't respond, he got up, stretched, and then left, turning out the light behind him. Reluctantly, I followed.

As I climbed the stairs, I felt the last of the afternoon's abnormal sense of well-being drain from my system, replaced by a dull fear at the thought of what I was going to have to live through now.

I wasn't numb anymore. Tonight would, no doubt, be as horrific as last night. I lay down on my bed and curled into a ball in preparation for the onslaught. I squeezed my eyes shut and . . . the next thing I next I knew, it was morning.

I stared at the pale silver light coming through my window, stunned.

For the first time in more than four months, I'd slept without dreaming. Dreaming *or* screaming. I couldn't tell which emotion was stronger—the relief or the shock.

I lay still in my bed for a few minutes, waiting for it to come back. Because something must be coming. If not the pain, then the numbness. I waited, but nothing happened. I felt more rested than I had in a long time.

I didn't trust this to last. It was a slippery, precarious edge that I balanced on, and it wouldn't take much to knock me back down. Just glancing around my room with these suddenly clear eyes—noticing how strange it looked, too tidy, like I didn't live here at all—was dangerous.

I pushed that thought from my mind, and concentrated, as I got dressed, on the fact that I was going to see Jacob again today. The thought made me feel almost . . . hopeful. Maybe it would be the same as yesterday. Maybe I wouldn't have to remind myself to look interested and to nod or smile at appropriate intervals, the way I had to with everyone else. Maybe . . . but I wouldn't trust this to last, either. Wouldn't trust it to be the same—so easy— as yesterday. I wasn't going to set myself up for disappointment like that.

At breakfast, Charlie was being careful, too. He tried to hide his scrutiny, keeping his eyes on his eggs until he thought I wasn't looking.

"What are you up to today?" he asked, eyeing a loose thread on the edge of his cuff like he wasn't paying much attention to my answer.

"I'm going to hang out with Jacob again."

He nodded without looking up. "Oh," he said.

"Do you mind?" I pretended to worry. "I could stay. . . ."

He glanced up quickly, a hint of panic in his eyes. "No, no! You go ahead. Harry was going to come up to watch the game with me anyway."

"Maybe Harry could give Billy a ride up," I suggested. The fewer witnesses the better.

"That's a great idea."

I wasn't sure if the game was just an excuse for kicking me out, but he looked excited enough now. He headed to the phone while I donned my rain jacket. I felt self-conscious with the checkbook shoved in my jacket pocket. It was something I never used.

Outside, the rain came down like water slopped from a bucket. I had to drive more slowly than I wanted to; I could hardly see a car length in front of the truck. But I finally made it through the muddy lanes to Jacob's house. Before I'd killed the engine, the front door opened and Jacob came running out with a huge black umbrella.

He held it over my door while I opened it.

"Charlie called—said you were on your way," Jacob explained with a grin.

Effortlessly, without a conscious command to the muscles around my lips, my answering smile spread across my face. A strange feeling of warmth bubbled up in my throat, despite the icy rain splattering on my cheeks.

"Hi, Jacob."

"Good call on inviting Billy up." He held up his hand for a high five.

I had to reach so high to slap his hand that he laughed.

Harry showed up to get Billy just a few minutes later. Jacob took me on a brief tour of his tiny room while we waited to be unsupervised.

"So where to, Mr. Goodwrench?" I asked as soon as the door closed behind Billy.

Jacob pulled a folded paper out of his pocket and smoothed it out. "We'll start at the dump first, see if we can get lucky. This could get a little expensive," he warned me. "Those bikes are going to need a lot of help before they'll run again." My face didn't look worried enough, so he continued. "I'm talking about maybe more than a hundred dollars here."

I pulled my checkbook out, fanned myself with it, and rolled my eyes at his worries. "We're covered."

It was a very strange kind of day. I enjoyed myself. Even at the dump, in the slopping rain and ankle-deep mud. I wondered at first if it was just the aftershock of losing the numbness, but I didn't think that was enough of an explanation.

I was beginning to think it was mostly Jacob. It wasn't just that he was always so happy to see me, or that he didn't watch me out of the corner of his eye, waiting for me to do something that would mark me as crazy or depressed. It was nothing that related to me at all.

It was Jacob himself. Jacob was simply a perpetually happy person, and he carried that happiness with him like an aura, sharing it with whoever was near him. Like an earthbound sun, whenever someone was within his gravitational pull, Jacob warmed them. It was natural, a part of who he was. No wonder I was so eager to see him.

Even when he commented on the gaping hole in my dashboard, it didn't send me into a panic like it should have.

"Did the stereo break?" he wondered.

"Yeah," I lied.

He poked around in the cavity. "Who took it out? There's a lot of damage. . . ."

"I did," I admitted.

He laughed. "Maybe you shouldn't touch the motorcycles too much."

"No problem."

According to Jacob, we did get lucky at the dump. He was very excited about several grease-blackened pieces of twisted metal that he found; I was just impressed that he could tell what they were supposed to be.

From there we went to the Checker Auto Parts down in Hoquiam. In my truck, it was more than a two hour drive south on the winding freeway, but the time passed easily with Jacob. He chattered about his friends and his school, and I found myself asking questions, not even pretending, truly curious to hear what he had to say.

"I'm doing all the talking," he complained after a long story about Quil and the trouble he'd stirred up by asking out a senior's steady girlfriend. "Why don't you take a turn? What's going on in Forks? It has to be more exciting than La Push."

"Wrong," I sighed. "There's really nothing. Your friends are a lot more interesting than mine. I like your friends. Quil's funny."

He frowned. "I think Quil likes you, too."

I laughed. "He's a little young for me."

Jacob's frown deepened. "He's not that much younger than you. It's just a year and a few months."

I had a feeling we weren't talking about Quil anymore. I kept my voice light, teasing. "Sure, but, considering the difference in maturity between guys and girls, don't you have to count that in dog years? What does that make me, about twelve years older?"

He laughed, rolling his eyes. "Okay, but if you're going

to get picky like that, you have to average in size, too. You're so small, I'll have to knock ten years off your total."

"Five foot four is perfectly average." I sniffed. "It's not my fault you're a freak."

We bantered like that till Hoquiam, still arguing over the correct formula to determine age—I lost two more years because I didn't know how to change a tire, but gained one back for being in charge of the bookkeeping at my house—until we were in Checker, and Jacob had to concentrate again. We found everything left on his list, and Jacob felt confident that he could make a lot of progress with our haul.

By the time we got back to La Push, I was twenty-three and he was thirty—he was definitely weighting skills in his favor.

I hadn't forgotten the reason for what I was doing. And, even though I was enjoying myself more than I'd thought possible, there was no lessening of my original desire. I still wanted to cheat. It was senseless, and I really didn't care. I was going to be as reckless as I could possibly manage in Forks. I would not be the only keeper of an empty contract. Getting to spend time with Jacob was just a much bigger perk than I'd expected.

Billy wasn't back yet, so we didn't have to be sneaky about unloading our day's spoils. As soon as we had everything laid out on the plastic floor next to Jacob's toolbox, he went right to work, still talking and laughing while his fingers combed expertly through the metal pieces in front of him.

Jacob's skill with his hands was fascinating. They looked too big for the delicate tasks they performed with ease and precision. While he worked, he seemed almost graceful. Unlike when he was on his feet; there, his height and big feet made him nearly as dangerous as I was.

Quil and Embry did not show up, so maybe his threat yesterday had been taken seriously.

The day passed too quickly. It got dark outside the mouth of the garage before I was expecting it, and then we heard Billy calling for us.

I jumped up to help Jacob put things away, hesitating because I wasn't sure what I should touch.

"Just leave it," he said. "I'll work on it later tonight."

"Don't forget your schoolwork or anything," I said, feeling a little guilty. I didn't want him to get in trouble. That plan was just for me.

"Bella?"

Both our heads snapped up as Charlie's familiar voice wafted through the trees, sounding closer than the house.

"Shoot," I muttered. "Coming!" I yelled toward the house.

"Let's go." Jacob smiled, enjoying the cloak-and-dagger. He snapped the light off, and for a moment I was blind. Jacob grabbed my hand and towed me out of the garage and through the trees, his feet finding the familiar path easily. His hand was rough, and very warm.

Despite the path, we were both tripping over our feet in the darkness. So we were also both laughing when the house came into view. The laughter did not go deep; it was light and superficial, but still nice. I was sure he wouldn't notice the faint hint of hysteria. I wasn't used to laughing, and it felt right and also very wrong at the same time.

Charlie was standing under the little back porch, and Billy was sitting in the doorway behind them.

"Hey, Dad," we both said at the same time, and that started us laughing again.

Charlie stared at me with wide eyes that flashed down to note Jacob's hand around mine.

"Billy invited us for dinner," Charlie said to us in an absentminded tone.

"My super secret recipe for spaghetti. Handed down for generations," Billy said gravely.

Jacob snorted. "I don't think Ragu's actually been around that long."

The house was crowded. Harry Clearwater was there, too, with his family—his wife, Sue, whom I knew vaguely from my childhood summers in Forks, and his two children. Leah was a senior like me, but a year older. She was beautiful in an exotic way—perfect copper skin, glistening black hair, eyelashes like feather dusters—and preoccupied. She was on Billy's phone when we got in, and she never let it go. Seth was fourteen; he hung on Jacob's every word with idolizing eyes.

There were too many of us for the kitchen table, so Charlie and Harry brought chairs out to the yard, and we ate spaghetti off plates on our laps in the dim light from Billy's open door. The men talked about the game, and Harry and Charlie made fishing plans. Sue teased her husband about his cholesterol and tried, unsuccessfully, to shame him into eating something green and leafy. Jacob talked mostly to me and Seth, who interrupted eagerly whenever Jacob seemed in danger of forgetting him. Charlie watched me, trying to be inconspicuous about it, with pleased but cautious eyes.

It was loud and sometimes confusing as everyone talked over everyone else, and the laughter from one joke interrupted the telling of another. I didn't have to speak often, but I smiled a lot, and only because I felt like it.

I didn't want to leave.

This was Washington, though, and the inevitable rain eventually broke up the party; Billy's living room was much too small to provide an option for continuing the get-together. Harry had driven Charlie down, so we rode together in my truck on the way back home. He asked about my day, and I told mostly the truth—that I'd gone with Jacob to look at parts and then watched him work in his garage.

"You think you'll visit again anytime soon?" he wondered, trying to be casual about it.

"Tomorrow after school," I admitted. "I'll take homework, don't worry."

"You be sure to do that," he ordered, trying to disguise his satisfaction.

I was nervous when we got to the house. I didn't want to go upstairs. The warmth of Jacob's presence was fading and, in its absence, the anxiety grew stronger. I was sure I wouldn't get away with two peaceful nights of sleep in a row.

To put bedtime off, I checked my e-mail; there was a new message from Reneé.

She wrote about her day, a new book club that filled the time slot of the meditation classes she'd just quit, her week subbing in the second grade, missing her kindergarteners. She wrote that Phil was enjoying his new coaching job, and that they were planning a second honeymoon trip to Disney World.

And I noticed that the whole thing read like a journal entry, rather than a letter to someone else. Remorse flooded through me, leaving an uncomfortable sting behind. Some daughter I was.

I wrote back to her quickly, commenting on each part of her letter, volunteering information of my own—describing the spaghetti party at Billy's and how I felt watching Jacob build useful things out of small pieces of metal—awed and slightly envious. I made no reference to the change this letter would be from the ones she'd received in the last several months. I could barely remember what I'd written to her even as recently as last week, but I was sure it wasn't very responsive. The more I thought about it, the guiltier I felt; I really must have worried her.

I stayed up extra late after that, finishing more homework than strictly necessary. But neither sleep deprivation nor the time spent with Jacob—being almost happy in a shallow kind of way—could keep the dream away for two nights in a row.

I woke shuddering, my scream muffled by the pillow.

As the dim morning light filtered through the fog outside my window, I lay still in bed and tried to shake off the dream. There had been a small difference last night, and I concentrated on that.

Last night I had not been alone in the woods. Sam Uley—the man who had pulled me from the forest floor that night I couldn't bear to think of consciously—was there. It was an odd, unexpected alteration. The man's dark eyes had been surprisingly unfriendly, filled with some secret he didn't seem inclined to share. I'd stared at him as often as my frantic searching had allowed; it made me uncomfortable, under all the usual panic, to have him there. Maybe that was because, when I didn't look directly at him, his shape seemed to shiver and change in my peripheral vision. Yet he did nothing but stand and watch. Unlike the time when we had met in reality, he did not offer me his help.

Charlie stared at me during breakfast, and I tried to ignore him. I supposed I deserved it. I couldn't expect him not to worry. It would probably be weeks before he stopped watching for the return of the zombie, and I would just have to try to not let it bother me. After all, I would be watching for the return of the zombie, too. Two days was hardly long enough to call me cured.

School was the opposite. Now that I was paying attention, it was clear that no one was watching here.

I remembered the first day I'd come to Forks High School—how desperately I'd wished that I could turn gray, fade into the wet concrete of the sidewalk like an oversized chameleon. It seemed I was getting that wish answered, a year late.

It was like I wasn't there. Even my teachers' eyes slid past my seat as if it were empty.

I listened all through the morning, hearing once again the voices of the people around me. I tried to catch up on what was going on, but the conversations were so disjointed that I gave up.

Jessica didn't look up when I sat down next to her in Calculus.

"Hey, Jess," I said with put-on nonchalance. "How was the rest of your weekend?"

She looked at me with suspicious eyes. Could she still be angry? Or was she just too impatient to deal with a crazy person?

"Super," she said, turning back to her book.

"That's good," I mumbled.

The figure of speech *cold shoulder* seemed to have some literal truth to it. I could feel the warm air blowing from the floor vents, but I was still too cold. I took the jacket off the back of my chair and put it on again.

My fourth hour class got out late, and the lunch table I always sat at was full by the time I arrived. Mike was there, Jessica and Angela, Conner, Tyler, Eric and Lauren. Katie Marshall, the redheaded junior who lived around the corner from me, was sitting with Eric, and Austin Marks—older brother to the boy with the motorcycles—was next to her. I wondered how long they'd been sitting here, unable to remember if this was the first day or something that was a regular habit.

I was beginning to get annoyed with myself. I might as well have been packed in Styrofoam peanuts through the last semester.

No one looked up when I sat down next to Mike, even though the chair squealed stridently against the linoleum as I dragged it back.

I tried to catch up with the conversation.

Mike and Conner were talking sports, so I gave up on that one at once.

"Where's Ben today?" Lauren was asking Angela. I perked up, interested. I wondered if that meant Angela and Ben were still together.

I barely recognized Lauren. She'd cut off all her blond, corn-silk hair—now she had a pixie cut so short that the back was shaved like a boy. What an odd thing for her to do. I wished I knew the reason behind it. Did she get gum stuck in it? Did she sell it? Had all the people she was habitually nasty to caught her behind the gym and scalped her? I decided it wasn't fair for me to judge her now by my former opinion. For all I knew, she'd turned into a nice person.

"Ben's got the stomach flu," Angela said in her quiet, calm voice. "Hopefully it's just some twenty-four hour thing. He was really sick last night."

Angela had changed her hair, too. She'd grown out her layers.

"What did you two do this weekend?" Jessica asked, not sounding as if she cared about the answer. I'd bet that this was just an opener so she could tell her own stories. I wondered if she would talk about Port Angeles with me sitting two seats away? Was I that invisible, that no one would feel uncomfortable discussing me while I was here?

"We were going to have a picnic Saturday, actually,

but . . . we changed our minds," Angela said. There was an edge to her voice that caught my interest.

Jess, not so much. "That's too bad," she said, about to launch into her story. But I wasn't the only one who was paying attention.

"What happened?" Lauren asked curiously.

"Well," Angela said, seeming more hesitant than usual, though she was always reserved, "we drove up north, almost to the hot springs—there's a good spot just about a mile up the trail. But, when we were halfway there . . . we saw something."

"Saw something? What?" Lauren's pale eyebrows pulled together. Even Jess seemed to be listening now.

"I don't know," Angela said. "We *think* it was a bear. It was black, anyway, but it seemed . . . too big."

Lauren snorted. "Oh, not you, too!" Her eyes turned mocking, and I decided I didn't need to give her the benefit of the doubt. Obviously her personality had not changed as much as her hair. "Tyler tried to sell me that one last week."

"You're not going to see any bears that close to the resort," Jessica said, siding with Lauren.

"Really," Angela protested in a low voice, looking down at the table. "We did see it."

Lauren snickered. Mike was still talking to Conner, not paying attention to the girls.

"No, she's right," I threw in impatiently. "We had a hiker in just Saturday who saw the bear, too, Angela. He said it was huge and black and just outside of town, didn't he, Mike?"

There was a moment of silence. Every pair of eyes at the table turned to stare at me in shock. The new girl, Katie, had her mouth hanging open like she'd just witnessed an explosion. Nobody moved.

"Mike?" I muttered, mortified. "Remember the guy with the bear story?"

"S-sure," Mike stuttered after a second. I didn't know why he was looking at me so strangely. I talked to him at work, didn't I? Did I? I thought so. . . .

Mike recovered. "Yeah, there was a guy who said he saw a huge black bear right at the trailhead—bigger than a grizzly," he confirmed.

"Hmph." Lauren turned to Jessica, her shoulders stiff, and changed the subject.

"Did you hear back from USC?" she asked.

Everyone else looked away, too, except for Mike and Angela. Angela smiled at me tentatively, and I hurried to return the smile.

"So, what did you do this weekend, Bella?" Mike asked, curious, but oddly wary.

Everyone but Lauren looked back, waiting for my response.

"Friday night, Jessica and I went to a movie in Port Angeles. And then I spent Saturday afternoon and most of Sunday down at La Push."

The eyes flickered to Jessica and back to me. Jess looked irritated. I wondered if she didn't want anyone to know she'd gone out with me, or whether she just wanted to be the one to tell the story.

"What movie did you see?" Mike asked, starting to smile.

"*Dead End*—the one with the zombies." I grinned in encouragement. Maybe some of the damage I'd done in these past zombie months was reparable.

"I heard that was scary. Did you think so?" Mike was eager to continue the conversation.

"Bella had to leave at the end, she was so freaked," Jessica inserted with a sly smile.

I nodded, trying to look embarrassed. "It was pretty scary."

Mike didn't stop asking me questions till lunch was over. Gradually, the others were able to start up their own conversations again, though they still looked at me a lot. Angela talked mostly to Mike and me, and, when I got up to dump my tray, she followed.

"Thanks," she said in a low voice when we were away from the table.

"For what?"

"Speaking up, sticking up for me."

"No problem."

She looked at me with concern, but not the offensive, maybe-she's-lost-it kind. "Are you okay?"

This is why I'd picked Jessica over Angela—though I'd always liked Angela more—for the girls' night movie. Angela was too perceptive.

"Not completely," I admitted. "But I'm a little bit better."

"I'm glad," she said. "I've missed you."

Lauren and Jessica strolled by us then, and I heard Lauren whisper loudly, "Oh, *joy*. Bella's back."

Angela rolled her eyes at them, and smiled at me in encouragement.

I sighed. It was like I was starting all over again.

"What's today's date?" I wondered suddenly.

"It's January nineteenth."

"Hmm."

"What is it?" Angela asked.

"It was a year ago yesterday that I had my first day here," I mused.

"Nothing's changed much," Angela muttered, looking after Lauren and Jessica.

"I know," I agreed. "I was just thinking the same thing."

7. REPETITION

I WASN'T SURE WHAT THE HELL I WAS DOING HERE.

Was I *trying* to push myself back into the zombie stupor? Had I turned masochistic—developed a taste for torture? I should have gone straight down to La Push. I felt much, much healthier around Jacob. *This* was not a healthy thing to do.

But I continued to drive slowly down the overgrown lane, twisting through the trees that arched over me like a green, living tunnel. My hands were shaking, so I tightened my grip on the steering wheel.

I knew that part of the reason I did this was the nightmare; now that I was really awake, the nothingness of the dream gnawed on my nerves, a dog worrying a bone.

There *was* something to search for. Unattainable and impossible, uncaring and distracted . . . but *he* was out there, somewhere. I had to believe that.

The other part was the strange sense of repetition I'd felt at school today, the coincidence of the date. The feeling that I was starting over—perhaps the way my first day would have gone if I'd really been the most unusual person in the cafeteria that afternoon.

The words ran through my head, tonelessly, like I was reading them rather than hearing them spoken:

It will be as if I'd never existed.

I was lying to myself by splitting my reason for coming here into just two parts. I didn't want to admit the strongest motivation. Because it was mentally unsound.

The truth was that I wanted to hear his voice again, like I had in the strange delusion Friday night. For that brief moment, when his voice came from some other part of me than my conscious memory, when his voice was perfect and honey smooth rather than the pale echo my memories usually produced, I was able to remember without pain. It hadn't lasted; the pain had caught up with me, as I was sure it would for this fool's errand. But those precious moments when I could hear him again were an irresistible lure. I had to find some way to repeat the experience . . . or maybe the better word was *episode*.

I was hoping that déjà vu was the key. So I was going to his home, a place I hadn't been since my ill-fated birthday party, so many months ago.

The thick, almost jungle-like growth crawled slowly past my windows. The drive wound on and on. I started to go faster, getting edgy. How long had I been driving? Shouldn't I have reached the house yet? The lane was so overgrown that it did not look familiar.

What if I couldn't find it? I shivered. What if there was no tangible proof at all?

Then there was the break in the trees that I was looking for, only it was not so pronounced as before. The flora here did not wait long to reclaim any land that was left unguarded. The tall ferns had infiltrated the meadow around the house, crowding against the trunks of the cedars, even the wide porch. It was like the lawn had been flooded—waist-high—with green, feathery waves.

And the house *was* there, but it was not the same. Though nothing had changed on the outside, the emptiness screamed from the blank windows. It was creepy. For the first time since I'd seen the beautiful house, it looked like a fitting haunt for vampires.

I hit the brakes, looking away. I was afraid to go farther.

But nothing happened. No voice in my head.

So I left the engine running and jumped out into the fern sea. Maybe, like Friday night, if I walked forward . . .

I approached the barren, vacant face slowly, my truck rumbling out a comforting roar behind me. I stopped when I got to the porch stairs, because there was nothing here. No lingering sense of their presence . . . of his presence. The house was solidly here, but it meant little. Its concrete reality would not counteract the nothingness of the nightmares.

I didn't go any closer. I didn't want to look in the

windows. I wasn't sure which would be harder to see. If the rooms were bare, echoing empty from floor to ceiling, that would certainly hurt. Like my grandmother's funeral, when my mother had insisted that I stay outside during the viewing. She had said that I didn't need to see Gran that way, to remember her that way, rather than alive.

But wouldn't it be worse if there were no change? If the couches sat just as I'd last seen them, the paintings on the walls—worse still, the piano on its low platform? It would be second only to the house disappearing all together, to see that there was no physical possession that tied them in anyway. That everything remained, untouched and forgotten, behind them.

Just like me.

I turned my back on the gaping emptiness and hurried to my truck. I nearly ran. I was anxious to be gone, to get back to the human world. I felt hideously empty, and I wanted to see Jacob. Maybe I was developing a new kind of sickness, another addiction, like the numbness before. I didn't care. I pushed my truck as fast as it would go as I barreled toward my fix.

Jacob was waiting for me. My chest seemed to relax as soon as I saw him, making it easier to breathe.

"Hey, Bella," he called.

I smiled in relief. "Hey, Jacob." I waved at Billy, who was looking out the window.

"Let's get to work," Jacob said in a low but eager voice.

I was somehow able to laugh. "You seriously aren't sick of me yet?" I wondered. He must be starting to ask himself how desperate I was for company.

Jacob led the way around the house to his garage.

"Nope. Not yet."

"Please let me know when I start getting on your nerves. I don't want to be a pain."

"Okay." He laughed, a throaty sound. "I wouldn't hold your breath for that, though."

When I walked into the garage, I was shocked to see the red bike standing up, looking like a motorcycle rather than a pile of jagged metal.

"Jake, you're amazing," I breathed.

He laughed again. "I get obsessive when I have a project." He shrugged. "If I had any brains I'd drag it out a little bit."

"Why?"

He looked down, pausing for so long that I wondered if he hadn't heard my question. Finally, he asked me, "Bella, if I told you that I couldn't fix these bikes, what would you say?"

I didn't answer right away, either, and he glanced up to check my expression.

"I would say . . . that's too bad, but I'll bet we could figure out something else to do. If we got really desperate, we could even do homework."

Jacob smiled, and his shoulders relaxed. He sat down next to the bike and picked up a wrench. "So you think you'll still come over when I'm done, then?"

"Is that what you meant?" I shook my head. "I guess I *am* taking advantage of your very underpriced mechanical skills. But as long as you let me come over, I'll be here."

"Hoping to see Quil again?" he teased.

"You caught me."

He chuckled. "You really like spending time with me?" he asked, marveling.

"Very, very much. And I'll prove it. I have to work tomorrow, but Wednesday we'll do something nonmechanical."

"Like what?"

"I have no idea. We can go to my place so you won't be tempted to be obsessive. You could bring your schoolwork—you have to be getting behind, because I know I am."

"Homework might be a good idea." He made a face, and I wondered how much he was leaving undone to be with me.

"Yes," I agreed. "We'll have to start being responsible occasionally, or Billy and Charlie aren't going to be so easygoing about this." I made a gesture indicating the two of us as a single entity. He liked that—he beamed.

"Homework once a week?" he proposed.

"Maybe we'd better go with twice," I suggested, thinking of the pile I'd just been assigned today.

He sighed a heavy sigh. Then he reached over his toolbox to a paper grocery sack. He pulled out two cans of soda, cracking one open and handing it to me. He opened the second, and held it up ceremoniously.

"Here's to responsibility," he toasted. "Twice a week."

"And recklessness every day in between," I emphasized.

He grinned and touched his can to mine.

I got home later than I'd planned and found Charlie had ordered a pizza rather than wait for me. He wouldn't let me apologize.

"I don't mind," he assured me. "You deserve a break from all the cooking, anyway."

I knew he was just relieved that I was still acting like a normal person, and he was not about to rock the boat.

I checked my e-mail before I started on my homework, and there was a long one from Renée. She gushed over every detail I'd provided her with, so I sent back another exhaustive description of my day. Everything but the motorcycles. Even happy-go-lucky Renée was likely to be alarmed by that.

School Tuesday had its ups and downs. Angela and Mike seemed ready to welcome me back with open arms—to kindly overlook my few months of aberrant behavior. Jess was more resistant. I wondered if she needed a formal written apology for the Port Angeles incident.

Mike was animated and chatty at work. It was like he'd stored up the semester's worth of talk, and it was all spilling out now. I found that I was able to smile and laugh with him, though it wasn't as effortless as it was with Jacob. It seemed harmless enough, until quitting time.

Mike put the closed sign in the window while I folded my vest and shoved it under the counter.

"This was fun tonight," Mike said happily.

"Yeah," I agreed, though I'd much rather have spent the afternoon in the garage.

"It's too bad that you had to leave the movie early last week."

I was a little confused by his train of thought. I shrugged. "I'm just a wimp, I guess."

"What I mean is, you should go to a better movie, something you'd enjoy," he explained.

"Oh," I muttered, still confused.

"Like maybe this Friday. With me. We could go see something that isn't scary at all."

I bit my lip.

I didn't want to screw things up with Mike, not when he was one of the only people ready to forgive me for being crazy. But this, again, felt far too familiar. Like the last year had never happened. I wished I had Jess as an excuse this time.

"Like a date?" I asked. Honesty was probably the best policy at this point. Get it over with.

He processed the tone of my voice. "If you want. But it doesn't have to be like that."

"I don't date," I said slowly, realizing how true that was. That whole world seemed impossibly distant.

"Just as friends?" he suggested. His clear blue eyes were not as eager now. I hoped he really meant that we could be friends anyway.

"That would be fun. But I actually have plans already this Friday, so maybe next week?"

"What are you doing?" he asked, less casually than I think he wanted to sound.

"Homework. I have a . . . study session planned with a friend."

"Oh. Okay. Maybe next week."

He walked me to my car, less exuberant than before. It reminded me so clearly of my first months in Forks. I'd come full circle, and now everything felt like an echo—an empty echo, devoid of the interest it used to have.

The next night, Charlie didn't seem the smallest bit surprised to find Jacob and me sprawled across the living room floor with our books scattered around us, so I guessed that he and Billy were talking behind our backs.

"Hey, kids," he said, his eyes straying to the kitchen. The smell of the lasagna I'd spent the afternoon making— while Jacob watched and occasionally sampled—wafted down the hall; I was being good, trying to atone for all the pizza.

Jacob stayed for dinner, and took a plate home for Billy. He grudgingly added another year to my negotiable age for being a good cook.

Friday was the garage, and Saturday, after my shift at Newton's, was homework again. Charlie felt secure enough in my sanity to spend the day fishing with Harry. When he got back, we were all done—feeling very sensible and mature about it, too—and watching *Monster Garage* on the Discovery Channel.

"I probably ought to go." Jacob sighed. "It's later than I thought."

"Okay, fine," I grumbled. "I'll take you home."

He laughed at my unwilling expression—it seemed to please him.

"Tomorrow, back to work," I said as soon as we were safe in the truck. "What time do you want me to come up?"

There was an unexplained excitement in his answering smile. "I'll call you first, okay?"

"Sure." I frowned to myself, wondering what was up. His smile widened.

I cleaned the house the next morning—waiting for Jacob to call and trying to shake off the latest nightmare. The scenery had changed. Last night I'd wandered in a wide sea of ferns interspersed with huge hemlock trees. There was nothing else there, and I was lost, wandering aimless and alone, searching for nothing. I wanted to kick myself for the stupid field trip last week. I shoved the dream out of my conscious mind, hoping it would stay locked up somewhere and not escape again.

Charlie was outside washing the cruiser, so when the phone rang, I dropped the toilet brush and ran downstairs to answer it.

"Hello?" I asked breathlessly.

"Bella," Jacob said, a strange, formal tone to his voice.

"Hey, Jake."

"I believe that . . . we have a *date*," he said, his tone thick with implications.

It took me a second before I got it. "They're done? I can't believe it!" What perfect timing. I needed something to distract me from nightmares and nothingness.

"Yeah, they run and everything."

"Jacob, you are absolutely, without a doubt, the most talented and wonderful person I know. You get ten years for this one."

"Cool! I'm middle-aged now."

I laughed. "I'm on my way up!"

I threw the cleaning supplies under the bathroom counter and grabbed my jacket.

"Headed to see Jake," Charlie said when I ran past him. It wasn't really a question.

"Yep," I replied as I jumped in my truck.

"I'll be at the station later," Charlie called after me.

"Okay," I yelled back, turning the key.

Charlie said something else, but I couldn't hear him clearly over the roar of the engine. It sounded sort of like, "Where's the fire?"

I parked my truck off to the side of the Blacks' house, close to the trees, to make it easier for us to sneak the bikes out. When I got out, a splash of color caught my eye—two shiny motorcycles, one red, one black, were hidden under a spruce, invisible from the house. Jacob was prepared.

There was a piece of blue ribbon tied in a small bow around each of the handlebars. I was laughing at that when Jacob ran out of the house.

"Ready?" he asked in a low voice, his eyes sparkling.

I glanced over his shoulder, and there was no sign of Billy.

"Yeah," I said, but I didn't feel quite as excited as before; I was trying to imagine myself actually *on* the motorcycle.

Jacob loaded the bikes into the bed of the truck with ease, laying them carefully on their sides so they didn't show.

"Let's go," he said, his voice higher than usual with

excitement. "I know the perfect spot—no one will catch us there."

We drove south out of town. The dirt road wove in and out of the forest—sometimes there was nothing but trees, and then there would suddenly be a breathtaking glimpse of the Pacific Ocean, reaching to the horizon, dark gray under the clouds. We were above the shore, on top of the cliffs that bordered the beach here, and the view seemed to stretch on forever.

I was driving slowly, so that I could safely stare out across the ocean now and then, as the road wound closer to the sea cliffs. Jacob was talking about finishing the bikes, but his descriptions were getting technical, so I wasn't paying close attention.

That was when I noticed four figures standing on a rocky ledge, much too close to the precipice. I couldn't tell from the distance how old they were, but I assumed they were men. Despite the chill in the air today, they seemed to be wearing only shorts.

As I watched, the tallest person stepped closer to the brink. I slowed automatically, my foot hesitating over the brake pedal.

And then he threw himself off the edge.

"No!" I shouted, stomping down on the brake.

"What's wrong?" Jacob shouted back, alarmed.

"That guy—he just *jumped* off the *cliff*! Why didn't they stop him? We've got to call an ambulance!" I threw open my door and started to get out, which made no sense at all. The fastest way to a phone was to drive back to

Billy's. But I couldn't believe what I'd just seen. Maybe, subconsciously, I hoped I would see something different without the glass of the windshield in the way.

Jacob laughed, and I spun to stare at him wildly. How could he be so calloused, so cold-blooded?

"They're just cliff diving, Bella. Recreation. La Push doesn't have a mall, you know." He was teasing, but there was a strange note of irritation in his voice.

"Cliff diving?" I repeated, dazed. I stared in disbelief as a second figure stepped to the edge, paused, and then very gracefully leaped into space. He fell for what seemed like an eternity to me, finally cutting smoothly into the dark gray waves below.

"Wow. It's so high." I slid back into my seat, still staring wide-eyed at the two remaining divers. "It must be a hundred feet."

"Well, yeah, most of us jump from lower down, that rock that juts out from the cliff about halfway." He pointed out his window. The place he indicated did seem much more reasonable. "*Those* guys are insane. Probably showing off how tough they are. I mean, really, it's freezing today. That water can't feel good." He made a disgruntled face, as if the stunt personally offended him. It surprised me a little. I would have thought Jacob was nearly impossible to upset.

"*You* jump off the cliff?" I hadn't missed the "us."

"Sure, sure." He shrugged and grinned. "It's fun. A little scary, kind of a rush."

I looked back at the cliffs, where the third figure was

pacing the edge. I'd never witnessed anything so reckless in all my life. My eyes widened, and I smiled. "Jake, you have to take me cliff diving."

He frowned back at me, his face disapproving. "Bella, you just wanted to call an ambulance for Sam," he reminded me. I was surprised that he could tell who it was from this distance.

"I want to try," I insisted, starting to get out of the car again.

Jacob grabbed my wrist. "Not today, all right? Can we at least wait for a warmer day?"

"Okay, fine," I agreed. With the door open, the glacial breeze was raising goose bumps on my arm. "But I want to go soon."

"Soon." He rolled his eyes. "Sometimes you're a little strange, Bella. Do you know that?"

I sighed. "Yes."

"And we're not jumping off the top."

I watched, fascinated, as the third boy made a running start and flung himself farther into the empty air than the other two. He twisted and cartwheeled through space as he fell, like he was skydiving. He looked absolutely free— unthinking and utterly irresponsible.

"Fine," I agreed. "Not the first time, anyway."

Now Jacob sighed.

"Are we going to try out the bikes or not?" he demanded.

"Okay, okay," I said, tearing my eyes away from the last person waiting on the cliff. I put my seat belt back on and closed the door. The engine was still running, roaring as it idled. We started down the road again.

"So who were those guys—the crazy ones?" I wondered.

He made a disgusted sound in the back of his throat. "The La Push gang."

"You have a gang?" I asked. I realized that I sounded impressed.

He laughed once at my reaction. "Not like that. I swear, they're like hall monitors gone bad. They don't start fights, they keep the peace." He snorted. "There was this guy from up somewhere by the Makah rez, big guy too, scary-looking. Well, word got around that he was selling meth to kids, and Sam Uley and his *disciples* ran him off our land. They're all about *our land*, and *tribe pride* . . . it's getting ridiculous. The worst part is that the council takes them seriously. Embry said that the council actually meets with Sam." He shook his head, face full of resentment. "Embry also heard from Leah Clearwater that they call themselves 'protectors' or something like that."

Jacob's hands were clenched into fists, as if he'd like to hit something. I'd never seen this side of him.

I was surprised to hear Sam Uley's name. I didn't want it to bring back the images from my nightmare, so I made a quick observation to distract myself. "You don't like them very much."

"Does it show?" he asked sarcastically.

"Well . . . It doesn't sound like they're doing anything

bad." I tried to soothe him, to make him cheerful again. "Just sort of annoyingly goody-two-shoes for a gang."

"Yeah. Annoying is a good word. They're always showing off—like the cliff thing. They act like . . . like, I don't know. Like tough guys. I was hanging out at the store with Embry and Quil once, last semester, and Sam came by with his *followers*, Jared and Paul. Quil said something, you know how he's got a big mouth, and it pissed Paul off. His eyes got all dark, and he sort of smiled—no, he showed his teeth but he didn't smile—and it was like he was so mad he was shaking or something. But Sam put his hand against Paul's chest and shook his head. Paul looked at him for a minute and calmed down. Honestly, it was like Sam was holding him back—like Paul was going to tear us up if Sam didn't stop him." He groaned. "Like a bad western. You know, Sam's a pretty big guy, he's twenty. But Paul's just sixteen, too, shorter than me and not as beefy as Quil. I think any one of us could take him."

"Tough guys," I agreed. I could see it in my head as he described it, and it reminded me of something . . . a trio of tall, dark men standing very still and close together in my father's living room. The picture was sideways, because my head was lying against the couch while Dr. Gerandy and Charlie leaned over me. . . . Had that been Sam's gang?

I spoke quickly again to divert myself from the bleak memories. "Isn't Sam a little too old for this kind of thing?"

"Yeah. He was supposed to go to college, but he stayed. And no one gave him any crap about it, either. The whole council pitched a fit when my sister turned down a partial scholarship and got married. But, oh no, Sam Uley can do no wrong."

His face was set in unfamiliar lines of outrage—outrage and something else I didn't recognize at first.

"It all sounds really annoying and . . . strange. But I don't get why you're taking it so personally." I peeked over at his face, hoping I hadn't offended him. He was suddenly calm, staring out the side window.

"You just missed the turn," he said in an even voice.

I executed a very wide U-turn, nearly hitting a tree as my circle ran the truck halfway off the road.

"Thanks for the heads-up," I muttered as I started up the side road.

"Sorry, I wasn't paying attention."

It was quiet for a brief minute.

"You can stop anywhere along here," he said softly.

I pulled over and cut the engine. My ears rang in the silence that followed. We both got out, and Jacob headed around to the back to get the bikes. I tried to read his expression. Something more was bothering him. I'd hit a nerve.

He smiled halfheartedly as he pushed the red bike to my side. "Happy late birthday. Are you ready for this?"

"I think so." The bike suddenly looked intimidating, frightening, as I realized I would soon be astride it.

"We'll take it slow," he promised. I gingerly leaned the

motorcycle against the truck's fender while he went to get his.

"Jake . . ." I hesitated as he came back around the truck.

"Yeah?"

"What's really bothering you? About the Sam thing, I mean? Is there something else?" I watched his face. He grimaced, but he didn't seem angry. He looked at the dirt and kicked his shoe against the front tire of his bike again and again, like he was keeping time.

He sighed. "It's just . . . the way they treat me. It creeps me out." The words started to rush out now. "You know, the council is supposed to be made up of equals, but if there was a leader, it would be my dad. I've never been able to figure out why people treat him the way they do. Why his opinion counts the most. It's got something to do with his father and his father's father. My great-grandpa, Ephraim Black, was sort of the last chief we had, and they still listen to Billy, maybe because of that.

"But I'm just like everyone else. Nobody treats *me* special . . . until now."

That caught me off guard. "Sam treats you special?"

"Yeah," he agreed, looking up at me with troubled eyes. "He looks at me like he's waiting for something . . . like I'm going to join his stupid gang someday. He pays more attention to me than any of the other guys. I hate it."

"You don't have to join anything." My voice was angry. This was really upsetting Jacob, and that infuriated me. Who did these "protectors" think they were?

"Yeah." His foot kept up its rhythm against the tire.

"What?" I could tell there was more.

He frowned, his eyebrows pulling up in a way that looked sad and worried rather than angry. "It's Embry. He's been avoiding me lately."

The thoughts didn't seem connected, but I wondered if I was to blame for the problems with his friend. "You've been hanging out with me a lot," I reminded him, feeling selfish. I'd been monopolizing him.

"No, that's not it. It's not just me—it's Quil, too, and everyone. Embry missed a week of school, but he was never home when we tried to see him. And when he came back, he looked . . . he looked freaked out. Terrified. Quil and I both tried to get him to tell us what was wrong, but he wouldn't talk to either one of us."

I stared at Jacob, biting my lip anxiously—he was really frightened. But he didn't look at me. He watched his own foot kicking the rubber as if it belonged to someone else. The tempo increased.

"Then this week, out of nowhere, Embry's hanging out with Sam and the rest of them. He was out on the cliffs today." His voice was low and tense.

He finally looked at me. "Bella, they bugged him even more than they bother me. He didn't want anything to do with them. And now Embry's following Sam around like he's joined a cult.

"And that's the way it was with Paul. Just exactly the same. He wasn't friends with Sam at all. Then he stopped coming to school for a few weeks, and, when he came back, suddenly Sam owned him. I don't know what it means. I can't figure it out, and I feel like I have to, because Embry's my friend and . . . Sam's looking at me funny . . . and . . ." He trailed off.

"Have you talked to Billy about this?" I asked. His horror was spreading to me. I had chills running on the back of my neck.

Now there was anger on his face. "Yes," he snorted. "That was helpful."

"What did he say?"

Jacob's expression was sarcastic, and when he spoke, his voice mocked the deep tones of his father's voice. "It's nothing you need to worry about now, Jacob. In a few years, if you don't . . . well, I'll explain later." And then his voice was his own. "What am I supposed to get from that? Is he trying to say it's some stupid puberty, coming-of-age thing? This is something else. Something wrong."

He was biting his lower lip and clenching his hands. He looked like he was about to cry.

I threw my arms around him instinctively, wrapping them around his waist and pressing my face against his chest. He was so big, I felt like I was a child hugging a grown-up.

"Oh, Jake, it'll be okay!" I promised. "If it gets worse you can come live with me and Charlie. Don't be scared, we'll think of something!"

He was frozen for a second, and then his long arms wrapped hesitantly around me. "Thanks, Bella." His voice was huskier than usual.

We stood like that for a moment, and it didn't upset me; in fact, I felt comforted by the contact. This didn't feel anything like the last time someone had embraced me this way. This was friendship. And Jacob was very warm.

It was strange for me, being this close—emotionally rather than physically, though the physical was strange for me, too—to another human being. It wasn't my usual style. I didn't normally relate to people so easily, on such a basic level.

Not human beings.

"If this is how you're going to react, I'll freak out more often." Jacob's voice was light, normal again, and his laughter rumbled against my ear. His fingers touched my hair, soft and tentative.

Well, it was friendship for me.

I pulled away quickly, laughing with him, but determined to put things back in perspective at once.

"It's hard to believe I'm two years older than you," I said, emphasizing the word *older*. "You make me feel like a dwarf." Standing this close to him, I really had to crane my neck to see his face.

"You're forgetting I'm in my forties, of course."

"Oh, that's right."

He patted my head. "You're like a little doll," he teased. "A porcelain doll."

I rolled my eyes, taking another step away. "Let's not start with the albino cracks."

"Seriously, Bella, are you sure you're not?" He stretched his russet arm out next to mine. The difference wasn't flattering. "I've never seen anyone paler than you . . . well, except for—" He broke off, and I looked away, trying to not understand what he had been about to say.

"So are we going to ride or what?"

"Let's do it," I agreed, more enthusiastic than I would have been half a minute ago. His unfinished sentence reminded me of why I was here.

8. ADRENALINE

"OKAY, WHERE'S YOUR CLUTCH?"

I pointed to the lever on my left handlebar. Letting go of the grip was a mistake. The heavy bike wobbled underneath me, threatening to knock me sidewise. I grabbed the handle again, trying to hold it straight.

"Jacob, it won't stay up," I complained.

"It will when you're moving," he promised. "Now where's your brake?"

"Behind my right foot."

"Wrong."

He grabbed my right hand and curled my fingers around the lever over the throttle.

"But you said—"

"This is the brake you want. Don't use the back brake now, that's for later, when you know what you're doing."

"That doesn't sound right," I said suspiciously. "Aren't both brakes kind of important?"

"Forget the back brake, okay? Here—" He wrapped his hand around mine and made me squeeze the lever down. *"That* is how you brake. Don't forget." He squeezed my hand another time.

"Fine," I agreed.

"Throttle?"

I twisted the right grip.

"Gearshift?"

I nudged it with my left calf.

"Very good. I think you've got all the parts down. Now you just have to get it moving."

"Uh-huh," I muttered, afraid to say more. My stomach was contorting strangely and I thought my voice might crack. I was terrified. I tried to tell myself that the fear was pointless. I'd already lived through the worst thing possible. In comparison with that, why should anything frighten me now? I should be able to look death in the face and laugh.

My stomach wasn't buying it.

I stared down the long stretch of dirt road, bordered by thick misty green on every side. The road was sandy and damp. Better than mud.

"I want you to hold down the clutch," Jacob instructed.

I wrapped my fingers around the clutch.

"Now this is crucial, Bella," Jacob stressed. "Don't let

go of that, okay? I want you to pretend that I've handed you a live grenade. The pin is out and you are holding down the spoon."

I squeezed tighter.

"Good. Do you think you can kick-start it?"

"If I move my foot, I will fall over," I told him through gritted teeth, my fingers tight around my live grenade.

"Okay, I'll do it. Don't let go of the clutch."

He took a step back, and then suddenly slammed his foot down on the pedal. There was a short ripping noise, and the force of his thrust rocked the bike. I started to fall sideways, but Jake caught the bike before it knocked me to the ground.

"Steady there," he encouraged. "Do you still have the clutch?"

"Yes," I gasped.

"Plant your feet—I'm going to try again." But he put his hand on the back of the seat, too, just to be safe.

It took four more kicks before the ignition caught. I could feel the bike rumbling beneath me like an angry animal. I gripped the clutch until my fingers ached.

"Try out the throttle," he suggested. "Very lightly. And don't let go of the clutch."

Hesitantly, I twisted the right handle. Though the movement was tiny, the bike snarled beneath me. It sounded angry *and* hungry now. Jacob smiled in deep satisfaction.

"Do you remember how to put it into first gear?" he asked.

"Yes."

"Well, go ahead and do it."

"Okay."

He waited for a few seconds.

"Left foot," he prompted.

"I *know*," I said, taking a deep breath.

"Are you sure you want to do this?" Jacob asked. "You look scared."

"I'm fine," I snapped. I kicked the gearshift down one notch.

"Very good," he praised me. "Now, *very* gently, ease up on the clutch."

He took a step away from the bike.

"You want me to let go of the grenade?" I asked in disbelief. No wonder he was moving back.

"That's how you move, Bella. Just do it little by little."

As I began to loosen my grip, I was shocked to be interrupted by a voice that did not belong to the boy standing next to me.

"This is reckless and childish and idiotic, Bella," the velvet voice fumed.

"Oh!" I gasped, and my hand fell off the clutch.

The bike bucked under me, yanking me forward and then collapsing to the ground half on top of me. The growling engine choked to a stop.

"Bella?" Jacob jerked the heavy bike off me with ease. "Are you hurt?"

But I wasn't listening.

"I told you so," the perfect voice murmured, crystal clear.

"Bella?" Jacob shook my shoulder.

"I'm fine," I mumbled, dazed.

More than fine. The voice in my head was back. It still rang in my ears—soft, velvety echoes.

My mind ran swiftly through the possibilities. There was no familiarity here—on a road I'd never seen, doing something I'd never done before—no déjà vu. So the hallucinations must be triggered by something else. . . . I felt the adrenaline coursing through my veins again, and I thought I had the answer. Some combination of adrenaline and danger, or maybe just stupidity.

Jacob was pulling me to my feet.

"Did you hit your head?" he asked.

"I don't think so." I shook it back and forth, checking. "I didn't hurt the bike, did I?" This thought worried me. I was anxious to try again, right away. Being reckless was paying off better than I'd thought. Forget cheating. Maybe I'd found a way to generate the hallucinations— that was much more important.

"No. You just stalled the engine," Jacob said, interrupting my quick speculations. "You let go of the clutch too fast."

I nodded. "Let's try again."

"Are you sure?" Jacob asked.

"Positive."

This time I tried to get the kick-start myself. It was complicated; I had to jump a little to slam down on the pedal with enough force, and every time I did that, the bike tried to knock me over. Jacob's hand hovered over the handlebars, ready to catch me if I needed him.

It took several good tries, and even more poor tries,

before the engine caught and roared to life under me. Remembering to hold on to the grenade, I revved the throttle experimentally. It snarled at the slightest touch. My smile mirrored Jacob's now.

"Easy on the clutch," he reminded me.

"Do you *want* to kill yourself, then? Is that what this is about?" the other voice spoke again, his tone severe.

I smiled tightly—it was still working—and ignored the questions. Jacob wasn't going to let anything serious happen to me.

"Go home to Charlie," the voice ordered. The sheer beauty of it amazed me. I couldn't allow my memory to lose it, no matter the price.

"Ease off slowly," Jacob encouraged me.

"I will," I said. It bothered me a bit when I realized I was answering both of them.

The voice in my head growled against the roar of the motorcycle.

Trying to focus this time, to not let the voice startle me again, I relaxed my hand by tiny degrees. Suddenly, the gear caught and wrenched me forward.

And I was flying.

There was wind that wasn't there before, blowing my skin against my skull and flinging my hair back behind me with enough force that it felt like someone was tugging on it. I'd left my stomach back at the starting point; the adrenaline coursed through my body, tingling in my veins. The trees raced past me, blurring into a wall of green.

But this was only first gear. My foot itched toward the gearshift as I twisted for more gas.

"No, Bella!" the angry, honey-sweet voice ordered in my ear. "Watch what you're doing!"

It distracted me enough from the speed to realize that the road was starting a slow curve to the left, and I was still going straight. Jacob hadn't told me how to turn.

"Brakes, brakes," I muttered to myself, and I instinctively slammed down with my right foot, like I would in my truck.

The bike was suddenly unstable underneath me, shivering first to one side and then the other. It was dragging me toward the green wall, and I was going too fast. I tried to turn the handlebar the other direction, and the sudden shift of my weight pushed the bike toward the ground, still spinning toward the trees.

The motorcycle landed on top of me again, roaring loudly, pulling me across the wet sand until it hit something stationary. I couldn't see. My face was mashed into the moss. I tried to lift my head, but there was something in the way.

I was dizzy and confused. It sounded like there were three things snarling—the bike over me, the voice in my head, and something else. . . .

"Bella!" Jacob yelled, and I heard the roar of the other bike cut off.

The motorcycle no longer pinned me to the ground, and I rolled over to breathe. All the growling went silent.

"Wow," I murmured. I was thrilled. This had to be it,

the recipe for a hallucination—adrenaline plus danger plus stupidity. Something close to that, anyway.

"Bella!" Jacob was crouching over me anxiously. "Bella, are you alive?"

"I'm great!" I enthused. I flexed my arms and legs. Everything seemed to be working correctly. "Let's do it again."

"I don't think so." Jacob still sounded worried. "I think I'd better drive you to the hospital first."

"I'm fine."

"Um, Bella? You've got a huge cut on your forehead, and it's gushing blood," he informed me.

I clapped my hand over my head. Sure enough, it was wet and sticky. I could smell nothing but the damp moss on my face, and that held off the nausea.

"Oh, I'm so sorry, Jacob." I pushed hard against the gash, as if I could force the blood back inside my head.

"Why are you apologizing for bleeding?" he wondered as he wrapped a long arm around my waist and pulled me to my feet. "Let's go. I'll drive." He held out his hand for the keys.

"What about the bikes?" I asked, handing them over.

He thought for a second. "Wait here. And take this." He pulled off his T-shirt, already spotted with blood, and threw it to me. I wadded it up and held it tightly to my forehead. I was starting to smell the blood; I breathed deeply through my mouth and tried to concentrate on something else.

Jacob jumped on the black motorcycle, kicked it to a start in one try, and raced back down the road, spraying sand and pebbles behind him. He looked athletic and professional as he leaned over the handlebars, head low, face forward, his shiny hair whipping against the russet skin of his back. My eyes narrowed enviously. I was sure I hadn't looked like that on my motorcycle.

I was surprised at how far I'd gone. I could barely see Jacob in the distance when he finally got to the truck. He threw the bike into the bed and sprinted to the driver's side.

I really didn't feel bad at all as he coaxed my truck to a deafening roar in his hurry to get back to me. My head stung a little, and my stomach was uneasy, but the cut wasn't serious. Head wounds just bled more than most. His urgency wasn't necessary.

Jacob left the truck running as he raced back to me, wrapping his arm around my waist again.

"Okay, let's get you in the truck."

"I'm honestly fine," I assured him as he helped me in. "Don't get worked up. It's just a little blood."

"Just a *lot* of blood," I heard him mutter as he went back for my bike.

"Now, let's think about this for a second," I began when he got back in. "If you take me to the ER like this, Charlie is sure to hear about it." I glanced down at the sand and dirt caked into my jeans.

"Bella, I think you need stitches. I'm not going to let you bleed to death."

"I won't," I promised. "Let's just take the bikes back first, and then we'll make a stop at my house so I can dispose of the evidence before we go to the hospital."

"What about Charlie?"

"He said he had to work today."

"Are you really sure?"

"Trust me. I'm an easy bleeder. It's not nearly as dire as it looks."

Jacob wasn't happy—his full mouth turned down in an uncharacteristic frown—but he didn't want to get me in trouble. I stared out the window, holding his ruined shirt to my head, while he drove me to Forks.

The motorcycle was better than I'd dreamed. It had served its original purpose. I'd cheated—broken my promise. I'd been needlessly reckless. I felt a little less pathetic now that the promises had been broken on both sides.

And then to discover the key to the hallucinations! At least, I hoped I had. I was going to test the theory as soon as possible. Maybe they'd get through with me quickly in the ER, and I could try again tonight.

Racing down the road like that had been amazing. The feel of the wind in my face, the speed and the freedom . . . it reminded me of a past life, flying through the thick forest without a road, piggyback while *he* ran—I stopped thinking right there, letting the memory break off in the sudden agony. I flinched.

"You still okay?" Jacob checked.

"Yeah." I tried to sound as convincing as before.

"By the way," he added. "I'm going to disconnect your foot brake tonight."

At home, I went to look at myself in the mirror first thing; it was pretty gruesome. Blood was drying in thick streaks across my cheek and neck, matting in my muddy hair. I examined myself clinically, pretending the blood was paint so it wouldn't upset my stomach. I breathed through my mouth, and was fine.

I washed up as well as I could. Then I hid my dirty, bloody clothes in the bottom of my laundry basket, putting on new jeans and a button-up shirt (that I didn't have to pull over my head) as carefully as I could. I managed to do this one-handed and keep both garments blood-free.

"Hurry up," Jacob called.

"Okay, okay," I shouted back. After making sure I left nothing incriminating behind me, I headed downstairs.

"How do I look?" I asked him.

"Better," he admitted.

"But do I look like I tripped in your garage and hit my head on a hammer?"

"Sure, I guess so."

"Let's go then."

Jacob hurried me out the door, and insisted on driving again. We were halfway to the hospital when I realized he was still shirtless.

I frowned guiltily. "We should have grabbed you a jacket."

"That would have given us away," he teased. "Besides, it's not cold."

"Are you kidding?" I shivered and reached out to turn the heat on.

I watched Jacob to see if he was just playing tough so I wouldn't worry, but he looked comfortable enough. He had one arm over the back of my seat, though I was huddled up to keep warm.

Jacob really did look older than sixteen—not quite forty, but maybe older than me. Quil didn't have too much on him in the muscle department, for all that Jacob claimed to be a skeleton. The muscles were the long wiry kind, but they were definitely there under the smooth skin. His skin was such a pretty color, it made me jealous.

Jacob noticed my scrutiny.

"What?" he asked, suddenly self-conscious.

"Nothing. I just hadn't realized before. Did you know, you're sort of beautiful?"

Once the words slipped out, I worried that he might take my impulsive observation the wrong way.

But Jacob just rolled his eyes. "You hit your head pretty hard, didn't you?"

"I'm serious."

"Well, then, thanks. Sort of."

I grinned. "You're sort of welcome."

I had to have seven stitches to close the cut on my forehead. After the sting of the local anesthetic, there was no pain in the procedure. Jacob held my hand while Dr. Snow was sewing, and I tried not to think about why that was ironic.

We were at the hospital forever. By the time I was done, I had to drop Jacob off at his home and hurry back to cook dinner for Charlie. Charlie seemed to buy my story about falling in Jacob's garage. After all, it wasn't like I hadn't been able to land myself in the ER before with no more help than my own feet.

This night was not as bad as that first night, after I'd

heard the perfect voice in Port Angeles. The hole came back, the way it always did when I was away from Jacob, but it didn't throb so badly around the edges. I was already planning ahead, looking forward to more delusions, and that was a distraction. Also, I knew I would feel better tomorrow when I was with Jacob again. That made the empty hole and the familiar pain easier to bear; relief was in sight. The nightmare, too, had lost a little of its potency. I was horrified by the nothingness, as always, but I was also strangely impatient as I waited for the moment that would send me screaming into consciousness. I knew the nightmare had to end.

The next Wednesday, before I could get home from the ER, Dr. Gerandy called to warn my father that I might possibly have a concussion and advised him to wake me up every two hours through the night to make sure it wasn't serious. Charlie's eyes narrowed suspiciously at my weak explanation about tripping again.

"Maybe you should just stay out of the garage altogether, Bella," he suggested that night during dinner.

I panicked, worried that Charlie was about to lay down some kind of edict that would prohibit La Push, and consequently my motorcycle. And I wasn't giving it up—I'd had the most amazing hallucination today. My velvet-voiced delusion had yelled at me for almost five minutes before I'd hit the brake too abruptly and launched myself into the tree. I'd take whatever pain that would cause me tonight without complaint.

"This didn't happen in the garage," I protested quickly. "We were hiking, and I tripped over a rock."

"Since when do you hike?" Charlie asked skeptically.

"Working at Newton's was bound to rub off sometime," I pointed out. "Spend every day selling all the virtues of the outdoors, eventually you get curious."

Charlie glared at me, unconvinced.

"I'll be more careful," I promised, surreptitiously crossing my fingers under the table.

"I don't mind you hiking right there around La Push, but keep close to town, okay?"

"Why?"

"Well, we've been getting a lot of wildlife complaints lately. The forestry department is going to check into it, but for the time being . . ."

"Oh, the big bear," I said with sudden comprehension. "Yeah, some of the hikers coming through Newton's have seen it. Do you think there's really some giant mutated grizzly out there?"

His forehead creased. "There's something. Keep it close to town, okay?"

"Sure, sure," I said quickly. He didn't look completely appeased.

"Charlie's getting nosy," I complained to Jacob when I picked him up after school Friday.

"Maybe we should cool it with the bikes." He saw my objecting expression and added, "At least for a week or so. You could stay out of the hospital for a week, right?"

"What are we going to do?" I griped.

He smiled cheerfully. "What ever you want."

I thought about that for a minute—about what I wanted.

I hated the idea of losing even my brief seconds of closeness with the memories that didn't hurt—the ones that came on their own, without me thinking of them consciously. If I couldn't have the bikes, I was going to have to find some other avenue to the danger and the adrenaline, and that was going to take serious thought and creativity. Doing nothing in the meantime was not appealing. Suppose I got depressed again, even with Jake? I had to keep occupied.

Maybe there was some other way, some other recipe . . . some other place.

The house had been a mistake, certainly. But *his* presence must be stamped somewhere, somewhere other than inside me. There had to be a place where he seemed more real than among all the familiar landmarks that were crowded with other human memories.

I could think of one place where that might hold true. One place that would always belong to *him* and no one else. A magic place, full of light. The beautiful meadow I'd seen only once in my life, lit by sunshine and the sparkle of his skin.

This idea had a huge potential for backfiring—it might be dangerously painful. My chest ached with emptiness even to think of it. It was hard to hold myself upright, to not give myself away. But surely, there of all places, I could hear his voice. And I'd already told Charlie I was hiking. . . .

"What are you thinking about so hard?" Jacob asked.

"Well . . . ," I began slowly. "I found this place in the forest once—I came across it when I was, um, hiking. A little meadow, the most beautiful place. I don't know if I could track it down again on my own. It would definitely take a few tries. . . ."

"We could use a compass and a grid pattern," Jacob said with confident helpfulness. "Do you know where you started from?"

"Yes, just below the trailhead where the one-ten ends. I was going mostly south, I think."

"Cool. We'll find it." As always, Jacob was game for anything I wanted. No matter how strange it was.

So, Saturday afternoon, I tied on my new hiking boots—purchased that morning using my twenty-percent-off employee discount for the first time—grabbed my new topographical map of the Olympic Peninsula, and drove to La Push.

We didn't get started immediately; first, Jacob sprawled across the living room floor—taking up the whole room—and, for a full twenty minutes, drew a complicated web across the key section of the map while I perched on a kitchen chair and talked to Billy. Billy didn't seem at all concerned about our proposed hiking trip. I was surprised that Jacob had told him where we were going, given the fuss people were making about the bear sightings. I wanted to ask Billy not to say anything about this to Charlie, but I was afraid that making the request would cause the opposite result.

"Maybe we'll see the super bear," Jacob joked, eyes on his design.

I glanced at Billy swiftly, fearing a Charlie-style reaction.

But Billy just laughed at his son. "Maybe you should take a jar of honey, just in case."

Jake chuckled. "Hope your new boots are fast, Bella. One little jar isn't going to keep a hungry bear occupied for long."

"I only have to be faster than you."

"Good luck with that!" Jacob said, rolling his eyes as he refolded the map. "Let's go."

"Have fun," Billy rumbled, wheeling himself toward the refrigerator.

Charlie was not a hard person to live with, but it looked to me like Jacob had it even easier than I did.

I drove to the very end of the dirt road, stopping near the sign that marked the beginning of the trailhead. It had been a long time since I'd been here, and my stomach reacted nervously. This might be a very bad thing. But it would be worth it, if I got to hear *him*.

I got out and looked at the dense wall of green.

"I went this way," I murmured, pointing straight ahead.

"Hmm," Jake muttered.

"What?"

He looked at the direction I'd pointed, then at the clearly marked trail, and back.

"I would have figured you for a trail kind of girl."

"Not me." I smiled bleakly. "I'm a rebel."

He laughed, and then pulled out our map.

"Give me a second." He held the compass in a skilled way, twisting the map around till it angled the way he wanted.

"Okay—first line on the grid. Let's do it."

I could tell that I was slowing Jacob up, but he didn't complain. I tried not to dwell on my last trip through this part of the forest, with a very different companion. Normal memories were still dangerous. If I let myself slip up, I'd end up with my arms clutching my chest to hold it together, gasping for air, and how would I explain that to Jacob?

It wasn't as hard as I would have thought to keep focused on the present. The forest looked a lot like any other part of the peninsula, and Jacob set a vastly different mood.

He whistled cheerfully, an unfamiliar tune, swinging his arms and moving easily through the rough undergrowth. The shadows didn't seem as dark as usual. Not with my personal sun along.

Jacob checked the compass every few minutes, keeping us in a straight line with one of the radiating spokes of his grid. He really looked like he knew what he was doing. I was going to compliment him, but I caught myself. No doubt he'd add another few years to his inflated age.

My mind wandered as I walked, and I grew curious. I hadn't forgotten the conversation we'd had by the sea cliffs—I'd been waiting for him to bring it up again, but it didn't look like that was going to happen.

"Hey . . . Jake?" I asked hesitantly.

"Yeah?"

"How are things . . . with Embry? Is he back to normal yet?"

Jacob was silent for a minute, still moving forward with

long paces. When he was about ten feet ahead, he stopped to wait for me.

"No. He's not back to normal," Jacob said when I reached him, his mouth pulling down at the corners. He didn't start walking again. I immediately regretted bringing it up.

"Still with Sam."

"Yup."

He put his arm around my shoulder, and he looked so troubled that I didn't playfully shake it off, as I might have otherwise.

"Are they still looking at you funny?" I half-whispered.

Jacob stared through the trees. "Sometimes."

"And Billy?"

"As helpful as ever," he said in a sour, angry voice that disturbed me.

"Our couch is always open," I offered.

He laughed, breaking out of the unnatural gloom. "But think of the position that would put Charlie in—when Billy calls the police to report my kidnapping."

I laughed too, glad to have Jacob back to normal.

We stopped when Jacob said we'd gone six miles, cut west for a short time, and headed back along another line of his grid. Everything looked exactly the same as the way in, and I had a feeling that my silly quest was pretty much doomed. I admitted as much when it started to get darker, the sunless day fading toward a starless night, but Jacob was more confident.

"As long as you're sure we're starting from the right place . . ." He glanced down at me.

"Yes, I'm sure."

"Then we'll find it," he promised, grabbing my hand and pulling me through a mass of ferns. On the other side was the truck. He gestured toward it proudly. "Trust me."

"You're good," I admitted. "Next time we bring flashlights, though."

"We'll save hiking for Sundays from now on. I didn't know you were that slow."

I yanked my hand back and stomped around to the driver's side while he chuckled at my reaction.

"So you up for another try tomorrow?" he asked, sliding into the passenger seat.

"Sure. Unless you want to go without me so I don't tie you down to my gimpy pace."

"I'll survive," he assured me. "If we're hiking again, though, you might want to pick up some moleskin. I bet you can feel those new boots right now."

"A little," I confessed. It felt like I had more blisters than I had space to fit them.

"I hope we see the bear tomorrow. I'm sort of disappointed about that."

"Yes, me, too," I agreed sarcastically. "Maybe we'll get lucky tomorrow and something will eat us!"

"Bears don't want to eat people. We don't taste that good." He grinned at me in the dark cab. "Of course, you *might* be an exception. I bet you'd taste good."

"Thanks so much," I said, looking away. He wasn't the first person to tell me that.

9. THIRD WHEEL

TIME BEGAN TO TRIP ALONG MUCH MORE QUICKLY THAN before. School, work, and Jacob—though not necessarily in that order—created a neat and effortless pattern to follow. And Charlie got his wish: I wasn't miserable anymore. Of course, I couldn't fool myself completely. When I stopped to take stock of my life, which I tried not to do too often, I couldn't ignore the implications of my behavior.

I was like a lost moon—my planet destroyed in some cataclysmic, disaster-movie scenario of desolation—that continued, nevertheless, to circle in a tight little orbit around the empty space left behind, ignoring the laws of gravity.

I was getting better with my bike, which meant fewer bandages to worry Charlie. But it also meant that the voice in my head began to fade, until I heard it no more. Quietly, I panicked. I threw myself into the search for the meadow with slightly frenzied intensity. I racked my brain for other adrenaline-producing activities.

I didn't keep track of the days that passed—there was no reason, as I tried to live as much in the present as possible, no past fading, no future impending. So I was surprised by the date when Jacob brought it up on one of our homework days. He was waiting when I pulled up in front of his house.

"Happy Valentine's Day," Jacob said, smiling, but ducking his head as he greeted me.

He held out a small, pink box, balancing it on his palm. Conversation hearts.

"Well, I feel like a schmuck," I mumbled. "Is today Valentine's Day?"

Jacob shook his head with mock sadness. "You can be so out of it sometimes. Yes, it is the fourteenth day of February. So are you going to be my Valentine? Since you didn't get me a fifty-cent box of candy, it's the least you can do."

I started to feel uncomfortable. The words were teasing, but only on the surface.

"What exactly does that entail?" I hedged.

"The usual—slave for life, that kind of thing."

"Oh, well, if that's all . . ." I took the candy. But I was trying to think of some way to make the boundaries clear. Again. They seemed to get blurred a lot with Jacob.

"So, what are we doing tomorrow? Hiking, or the ER?"

"Hiking," I decided. "You're not the only one who can be obsessive. I'm starting to think I imagined that place. . . ." I frowned into space.

"We'll find it," he assured me. "Bikes Friday?" he offered.

I saw a chance and took it without taking time to think it through.

"I'm going to a movie Friday. I've been promising my cafeteria crowd that I would go out forever." Mike would be pleased.

But Jacob's face fell. I caught the expression in his dark eyes before he dropped them to look at the ground.

"You'll come too, right?" I added quickly. "Or will it be too much of a drag with a bunch of boring seniors?" So much for my chance to put some distance between us. I couldn't stand hurting Jacob; we seemed to be connected in an odd way, and his pain set off little stabs of my own. Also, the idea of having his company for the ordeal— I *had* promised Mike, but really didn't feel any enthusiasm at the thought of following through—was just too tempting.

"You'd like me to come, with your friends there?"

"Yes," I admitted honestly, knowing as I continued that I was probably shooting myself in the foot with my words. "I'll have a lot more fun if you're there. Bring Quil, and we'll make it a party."

"Quil's gonna freak. Senior girls." He chortled and rolled his eyes. I didn't mention Embry, and neither did he.

I laughed, too. "I'll try to get him a good selection."

I broached the subject with Mike in English.

"Hey, Mike," I said when class was over. "Are you free Friday night?"

He looked up, his blue eyes instantly hopeful. "Yeah, I am. You want to go out?"

I worded my reply carefully. "I was thinking about getting a *group*"—I emphasized the word—"together to go see *Crosshairs*." I'd done my homework this time—even reading the movie spoilers to be sure I wouldn't be caught off guard. This movie was supposed to be a bloodbath from start to finish. I wasn't so recovered that I could stand to sit through a romance. "Does that sound like fun?"

"Sure," he agreed, visibly less eager.

"Cool."

After a second, he perked back up to near his former excitement level. "How about we get Angela and Ben? Or Eric and Katie?"

He was determined to make this some kind of double date, apparently.

"How about both?" I suggested. "And Jessica, too, of course. And Tyler and Conner, and maybe Lauren," I tacked on grudgingly. I *had* promised Quil variety.

"Okay," Mike muttered, foiled.

"And," I continued, "I've got a couple of friends from

La Push I'm inviting. So it sounds like we'll need your Suburban if everyone comes."

Mike's eyes narrowed in suspicion.

"These are the friends you spend all your time studying with now?"

"Yep, the very ones," I answered cheerfully. "Though you could look at it as tutoring—they're only sophomores."

"Oh," Mike said, surprised. After a second of thought, he smiled.

In the end, though, the Suburban wasn't necessary.

Jessica and Lauren claimed to be busy as soon as Mike let it slip that I was involved in the planning. Eric and Katie already had plans—it was their three-week anniversary or something. Lauren got to Tyler and Conner before Mike could, so those two were also busy. Even Quil was out—grounded for fighting at school. In the end, only Angela and Ben, and, of course Jacob, were able to go.

The diminished numbers didn't dampen Mike's anticipation, though. It was all he could talk about Friday.

"Are you sure you don't want to see *Tomorrow and Forever* instead?" he asked at lunch, naming the current romantic comedy that was ruling the box office. "Rotten Tomatoes gave it a better review."

"I want to see *Crosshairs*," I insisted. "I'm in the mood for action. Bring on the blood and guts!"

"Okay." Mike turned away, but not before I saw his maybe-she's-crazy-after-all expression.

When I got home from school, a very familiar car was

parked in front of my house. Jacob was leaning against the hood, a huge grin lighting up his face.

"No way!" I shouted as I jumped out of the truck. "You're done! I can't believe it! You finished the Rabbit!"

He beamed. "Just last night. This is the maiden voyage."

"Incredible." I held my hand up for a high five.

He smacked his hand against mine, but left it there, twisting his fingers through mine. "So do I get to drive tonight?"

"Definitely," I said, and then I sighed.

"What's wrong?"

"I'm giving up—I can't top this one. So you win. You're oldest."

He shrugged, unsurprised by my capitulation. "Of course I am."

Mike's Suburban chugged around the corner. I pulled my hand out of Jacob's, and he made a face that I wasn't meant to see.

"I remember this guy," he said in a low voice as Mike parked across the street. "The one who thought you were his girlfriend. Is he still confused?"

I raised one eyebrow. "Some people are hard to discourage."

"Then again," Jacob said thoughtfully, "sometimes persistence pays off."

"Most of the time it's just annoying, though."

Mike got out of his car and crossed the road.

"Hey, Bella," he greeted me, and then his eyes turned wary as he looked up at Jacob. I glanced briefly at Jacob, too, trying to be objective. He really didn't look like a sophomore at all. He was just so big—Mike's head barely cleared Jacob's shoulder; I didn't even want to think where I measured next to him—and then his face was older-looking than it used to be, even a month ago.

"Hey, Mike! Do you remember Jacob Black?"

"Not really." Mike held out his hand.

"Old family friend," Jacob introduced himself, shaking hands. They locked hands with more force than necessary. When their grip broke, Mike flexed his fingers.

I heard the phone ringing from the kitchen.

"I'd better get that—it might be Charlie," I told them, and dashed inside.

It was Ben. Angela was sick with the stomach flu, and he didn't feel like coming without her. He apologized for bailing on us.

I walked slowly back to the waiting boys, shaking my head. I really hoped Angela would feel better soon, but I had to admit that I was selfishly upset by this development. Just the three of us, Mike and Jacob and me, together for the evening—this had worked out brilliantly, I thought with grim sarcasm.

It didn't seem like Jake and Mike had made any progress towards friendship in my absence. They were several yards apart, facing away from each other as they waited for me; Mike's expression was sullen, though Jacob's was cheerful as always.

"Ang is sick," I told them glumly. "She and Ben aren't coming."

"I guess the flu is making another round. Austin and

Conner were out today, too. Maybe we should do this another time," Mike suggested.

Before I could agree, Jacob spoke.

"I'm still up for it. But if you'd rather to stay behind,
Mike—"

"No, I'm coming," Mike interrupted. "I was just thinking of Angela and Ben. Let's go." He started toward his
Suburban.

"Hey, do you mind if Jacob drives?" I asked. "I told
him he could—he just finished his car. He built it from
scratch, all by himself," I bragged, proud as a PTA mom
with a student on the principal's list.

"Fine," Mike snapped.

"All right, then," Jacob said, as if that settled everything. He seemed more comfortable than anyone else.

Mike climbed in the backseat of the Rabbit with a disgusted expression.

Jacob was his normal sunny self, chattering away
until I'd all but forgotten Mike sulking silently in the
back.

And then Mike changed his strategy. He leaned forward,
resting his chin on the shoulder of my seat; his cheek almost
touched mine. I shifted away, turning my back toward the
window.

"Doesn't the radio work in this thing?" Mike asked
with a hint of petulance, interrupting Jacob mid-sentence.

"Yes," Jacob answered. "But Bella doesn't like music."

I stared at Jacob, surprised. I'd never told him that.

"Bella?" Mike asked, annoyed.

"He's right," I mumbled, still looking at Jacob's serene profile.

"How can you not like music?" Mike demanded.

I shrugged. "I don't know. It just irritates me."

"Hmph." Mike leaned away.

When we got to the theater, Jacob handed me a ten-dollar bill.

"What's this?" I objected.

"I'm not old enough to get into this one," he reminded me.

I laughed out loud. "So much for relative ages. Is Billy going to kill me if I sneak you in?"

"No. I told him you were planning to corrupt my youthful innocence."

I snickered, and Mike quickened his pace to keep up with us.

I almost wished that Mike had decided to bow out. He was still sullen—not much of an addition to the party. But I didn't want to end up on a date alone with Jacob, either. That wouldn't help anything.

The movie was exactly what it professed to be. In just the opening credits, four people got blown up and one got beheaded. The girl in front of me put her hands over her eyes and turned her face into her date's chest. He patted her shoulder, and winced occasionally, too. Mike didn't look like he was watching. His face was stiff as he glared toward the fringe of curtain above the screen.

I settled in to endure the two hours, watching the colors and the movement on the screen rather than seeing the shapes of people and cars and houses. But then Jacob started sniggering.

"What?" I whispered.

"Oh, c'mon!" he hissed back. "The blood squirted twenty feet out of that guy. How fake can you get?"

He chuckled again, as a flagpole speared another man into a concrete wall.

After that, I really watched the show, laughing with him as the mayhem got more and more ridiculous. How was I ever going to fight the blurring lines in our relationship when I enjoyed being with him so much?

Both Jacob and Mike had claimed the armrests on either side of me. Both of their hands rested lightly, palms up, in an unnatural looking position. Like steel bear traps, open and ready. Jacob was in the habit of taking my hand whenever the opportunity presented itself, but here in the darkened movie theater, with Mike watching, it would have a different significance—and I was sure he knew that. I couldn't believe that Mike was thinking the same thing, but his hand was placed exactly like Jacob's.

I folded my arms tightly across my chest and hoped that both their hands fell asleep.

Mike gave up first. About halfway through the movie, he pulled his arm back, and leaned forward to put his head in his hands. At first I thought he was reacting to something on the screen, but then he moaned.

"Mike, are you okay?" I whispered.

The couple in front of us turned to look at him as he groaned again.

"No," he gasped. "I think I'm sick."

I could see the sheen of sweat across his face in the light from the screen.

Mike groaned again, and bolted for the door. I got up to follow him, and Jacob copied me immediately.

"No, stay," I whispered. "I'll make sure he's okay."

Jacob came with me anyway.

"You don't have to come. Get your eight bucks worth of carnage," I insisted as we walked up the aisle.

"That's okay. You sure can pick them, Bella. This movie really sucks." His voice rose from a whisper to its normal pitch as we walked out of the theater.

There was no sign of Mike in the hallway, and I was glad then that Jacob had come with me—he ducked into the men's bathroom to check for him there.

Jacob was back in a few seconds.

"Oh, he's in there, all right," he said, rolling his eyes. "What a marshmallow. You should hold out for someone with a stronger stomach. Someone who laughs at the gore that makes weaker men vomit."

"I'll keep my eyes open for someone like that."

We were all alone in the hallway. Both theaters were halfway through the movie, and it was deserted—quiet enough for us to hear the popcorn popping at the concession counter in the lobby.

Jacob went to sit on the velveteen-upholstered bench against the wall, patting the space beside him.

"He sounded like he was going to be in there for a while," he said, stretching his long legs out in front of him as he settled in to wait.

I joined him with a sigh. He looked like he was

thinking about blurring more lines. Sure enough, as soon as I sat down, he shifted over to put his arm around my shoulders.

"Jake," I protested, leaning away. He dropped his arm, not looking bothered at all by the minor rejection. He reached out and took my hand firmly, wrapping his other hand around my wrist when I tried to pull away again. Where did he get the confidence from?

"Now, just hold on a minute, Bella," he said in a calm voice. "Tell me something."

I grimaced. I didn't want to do this. Not just not now, but not ever. There was nothing left in my life at this point that was more important than Jacob Black. But he seemed determined to ruin everything.

"What?" I muttered sourly.

"You like me, right?"

"You know I do."

"Better than that joker puking his guts out in there?" He gestured toward the bathroom door.

"Yes," I sighed.

"Better than any of the other guys you know?" He was calm, serene—as if my answer didn't matter, or he already knew what it was.

"Better than the girls, too," I pointed out.

"But that's all," he said, and it wasn't a question.

It was hard to answer, to say the word. Would he get hurt and avoid me? How would I stand that?

"Yes," I whispered.

He grinned down at me. "That's okay, you know. As long as you like me the best. *And* you think I'm good-looking—sort of. I'm prepared to be annoyingly persistent."

"I'm not going to change," I said, and though I tried to keep my voice normal, I could hear the sadness in it.

His face was thoughtful, no longer teasing. "It's still the other one, isn't it?"

I cringed. Funny how he seemed to know not to say the name—just like before in the car with the music. He picked up on so much about me that I never said.

"You don't have to talk about it," he told me.

I nodded, grateful.

"But don't get mad at me for hanging around, okay?" Jacob patted the back of my hand. "Because I'm not giving up. I've got loads of time."

I sighed. "You shouldn't waste it on me," I said, though I wanted him to. Especially if he was willing to accept me the way I was—damaged goods, as is.

"It's what I want to do, as long as you still like to be with me."

"I can't imagine how I could *not* like being with you," I told him honestly.

Jacob beamed. "I can live with that."

"Just don't expect more," I warned him, trying to pull my hand away. He held onto it obstinately.

"This doesn't really bother you, does it?" he demanded, squeezing my fingers.

"No," I sighed. Truthfully, it felt nice. His hand was so much warmer than mine; I always felt too cold these days.

"And you don't care what *he* thinks." Jacob jerked his thumb toward the bathroom.

"I guess not."

"So what's the problem?"

"The problem," I said, "is that it means something different to me than it does to you."

"Well." He tightened his hand around mine. "That's *my* problem, isn't it?"

"Fine," I grumbled. "Don't forget it, though."

"I won't. The pin's out of the grenade for me, now, eh?" He poked me in the ribs.

I rolled my eyes. I guess if he felt like making a joke out of it, he was entitled.

He chuckled quietly for a minute while his pinky finger absently traced designs against the side of my hand.

"That's a funny scar you've got there," he suddenly said, twisting my hand to examine it. "How did that happen?"

The index finger of his free hand followed the line of the long silvery crescent that was barely visible against my pale skin.

I scowled. "Do you honestly expect me to remember where all my scars come from?"

I waited for the memory to hit—to open the gaping hole. But, as it so often did, Jacob's presence kept me whole.

"It's cold," he murmured, pressing lightly against the place where James had cut me with his teeth.

And then Mike stumbled out of the bathroom, his face ashen and covered in sweat. He looked horrible.

"Oh, Mike," I gasped.

"Do you mind leaving early?" he whispered.

"No, of course not." I pulled my hand free and went to help Mike walk. He looked unsteady.

"Movie too much for you?" Jacob asked heartlessly.

Mike's glare was malevolent. "I didn't actually see any of it," he mumbled. "I was nauseated before the lights went down."

"Why didn't you say something?" I scolded as we staggered toward the exit.

"I was hoping it would pass," he said.

"Just a sec," Jacob said as we reached the door. He walked quickly back to the concession stand.

"Could I have an empty popcorn bucket?" he asked the salesgirl. She looked at Mike once, and then thrust a bucket at Jacob.

"Get him outside, please," she begged. She was obviously the one who would have to clean the floor.

I towed Mike out into the cool, wet air. He inhaled deeply. Jacob was right behind us. He helped me get Mike into the back of the car, and handed him the bucket with a serious gaze.

"Please," was all Jacob said.

We rolled down the windows, letting the icy night air blow through the car, hoping it would help Mike. I curled my arms around my legs to keep warm.

"Cold, again?" Jacob asked, putting his arm around me before I could answer.

"You're not?"

He shook his head.

"You must have a fever or something," I grumbled. It

was freezing. I touched my fingers to his forehead, and his head *was* hot.

"Whoa, Jake—you're burning up!"

"I feel fine." He shrugged. "Fit as a fiddle."

I frowned and touched his head again. His skin blazed under my fingers.

"Your hands are like ice," he complained.

"Maybe it's me," I allowed.

Mike groaned in the backseat, and threw up in the bucket. I grimaced, hoping my own stomach could stand the sound and smell. Jacob checked anxiously over his shoulder to make sure his car wasn't defiled.

The road felt longer on the way back.

Jacob was quiet, thoughtful. He left his arm around me, and it was so warm that the cold wind felt good.

I stared out the windshield, consumed with guilt.

It was so wrong to encourage Jacob. Pure selfishness. It didn't matter that I'd tried to make my position clear. If he felt any hope at all that this could turn into something other than friendship, then I hadn't been clear enough.

How could I explain so that he would understand? I was an empty shell. Like a vacant house—condemned— for months I'd been utterly uninhabitable. Now I was a little improved. The front room was in better repair. But that was all—just the one small piece. He deserved better than that—better than a one-room, falling-down fixer-upper. No amount of investment on his part could put me back in working order.

Yet I knew that I wouldn't send him away, regardless. I needed him too much, and I was selfish. Maybe I could make my side more clear, so that he would know to leave me. The thought made me shudder, and Jacob tightened his arm around me.

I drove Mike home in his Suburban, while Jacob followed behind us to take me home. Jacob was quiet all the way back to my house, and I wondered if he were thinking the same things that I was. Maybe he was changing his mind.

"I would invite myself in, since we're early," he said as we pulled up next to my truck. "But I think you might be right about the fever. I'm starting to feel a little . . . strange."

"Oh no, not you, too! Do you want me to drive you home?"

"No." He shook his head, his eyebrows pulling together. "I don't feel sick yet. Just . . . wrong. If I have to, I'll pull over."

"Will you call me as soon as you get in?" I asked anxiously.

"Sure, sure." He frowned, staring ahead into the darkness and biting his lip.

I opened my door to get out, but he grabbed my wrist lightly and held me there. I noticed again how hot his skin felt on mine.

"What is it, Jake?" I asked.

"There's something I want to tell you, Bella . . . but I think it's going to sound kind of corny."

I sighed. This would be more of the same from the theater. "Go ahead."

"It's just that, I know how you're unhappy a lot. And, maybe it doesn't help anything, but I wanted you to know that I'm always here. I won't ever let you down—I promise that you can always count on me. Wow, that does sound corny. But you know that, right? That I would never, ever hurt you?"

"Yeah, Jake. I know that. And I already do count on you, probably more than you know."

The smile broke across his face the way the sunrise set the clouds on fire, and I wanted to cut my tongue out. I hadn't said one word that was a lie, but I should have lied. The truth was wrong, it would hurt him. *I* would let *him* down.

A strange look crossed his face. "I really think I'd better go home now," he said.

I got out quickly.

"Call me!" I yelled as he pulled away.

I watched him go, and he seemed to be in control of the car, at least. I stared at the empty street when he was gone, feeling a little sick myself, but not for any physical reason.

How much I wished that Jacob Black had been born my brother, my flesh-and-blood brother, so that I would have some legitimate claim on him that still left me free of any blame now. Heaven knows I had never wanted to use Jacob, but I couldn't help but interpret the guilt I felt now to mean that I had.

Even more, I had never meant to love him. One thing I truly knew—knew it in the pit of my stomach, in the center of my bones, knew it from the crown of my head to the soles of my feet, knew it deep in my empty chest—was how love gave someone the power to break you.

I'd been broken beyond repair.

But I needed Jacob now, needed him like a drug. I'd used him as a crutch for too long, and I was in deeper than I'd planned to go with anyone again. Now I couldn't bear for him to be hurt, and I couldn't keep from hurting him, either. He thought time and patience would change me, and, though I knew he was dead wrong, I also knew that I would let him try.

He was my best friend. I would always love him, and it would never, ever be enough.

I went inside to sit by the phone and bite my nails.

"Movie over already?" Charlie asked in surprise when I came in. He was on the floor, just a foot from the TV. Must be an exciting game.

"Mike got sick," I explained. "Some kind of stomach flu."

"You okay?"

"I feel fine now," I said doubtfully. Clearly, I'd been exposed.

I leaned against the kitchen counter, my hand inches from the phone, and tried to wait patiently. I thought of the strange look on Jacob's face before he drove away, and my fingers started drumming against the counter. I should have insisted on driving him home.

I watched the clock as the minutes ticked by. Ten. Fifteen. Even when I was driving, it took only fifteen minutes, and Jacob drove faster than I did. Eighteen minutes. I picked up the phone and dialed.

It rang and rang. Maybe Billy was asleep. Maybe I'd dialed wrong. I tried again.

On the eighth ring, just as I was about to hang up, Billy answered.

"Hello?" he asked. His voice was wary, like he was expecting bad news.

"Billy, it's me, Bella—did Jake make it home yet? He left here about twenty minutes ago."

"He's here," Billy said tonelessly.

"He was supposed to call me." I was a little irritated. "He was getting sick when he left, and I was worried."

"He was . . . too sick to call. He's not feeling well right now." Billy sounded distant. I realized he must want to be with Jacob.

"Let me know if you need any help," I offered. "I could come down." I thought of Billy, stuck in his chair, and Jake fending for himself. . . .

"No, no," Billy said quickly. "We're fine. Stay at your place."

The way he said it was almost rude.

"Okay," I agreed.

"Bye, Bella."

The line disconnected.

"Bye," I muttered.

Well, at least he'd made it home. Oddly, I didn't feel less worried. I trudged up the stairs, fretting. Maybe I would go down before work tomorrow to check on him. I could take soup—we had to have a can of Campbell's around here somewhere.

I realized all such plans were canceled when I woke up early—my clock said four thirty—and sprinted to the bathroom. Charlie found me there a half hour later, lying on the floor, my cheek pressed against the cold edge of the bathtub.

He looked at me for a long moment.

"Stomach flu," he finally said.

"Yes," I moaned.

"You need something?" he asked.

"Call the Newtons for me, please," I instructed hoarsely. "Tell them I have what Mike has, and that I can't make it in today. Tell them I'm sorry."

"Sure, no problem," Charlie assured me.

I spent the rest of the day on the bathroom floor, sleeping for a few hours with my head on a crumpled up towel. Charlie claimed that he had to work, but I suspected that he just wanted access to a bathroom. He left a glass of water on the floor beside me to keep me hydrated.

It woke me up when he came back home. I could see that it was dark in my room—after nightfall. He clumped up the stairs to check on me.

"Still alive?"

"Sort of," I said.

"Do you want anything?"

"No, thanks."

He hesitated, clearly out of his element. "Okay, then," he said, and then he went back down to the kitchen.

I heard the phone ring a few minutes later. Charlie spoke to someone in a low voice for a moment, and then hung up.

"Mike feels better," he called up to me.

Well, that was encouraging. He'd only gotten sick eight hours or so before me. Eight more hours. The thought made my stomach turn, and I pulled myself up to lean over the toilet.

I fell asleep on the towel again, but when I woke up I was in my bed and it was light outside my window. I didn't remember moving; Charlie must have carried me to my room—he'd also put the glass of water on my bedside table. I felt parched. I chugged it down, though it tasted funny from sitting stagnant all night.

I got up slowly, trying not to trigger the nausea again. I was weak, and my mouth tasted horrible, but my stomach felt fine. I looked at my clock.

My twenty-four hours were up.

I didn't push it, eating nothing but saltine crackers for breakfast. Charlie looked relieved to see me recovered.

As soon as I was sure that I wasn't going to have to spend the day on the bathroom floor again, I called Jacob.

Jacob was the one who answered, but when I heard his greeting I knew he wasn't over it.

"Hello?" His voice was broken, cracking.

"Oh, Jake," I groaned sympathetically. "You sound horrible."

"I feel horrible," he whispered.

"I'm so sorry I made you go out with me. This sucks."

"I'm glad I went." His voice was still a whisper. "Don't blame yourself. This isn't your fault."

"You'll get better soon," I promised. "I woke up this morning, and I was fine."

"You were sick?" he asked dully.

"Yes, I got it, too. But I'm fine now."

"That's good." His voice was dead.

"So you'll probably be better in a few hours," I encouraged.

I could barely hear his answer. "I don't think I have the same thing you did."

"Don't you have the stomach flu?" I asked, confused.

"No. This is something else."

"What's wrong with you?"

"Everything," he whispered. "Every part of me hurts."

The pain in his voice was nearly tangible.

"What can I do, Jake? What can I bring you?"

"Nothing. You can't come here." He was abrupt. It reminded me of Billy the other night.

"I've already been exposed to whatever you have," I pointed out.

He ignored me. "I'll call you when I can. I'll let you know when you can come down again."

"Jacob—"

"I've got to go," he said with sudden urgency.

"Call me when you feel better."

"Right," he agreed, and his voice had a strange, bitter edge.

He was silent for a moment. I was waiting for him to say goodbye, but he waited too.

"I'll see you soon," I finally said.

"Wait for me to call," he said again.

"Okay. . . . Bye, Jacob."

"Bella," he whispered my name, and then hung up the phone.

10. THE MEADOW

JACOB DIDN'T CALL.

The first time I called, Billy answered and told me that Jacob was still in bed. I got nosy, checking to make sure that Billy had taken him to a doctor. Billy said he had, but, for some reason I couldn't nail down, I didn't really believe him. I called again, several times a day, for the next two days, but no one was ever there.

Saturday, I decided to go see him, invitation be damned. But the little red house was empty. This frightened me— was Jacob so sick that he'd needed to go to the hospital? I stopped by the hospital on the way back home, but the nurse at the front desk told me neither Jacob or Billy had been in.

I made Charlie call Harry Clearwater as soon as he got home from work. I waited, anxious, while Charlie chatted with his old friend; the conversation seemed to go on forever without Jacob even being mentioned. It seemed that *Harry* had been in the hospital . . . some kind of tests for his heart. Charlie's forehead got all pinched together, but Harry joked with him, blowing it off, until Charlie was laughing again. Only then did Charlie ask about Jacob, and now his side of the conversation didn't give me much to work with, just a lot of *hmm*s and *yeah*s. I drummed my fingers against the counter beside him until he put a hand over mine to stop me.

Finally, Charlie hung up the phone and turned to me.

"Harry says there's been some trouble with the phone lines, and that's why you haven't been able to get through. Billy took Jake to the doc down there, and it looks like he has mono. He's real tired, and Billy said no visitors," he reported.

"No visitors?" I demanded in disbelief.

Charlie raised one eyebrow. "Now don't you go making a pest of yourself, Bells. Billy knows what's best for Jake. He'll be up and around soon enough. Be patient."

I didn't push it. Charlie was too worried about Harry. That was clearly the more important issue—it wouldn't be right to bug him with my lesser concerns. Instead, I went straight upstairs and turned on my computer. I found a medical site online and typed "mononucleosis" into the search box.

All I knew about mono was that you were supposed to get it from kissing, which was clearly not the case with

Jake. I read through the symptoms quickly—the fever he definitely had, but what about the rest of it? No horrible sore throat, no exhaustion, no headaches, at least not before he'd gone home from the movie; he'd said he felt "fit as a fiddle." Did it really come on so fast? The article made it sound like the sore stuff showed up first.

I glared at the computer screen and wondered why, exactly, I was doing this. Why did I feel so . . . so *suspicious*, like I didn't believe Billy's story? Why would Billy lie to Harry?

I was being silly, probably. I was just worried, and, to be honest, I was afraid of not being allowed to see Jacob—that made me nervous.

I skimmed through the rest of the article, looking for more information. I stopped when I got to the part about how mono could last more than a month.

A month? My mouth fell open.

But Billy couldn't enforce the no-visitors thing that long. Of course not. Jake would go crazy stuck in bed that long without anyone to talk to.

What was Billy afraid of, anyway? The article said that a person with mono needed to avoid physical activity, but there was nothing about visitors. The disease wasn't very infectious.

I'd give Billy a week, I decided, before I got pushy. A week was generous.

A week was *long*. By Wednesday, I was sure I wasn't going to live till Saturday.

When I'd decided to leave Billy and Jacob alone for a

week, I hadn't really believed that Jacob would go along with Billy's rule. Every day when I got home from school, I ran to the phone to check for messages. There never were any.

I cheated three times by trying to call him, but the phone lines still weren't working.

I was in the house much too much, and much too alone. Without Jacob, and my adrenaline and my distractions, everything I'd been repressing started creeping up on me. The dreams got hard again. I could no longer see the end coming. Just the horrible nothingness—half the time in the forest, half the time in the empty fern sea where the white house no longer existed. Sometimes Sam Uley was there in the forest, watching me again. I paid him no attention—there was no comfort in his presence; it made me feel no less alone. It didn't stop me from screaming myself awake, night after night.

The hole in my chest was worse than ever. I'd thought that I'd been getting it under control, but I found myself hunched over, day after day, clutching my sides together and gasping for air.

I wasn't handling alone well.

I was relieved beyond measure the morning I woke up—screaming, of course—and remembered that it was Saturday. Today I could call Jacob. And if the phone lines still weren't working, then I was going to La Push. One way or another, today would be better than the last lonely week.

I dialed, and then waited without high expectations.

It caught me off guard when Billy answered on the second ring.

"Hello?"

"Oh, hey, the phone is working again! Hi, Billy. It's Bella. I was just calling to see how Jacob is doing. Is he up for visitors yet? I was thinking about dropping by—"

"I'm sorry, Bella," Billy interrupted, and I wondered if he were watching TV; he sounded distracted. "He's not in."

"Oh." It took me a second. "So he's feeling better then?"

"Yeah," Billy hesitated for an instant too long. "Turns out it wasn't mono after all. Just some other virus."

"Oh. So . . . where is he?"

"He's giving some friends a ride up to Port Angeles— I think they were going to catch a double feature or something. He's gone for the whole day."

"Well, that's a relief. I've been so worried. I'm glad he felt good enough to get out." My voice sounded horribly phony as I babbled on.

Jacob was better, but not well enough to call me. He was out with friends. I was sitting home, missing him more every hour. I was lonely, worried, bored . . . perforated— and now also desolate as I realized that the week apart had not had the same effect on him.

"Is there anything in particular you wanted?" Billy asked politely.

"No, not really."

"Well, I'll tell him that you called," Billy promised. "Bye, Bella."

"Bye," I replied, but he'd already hung up.

I stood for a moment with the phone still in my hand.

Jacob must have changed his mind, just like I'd feared. He was going to take my advice and not waste any more time on someone who couldn't return his feelings. I felt the blood run out of my face.

"Something wrong?" Charlie asked as he came down the stairs.

"No," I lied, hanging up the phone. "Billy says Jacob is feeling better. It wasn't mono. So that's good."

"Is he coming here, or are you going there?" Charlie asked absentmindedly as he started poking through the fridge.

"Neither," I admitted. "He's going out with some other friends."

The tone of my voice finally caught Charlie's attention. He looked up at me with sudden alarm, his hands frozen around a package of cheese slices.

"Isn't it a little early for lunch?" I asked as lightly as I could manage, trying to distract him.

"No, I'm just packing something to take out to the river. . . ."

"Oh, fishing today?"

"Well, Harry called . . . and it's not raining." He was creating a stack of food on the counter as he spoke. Suddenly he looked up again as if he'd just realized something. "Say, did you want me to stay with you, since Jake's out?"

"That's okay, Dad," I said, working to sound indifferent. "The fish bite better when the weather's nice."

He stared at me, indecision clear on his face. I knew

that he was worrying, afraid to leave me alone, in case I got "mopey" again.

"Seriously, Dad. I think I'll call Jessica," I fibbed quickly. I'd rather be alone than have him watching me all day. "We have a Calculus test to study for. I could use her help." That part was true. But I'd have to make do without it.

"That's a good idea. You've been spending so much time with Jacob, your other friends are going to think you've forgotten them."

I smiled and nodded as if I cared what my other friends thought.

Charlie started to turn, but then spun back with a worried expression. "Hey, you'll study here or at Jess's, right?"

"Sure, where else?"

"Well, it's just that I want you to be careful to stay out of the woods, like I told you before."

It took me a minute to understand, distracted as I was. "More bear trouble?"

Charlie nodded, frowning. "We've got a missing hiker—the rangers found his camp early this morning, but no sign of him. There were some really big animal prints . . . of course those could have come later, smelling the food. . . . Anyway, they're setting traps for it now."

"Oh," I said vaguely. I wasn't really listening to his warnings; I was much more upset by the situation with Jacob than by the possibility of being eaten by a bear.

I was glad that Charlie was in a hurry. He didn't wait for me to call Jessica, so I didn't have to put on that charade. I went through the motions of gathering my school-books on the kitchen table to pack them in my bag; that was probably too much, and if he hadn't been eager to hit the holes, it might have made him suspicious.

I was so busy looking busy that the ferociously empty day ahead didn't really crash down on me until after I'd watched him drive away. It only took about two minutes of staring at the silent kitchen phone to decide that I wasn't staying home today. I considered my options.

I wasn't going to call Jessica. As far as I could tell, Jessica had crossed over to the dark side.

I could drive to La Push and get my motorcycle—an appealing thought but for one minor problem: who was going to drive me to the emergency room if I needed it afterward?

Or . . . I already had our map and compass in the truck. I was pretty sure I understood the process well enough by now that I wouldn't get lost. Maybe I could eliminate two lines today, putting us ahead of schedule for whenever Jacob decided to honor me with his presence again. I refused to think about how long that might be. Or if it was going to be never.

I felt a brief twinge of guilt as I realized how Charlie would feel about this, but I ignored it. I just couldn't stay in the house again today.

A few minutes later I was on the familiar dirt road that led to nowhere in particular. I had the windows rolled down and I drove as fast as was healthy for my truck, trying to enjoy the wind against my face. It was cloudy, but almost dry—a very nice day, for Forks.

Getting started took me longer than it would have taken Jacob. After I parked in the usual spot, I had to spend a good fifteen minutes studying the little needle on the compass face and the markings on the now worn map. When I was reasonably certain that I was following the right line of the web, I set off into the woods.

The forest was full of life today, all the little creatures enjoying the momentary dryness. Somehow, though, even with the birds chirping and cawing, the insects buzzing noisily around my head, and the occasional scurry of the field mice through the shrubs, the forest seemed creepier today; it reminded me of my most recent nightmare. I knew it was just because I was alone, missing Jacob's care-free whistle and the sound of another pair of feet squishing across the damp ground.

The sense of unease grew stronger the deeper I got into the trees. Breathing started to get more difficult—not because of exertion, but because I was having trouble with the stupid hole in my chest again. I kept my arms tight around my torso and tried to banish the ache from my thoughts. I almost turned around, but I hated to waste the effort I'd already expended.

The rhythm of my footsteps started to numb my mind and my pain as I trudged on. My breathing evened out eventually, and I was glad I hadn't quit. I was getting better at this bushwhacking thing; I could tell I was faster.

I didn't realize quite how much more efficiently I was moving. I thought I'd covered maybe four miles, and I wasn't even starting to look around for it yet. And then, with an abruptness that disoriented me, I stepped through a low arch made by two vine maples—pushing past the chest-high ferns—into the meadow.

It was the same place, of that I was instantly sure. I'd never seen another clearing so symmetrical. It was as perfectly round as if someone had intentionally created the flawless circle, tearing out the trees but leaving no evidence of that violence in the waving grass. To the east, I could hear the stream bubbling quietly.

The place wasn't nearly so stunning without the sunlight, but it was still very beautiful and serene. It was the wrong season for wildflowers; the ground was thick with tall grass that swayed in the light breeze like ripples across a lake.

It was the same place . . . but it didn't hold what I had been searching for.

The disappointment was nearly as instantaneous as the recognition. I sank down right where I was, kneeling there at the edge of the clearing, beginning to gasp.

What was the point of going any farther? Nothing lingered here. Nothing more than the memories that I could have called back whenever I wanted to, if I was ever willing to endure the corresponding pain—the pain that had me now, had me cold. There was nothing special about this place without *him*. I wasn't exactly sure what I'd hoped to feel here, but the meadow was empty of atmosphere, empty of everything, just like everywhere else. Just like my nightmares. My head swirled dizzily.

At least I'd come alone. I felt a rush of thankfulness as I realized that. If I'd discovered the meadow with Jacob . . . well, there was no way I could have disguised the abyss I was plunging into now. How could I have explained the way I was fracturing into pieces, the way I had to curl into a ball to keep the empty hole from tearing me apart? It was so much better that I didn't have an audience.

And I wouldn't have to explain to anyone why I was in such a hurry to leave, either. Jacob would have assumed, after going to so much trouble to locate the stupid place, I would want to spend more than a few seconds here. But I was already trying to find the strength to get to my feet again, forcing myself out of the ball so that I could escape. There was too much pain in this empty place to bear—I would crawl away if I had to.

How lucky that I was alone!

Alone. I repeated the word with grim satisfaction as I wrenched myself to my feet despite the pain. At precisely that moment, a figure stepped out from the trees to the north, some thirty paces away.

A dizzying array of emotions shot through me in a second. The first was surprise; I was far from any trail here, and I didn't expect company. Then, as my eyes focused on the motionless figure, seeing the utter stillness, the pallid skin, a rush of piercing hope rocked through me. I suppressed it viciously, fighting against the equally sharp lash of agony as my eyes continued to the face beneath the black hair, the face that wasn't the one I wanted to see. Next was fear; this was not the face I grieved for, but it was close enough for me to know that the man facing me was no stray hiker.

And finally, in the end, recognition.

"Laurent!" I cried in surprised pleasure.

It was an irrational response. I probably should have stopped at fear.

Laurent had been one of James's coven when we'd first met. He hadn't been involved with the hunt that followed—the hunt where I was the quarry—but that was only because he was afraid; I was protected by a bigger coven than his own. It would have been different if that wasn't the case—he'd had no compunctions, at the time, against making a meal of me. Of course, he must have changed, because he'd gone to Alaska to live with the other civilized coven there, the other family that refused to drink human blood for ethical reasons. The other family like . . . but I couldn't let myself think the name.

Yes, fear would have made more sense, but all I felt was an overwhelming satisfaction. The meadow was a magic place again. A darker magic than I'd expected, to be sure, but magic all the same. Here was the connection I'd sought. The proof, however remote, that—somewhere in the same world where I lived—*he* did exist.

It was impossible how exactly the same Laurent looked. I suppose it was very silly and human to expect some kind of change in the last year. But there was something . . . I couldn't quite put my finger on it.

"Bella?" he asked, looking more astonished than I felt.

"You remember." I smiled. It was ridiculous that I should be so elated because a vampire knew my name.

He grinned. "I didn't expect to see you here." He strolled toward me, his expression bemused.

"Isn't it the other way around? I do live here. I thought you'd gone to Alaska."

He stopped about ten paces away, cocking his head to

the side. His face was the most beautiful face I'd seen in what felt like an eternity. I studied his features with a strangely greedy sense of release. Here was someone I didn't have to pretend for—someone who already knew everything I could never say.

"You're right," he agreed. "I did go to Alaska. Still, I didn't expect . . . When I found the Cullen place empty, I thought they'd moved on."

"Oh." I bit my lip as the name set the raw edges of my wound throbbing. It took me a second to compose myself. Laurent waited with curious eyes.

"They did move on," I finally managed to tell him.

"Hmm," he murmured. "I'm surprised they left you behind. Weren't you sort of a pet of theirs?" His eyes were innocent of any intended offense.

I smiled wryly. "Something like that."

"Hmm," he said, thoughtful again.

At that precise moment, I realized why he looked the same—*too much* the same. After Carlisle told us that Laurent had stayed with Tanya's family, I'd begun to picture him, on the rare occasions that I thought of him at all, with the same golden eyes that the . . . Cullens—I forced the name out, wincing—had. That all *good* vampires had.

I took an involuntary step back, and his curious, dark red eyes followed the movement.

"Do they visit often?" he asked, still casual, but his weight shifted toward me.

"Lie," the beautiful velvet voice whispered anxiously from my memory.

I started at the sound of *his* voice, but it should not have surprised me. Was I not in the worst danger imaginable? The motorcycle was safe as kittens next to this.

I did what the voice said to do.

"Now and again." I tried to make my voice light, relaxed. "The time seems longer to me, I imagine. You know how they get distracted. . . ." I was beginning to babble. I had to work to shut myself up.

"Hmm," he said again. "The house smelled like it had been vacant for a while. . . ."

"You must lie better than that, Bella," the voice urged.

I tried. "I'll have to mention to Carlisle that you stopped by. He'll be sorry they missed your visit." I pretended to deliberate for a second. "But I probably shouldn't mention it to . . . Edward, I suppose—" I barely managed to say his name, and it twisted my expression on the way out, ruining my bluff "—he has such a temper . . . well, I'm sure you remember. He's still touchy about the whole James thing." I rolled my eyes and waved one hand dismissively, like it was all ancient history, but there was an edge of hysteria to my voice. I wondered if he would recognize what it was.

"Is he really?" Laurent asked pleasantly . . . skeptically.

I kept my reply short, so that my voice wouldn't betray my panic. "Mm-hmm."

Laurent took a casual step to the side, gazing around at the little meadow. I didn't miss that the step brought him closer to me. In my head, the voice responded with a low snarl.

"So how are things working out in Denali? Carlisle said you were staying with Tanya?" My voice was too high.

The question made him pause. "I like Tanya very much," he mused. "And her sister Irina even more. . . . I've never stayed in one place for so long before, and I enjoy the advantages, the novelty of it. But, the restrictions are difficult. . . . I'm surprised that any of them can keep it up for long." He smiled at me conspiratorially. "Sometimes I cheat."

I couldn't swallow. My foot started to ease back, but I froze when his red eyes flickered down to catch the movement.

"Oh," I said in a faint voice. "Jasper has problems with that, too."

"Don't move," the voice whispered. I tried to do what he instructed. It was hard; the instinct to take flight was nearly uncontrollable.

"Really?" Laurent seemed interested. "Is that why they left?"

"No," I answered honestly. "Jasper is more careful at home."

"Yes," Laurent agreed. "I am, too."

The step forward he took now was quite deliberate.

"Did Victoria ever find you?" I asked, breathless, desperate to distract him. It was the first question that popped into my head, and I regretted it as soon as the words were spoken. Victoria—who *had* hunted me with James, and then disappeared—was not someone I wanted to think of at this particular moment.

But the question did stop him.

"Yes," he said, hesitating on that step. "I actually came here as a favor to her." He made a face. "She won't be happy about this."

"About what?" I said eagerly, inviting him to continue. He was glaring into the trees, away from me. I took advantage of his diversion, taking a furtive step back.

He looked back at me and smiled—the expression made him look like a black-haired angel.

"About me killing you," he answered in a seductive purr.

I staggered back another step. The frantic growling in my head made it hard to hear.

"She wanted to save that part for herself," he went on blithely. "She's sort of . . . put out with you, Bella."

"Me?" I squeaked.

He shook his head and chuckled. "I know, it seems a little backward to me, too. But James was her mate, and your Edward killed him."

Even here, on the point of death, his name tore against my unhealed wounds like a serrated edge.

Laurent was oblivious to my reaction. "She thought it more appropriate to kill you than Edward—fair turnabout, mate for mate. She asked me to get the lay of the land for her, so to speak. I didn't imagine you would be so easy to get to. So maybe her plan was flawed—apparently it wouldn't be the revenge she imagined, since you must not mean very much to him if he left you here unprotected."

Another blow, another tear through my chest.

Laurent's weight shifted slightly, and I stumbled another step back.

He frowned. "I suppose she'll be angry, all the same."

"Then why not wait for her?" I choked out.

A mischievous grin rearranged his features. "Well, you've

caught me at a bad time, Bella. I didn't come to *this* place on Victoria's mission—I was hunting. I'm quite thirsty, and you do smell . . . simply mouthwatering."

Laurent looked at me with approval, as if he meant it as a compliment.

"Threaten him," the beautiful delusion ordered, his voice distorted with dread.

"He'll know it was you," I whispered obediently. "You won't get away with this."

"And why not?" Laurent's smile widened. He gazed around the small opening in the trees. "The scent will wash away with the next rain. No one will find your body— you'll simply go missing, like so many, many other humans. There's no reason for Edward to think of me, if he cares enough to investigate. This is nothing personal, let me assure you, Bella. Just thirst."

"Beg," my hallucination begged.

"Please," I gasped.

Laurent shook his head, his face kind. "Look at it this way, Bella. You're very lucky I was the one to find you."

"Am I?" I mouthed, faltering another step back.

Laurent followed, lithe and graceful.

"Yes," he assured me. "I'll be very quick. You won't feel a thing, I promise. Oh, I'll lie to Victoria about that later, naturally, just to placate her. But if you knew what she had planned for you, Bella . . ." He shook his head with a slow movement, almost as if in disgust. "I swear you'd be thanking me for this."

I stared at him in horror.

He sniffed at the breeze that blew threads of my hair in

his direction. "Mouthwatering," he repeated, inhaling deeply.

I tensed for the spring, my eyes squinting as I cringed away, and the sound of Edward's furious roar echoed distantly in the back of my head. His name burst through all the walls I'd built to contain it. *Edward, Edward, Edward.* I was going to die. It shouldn't matter if I thought of him now. *Edward, I love you.*

Through my narrowed eyes, I watched as Laurent paused in the act of inhaling and whipped his head abruptly to the left. I was afraid to look away from him, to follow his glance, though he hardly needed a distraction or any other trick to overpower me. I was too amazed to feel relief when he started slowly backing away from me.

"I don't believe it," he said, his voice so low that I barely heard it.

I had to look then. My eyes scanned the meadow, searching for the interruption that had extended my life by a few seconds. At first I saw nothing, and my gaze flickered back to Laurent. He was retreating more quickly now, his eyes boring into the forest.

Then I saw it; a huge black shape eased out of the trees, quiet as a shadow, and stalked deliberately toward the vampire. It was enormous—as tall as a horse, but thicker, much more muscular. The long muzzle grimaced, revealing a line of dagger-like incisors. A grisly snarl rolled out from between the teeth, rumbling across the clearing like a prolonged crack of thunder.

The bear. Only, it wasn't a bear at all. Still, this gigantic black monster had to be the creature causing all the alarm. From a distance, anyone would assume it was a bear. What else could be so vast, so powerfully built?

I wished I were lucky enough to see it from a distance. Instead, it padded silently through the grass a mere ten feet from where I stood.

"Don't move an inch," Edward's voice whispered.

I stared at the monstrous creature, my mind boggling as I tried to put a name to it. There was a distinctly canine cast to the shape of it, the way it moved. I could only think of one possibility, locked in horror as I was. Yet I'd never imagined that a wolf could get so *big*.

Another growl rumbled in its throat, and I shuddered away from the sound.

Laurent was backing toward the edge of the trees, and, under the freezing terror, confusion swept through me. Why was Laurent retreating? Granted, the wolf was monstrous in size, but it was just an animal. What reason would a vampire have for fearing an animal? And Laurent *was* afraid. His eyes were wide with horror, just like mine.

As if in answer to my question, suddenly the mammoth wolf was not alone. Flanking it on either side, another two gigantic beasts prowled silently into the meadow. One was a deep gray, the other brown, neither one quite as tall as the first. The gray wolf came through the trees only a few feet from me, its eyes locked on Laurent.

Before I could even react, two more wolves followed, lined up in a V, like geese flying south. Which meant that the rusty brown monster that shrugged through the brush last was close enough for me to touch.

I gave an involuntary gasp and jumped back—which

was the stupidest thing I could have done. I froze again, waiting for the wolves to turn on me, the much weaker of the available prey. I wished briefly that Laurent would get on with it and crush the wolf pack—it should be so simple for him. I guessed that, between the two choices before me, being eaten by wolves was almost certainly the worse option.

The wolf closest to me, the reddish brown one, turned its head slightly at the sound of my gasp.

The wolf's eyes were dark, nearly black. It gazed at me for a fraction of a second, the deep eyes seeming too intelligent for a wild animal.

As it stared at me, I suddenly thought of Jacob—again, with gratitude. At least I'd come here alone, to this fairy-tale meadow filled with dark monsters. At least Jacob wasn't going to die, too. At least I wouldn't have his death on my hands.

Then another low growl from the leader caused the russet wolf to whip his head around, back toward Laurent.

Laurent was staring at the pack of monster wolves with unconcealed shock and fear. The first I could understand. But I was stunned when, without warning, he spun and disappeared into the trees.

He ran away.

The wolves were after him in a second, sprinting across the open grass with a few powerful bounds, snarling and snapping so loudly that my hands flew up instinctively to cover my ears. The sound faded with surprising swiftness once they disappeared into the woods.

And then I was alone again.

My knees buckled under me, and I fell onto my hands, sobs building in my throat.

I knew I needed to leave, and leave now. How long would the wolves chase Laurent before they doubled back for me? Or would Laurent turn on them? Would he be the one that came looking?

I couldn't move at first, though; my arms and legs were shaking, and I didn't know how to get back to my feet.

My mind couldn't move past the fear, the horror or the confusion. I didn't understand what I'd just witnessed.

A vampire should not have run from overgrown dogs like that. What good would their teeth be against his granite skin?

And the wolves should have given Laurent a wide berth. Even if their extraordinary size had taught them to fear nothing, it still made no sense that they would pursue him. I doubted his icy marble skin would smell anything like food. Why would they pass up something warm-blooded and weak like me to chase after Laurent?

I couldn't make it add up.

A cold breeze whipped through the meadow, swaying the grass like something was moving through it.

I scrambled to my feet, backing away even though the wind brushed harmlessly past me. Stumbling in panic, I turned and ran headlong into the trees.

The next few hours were agony. It took me three times as long to escape the trees as it had to get to the meadow.

At first I paid no attention to where I was headed, focused only on what I was running from. By the time I collected myself enough to remember the compass, I was deep in the unfamiliar and menacing forest. My hands were shaking so violently that I had to set the compass on the muddy ground to be able to read it. Every few minutes I would stop to put the compass down and check that I was still heading northwest, hearing—when the sounds weren't hidden behind the frantic squelching of my footsteps—the quiet whisper of unseen things moving in the leaves.

The call of a jaybird made me leap back and fall into a thick stand of young spruce, scraping up my arms and tangling my hair with sap. The sudden rush of a squirrel up a hemlock made me scream so loud it hurt my own ears.

At last there was a break in the trees ahead. I came out onto the empty road a mile or so south of where I'd left the truck. Exhausted as I was, I jogged up the lane until I found it. By the time I pulled myself into the cab, I was sobbing again. I fiercely shoved down both stiff locks before I dug my keys out of my pocket. The roar of the engine was comforting and sane. It helped me control the tears as I sped as fast as my truck would allow toward the main highway.

I was calmer, but still a mess when I got home. Charlie's cruiser was in the driveway—I hadn't realized how late it was. The sky was already dusky.

"Bella?" Charlie asked when I slammed the front door behind me and hastily turned the locks.

"Yeah, it's me." My voice was unsteady.

"Where have you been?" he thundered, appearing through the kitchen doorway with an ominous expression.

I hesitated. He'd probably called the Stanleys. I'd better stick to the truth.

"I was hiking," I admitted.

His eyes were tight. "What happened to going to Jessica's?"

"I didn't feel like Calculus today."

Charlie folded his arms across his chest. "I thought I asked you to stay out of the forest."

"Yeah, I know. Don't worry, I won't do it again." I shuddered.

Charlie seemed to really look at me for the first time. I remembered that I had spent some time on the forest floor today; I must be a mess.

"What happened?" Charlie demanded.

Again, I decided that the truth, or part of it anyway, was the best option. I was too shaken to pretend that I'd spent an uneventful day with the flora and fauna.

"I saw the bear." I tried to say it calmly, but my voice was high and shaky. "It's not a bear, though—it's some kind of wolf. And there are five of them. A big black one, and gray, and reddish-brown . . ."

Charlie's eyes grew round with horror. He strode quickly to me and grabbed the tops of my arms.

"Are you okay?"

My head bobbed in a weak nod.

"Tell me what happened."

"They didn't pay any attention to me. But after they were gone, I ran away and I fell down a lot."

He let go of my shoulders and wrapped his arms around me. For a long moment, he didn't say anything.

"Wolves," he murmured.

"What?"

"The rangers said the tracks were wrong for a bear—but wolves just don't get that big. . . ."

"These were *huge*."

"How many did you say you saw?"

"Five."

Charlie shook his head, frowning with anxiety. He finally spoke in a tone that allowed no argument. "No more hiking."

"No problem," I promised fervently.

Charlie called the station to report what I'd seen. I fudged a little bit about where exactly I'd seen the wolves—claiming I'd been on the trail that led to the north. I didn't want my dad to know how deep I'd gone into the forest against his wishes, and, more importantly, I didn't want anyone wandering near where Laurent might be searching for me. The thought of it made me feel sick.

"Are you hungry?" he asked me when he hung up the phone.

I shook my head, though I must have been starving. I hadn't eaten all day.

"Just tired," I told him. I turned for the stairs.

"Hey," Charlie said, his voice suddenly suspicious again. "Didn't you say Jacob was gone for the day?"

"That's what Billy said," I told him, confused by his question.

He studied my expression for a minute, and seemed satisfied with what he saw there.

"Huh."

"Why?" I demanded. It sounded like he was implying that I'd been lying to him this morning. About something besides studying with Jessica.

"Well, it's just that when I went to pick up Harry, I saw Jacob out in front of the store down there with some of his friends. I waved hi, but he . . . well, I guess I don't know if he saw me. I think maybe he was arguing with his friends. He looked strange, like he was upset about something. And . . . different. It's like you can watch that kid growing! He gets bigger every time I see him."

"Billy said Jake and his friends were going up to Port Angeles to see some movies. They were probably just waiting for someone to meet them."

"Oh." Charlie nodded and headed for the kitchen.

I stood in the hall, thinking about Jacob arguing with his friends. I wondered if he had confronted Embry about the situation with Sam. Maybe that was the reason he'd ditched me today—if it meant he could sort things out with Embry, I was glad he had.

I paused to check the locks again before I went to my room. It was a silly thing to do. What difference would a lock make to any of the monsters I'd seen this afternoon? I assumed the handle alone would stymie the wolves, not having opposable thumbs. And if Laurent came here . . .

Or . . . *Victoria.*

I lay down on my bed, but I was shaking too hard to hope for sleep. I curled into a cramped ball under my quilt, and faced the horrifying facts.

There was nothing I could do. There were no precautions I could take. There was no place I could hide. There was no one who could help me.

I realized, with a nauseous roll of my stomach, that the situation was worse than even that. Because all those facts applied to Charlie, too. My father, sleeping one room away from me, was just a hairsbreadth off the heart of the target that was centered on me. My scent would lead them here, whether I was here or not.

The tremors rocked me until my teeth chattered.

To calm myself, I fantasized the impossible: I imagined the big wolves catching up to Laurent in the woods and massacring the indestructible immortal the way they would any normal person. Despite the absurdity of such a vision, the idea comforted me. If the wolves got him, then he couldn't tell Victoria I was here all alone. If he didn't return, maybe she'd think the Cullens were still protecting me. If only the wolves could win such a fight. . . .

My good vampires were never coming back; how soothing it was to imagine that the *other* kind could also disappear.

I squeezed my eyes tight together and waited for unconsciousness—almost eager for my nightmare to start. Better that than the pale, beautiful face that smiled at me now from behind my lids.

In my imagination, Victoria's eyes were black with thirst, bright with anticipation, and her lips curled back from her gleaming teeth in pleasure. Her red hair was brilliant as fire; it blew chaotically around her wild face.

Laurent's words repeated in my head. *If you knew what she had planned for you . . . .*

I pressed my fist against my mouth to keep from screaming.

11. CULT

EACH TIME THAT I OPENED MY EYES TO THE MORNING
light and realized I'd lived through another night was a
surprise to me. After the surprise wore off, my heart would
start to race and my palms would sweat; I couldn't really
breathe again until I'd gotten up and ascertained that
Charlie had survived as well.

I could tell he was worried—watching me jump at any
loud sound, or my face suddenly go white for no reason
that he could see. From the questions he asked now and
then, he seemed to blame the change on Jacob's continued
absence.

The terror that was always foremost in my thoughts
usually distracted me from the fact that another week

had passed, and Jacob still hadn't called me. But when I was able to concentrate on my normal life—if my life was really ever normal—this upset me.

I missed him horribly.

It had been bad enough to be alone before I was scared silly. Now, more than ever, I yearned for his carefree laugh and his infectious grin. I needed the safe sanity of his homemade garage and his warm hand around my cold fingers.

I'd half expected him to call on Monday. If there had been some progress with Embry, wouldn't he want to report it? I wanted to believe that it was worry for his friend that was occupying all his time, not that he was just giving up on me.

I called him Tuesday, but no one answered. Were the phone lines still having problems? Or had Billy invested in caller I.D.?

On Wednesday I called every half hour until after eleven at night, desperate to hear the warmth of Jacob's voice.

Thursday I sat in my truck in front of my house—with the locks pushed down—keys in hand, for a solid hour. I was arguing with myself, trying to justify a quick trip to La Push, but I couldn't do it.

I knew that Laurent had gone back to Victoria by now. If I went to La Push, I took the chance of leading one of them there. What if they caught up to me when Jake was nearby? As much as it hurt me, I knew it was better for Jacob that he was avoiding me. Safer for him.

It was bad enough that I couldn't figure out a way to

keep Charlie safe. Nighttime was the most likely time that they would come looking for me, and what could I say to get Charlie out of the house? If I told him the truth, he'd have me locked up in a rubber room somewhere. I would have endured that—welcomed it, even—if it could have kept him safe. But Victoria would still come to his house first, looking for me. Maybe, if she found me here, that would be enough for her. Maybe she would just leave when she was done with me.

So I couldn't run away. Even if I could, where would I go? To Renée? I shuddered at the thought of dragging my lethal shadows into my mother's safe, sunny world. I would never endanger her that way.

The worry was eating a hole in my stomach. Soon I would have matching punctures.

That night, Charlie did me another favor and called Harry again to see if the Blacks were out of town. Harry reported that Billy had attended the council meeting Wednesday night, and never mentioned anything about leaving. Charlie warned me not to make a nuisance of myself—Jacob would call when he got around to it.

Friday afternoon, as I drove home from school, it hit me out of the blue.

I wasn't paying attention to the familiar road, letting the sound of the engine deaden my brain and silence the worries, when my subconscious delivered a verdict it must have been working on for some time without my knowledge.

As soon as I thought of it, I felt really stupid for not seeing it sooner. Sure, I'd had a lot on my mind—revenge-obsessed vampires, giant mutant wolves, a ragged hole in the center of my chest—but when I laid the evidence out, it was embarrassingly obvious.

Jacob avoiding me. Charlie saying he looked strange, upset. . . . Billy's vague, unhelpful answers.

Holy crow, I knew exactly what was going on with Jacob.

It was Sam Uley. Even my nightmares had been trying to tell me that. Sam had gotten to Jacob. Whatever was happening to the other boys on the reservation had reached out and stolen my friend. He'd been sucked into Sam's cult.

He hadn't given up on me at all, I realized with a rush of feeling.

I let my truck idle in front of my house. What should I do? I weighed the dangers against each other.

If I went looking for Jacob, I risked the chance of Victoria or Laurent finding me with him.

If I didn't go after him, Sam would pull him deeper into his frightening, compulsory gang. Maybe it would be too late if I didn't act soon.

It had been a week, and no vampires had come for me yet. A week was more than enough time for them to have returned, so I must not be a priority. Most likely, as I'd decided before, they would come for me at night. The chances of them following me to La Push were much lower than the chance of losing Jacob to Sam.

It was worth the danger of the secluded forest road. This was no idle visit to see what was going on. I *knew* what was going on. This was a rescue mission. I was going to talk to Jacob—kidnap him if I had to. I'd once seen a PBS show on deprogramming the brainwashed. There had to be some kind of cure.

I decided I'd better call Charlie first. Maybe whatever was going on down in La Push was something the police should be involved in. I dashed inside, in a hurry to be on my way.

Charlie answered the phone at the station himself.

"Chief Swan."

"Dad, it's Bella."

"What's wrong?"

I couldn't argue with his doomsday assumption this time. My voice was shaking.

"I'm worried about Jacob."

"Why?" he asked, surprised by the unexpected topic.

"I think . . . I think something weird is going on down at the reservation. Jacob told me about some strange stuff happening with the other boys his age. Now he's acting the same way and I'm scared."

"What kind of stuff?" He used his professional, police business voice. That was good; he was taking me seriously.

"First he was scared, and then he was avoiding me, and now . . . I'm afraid he's part of that bizarre gang down there, Sam's gang. Sam Uley's gang."

"Sam Uley?" Charlie repeated, surprised again.

"Yes."

Charlie's voice was more relaxed when he answered. "I think you've got it wrong, Bells. Sam Uley is a great kid. Well, he's a man now. A good son. You should hear Billy talk about him. He's really doing wonders with the youth on the reservation. He's the one who—" Charlie broke off mid-sentence, and I guessed that he had been about to make a reference to the night I'd gotten lost in the woods. I moved on quickly.

"Dad, it's not like that. Jacob was *scared* of him."

"Did you talk to Billy about this?" He was trying to soothe me now. I'd lost him as soon as I'd mentioned Sam.

"Billy's not concerned."

"Well, Bella, then I'm sure it's okay. Jacob's a kid; he was probably just messing around. I'm sure he's fine. He can't spend every waking minute with you, after all."

"This isn't about me," I insisted, but the battle was lost.

"I don't think you need to worry about this. Let Billy take care of Jacob."

"Charlie . . ." My voice was starting to sound whiney.

"Bells, I got a lot on my plate right now. Two tourists have gone missing off a trail outside crescent lake." There was an anxious edge to his voice. "This wolf problem is getting out of hand."

I was momentarily distracted—stunned, really—by his news. There was no way the wolves could have survived a match-up with Laurent. . . .

"Are you sure that's what happened to them?" I asked.

"Afraid so, honey. There was—" He hesitated. "There were tracks again, and . . . some blood this time."

"Oh!" It must not have come to a confrontation, then. Laurent must have simply outrun the wolves, but why? What I'd seen in the meadow just got stranger and stranger—more impossible to understand.

"Look, I really have to go. Don't worry about Jake, Bella. I'm sure it's nothing."

"Fine," I said curtly, frustrated as his words reminded me of the more urgent crisis at hand. "Bye." I hung up.

I stared at the phone for a long minute. *What the hell*, I decided.

Billy answered after two rings.

"Hello?"

"Hey, Billy," I almost growled. I tried to sound more friendly as I continued. "Can I talk to Jacob, please?"

"Jake's not here."

What a shock. "Do you know where he is?"

"He's out with his friends." Billy's voice was careful.

"Oh yeah? Anyone I know? Quil?" I could tell the words didn't come across as casually as I'd meant them to.

"No," Billy said slowly. "I don't think he's with Quil today."

I knew better than to mention Sam's name.

"Embry?" I asked.

Billy seemed happier to answer this one. "Yeah, he's with Embry."

That was enough for me. Embry was one of them.

"Well, have him call me when he gets in, all right?"

"Sure, sure. No problem." *Click.*

"See you soon, Billy," I muttered into the dead phone.

I drove to La Push determined to wait. I'd sit out front of his house all night if I had to. I'd miss school. The boy was going to have to come home sometime, and when he did, he was going to have to talk to me.

My mind was so preoccupied that the trip I'd been

terrified of making seemed to take only a few seconds. Before I was expecting it, the forest began to thin, and I knew I would soon be able to see the first little houses of the reservation.

Walking away, along the left side of the road, was a tall boy with a baseball cap.

My breath caught for just a moment in my throat, hopeful that luck was with me for once, and I'd stumbled across Jacob without hardly trying. But this boy was too wide, and the hair was short under the hat. Even from behind, I was sure it was Quil, though he looked bigger than the last time I'd seen him. What was with these Quileute boys? Were they feeding them experimental growth hormones?

I crossed over to the wrong side of the road to stop next to him. He looked up when the roar of my truck approached.

Quil's expression frightened me more than it surprised me. His face was bleak, brooding, his forehead creased with worry.

"Oh, hey, Bella," he greeted me dully.

"Hi, Quil. . . . Are you okay?"

He stared at me morosely. "Fine."

"Can I give you a ride somewhere?" I offered.

"Sure, I guess," he mumbled. He shuffled around the front of the truck and opened the passenger door to climb in.

"Where to?"

"My house is on the north side, back behind the store," he told me.

"Have you seen Jacob today?" The question burst from me almost before he'd finished speaking.

I looked at Quil eagerly, waiting for his answer. He stared out the windshield for a second before he spoke. "From a distance," he finally said.

"A distance?" I echoed.

"I tried to follow them—he was with Embry." His voice was low, hard to hear over the engine. I leaned closer. "I know they saw me. But they turned and just disappeared into the trees. I don't think they were alone—I think Sam and his crew might have been with them.

"I've been stumbling around in the forest for an hour, yelling for them. I just barely found the road again when you drove up."

"So Sam did get to him." The words were a little distorted—my teeth were gritted together.

Quil stared at me. "You know about that?"

I nodded. "Jake told me . . . before."

"Before," Quil repeated, and sighed.

"Jacob's just as bad as the others now?"

"Never leaves Sam's side." Quil turned his head and spit out the open window.

"And before that—did he avoid everyone? Was he acting upset?"

His voice was low and rough. "Not for as long as the others. Maybe one day. Then Sam caught up with him."

"What do you think it is? Drugs or something?"

"I can't see Jacob or Embry getting into anything like that . . . but what do I know? What else could it be? And why aren't the old people worried?" He shook his head, and the fear showed in his eyes now. "Jacob didn't want to be a part of this . . . cult. I don't understand what could change him." He stared at me, his face frightened. "*I don't want to be next.*"

My eyes mirrored his fear. That was the second time I'd heard it described as a cult. I shivered. "Are your parents any help?"

He grimaced. "Right. My grandfather's on the council with Jacob's dad. Sam Uley is the best thing that ever happened to this place, as far as he's concerned."

We stared at each other for a prolonged moment. We were in La Push now, and my truck was barely crawling along the empty road. I could see the village's only store not too far ahead.

"I'll get out now," Quil said. "My house is right over there." He gestured toward the small wooden rectangle behind the store. I pulled over to the shoulder, and he jumped out.

"I'm going to go wait for Jacob," I told him in a hard voice.

"Good luck." He slammed the door and shuffled forward along the road, his head bent forward, his shoulders slumped.

Quil's face haunted me as I made a wide U-turn and headed back toward the Blacks'. He was terrified of being next. What was happening here?

I stopped in front of Jacob's house, killing the motor and rolling down the windows. It was stuffy today, no breeze. I put my feet up on the dashboard and settled in to wait.

A movement flashed in my peripheral vision—I turned and spotted Billy looking at me through the front window with a confused expression. I waved once and smiled a tight smile, but stayed where I was.

His eyes narrowed; he let the curtain fall across the glass.

I was prepared to stay as long as it took, but I wished I had something to do. I dug up a pen out of the bottom of my backpack, and an old test. I started to doodle on the back of the scrap.

I'd only had time to scrawl one row of diamonds when there was a sharp tap against my door.

I jumped, looking up, expecting Billy.

"What are you doing here, Bella?" Jacob growled.

I stared at him in blank astonishment.

Jacob had changed radically in the last weeks since I'd seen him. The first thing I noticed was his hair—his beautiful hair was all gone, cropped quite short, covering his head with an inky gloss like black satin. The planes of his face seemed to have hardened subtly, tightened . . . aged. His neck and his shoulders were different, too, thicker somehow. His hands, where they gripped the window frame, looked enormous, with the tendons and veins more prominent under the russet skin. But the physical changes were insignificant.

It was his expression that made him almost completely unrecognizable. The open, friendly smile was gone like the hair, the warmth in his dark eyes altered to a brooding resentment that was instantly disturbing. There was a darkness in Jacob now. Like my sun had imploded.

"Jacob?" I whispered.

He just stared at me, his eyes tense and angry.

I realized we weren't alone. Behind him stood four others; all tall and russet-skinned, black hair chopped short just like Jacob's. They could have been brothers—I couldn't even pick Embry out of the group. The resemblance was only intensified by the strikingly similar hostility in every pair of eyes.

Every pair but one. The oldest by several years, Sam stood in the very back, his face serene and sure. I had to swallow back the bile that rose in my throat. I wanted to take a swing at him. No, I wanted to do more than that. More than anything, I wanted to be fierce and deadly, someone no one would dare mess with. Someone who would scare Sam Uley silly.

I wanted to be a vampire.

The violent desire caught me off guard and knocked the wind out of me. It was the most forbidden of all wishes—even when I only wished it for a malicious reason like this, to gain an advantage over an enemy—because it was the most painful. That future was lost to me forever, had never really been within my grasp. I scrambled to gain control of myself while the hole in my chest ached hollowly.

"What do you want?" Jacob demanded, his expression growing more resentful as he watched the play of emotion across my face.

"I want to talk to you," I said in a weak voice. I tried to focus, but I was still reeling against the escape of my taboo dream.

"Go ahead," he hissed through his teeth. His glare was vicious. I'd never seen him look at anyone like that, least of all me. It hurt with a surprising intensity—a physical pain, a stabbing in my head.

"Alone!" I hissed, and my voice was stronger.

He looked behind him, and I knew where his eyes would go. Every one of them was turned for Sam's reaction.

Sam nodded once, his face unperturbed. He made a brief comment in an unfamiliar, liquid language—I could only be positive that it wasn't French or Spanish, but I guessed that it was Quileute. He turned and walked into Jacob's house. The others, Paul, Jared, and Embry, I assumed, followed him in.

"Okay." Jacob seemed a bit less furious when the others were gone. His face was a little calmer, but also more hopeless. His mouth seemed permanently pulled down at the corners.

I took a deep breath. "You know what I want to know."

He didn't answer. He just stared at me bitterly.

I stared back and the silence stretched on. The pain in his face unnerved me. I felt a lump beginning to build in my throat.

"Can we walk?" I asked while I could still speak.

He didn't respond in any way; his face didn't change.

I got out of the car, feeling unseen eyes behind the windows on me, and started walking toward the trees to the north. My feet squished in the damp grass and mud beside the road, and, as that was the only sound, at first I thought he wasn't following me. But when I glanced around, he was right beside me, his feet having somehow found a less noisy path than mine.

I felt better in the fringe of trees, where Sam couldn't possibly be watching. As we walked, I struggled for the right thing to say, but nothing came. I just got more and more angry that Jacob had gotten sucked in . . . that Billy had allowed this . . . that Sam was able to stand there so assured and calm. . . .

Jacob suddenly picked up the pace, striding ahead of me easily with his long legs, and then swinging around to face me, planting himself in my path so I would have to stop too.

I was distracted by the overt grace of his movement. Jacob had been nearly as klutzy as me with his never-ending growth spurt. When did that change?

But Jacob didn't give me time to think about it.

"Let's get this over with," he said in a hard, husky voice.

I waited. He knew what I wanted.

"It's not what you think." His voice was abruptly weary. "It's not what I thought—I was way off."

"So what is it, then?"

He studied my face for a long moment, speculating. The anger never completely left his eyes. "I can't tell you," he finally said.

My jaw tightened, and I spoke through my teeth. "I thought we were friends."

"We were." There was a slight emphasis on the past tense.

"But you don't need friends anymore," I said sourly. "You have Sam. Isn't that nice—you've always looked up to him so much."

"I didn't understand him before."

"And now you've seen the light. Hallelujah."

"It wasn't like I thought it was. This isn't Sam's fault. He's helping me as much as he can." His voice turned brittle and he looked over my head, past me, rage burning out from his eyes.

"He's helping you," I repeated dubiously. "Naturally."

But Jacob didn't seem to be listening. He was taking deep, deliberate breaths, trying to calm himself. He was so mad that his hands were shaking.

"Jacob, please," I whispered. "Won't you tell me what happened? Maybe I can help."

"No one can help me now." The words were a low moan; his voice broke.

"What did he do to you?" I demanded, tears collecting in my eyes. I reached out to him, as I had once before, stepping forward with my arms wide.

This time he cringed away, holding his hands up defensively. "Don't touch me," he whispered.

"Is Sam catching?" I mumbled. The stupid tears had escaped the corners of my eyes. I wiped them away with the back of my hand, and folded my arms across my chest.

"Stop blaming Sam." The words came out fast, like a reflex. His hands reached up to twist around the hair that was no longer there, and then fell limply at his sides.

"Then who should I blame?" I retorted.

He halfway smiled; it was a bleak, twisted thing.

"You don't want to hear that."

"The hell I don't!" I snapped. "I want to know, and I want to know *now*."

"You're wrong," he snapped back.

"Don't you dare tell me I'm wrong—I'm not the one who got brainwashed! Tell me now whose fault this all is, if it's not your precious Sam!"

"You asked for it," he growled at me, eyes glinting hard. "If you want to blame someone, why don't you point your finger at those filthy, *reeking* bloodsuckers that you love so much?"

My mouth fell open and my breath came out with a *whoosh*ing sound. I was frozen in place, stabbed through with his double-edged words. The pain twisted in familiar patterns through my body, the jagged hole ripping me open from the inside out, but it was second place, background music to the chaos of my thoughts. I couldn't believe that I'd heard him correctly. There was no trace of indecision in his face. Only fury.

My mouth still hung wide.

"I told you that you didn't want to hear it," he said.

"I don't understand who you mean," I whispered.

He raised one eyebrow in disbelief. "I think you understand exactly who I mean. You're not going to make me say it, are you? I don't like hurting you."

"I don't understand who you mean," I repeated mechanically.

"The *Cullens*," he said slowly, drawing out the word, scrutinizing my face as he spoke it. "I saw that—I can see in your eyes what it does to you when I say their name."

I shook my head back and forth in denial, trying to clear it at the same time. How did he know this? And how did it have anything to do with Sam's cult? Was it a gang of vampire-haters? What was the point of forming such a society when no vampires lived in Forks anymore? Why would Jacob start believing the stories about the Cullens now, when the evidence of them was long gone, never to return?

It took me too long to come up with the correct response. "Don't tell me you're listening to Billy's superstitious nonsense now," I said with a feeble attempt at mockery.

"He knows more than I gave him credit for."

"Be serious, Jacob."

He glared at me, his eyes critical.

"Superstitions aside," I said quickly. "I still don't see what you're accusing the . . . Cullens"—wince—"of. They left more than half a year ago. How can you blame them for what Sam is doing now?"

"Sam isn't *doing* anything, Bella. And I know they're gone. But sometimes . . . things are set in motion, and then it's too late."

"What's set in motion? What's too late? What are you blaming them for?"

He was suddenly right in my face, his fury glowing in his eyes. "For existing," he hissed.

I was surprised and distracted as the warning words came in Edward's voice again, when I wasn't even scared.

"Quiet now, Bella. Don't push him," Edward cautioned in my ear.

Ever since Edward's name had broken through the careful walls I'd buried it behind, I'd been unable to lock it up again. It didn't hurt now—not during the precious seconds when I could hear his voice.

Jacob was fuming in front of me, quivering with anger.

I didn't understand why the Edward delusion was unexpectedly in my mind. Jacob was livid, but he was Jacob. There was no adrenaline, no danger.

"Give him a chance to calm down," Edward's voice insisted.

I shook my head in confusion. "You're being ridiculous," I told them both.

"Fine," Jacob answered, breathing deeply again. "I won't argue it with you. It doesn't matter anyway, the damage is done."

"*What damage?*"

He didn't flinch as I shouted the words in his face.

"Let's head back. There's nothing more to say."

I gaped. "There's everything more to say! You haven't said anything yet!"

He walked past me, striding back toward the house.

"I ran into Quil today," I yelled after him.

He paused midstep, but didn't turn.

"You remember your friend, Quil? Yeah, he's terrified."

Jacob whirled to face me. His expression was pained. "Quil" was all he said.

"He's worried about you, too. He's freaked out."

Jacob stared past me with desperate eyes.

I goaded him further. "He's frightened that he's next."

Jacob clutched at a tree for support, his face turning a

strange shade of green under the red-brown surface. "He won't be next," Jacob muttered to himself. "He can't be. It's over now. This shouldn't still be happening. Why? Why?" His fist slammed against the tree. It wasn't a big tree, slender and only a few feet taller than Jacob. But it still surprised me when the trunk gave way and snapped off loudly under his blows.

Jacob stared at the sharp, broken point with shock that quickly turned to horror.

"I have to get back." He whirled and stalked away so swiftly that I had to jog to keep up.

"Back to Sam!"

"That's one way of looking at it," it sounded like he said. He was mumbling and facing away.

I chased him back to the truck. "Wait!" I called as he turned toward the house.

He spun around to face me, and I saw that his hands were shaking again.

"Go home, Bella. I can't hang out with you anymore."

The silly, inconsequential hurt was incredibly potent. The tears welled up again. "Are you . . . breaking up with me?" The words were all wrong, but they were the best way I could think to phrase what I was asking. After all, what Jake and I had was more than any schoolyard romance. Stronger.

He barked out a bitter laugh. "Hardly. If that were the case, I'd say 'Let's stay friends.' I can't even say that."

"Jacob . . . why? Sam won't let you have other friends? Please, Jake. You promised. I need you!" The blank empti-

ness of my life before—before Jacob brought some sem-
blance of reason back into it—reared up and confronted
me. Loneliness choked in my throat.

"I'm sorry, Bella," Jacob said each word distinctly in a
cold voice that didn't seem to belong to him.

I didn't believe that this was really what Jacob wanted
to say. It seemed like there was something else trying to be
said through his angry eyes, but I couldn't understand the
message.

Maybe this wasn't about Sam at all. Maybe this had
nothing to do with the Cullens. Maybe he was just trying
to pull himself out of a hopeless situation. Maybe I should
let him do that, if that's what was best for him. I should do
that. It would be right.

But I heard my voice escaping in a whisper.

"I'm sorry that I couldn't . . . before . . . I wish I could
change how I feel about you, Jacob." I was desperate, reaching, stretching the truth so far that it curved nearly into
the shape of a lie. "Maybe . . . maybe I would change," I
whispered. "Maybe, if you gave me some time . . . just
don't quit on me now, Jake. I can't take it."

His face went from anger to agony in a second. One
shaking hand reached out toward me.

"No. Don't think like that, Bella, please. Don't blame
yourself, don't think this is your fault. This one is *all* me.
I swear, it's not about you."

"It's not you, it's me," I whispered. "There's a new
one."

"I mean it, Bella. I'm not . . ." he struggled, his voice

going even huskier as he fought to control his emotion. His eyes were tortured. "I'm not good enough to be your friend anymore, or anything else. I'm not what I was before. I'm not good."

"What?" I stared at him, confused and appalled. "What are you *saying*? You're much better than I am, Jake. You are good! Who told you that you aren't? Sam? It's a vicious lie, Jacob! Don't let him tell you that!" I was suddenly yelling again.

Jacob's face went hard and flat. "No one had to tell me anything. I know what I am."

"You're my friend, that's what you are! Jake—don't!"

He was backing away from me.

"I'm sorry, Bella," he said again; this time it was a broken mumble. He turned and almost ran into the house.

I was unable to move from where I stood. I stared at the little house; it looked too small to hold four large boys and two larger men. There was no reaction inside. No flutter at the edge of the curtain, no sound of voices or movement. It faced me vacantly.

The rain started to drizzle, stinging here and there against my skin. I couldn't take my eyes off the house. Jacob would come back. He had to.

The rain picked up, and so did the wind. The drops were no longer falling from above; they slanted at an angle from the west. I could smell the brine from the ocean. My hair whipped in my face, sticking to the wet places and tangling in my lashes. I waited.

Finally the door opened, and I took a step forward in relief.

Billy rolled his chair into the door frame. I could see no one behind him.

"Charlie just called, Bella. I told him you were on your way home." His eyes were full of pity.

The pity made it final somehow. I didn't comment. I just turned robotically and climbed in my truck. I'd left the windows open and the seats were slick and wet. It didn't matter. I was already soaked.

Not as bad! Not as bad! my mind tried to comfort me. It was true. This wasn't as bad. This wasn't the end of the world, not again. This was just the end of what little peace there was left behind. That was all.

Not as bad, I agreed, then added, *but bad enough.*

I'd thought Jake had been healing the hole in me—or at least plugging it up, keeping it from hurting me so much. I'd been wrong. He'd just been carving out his own hole, so that I was now riddled through like Swiss cheese. I wondered why I didn't crumble into pieces.

Charlie was waiting on the porch. As I rolled to a stop, he walked out to meet me.

"Billy called. He said you got in fight with Jake—said you were pretty upset," he explained as he opened my door for me.

Then he looked at my face. A kind of horrified recognition registered in his expression. I tried to feel my face from the inside out, to know what he was seeing. My face felt empty and cold, and I realized what it would remind him of.

"That's not exactly how it happened," I muttered.

Charlie put his arm around me and helped me out of the car. He didn't comment on my sodden clothes.

"Then what did happen?" he asked when we were inside. He pulled the afghan off the back of the sofa as he spoke and wrapped it around my shoulders. I realized I was shivering still.

My voice was lifeless. "Sam Uley says Jacob can't be my friend anymore."

Charlie shot me a strange look. "Who told you that?"

"Jacob," I stated, though that wasn't exactly what he'd said. It was still true.

Charlie's eyebrows pulled together. "You really think there's something wrong with the Uley kid?"

"I know there is. Jacob wouldn't tell me what, though." I could hear the water from my clothes dripping to the floor and splashing on the linoleum. "I'm going to go change."

Charlie was lost in thought. "Okay," he said absently.

I decided to take a shower because I was so cold, but the hot water didn't seem to affect the temperature of my skin. I was still freezing when I gave up and shut the water off. In the sudden quiet, I could hear Charlie talking to someone downstairs. I wrapped a towel around me, and cracked the bathroom door.

Charlie's voice was angry. "I'm not buying that. It doesn't make any sense."

It was quiet then, and I realized he was on the phone. A minute passed.

"Don't you put this on Bella!" Charlie suddenly shouted.

I jumped. When he spoke again, his voice was careful and lower. "Bella's made it very clear all along that she and Jacob were just friends. . . . Well, if that was it, then why didn't you say so at first? No, Billy, I think she's right about this. . . . Because I know my daughter, and if she says Jacob was scared before—" He was cut off mid-sentence, and when he answered he was almost shouting again.

"What do you mean I don't know my daughter as well as I think I do!" He listened for a brief second, and his response was almost too low for me to hear. "If you think I'm going to remind her about that, then you had better think again. She's only just starting to get over it, and mostly because of Jacob, I think. If whatever Jacob has going on with this Sam character sends her back into that depression, then Jacob is going to have to answer to me. You're my friend, Billy, but this is hurting my family."

There was another break for Billy to respond.

"You got that right—those boys set one toe out of line and I'm going to know about it. We'll be keeping an eye on the situation, you can be sure of that." He was no longer Charlie; he was Chief Swan now.

"Fine. Yeah. Goodbye." The phone slammed into the cradle.

I tiptoed quickly across the hall into my room. Charlie was muttering angrily in the kitchen.

So Billy was going to blame me. I was leading Jacob on and he'd finally had enough.

It was strange, for I'd feared that myself, but after the

last thing Jacob had said this afternoon, I didn't believe it anymore. There was much more to this than an unrequited crush, and it surprised me that Billy would stoop to claiming that. It made me think that whatever secret they were keeping was bigger than I'd been imagining. At least Charlie was on my side now.

I put my pajamas on and crawled into bed. Life seemed dark enough at the moment that I let myself cheat. The hole—holes now—were already aching, so why not? I pulled out the memory—not a real memory that would hurt *too* much, but the false memory of Edward's voice in my mind this afternoon—and played it over and over in my head until I fell asleep with the tears still streaming calmly down my empty face.

It was a new dream tonight. Rain was falling and Jacob was walking soundlessly beside me, though beneath *my* feet the ground crunched like dry gravel. But he wasn't my Jacob; he was the new, bitter, graceful Jacob. The smooth suppleness of his walk reminded me of someone else, and, as I watched, his features started to change. The russet color of his skin leached away, leaving his face pale white like bone. His eyes turned gold, and then crimson, and then back to gold again. His shorn hair twisted in the breeze, turning bronze where the wind touched it. And his face became so beautiful that it shattered my heart. I reached for him, but he took a step away, raising his hands like a shield. And then Edward vanished.

I wasn't sure, when I woke in the dark, if I'd just begun crying, or if my tears had run while I slept and simply continued now. I stared at my dark ceiling. I could feel that it was the middle of the night—I was still half-asleep, maybe more than half. I closed my eyes wearily and prayed for a dreamless sleep.

That's when I heard the noise that must have wakened me in the first place. Something sharp scraped along the length of my window with a high-pitched squeal, like fingernails against the glass.

12. INTRUDER

My eyes flew wide open with fright, though I was so exhausted and muddled that I was not yet positive whether I was awake or asleep.

Something scratched against my window again with the same thin, high-pitched sound.

Confused and clumsy with sleep, I stumbled out of my bed and to the window, blinking the lingering tears from my eyes on the way.

A huge, dark shape wobbled erratically on the other side of the glass, lurching toward me like it was going to smash right through. I staggered back, terrified, my throat closing around a scream.

Victoria.

She'd come for me.

I was dead.

Not Charlie, too!

I choked back the building scream. I would have to keep quiet through this. Somehow. I had to keep Charlie from coming to investigate. . . .

And then a familiar, husky voice called from the dark shape.

"Bella!" it hissed. "Ouch! Damn it, open the window! OUCH!"

I needed two seconds to shake off the horror before I could move, but then I hurried to the window and shoved the glass out of the way. The clouds were dimly lit from behind, enough for me to make sense of the shapes.

"What are you *doing*?" I gasped.

Jacob was clinging precariously to the top of the spruce that grew in the middle of Charlie's little front yard. His weight had bowed the tree toward the house and he now swung—his legs dangling twenty feet above the ground— not a yard away from me. The thin branches at the tip of the tree scraped against the side of the house again with a grating squeal.

"I'm trying to keep"— he huffed, shifting his weight as the treetop bounced him—"my promise!"

I blinked my wet blurry eyes, suddenly sure that I was dreaming.

"When did you ever promise to kill yourself falling out of Charlie's tree?"

He snorted, unamused, swinging his legs to improve his balance. "Get out of the way," he ordered.

"What?"

He swung his legs again, backwards and forward, increasing his momentum. I realized what he was trying to do.

"No, Jake!"

But I ducked to the side, because it was too late. With a grunt, he launched himself toward my open window.

Another scream built in my throat as I waited for him to fall to his death—or at least maim himself against the wooden siding. To my shock, he swung agilely into my room, landing on the balls of his feet with a low thud.

We both looked to the door automatically, holding our breath, waiting to see if the noise had woken Charlie. A short moment of silence passed, and then we heard the muffled sound of Charlie's snore.

A wide grin spread slowly across Jacob's face; he seemed extremely pleased with himself. It wasn't the grin that I knew and loved—it was a new grin, one that was a bitter mockery of his old sincerity, on the new face that belonged to Sam.

That was a bit much for me.

I'd cried myself to sleep over this boy. His harsh rejection had punched a painful new hole in what was left of my chest. He'd left a new nightmare behind him, like an infection in a sore—the insult after the injury. And now he was here in my room, smirking at me as if none of that had passed. Worse than that, even though his arrival had been noisy and awkward, it reminded me of when Edward used to sneak in through my window at night, and the reminder picked viciously at the unhealed wounds.

All of this, coupled with the fact that I was dog-tired, did not put me in a friendly mood.

"Get out!" I hissed, putting as much venom into the whisper as I could.

He blinked, his face going blank with surprise.

"No," he protested. "I came to apologize."

"I don't *accept*!"

I tried to shove him back out the window—after all, if this was a dream, it wouldn't really hurt him. It was useless, though. I didn't budge him an inch. I dropped my hands quickly, and stepped away from him.

He wasn't wearing a shirt, though the air blowing in the window was cold enough to make me shiver, and it made me uncomfortable to have my hands on his bare chest. His skin was burning hot, like his head had been the last time I'd touched him. Like he was still sick with the fever.

He didn't look sick. He looked *huge*. He leaned over me, so big that he blacked out the window, tongue-tied by my furious reaction.

Suddenly, it was just more than I could handle—it felt as if all of my sleepless nights were crashing down on me en masse. I was so brutally tired that I thought I might collapse right there on the floor. I swayed unsteadily, and struggled to keep my eyes open.

"Bella?" Jacob whispered anxiously. He caught my elbow as I swayed again, and steered me back to the bed. My legs gave out when I reached the edge, and I plopped into a limp heap on the mattress.

"Hey, are you okay?" Jacob asked, worry creasing his forehead.

I looked up at him, the tears not yet dried on my cheeks. "Why in the world would I be okay, Jacob?"

Anguish replaced some of the bitterness in his face. "Right," he agreed, and took a deep breath. "Crap. Well . . . I—I'm so sorry, Bella." The apology was sincere, no doubt about it, though there was still an angry twist to his features.

"Why did you come here? I don't want apologies from you, Jake."

"I know," he whispered. "But I couldn't leave things the way I did this afternoon. That was horrible. I'm sorry."

I shook my head wearily. "I don't understand anything."

"I know. I want to explain—" He broke off suddenly, his mouth open, almost like something had cut off his air. Then he sucked in a deep breath. "But I can't explain," he said, still angry. "I wish I could."

I let my head fall into my hands. My question came out muffled by my arm. "Why?"

He was quiet for a moment. I twisted my head to the side—too tired to hold it up—to see his expression. It surprised me. His eyes were squinted, his teeth clenched, his forehead wrinkled in effort.

"What's wrong?" I asked.

He exhaled heavily, and I realized he'd been holding his breath, too. "I can't do it," he muttered, frustrated.

"Do what?"

He ignored my question. "Look, Bella, haven't you ever had a secret that you couldn't tell anyone?"

He looked at me with knowing eyes, and my thoughts jumped immediately to the Cullens. I hoped my expression didn't look guilty.

"Something you felt like you had to keep from Charlie, from your mom . . . ?" he pressed. "Something you won't even talk about with me? Not even now?"

I felt my eyes tighten. I didn't answer his question, though I knew he would take that as a confirmation.

"Can you understand that I might have the same kind of . . . situation?" He was struggling again, seeming to fight for the right words. "Sometimes, loyalty gets in the way of what you want to do. Sometimes, it's not your secret to tell."

So, I couldn't argue with that. He was exactly right—I had a secret that wasn't mine to tell, yet a secret I felt bound to protect. A secret that, suddenly, he seemed to know all about.

I still didn't see how it applied to him, or Sam, or Billy. What was it to them, now that the Cullens were gone?

"I don't know why you came here, Jacob, if you were just going to give me riddles instead of answers."

"I'm sorry," he whispered. "This is so frustrating."

We looked at each other for a long moment in the dark room, both our faces hopeless.

"The part that kills me," he said abruptly, "is that you already *know*. I already *told* you everything!"

"What are you talking about?"

He sucked in a startled breath, and then leaned toward me, his face shifting from hopelessness to blazing intensity in a second. He stared fiercely into my eyes, and his voice was fast and eager. He spoke the words right into my face; his breath was as hot as his skin.

"I think I see a way to make this work out—because you know this, Bella! I can't tell you, but if you *guessed* it! That would let me right off the hook!"

"You want me to guess? Guess *what?*"

"*My* secret! You can do it—you know the answer!"

I blinked twice, trying to clear my head. I was so tired. Nothing he said made sense.

He took in my blank expression, and then his face tensed with effort again. "Hold on, let me see if I give you some help," he said. Whatever he was trying to do, it was so hard he was panting.

"Help?" I asked, trying to keep up. My lids wanted to slip closed, but I forced them open.

"Yeah," he said, breathing hard. "Like clues."

He took my face in his enormous, too-warm hands and held it just a few inches from his. He stared into my eyes while he whispered, as if to communicate something besides the words he spoke.

"Remember the first day we met—on the beach in La Push?"

"Of course I do."

"Tell me about it."

I took a deep breath and tried to concentrate. "You asked about my truck. . . ."

He nodded, urging me on.

"We talked about the Rabbit. . . ."

"Keep going."

"We went for a walk down the beach. . . ." My cheeks were growing warm under his palms as I remembered, but he wouldn't notice, hot as his skin was. I'd asked him to walk with me, flirting ineptly but successfully, in order to pump him for information.

He was nodding, anxious for more.

My voice was nearly soundless. "You told me scary stories . . . Quileute legends."

He closed his eyes and opened them again. "Yes." The word was tense, fervent, like he was on the edge of something vital. He spoke slowly, making each word distinct. "Do you remember what I said?"

Even in the dark, he must be able to see the change in the color of my face. How could I ever forget that? Without realizing what he was doing, Jacob had told me exactly what I needed to know that day—that Edward was a vampire.

He looked at me with eyes that knew too much. "Think hard," he told me.

"Yes, I remember," I breathed.

He inhaled deeply, struggling. "Do you remember *all* the stor—" He couldn't finish the question. His mouth popped open like something had stuck in his throat.

"All the stories?" I asked.

He nodded mutely.

My head churned. Only one story really mattered. I knew he'd begun with others, but I couldn't remember the inconsequential prelude, especially not while my brain was so clouded with exhaustion. I started to shake my head.

Jacob groaned and jumped off the bed. He pressed his fists against his forehead and breathed fast and angry. "You know this, you know this," he muttered to himself.

"Jake? Jake, please, I'm *exhausted*. I'm no good at this right now. Maybe in the morning . . ."

He took a steadying breath and nodded. "Maybe it will come back to you. I guess I understand why you only remember the one story," he added in a sarcastic, bitter tone. He plunked back onto the mattress beside me. "Do you mind if I ask you a question about that?" he asked, still sarcastic. "I've been dying to know."

"A question about what?" I asked warily.

"About the vampire story I told you."

I stared at him with guarded eyes, unable to answer. He asked his question anyway.

"Did you honestly not know?" he asked me, his voice turning husky. "Was I the one who told you what he was?"

How did he know this? Why did he decide to believe, why *now*? My teeth clenched together. I stared back at him, no intention of speaking. He could see that.

"See what I mean about loyalty?" he murmured, even huskier now. "It's the same for me, only worse. You can't imagine how tight I'm bound. . . ."

I didn't like that—didn't like the way his eyes closed as if he were in pain when he spoke of being bound. More than dislike—I realized I *hated* it, hated anything that caused him pain. Hated it fiercely.

Sam's face filled my mind.

For me, this was all essentially voluntary. I protected the Cullens' secret out of love; unrequited, but true. For Jacob, it didn't seem to be that way.

"Isn't there any way for you to get free?" I whispered, touching the rough edge at the back of his shorn hair.

His hands began to tremble, but he didn't open his eyes. "No. I'm in this for life. A life sentence." A bleak laugh. "Longer, maybe."

"No, Jake," I moaned. "What if we ran away? Just you and me. What if we left home, and left Sam behind?"

"It's not something I can run away from, Bella," he whispered. "I would run with you, though, if I could." His shoulders were shaking now, too. He took a deep breath. "Look, I've got to leave."

"Why?"

"For one thing, you look like you're going to pass out at any second. You need your sleep—I need you firing on all pistons. You're going to figure this out, you have to."

"And why else?"

He frowned. "I had to sneak out—I'm not supposed to see you. They've got to be wondering where I am." His mouth twisted. "I suppose I should go let them know."

"You don't have to tell them anything," I hissed.

"All the same, I will."

The anger flashed hot inside me. "I *hate* them!"

Jacob looked at me with wide eyes, surprised. "No, Bella. Don't hate the guys. It's not Sam's or any of the others' faults. I told you before—it's me. Sam is actually . . .

well, incredibly cool. Jared and Paul are great, too, though Paul is kind of . . . And Embry's always been my friend. Nothing's changed there—the *only* thing that hasn't changed. I feel really bad about the things I used to think about Sam. . . ."

Sam was incredibly cool? I glared at him in disbelief, but let it go.

"Then why aren't you supposed to see me?" I demanded.

"It's not safe," he mumbled, looking down.

His words sent a thrill of fear through me.

Did he know *that*, too? Nobody knew that besides me. But he was right—it was the middle of the night, the perfect time for hunting. Jacob shouldn't be here in my room. If someone came for me, I had to be alone.

"If I thought it was too . . . too risky," he whispered, "I wouldn't have come. But Bella," he looked at me again, "I made you a promise. I had no idea it would be so hard to keep, but that doesn't mean I'm not going to try."

He saw the incomprehension in my face. "After that stupid movie," he reminded me. "I promised you that I wouldn't ever hurt you. . . . So I really blew it this afternoon, didn't I?"

"I know you didn't want to do it, Jake. It's okay."

"Thanks, Bella." He took my hand. "I'm going to do what I can to be here for you, just like I promised." He grinned at me suddenly. The grin was not mine, nor Sam's, but some strange combination of the two. "It would really help if you could figure this out on your own, Bella. Put some honest effort into it."

I made a weak grimace. "I'll try."

"And I'll try to see you soon." He sighed. "And they'll try to talk me out of that."

"Don't listen to them."

"I'll try." He shook his head, as if he doubted his success. "Come and tell me as soon as you figure it out." Something occurred to him just then, something that made his hands shake. "If you . . . if you *want* to."

"Why wouldn't I want to see you?"

His face turned hard and bitter, one hundred percent the face that belonged to Sam. "Oh, I can think of a reason," he said in a harsh tone. "Look, I really have to go. Could you do something for me?"

I just nodded, frightened of the change in him.

"At least call me—if you don't want to see me again. Let me know if it's like that."

"That won't happen—"

He raised one hand, cutting me off. "Just let me know."

He stood and headed for the window.

"Don't be an idiot, Jake," I complained. "You'll break your leg. Use the door. Charlie's not going to catch you."

"I won't get hurt," he muttered, but he turned for the door. He hesitated as he passed me, staring at me with an expression like something was stabbing him. He held one hand out, pleading.

I took his hand, and suddenly he yanked me—too roughly—right off the bed so that I thudded against his chest.

"Just in case," he muttered against my hair, crushing me in a bear hug that about broke my ribs.

"Can't—breathe!" I gasped.

He dropped me at once, keeping one hand at my waist so I didn't fall over. He pushed me, more gently this time, back down on the bed.

"Get some sleep, Bells. You've got to get your head working. I know you can do this. I *need* you to understand. I won't lose you, Bella. Not for this."

He was to the door in one stride, opening it quietly, and then disappearing through it. I listened for him to hit the squeaky step in the stairs, but there was no sound.

I lay back on my bed, my head spinning. I was too confused, too worn out. I closed my eyes, trying to make sense of it, only to be swallowed up by unconsciousness so swiftly that it was disorienting.

It was not the peaceful, dreamless sleep I'd yearned for—of course not. I was in the forest again, and I started to wander the way I always did.

I quickly became aware that this was not the same dream as usual. For one thing, I felt no compulsion to wander or to search; I was merely wandering out of habit, because that was what was usually expected of me here. Actually, this wasn't even the same forest. The smell was different, and the light, too. It smelled, not like the damp earth of the woods, but like the brine of the ocean. I couldn't see the sky; still, it seemed like the sun must be shining—the leaves above were bright jade green.

This was the forest around La Push—near the beach there, I was sure of it. I knew that if I found the beach, I would be able to see the sun, so I hurried forward, following the faint sound of waves in the distance.

And then Jacob was there. He grabbed my hand, pulling me back toward the blackest part of the forest.

"Jacob, what's wrong?" I asked. His face was the frightened face of a boy, and his hair was beautiful again, swept back into a ponytail on the nape of his neck. He yanked with all his strength, but I resisted; I didn't want to go into the dark.

"Run, Bella, you have to run!" he whispered, terrified.

The abrupt wave of déjà vu was so strong it nearly woke me up.

I knew why I recognized this place now. It was because I'd been here before, in another dream. A million years ago, part of a different life entirely. This was the dream I'd had the night after I'd walked with Jacob on the beach, the first night I knew that Edward was a vampire. Reliving that day with Jacob must have dredged this dream out of my buried memories.

Detached from the dream now, I waited for it to play out. A light was coming toward me from the beach. In just a moment, Edward would walk through the trees, his skin faintly glowing and his eyes black and dangerous. He would beckon to me, and smile. He would be beautiful as an angel, and his teeth would be pointed and sharp. . . .

But I was getting ahead of myself. Something else had to happen first.

Jacob dropped my hand and yelped. Shaking and twitching, he fell to the ground at my feet.

"Jacob!" I screamed, but he was gone.

In his place was an enormous, red-brown wolf with dark, intelligent eyes.

The dream veered off course, like a train jumping the tracks.

This was not the same wolf that I'd dreamed of in another life. This was the great russet wolf I'd stood half a foot from in the meadow, just a week ago. This wolf was gigantic, monstrous, bigger than a bear.

This wolf stared intently at me, trying to convey something vital with his intelligent eyes. The black-brown, familiar eyes of Jacob Black.

I woke screaming at the top of my lungs.

I almost expected Charlie to come check on me this time. This wasn't my usual screaming. I buried my head in my pillow and tried to muffle the hysterics that my screams were building into. I pressed the cotton tight against my face, wondering if I couldn't also somehow smother the connection I'd just made.

But Charlie didn't come in, and eventually I was able to strangle the strange screeching coming out of my throat.

I remembered it all now—every word that Jacob had said to me that day on the beach, even the part before he got to the vampires, the "cold ones." Especially that first part.

"Do you know any of our old stories, about where we came from—the Quileutes, I mean?" he asked.

"Not really," I admitted.

"Well, there are lots of legends, some of them claiming to date

back to the Flood—supposedly, the ancient Quileutes tied their canoes to the tops of the tallest trees on the mountain to survive, like Noah and the ark." He smiled then, to show me how little stock he put in the histories. *"Another legend claims that we descended from wolves—and that the wolves are our brothers still. It's against tribal law to kill them.*

"Then there are the stories about the cold ones." His voice dropped a little lower.

"The cold ones?"

"Yes. There are stories of the cold ones as old as the wolf legends, and some much more recent. According to legend, my own great-grandfather knew some of them. He was the one who made the treaty that kept them off our land." Jacob rolled his eyes.

"Your great-grandfather?"

"He was a tribal elder, like my father. You see, the cold ones are the natural enemies of the wolf—well, not the wolf really, but the wolves that turn into men, like our ancestors. You would call them werewolves."

"Werewolves have enemies?"

"Only one."

There was something stuck in my throat, choking me. I tried to swallow it down, but it was lodged there, unmoving. I tried to spit it out.

"Werewolf," I gasped.

Yes, that was the word that I was choking on.

The whole world lurched, tilting the wrong way on its axis.

What kind of a place *was* this? Could a world really exist where ancient legends went wandering around the borders of tiny, insignificant towns, facing down mythical monsters? Did this mean every impossible fairy tale was grounded somewhere in absolute truth? Was there anything sane or normal at all, or was everything just magic and ghost stories?

I clutched my head in my hands, trying to keep it from exploding.

A small, dry voice in the back of my mind asked me what the big deal was. Hadn't I already accepted the existence of vampires long ago—and without all the hysterics that time?

Exactly, I wanted to scream back at the voice. Wasn't one myth enough for anyone, enough for a lifetime?

Besides, there'd never been one moment that I wasn't completely aware that Edward Cullen was above and beyond the ordinary. It wasn't such a surprise to find out what he was—because he so obviously was *something*.

But Jacob? Jacob, who was just Jacob, and nothing more than that? Jacob, my friend? Jacob, the only human I'd ever been able to relate to. . . .

And he wasn't even human.

I fought the urge to scream again.

What did this say about me?

I knew the answer to that one. It said that there was something deeply wrong with me. Why else would my life be filled with characters from horror movies? Why else would I care so much about them that it would tear big chunks right out of my chest when they went off along their mythical ways?

In my head, everything spun and shifted, rearranging so that things that had meant one thing before, now meant something else.

There was no cult. There had never been a cult, never been a gang. No, it was much worse than that. It was a *pack*.

A pack of five mind-blowingly gigantic, multihued werewolves that had stalked right past me in Edward's meadow. . . .

Suddenly, I was in a frantic hurry. I glanced at the clock—it was way too early and I didn't care. I had to go to La Push *now*. I had to see Jacob so he could tell me that I hadn't lost my mind altogether.

I pulled on the first clean clothes I could find, not bothering to be sure they matched, and took the stairs two at a time. I almost ran into Charlie as I skidded into the hallway, headed for the door.

"Where are you going?" he asked, as surprised to see me as I was to see him. "Do you know what time it is?"

"Yeah. I have to go see Jacob."

"I thought the thing with Sam—"

"That doesn't matter, I have to talk to him right now."

"It's pretty early." He frowned when my expression didn't change. "Don't you want breakfast?"

"Not hungry." The words flew through my lips. He was blocking my path to the exit. I considered ducking around him and making a run for it, but I knew I would have to explain that to him later. "I'll be back soon, okay?"

Charlie frowned. "Straight to Jacob's house, right? No stops on the way?"

"Of course not, where would I stop?" My words were running together in my hurry.

"I don't know," he admitted. "It's just . . . well, there's been another attack—the wolves again. It was real close to the resort by the hot springs—there's a witness this time. The victim was only a dozen yards from the road when he disappeared. His wife saw a huge gray wolf just a few minutes later, while she was searching for him, and ran for help."

My stomach dropped like I'd hit a corkscrew on a roller coaster. "A wolf attacked him?"

"There's no sign of him—just a little blood again." Charlie's face was pained. "The rangers are going out armed, taking armed volunteers. There're a lot of hunters who are eager to be involved—there's a reward being offered for wolf carcasses. That's going to mean a lot of firepower out there in the forest, and it worries me." He shook his head. "When people get too excited, accidents happen. . . ."

"They're going to shoot the wolves?" My voice shot through three octaves.

"What else can we do? What's wrong?" he asked, his tense eyes studying my face. I felt faint; I must be whiter than usual. "You aren't turning into a tree-hugger on me, are you?"

I couldn't answer. If he hadn't been watching me, I would have put my head between my knees. I'd forgotten about the missing hikers, the bloody paw prints. . . . I hadn't connected those facts to my first realization.

"Look, honey, don't let this scare you. Just stay in town or on the highway—no stops—okay?"

"Okay," I repeated in a weak voice.

"I've got to go."

I looked at him closely for the first time, and saw that he had his gun strapped to his waist and hiking boots on.

"You aren't going out there after the wolves, are you, Dad?"

"I've got to help, Bells. People are disappearing."

My voice shot up again, almost hysterical now. "No! No, don't go. It's too dangerous!"

"I've got to do my job, kid. Don't be such a pessimist—I'll be fine." He turned for the door, and held it open. "You leaving?"

I hesitated, my stomach still spinning in uncomfortable loops. What could I say to stop him? I was too dizzy to think of a solution.

"Bells?"

"Maybe it's too early to go to La Push," I whispered.

"I agree," he said, and he stepped out into the rain, shutting the door behind him.

As soon as he was out of sight, I dropped to the floor and put my head between my knees.

Should I go after Charlie? What would I say?

And what about Jacob? Jacob was my best friend; I needed to warn him. If he really was a—I cringed and forced myself to think the word—werewolf (and I knew it was true, I could feel it), then people would be shooting at him! I needed to tell him *and* his friends that people would try to kill them if they went running around like gigantic wolves. I needed to tell them to stop.

They had to stop! Charlie was out there in the woods. Would they care about that? I wondered. . . . Up until now, only strangers had disappeared. Did that mean anything, or was it just chance?

I needed to believe that Jacob, at least, would care about that.

Either way, I had to warn him.

Or . . . did I?

Jacob was my best friend, but was he a monster, too? A real one? A bad one? *Should* I warn him, if he and his friends were . . . were *murderers*? If they were out slaughtering innocent hikers in cold blood? If they were truly creatures from a horror movie in every sense, would it be wrong to protect them?

It was inevitable that I would have to compare Jacob and his friends to the Cullens. I wrapped my arms around my chest, fighting the hole, while I thought of them.

I didn't know anything about werewolves, clearly. I would have expected something closer to the movies—big hairy half-men creatures or something—if I'd expected anything at all. So I didn't know what made them hunt, whether hunger or thirst or just a desire to kill. It was hard to judge, not knowing that.

But it couldn't be worse than what the Cullens endured in their quest to be good. I thought of Esme—the tears started when I pictured her kind, lovely face—and how, as motherly and loving as she was, she'd had to hold her nose, all ashamed, and run from me when I was bleeding. It couldn't be harder than that. I thought of Carlisle, the centuries upon centuries that he had struggled to teach himself to ignore blood, so that he could save lives as a doctor. Nothing could be harder than *that*.

The werewolves had chosen a different path.

Now, what should *I* choose?

13. KILLER

IF IT WAS ANYONE BUT JACOB, I THOUGHT TO MYSELF, shaking my head as I drove down the forest-lined highway to La Push.

I still wasn't sure if I was doing the right thing, but I'd made a compromise with myself.

I couldn't condone what Jacob and his friends, his pack, were doing. I understood now what he'd said last night—that I might not want to see him again—and I could have called him as he'd suggested, but that felt cowardly. I owed him a face-to-face conversation, at least. I would tell him to his face that I couldn't just overlook what was going on. I couldn't be friends with a killer and say nothing, let the killing continue . . . That would make me a monster, too.

But I couldn't *not* warn him, either. I had to do what I could to protect him.

I pulled up to the Blacks' house with my lips pressed together into a hard line. It was bad enough that my best friend was a werewolf. Did he have to be a monster, too?

The house was dark, no lights in the windows, but I didn't care if I woke them. My fist thudded against the front door with angry energy; the sound reverberated through the walls.

"Come in," I heard Billy call after a minute, and a light flicked on.

I twisted the knob; it was unlocked. Billy was leaning around an open doorway just off the little kitchen, a bathrobe around his shoulders, not in his chair yet. When he saw who it was, his eyes widened briefly, and then his face turned stoic.

"Well, good morning, Bella. What are you doing up so early?"

"Hey, Billy. I need to talk to Jake—where is he?"

"Um . . . I don't really know," he lied, straight-faced.

"Do you know what Charlie is doing this morning?" I demanded, sick of the stalling.

"Should I?"

"He and half the other men in town are all out in the woods with guns, hunting giant wolves."

Billy's expression flickered, and then went blank.

"So I'd like to talk to Jake about that, if you don't mind," I continued.

Billy pursed his thick lips for a long moment. "I'd bet he's still asleep," he finally said, nodding toward the tiny hallway off the front room. "He's out late a lot these days. Kid needs his rest—probably you shouldn't wake him."

"It's my turn," I muttered under my breath as I stalked to the hallway. Billy sighed.

Jacob's tiny closet of a room was the only door in the yard-long hallway. I didn't bother to knock. I threw the door open; it slammed against the wall with a bang.

Jacob—still wearing just the same black cut-off sweats he'd worn last night—was stretched diagonally across the double bed that took up all of his room but a few inches around the edges. Even on a slant, it wasn't long enough; his feet hung off the one end and his head off the other. He was fast asleep, snoring lightly with his mouth hanging open. The sound of the door hadn't even made him twitch.

His face was peaceful with deep sleep, all the angry lines smoothed out. There were circles under his eyes that I hadn't noticed before. Despite his ridiculous size, he looked very young now, and very weary. Pity shook me.

I stepped back out, and shut the door quietly behind me.

Billy stared with curious, guarded eyes as I walked slowly back into the front room.

"I think I'll let him get some rest."

Billy nodded, and then we gazed at each other for a minute. I was dying to ask him about his part in this.

What did he think of what his son had become? But I knew how he'd supported Sam from the very beginning, and so I supposed the murders must not bother him. How he justified that to himself I couldn't imagine.

I could see many questions for me in his dark eyes, but he didn't voice them either.

"Look," I said, breaking the loud silence. "I'll be down at the beach for a while. When he wakes up, tell him I'm waiting for him, okay?"

"Sure, sure," Billy agreed.

I wondered if he really would. Well, if he didn't, I'd tried, right?

I drove down to First Beach and parked in the empty dirt lot. It was still dark—the gloomy predawn of a cloudy day—and when I cut the headlights it was hard to see. I had to let my eyes adjust before I could find the path that led through the tall hedge of weeds. It was colder here, with the wind whipping off the black water, and I shoved my hands deep into the pockets of my winter jacket. At least the rain had stopped.

I paced down the beach toward the north seawall. I couldn't see St. James or the other islands, just the vague shape of the water's edge. I picked my way carefully across the rocks, watching out for driftwood that might trip me.

I found what I was looking for before I realized I was looking for it. It materialized out of the gloom when it was just a few feet away: a long bone-white driftwood tree stranded deep on the rocks. The roots twisted up at the seaward end, like a hundred brittle tentacles. I couldn't be sure that it was the same tree where Jacob and I had had our first conversation—a conversation that had begun so many different, tangled threads of my life—but it seemed to be in about the same place. I sat down where I'd sat before, and stared out across the invisible sea.

Seeing Jacob like that—innocent and vulnerable in sleep—had stolen all my revulsion, dissolved all my anger. I still couldn't turn a blind eye to what was happening, like Billy seemed to, but I couldn't condemn Jacob for it either. Love didn't work that way, I decided. Once you cared about a person, it was impossible to be logical about them anymore. Jacob was my friend whether he killed people or not. And I didn't know what I was going to do about that.

When I pictured him sleeping so peacefully, I felt an overpowering urge to *protect* him. Completely illogical.

Illogical or not, I brooded over the memory his peaceful face, trying to come up with some answer, some way to shelter him, while the sky slowly turned gray.

"Hi, Bella."

Jacob's voice came from the darkness and made me jump. It was soft, almost shy, but I'd been expecting some forewarning from the noisy rocks, and so it still startled me. I could see his silhouette against the coming sunrise—it looked enormous.

"Jake?"

He stood several paces away, shifting his weight from foot to foot anxiously.

"Billy told me you came by—didn't take you very long, did it? I knew you could figure it out."

"Yeah, I remember the right story now," I whispered.

It was quiet for a long moment and, though it was still too dark to see well, my skin prickled as if his eyes were searching my face. There must have been enough light for him to read my expression, because when he spoke again, his voice was suddenly acidic.

"You could have just called," he said harshly.

I nodded. "I know."

Jacob started pacing along the rocks. If I listened very hard, I could just hear the gentle brush of his feet on the rocks behind the sound of the waves. The rocks had clattered like castanets for me.

"Why did you come?" he demanded, not halting his angry stride.

"I thought it would be better face-to-face."

He snorted. "Oh, much better."

"Jacob, I have to warn you—"

"About the rangers and the hunters? Don't worry about it. We already know."

"Don't worry about it?" I demanded in disbelief. "Jake, they've got guns! They're setting traps and offering rewards and—"

"We can take care of ourselves," he growled, still pacing. "They're not going to catch anything. They're only making it more difficult—they'll start disappearing soon enough, too."

"Jake!" I hissed.

"What? It's just a fact."

My voice was pale with revulsion. "How can you . . .

feel that way? You know these people. Charlie's out there!"
The thought made my stomach twist.

He came to an abrupt stop. "What more can we do?"
he retorted.

The sun turned the clouds a slivery pink above us. I
could see his expression now; it was angry, frustrated, betrayed.

"Could you . . . well, try to *not* be a . . . werewolf?" I
suggested in a whisper.

He threw his hands up in the air. "Like I have a choice
about it!" he shouted. "And how would that help anything, if you're worried about people disappearing?"

"I don't understand you."

He glared at me, his eyes narrowing and his mouth
twisting into a snarl. "You know what makes me so mad I
could just spit?"

I flinched away from his hostile expression. He seemed
to be waiting for an answer, so I shook my head.

"You're such a hypocrite, Bella—there you sit, *terrified* of me! How is that fair?" His hands shook with
anger.

"*Hypocrite?* How does being afraid of a monster make
me a hypocrite?"

"Ugh!" he groaned, pressing his trembling fists to his
temples and squeezing his eyes shut. "Would you listen to
yourself?"

"What?"

He took two steps toward me, leaning over me and
glaring with fury. "Well, I'm so sorry that I can't be the

right kind of monster for you, Bella. I guess I'm just not as great as a bloodsucker, am I?"

I jumped to my feet and glared back. "No, you're not!" I shouted. "It's not what you *are*, stupid, it's what you *do*!"

"What's that supposed to mean?" He roared, his entire frame quivering with rage.

I was taken entirely by surprise when Edward's voice cautioned me. "Be very careful, Bella," his velvet voice warned. "Don't push him too far. You need to calm him down."

Even the voice in my head was making no sense today.

I listened to him, though. I would do anything for that voice.

"Jacob," I pleaded, making my tone soft and even. "Is it really necessary to *kill* people, Jacob? Isn't there some other way? I mean, if vampires can find a way to survive without murdering people, couldn't you give it a try, too?"

He straightened up with a jerk, like my words had sent an electric shock through him. His eyebrows shot up and his eyes stared wide.

"Killing people?" he demanded.

"What did you think we were talking about?"

He wasn't trembling anymore. He looked at me with half-hopeful disbelief. "*I* thought we were talking about your disgust for werewolves."

"No, Jake, no. It's not that you're a . . . wolf. That's fine," I promised him, and I knew as I said the words that I meant them. I really didn't care if he turned into a big wolf—he was still Jacob. "If you could just find a way not to hurt people . . . that's all that upsets me. These are innocent people, Jake, people like Charlie, and I can't just look the other way while you—"

"Is that all? Really?" he interrupted me, a smile breaking across his face. "You're just scared because I'm a murderer? That's the only reason?"

"Isn't that reason enough?"

He started to laugh.

"Jacob Black, this is *so* not funny!"

"Sure, sure," he agreed, still chortling.

He took one long stride and caught me in another vice-tight bear hug.

"You really, honestly don't mind that I morph into a giant dog?" he asked, his voice joyful in my ear.

"No," I gasped. "Can't—breathe—Jake!"

He let me go, but took both my hands. "I'm not a killer, Bella."

I studied his face, and it was clear that this was the truth. Relief pulsed through me.

"Really?" I asked.

"Really," he promised solemnly.

I threw my arms around him. It reminded me of that first day with the motorcycles—he was bigger, though, and I felt even more like a child now.

Like that other time, he stroked my hair.

"Sorry I called you a hypocrite," he apologized.

"Sorry I called you a murderer."

He laughed.

I thought of something then, and pulled away from him so that I could see his face. My eyebrows furrowed in anxiety. "What about Sam? And the others?"

He shook his head, smiling like a huge burden had been removed from his shoulders. "Of course not. Don't you remember what we call ourselves?"

The memory was clear—I'd just been thinking of that very day. "Protectors?"

"Exactly."

"But I don't understand. What's happening in the woods? The missing hikers, the blood?"

His face was serious, worried at once. "We're trying to do our job, Bella. We're trying to protect them, but we're always just a little too late."

"Protect them from what? Is there really a bear out there, too?"

"Bella, honey, we only protect people from one thing— our one enemy. It's the reason we exist—because they do."

I stared at him blankly for one second before I under- stood. Then the blood drained from my face and a thin, wordless cry of horror broke through my lips.

He nodded. "I thought you, of all people, would realize what was really going on."

"Laurent," I whispered. "He's still here."

Jacob blinked twice, and cocked his head to one side. "Who's Laurent?"

I tried to sort out the chaos in my head so that I could answer. "You know—you saw him in the meadow. You were there. . . ." The words came out in a wondering tone as it all sunk in. "You were there, and you kept him from killing me. . . ."

"Oh, the black-haired leech?" He grinned, a tight, fierce grin. "Was that his name?"

I shuddered. "What were you thinking?" I whispered. "He could have killed you! Jake, you don't realize how dangerous—"

Another laugh interrupted me. "Bella, one lone vampire isn't much of a problem for a pack as big as ours. It was so easy, it was hardly even fun!"

"What was so easy?"

"Killing the bloodsucker who was going to kill you. Now, I don't count that towards the whole murder thing," he added quickly. "Vampires don't count as people."

I could only mouth the words. "You . . . killed . . . Laurent?"

He nodded. "Well, it was a group effort," he qualified.

"Laurent is dead?" I whispered.

His expression changed. "You're not upset about that, are you? He was going to kill you—he was going for the kill, Bella, we were sure of that before we attacked. You know that, right?"

"I know that. No, I'm not upset—I'm . . ." I had to sit down. I stumbled back a step until I felt the driftwood against my calves, and then sank down onto it. "Laurent is dead. He's not coming back for me."

"You're not mad? He wasn't one of your friends or anything, was he?"

"My friend?" I stared up at him, confused and dizzy

with relief. I started babbling, my eyes getting moist. "No, Jake. I'm so . . . so *relieved*. I thought he was going to find me—I've been waiting for him every night, just hoping that he'd stop with me and leave Charlie alone. I've been so frightened, Jacob. . . . But how? He was a vampire! How did you kill him? He was so strong, so hard, like marble. . . ."

He sat down next to me and put one big arm around me comfortingly. "It's what we're made for, Bells. We're strong, too. I wish you would have told me that you were so afraid. You didn't need to be."

"You weren't around," I mumbled, lost in thought.

"Oh, right."

"Wait, Jake—I thought you knew, though. Last night, you said it wasn't safe for you to be in my room. I thought you knew that a vampire might be coming. Isn't that what you were talking about?"

He looked confused for a minute, and then he ducked his head. "No, that's not what I meant."

"Then why didn't you think it was safe for you there?"

He looked at me with guilt-ridden eyes. "I didn't say it wasn't safe for *me*. I was thinking of you."

"What do you mean?"

He looked down and kicked a rock. "There's more than one reason I'm not supposed to be around you, Bella. I wasn't supposed to tell you our secret, for one thing, but the other part is that it's not safe for *you*. If I get too mad . . . too upset . . . you might get hurt."

I thought about that carefully. "When you were mad

before . . . when I was yelling at you . . . and you were shaking . . . ?"

"Yeah." His face dropped even lower. "That was pretty stupid of me. I have to keep a better hold on myself. I swore I wasn't going to get mad, no matter what you said to me. But . . . I just got so upset that I was going to lose you . . . that you couldn't deal with what I am. . . ."

"What would happen . . . if you got too mad?" I whispered.

"I'd turn into a wolf," he whispered back.

"You don't need a full moon?"

He rolled his eyes. "Hollywood's version doesn't get much right." Then he sighed, and was serious again. "You don't need to be so stressed out, Bells. We're going to take care of this. And we're keeping a special eye on Charlie and the others—we won't let anything happen to him. Trust me on that."

Something very, very obvious, something I should have grasped at once—but I'd been so distracted by the idea of Jacob and his friends fighting with Laurent, that I'd completely missed it at the time—occurred to me only then, when Jacob used the present tense again.

We're going to take care of this.

It wasn't over.

"Laurent is dead," I gasped, and my entire body went ice cold.

"Bella?" Jacob asked anxiously, touching my ashen cheek.

"If Laurent died . . . a week ago . . . then someone else is killing people *now*."

Jacob nodded; his teeth clenched together, and he spoke through them. "There were two of them. We thought his mate would want to fight us—in our stories, they usually get pretty pissed off if you kill their mate— but she just keeps running away, and then coming back again. If we could figure out what she was after, it would be easier to take her down. But she makes no sense. She keeps dancing around the edges, like she's testing our defenses, looking for a way in—but *in* where? Where does she want to go? Sam thinks she's trying to separate us, so she'll have a better chance. . . ."

His voice faded until it sounded like it was coming through a long tunnel; I couldn't make out the individual words anymore. My forehead dewed with sweat and my stomach rolled like I had the stomach flu again. Exactly like I had the flu.

I turned away from him quickly, and leaned over the tree trunk. My body convulsed with useless heaves, my empty stomach contracting with horrified nausea, though there was nothing in it to expel.

Victoria was here. Looking for me. Killing strangers in the woods. The woods where Charlie was searching. . . .

My head spun sickeningly.

Jacob's hands caught my shoulders—kept me from sliding forward onto the rocks. I could feel his hot breath on my cheek. "Bella! What's wrong?"

"Victoria," I gasped as soon as I could catch my breath around the nauseous spasms.

In my head, Edward snarled in fury at the name.

I felt Jacob pull me up from my slump. He draped me

awkwardly across his lap, laying my limp head against his shoulder. He struggled to balance me, to keep me from sagging over, one way or the other. He brushed the sweaty hair back from my face.

"Who?" Jacob asked. "Can you hear me, Bella? Bella?"

"She wasn't Laurent's mate," I moaned into his shoulder. "They were just old friends. . . ."

"Do you need some water? A doctor? Tell me what to do," he demanded, frantic.

"I'm not sick—I'm scared," I explained in a whisper. The word *scared* didn't really seem to cover it.

Jacob patted my back. "Scared of this Victoria?"

I nodded, shuddering.

"Victoria is the red-haired female?"

I trembled again, and whimpered, "Yes."

"How do you know she wasn't his mate?"

"Laurent told me James was her mate," I explained, automatically flexing the hand with the scar.

He pulled my face around, holding it steady in his big hand. He stared intently into my eyes. "Did he tell you anything else, Bella? This is important. Do you know what she wants?"

"Of course," I whispered. "She wants *me*."

His eyes flipped wide, then narrowed into slits. "Why?" he demanded.

"Edward killed James," I whispered. Jacob held me so tightly that there was no need for me to clutch at the hole—he kept me in one piece. "She did get . . . pissed off. But Laurent said she thought it was fairer to kill me than

Edward. Mate for mate. She didn't know—still doesn't know, I guess—that . . . that . . ." I swallowed hard. "That things aren't like that with us anymore. Not for Edward, anyway."

Jacob was distracted by that, his face torn between several different expressions. "Is that what happened? Why the Cullens left?"

"I'm nothing but a human, after all. Nothing special," I explained, shrugging weakly.

Something like a growl—not a real growl, just a human approximation—rumbled in Jacob's chest under my ear. "If that idiot bloodsucker is honestly stupid enough—"

"Please," I moaned. "Please. Don't."

Jacob hesitated, then nodded once.

"This is important," he said again, his face all business now. "This is exactly what we needed to know. We've got to tell the others right away."

He stood, pulling me to my feet. He kept two hands on my waist until he was sure I wasn't going to fall.

"I'm okay," I lied.

He traded his hold on my waist for one of my hands. "Let's go."

He pulled me back toward the truck.

"Where are we going?" I asked.

"I'm not sure yet," he admitted. "I'll call a meeting. Hey, wait here for just a minute, okay?" He leaned me against the side of the truck and released my hand.

"Where are you going?"

"I'll be right back," he promised. Then he turned and

sprinted through the parking lot, across the road, and into the bordering forest. He flitted into the trees, swift and sleek as a deer.

"Jacob!" I yelled after him hoarsely, but he was already gone.

It was not a good time to be left alone. Seconds after Jacob was out of sight, I was hyperventilating. I dragged myself into the cab of the truck, and mashed the locks down at once. It didn't make me feel any better.

Victoria was already hunting me. It was just luck that she hadn't found me yet—just luck and five teenage werewolves. I exhaled sharply. No matter what Jacob said, the thought of him coming anywhere close to Victoria was horrifying. I didn't care what he could turn into when he got mad. I could see her in my head, her face wild, her hair like flames, deadly, indestructible. . . .

But, according to Jacob, Laurent was gone. Was that really possible? Edward—I clutched automatically at my chest—had told me how difficult it was to kill a vampire. Only another vampire could do the job. Yet Jake said this was what werewolves were made for . . .

He said they were keeping a special eye on Charlie— that I should trust the werewolves to keep my father safe. How could I trust that? None of us were safe! Jacob the very least of all, if he was trying to put himself between Victoria and Charlie . . . between Victoria and me.

I felt like I might be about to throw up again.

A sharp rap on the truck's window made me yelp in terror—but it was just Jacob, back already. I unlocked the door with trembling, grateful fingers.

"You're really scared, aren't you?" he asked as he climbed in.

I nodded.

"Don't be. We'll take care of you—and Charlie, too. I promise."

"The idea of you finding Victoria is scarier than the idea of her finding me," I whispered.

He laughed. "You've got to have a little more confidence in us than that. It's insulting."

I just shook my head. I'd seen too many vampires in action.

"Where did you go just now?" I asked.

He pursed his lips, and said nothing.

"What? Is it a secret?"

He frowned. "Not really. It's kind of weird, though. I don't want to freak you out."

"I'm sort of used to weird by this point, you know." I tried to smile without much success.

Jacob grinned back easily. "Guess you'd have to be. Okay. See, when we're wolves, we can . . . hear each other."

My eyebrows pulled down in confusion.

"Not hear sounds," he went on, "but we can hear . . . *thoughts*—each other's anyway—no matter how far away from each other we are. It really helps when we hunt, but it's a big pain otherwise. It's embarrassing—having no secrets like that. Freaky, eh?"

"Is that what you meant last night, when you said you would tell them you'd seen me, even though you didn't want to?"

"You're quick."

"Thanks."

"You're also very good with weird. I thought that would bother you."

"It's not . . . well, you're not the first person I've known who could do that. So it doesn't seem so weird to me."

"Really? . . . Wait—are you talking about your bloodsuckers?"

"I wish you wouldn't call them that."

He laughed. "Whatever. The Cullens, then?"

"Just . . . just Edward." I pulled one arm surreptitiously around my torso.

Jacob looked surprised—unpleasantly so. "I thought those were just stories. I've heard legends about vampires who could do . . . extra stuff, but I thought that was just a myth."

"Is anything just a myth anymore?" I asked him wryly.

He scowled. "Guess not. Okay, we're going to meet Sam and the others at the place we go to ride our bikes."

I started the truck and headed back up the road.

"So did you just turn into a wolf now, to talk to Sam?" I asked, curious.

Jacob nodded, seeming embarrassed. "I kept it real short—I tried not to think about you so they wouldn't know what was going on. I was afraid Sam would tell me I couldn't bring you."

"That wouldn't have stopped me." I couldn't get rid of my perception of Sam as the bad guy. My teeth clenched together whenever I heard his name.

"Well, it would have stopped *me*," Jacob said, morose now. "Remember how I couldn't finish my sentences last night? How I couldn't just tell you the whole story?"

"Yeah. You looked like you were choking on something."

He chuckled darkly. "Close enough. Sam told me I couldn't tell you. He's . . . the head of the pack, you know. He's the Alpha. When he tells us to do something, or not to do something—when he really means it, well, we can't just ignore him."

"Weird," I muttered.

"Very," he agreed. "It's kind of a wolf thing."

"Huh" was the best response I could think of.

"Yeah, there's a load of stuff like that—wolf things. I'm still learning. I can't imagine what it was like for Sam, trying to deal with this alone. It sucks bad enough to go through it with a whole pack for support."

"Sam was alone?"

"Yeah." Jacob's voice lowered. "When I . . . changed, it was the most . . . *horrible*, the most *terrifying* thing I've ever been through—worse than anything I could have imagined. But I wasn't alone—there were the voices there, in my head, telling me what had happened and what I had to do. That kept me from losing my mind, I think. But Sam . . ." He shook his head. "Sam had no help."

This was going to take some adjusting. When Jacob explained it like that, it was hard not to feel compassion for Sam. I had to keep reminding myself that there was no reason to hate him anymore.

"Will they be angry that I'm with you?" I asked.

He made a face. "Probably."

"Maybe I shouldn't—"

"No, it's okay," he assured me. "You know a ton of things that can help us. It's not like you're just some ignorant human. You're like a . . . I don't know, spy or something. You've been behind enemy lines."

I frowned to myself. Was that what Jacob would want from me? Insider information to help them destroy their enemies? I wasn't a spy, though. I hadn't been collecting that kind of information. Already, his words made me feel like a traitor.

But I wanted him to stop Victoria, didn't I?

No.

I *did* want Victoria to be stopped, preferably before she tortured me to death or ran into Charlie or killed another stranger. I just didn't want Jacob to be the one to stop her, or rather to try. I didn't want Jacob within a hundred miles of her.

"Like the stuff about the mind-reading bloodsucker," he continued, oblivious to my reverie. "That's the kind of thing we need to know about. That really sucks that *those* stories are true. It makes everything more complicated. Hey, do you think this Victoria can do anything special?"

"I don't think so," I hesitated, and then sighed. "He would have mentioned it."

"He? Oh, you mean Edward—oops, sorry. I forgot. You don't like to say his name. Or hear it."

I squeezed my midsection, trying to ignore the throbbing around the edges of my chest. "Not really, no."

"Sorry."

"How do you know me so well, Jacob? Sometimes it's like you can read *my* mind."

"Naw. I just pay attention."

We were on the little dirt road where Jacob had first taught me to ride the motorcycle.

"This good?" I asked.

"Sure, sure."

I pulled over and cut the engine.

"You're still pretty unhappy, aren't you?" he murmured.

I nodded, staring unseeingly into the gloomy forest.

"Did you ever think . . . that maybe . . . you're better off?"

I inhaled slowly, and then let my breath out. "No."

"'Cause he wasn't the best—"

"Please, Jacob," I interrupted, begging in a whisper. "Could we please not talk about this? I can't stand it."

"Okay." He took a deep breath. "I'm sorry I said anything."

"Don't feel bad. If things were different, it would be nice to finally be able to talk to someone about it."

He nodded. "Yeah, I had a hard time keeping a secret from you for two weeks. It must be hell to not be able to talk to *anyone*."

"Hell," I agreed.

Jacob sucked in a sharp breath. "They're here. Let's go."

"Are you sure?" I asked while he popped his door open. "Maybe I shouldn't be here."

"They'll deal with it," he said, and then he grinned. "Who's afraid of the big, bad wolf?"

"Ha ha," I said. But I got out of the truck, hurrying around the front end to stand close beside Jacob. I remembered only too clearly the giant monsters in the meadow. My hands were trembling like Jacob's had been before, but with fear rather than rage.

Jake took my hand and squeezed it. "Here we go."

14. FAMILY

I COWERED INTO JACOB'S SIDE, MY EYES SCANNING THE forest for the other werewolves. When they appeared, striding out from between the trees, they weren't what I was expecting. I'd gotten the image of the wolves stuck in my head. These were just four really big half-naked boys.

Again, they reminded me of brothers, quadruplets. Something about the way they moved almost in synchronization to stand across the road from us, the way they all had the same long, round muscles under the same red-brown skin, the same cropped black hair, and the way their expressions altered at exactly the same moment.

They started out curious and cautious. When they saw

me there, half-hidden beside Jacob, they all became furious in the same second.

Sam was still the biggest, though Jacob was getting close to catching up with him. Sam didn't really count as a boy. His face was older—not in the sense of lines or signs of aging, but in the maturity, the patience of his expression.

"What have you done, Jacob?" he demanded.

One of the others, one I didn't recognize—Jared or Paul—thrust past Sam and spoke before Jacob could defend himself.

"Why can't you just follow the rules, Jacob?" he yelled, throwing his arms in the air. "What the hell are you thinking? Is she more important than everything—than the whole tribe? Than the people getting killed?"

"She can help," Jacob said quietly.

"Help!" the angry boy shouted. His arms begin to quiver. "Oh, that's likely! I'm sure the leech-lover is just *dying* to help us out!"

"Don't talk about her like that!" Jacob shouted back, stung by the boy's criticism.

A shudder rippled through the other boy, along his shoulders and down his spine.

"Paul! Relax!" Sam commanded.

Paul shook his head back and forth, not in defiance, but as though he were trying to concentrate.

"Jeez, Paul," one of the other boys—probably Jared—muttered. "Get a grip."

Paul twisted his head toward Jared, his lips curling

back in irritation. Then he shifted his glare in my direction. Jacob took a step to put himself in front of me.

That did it.

"Right, protect *her*!" Paul roared in outrage. Another shudder, a convulsion, heaved through his body. He threw his head back, a real growl tearing from between his teeth.

"Paul!" Sam and Jacob shouted together.

Paul seemed to fall forward, vibrating violently. Halfway to the ground, there was a loud ripping noise, and the boy exploded.

Dark silver fur blew out from the boy, coalescing into a shape more than five-times his size—a massive, crouched shape, ready to spring.

The wolf's muzzle wrinkled back over his teeth, and another growl rolled through his colossal chest. His dark, enraged eyes focused on me.

In the same second, Jacob was running across the road straight for the monster.

"Jacob!" I screamed.

Mid-stride, a long tremor shivered down Jacob's spine. He leaped forward, diving headfirst into the empty air.

With another sharp tearing sound, Jacob exploded, too. He burst out of his skin—shreds of black and white cloth blasted up into the air. It happened so quickly that if I'd blinked, I'd have missed the entire transformation. One second it was Jacob diving into the air, and then it was the gigantic, russet brown wolf—so enormous that I couldn't make sense of its mass somehow fitting inside Jacob—charging the crouched silver beast.

Jacob met the other werewolf's attack head-on. Their angry snarls echoed like thunder off the trees.

The black and white scraps—the remains of Jacob's clothes—fluttered to the ground where he'd disappeared.

"Jacob!" I screamed again, staggering forward.

"Stay where you are, Bella," Sam ordered. It was hard to hear him over the roar of the fighting wolves. They were snapping and tearing at each other, their sharp teeth flashing toward each other's throats. The Jacob-wolf seemed to have the upper hand—he was visibly bigger than the other wolf, and it looked like he was stronger, too. He rammed his shoulder against the gray wolf again and again, knocking him back toward the trees.

"Take her to Emily's," Sam shouted toward the other boys, who were watching the conflict with rapt expressions. Jacob had successfully shoved the gray wolf off the road, and they were disappearing into the forest, though the sound of their snarls was still loud. Sam ran after them, kicking off his shoes on the way. As he darted into the trees, he was quivering from head to toe.

The growling and snapping was fading into the distance. Suddenly, the sound cut off and it was very quiet on the road.

One of the boys started laughing.

I turned to stare at him—my wide eyes felt frozen, like I couldn't even blink them.

The boy seemed to be laughing at my expression. "Well, there's something you don't see every day," he snickered. His face was vaguely familiar—thinner than the others. . . . Embry Call.

"I do," the other boy, Jared, grumbled. "Every single day."

"Aw, Paul doesn't lose his temper *every* day," Embry disagreed, still grinning. "Maybe two out of three."

Jared stopped to pick something white up off the ground. He held it up toward Embry; it dangled in limp strips from his hand.

"Totally shredded," Jared said. "Billy said this was the last pair he could afford—guess Jacob's going barefoot now."

"This one survived," Embry said, holding up a white sneaker. "Jake can hop," he added with a laugh.

Jared started collecting various pieces of fabric from the dirt. "Get Sam's shoes, will you? All the rest of this is headed for the trash."

Embry grabbed the shoes and then jogged into the trees where Sam had disappeared. He was back in a few seconds with a pair of cut-off jeans draped over his arm. Jared gathered the torn remnants of Jacob's and Paul's clothes and wadded them into a ball. Suddenly, he seemed to remember me.

He looked at me carefully, assessing.

"Hey, you're not going to faint or puke or anything?" he demanded.

"I don't *think* so," I gasped.

"You don't look so good. Maybe you should sit down."

"Okay," I mumbled. For the second time in one morning, I put my head between my knees.

"Jake should have warned us," Embry complained.

"He shouldn't have brought his girlfriend into this. What did he expect?"

"Well, the wolf's out of the bag now." Embry sighed. "Way to go, Jake."

I raised my head to glare at the two boys who seemed to be taking this all so lightly. "Aren't you worried about them at all?" I demanded.

Embry blinked once in surprise. "Worried? Why?"

"They could hurt each other!"

Embry and Jared guffawed.

"I *hope* Paul gets a mouthful of him," Jared said. "Teach him a lesson."

I blanched.

"Yeah, right!" Embry disagreed. "Did you *see* Jake? Even Sam couldn't have phased on the fly like that. He saw Paul losing it, and it took him, what, half a second to attack? The boy's got a gift."

"Paul's been fighting longer. I'll bet you ten bucks he leaves a mark."

"You're on. Jake's a natural. Paul doesn't have a prayer."

They shook hands, grinning.

I tried to comfort myself with their lack of concern, but I couldn't drive the brutal image of the fighting werewolves from my head. My stomach churned, sore and empty, my head ached with worry.

"Let's go see Emily. You know she'll have food waiting." Embry looked down at me. "Mind giving us a ride?"

"No problem," I choked.

Jared raised one eyebrow. "Maybe you'd better drive, Embry. She still looks like she might hurl."

"Good idea. Where are the keys?" Embry asked me.

"Ignition."

Embry opened the passenger-side door. "In you go," he said cheerfully, hauling me up from the ground with one hand and stuffing me into my seat. He appraised the available space. "You'll have to ride in the back," he told Jared.

"That's fine. I got a weak stomach. I don't want to be in there when she blows."

"I bet she's tougher than that. She runs with vampires."

"Five bucks?" Jared asked.

"Done. I feel guilty, taking your money like this."

Embry got in and started the engine while Jared leapt agilely into the bed. As soon as his door was closed, Embry muttered to me, "Don't throw up, okay? I've only got a ten, and if Paul got his teeth into Jacob . . ."

"Okay," I whispered.

Embry drove us back toward the village.

"Hey, how did Jake get around the injunction anyway?"

"The . . . what?"

"Er, the order. You know, to not spill the beans. How did he tell you about this?"

"Oh, that," I said, remembering Jacob trying to choke out the truth to me last night. "He didn't. I guessed right."

Embry pursed his lips, looking surprised. "Hmm. S'pose that would work."

"Where are we going?" I asked.

"Emily's house. She's Sam's girlfriend . . . no, fiancée, now, I guess. They'll meet us back there after Sam gives it to them for what just happened. And after Paul and Jake scrounge up some new clothes, if Paul even has any left."

"Does Emily know about . . . ?"

"Yeah. And hey, don't stare at her. That bugs Sam."

I frowned at him. "Why would I stare?"

Embry looked uncomfortable. "Like you saw just now, hanging out around werewolves has its risks." He changed the subject quickly. "Hey, are you okay about the whole thing with the black-haired bloodsucker in the meadow? It didn't look like he was a friend of yours, but . . ." Embry shrugged.

"No, he wasn't my friend."

"That's good. We didn't want to start anything, break the treaty, you know."

"Oh, yeah, Jake told me about the treaty once, a long time ago. Why would killing Laurent break the treaty?"

"Laurent," he repeated, snorting, like he was amused the vampire had had a name. "Well, we were technically on Cullen turf. We're not allowed to attack any of them, the Cullens, at least, off our land—unless they break the treaty first. We didn't know if the black-haired one was a relative of theirs or something. Looked like you knew him."

"How would they go about breaking the treaty?"

"If they bite a human. Jake wasn't so keen on the idea of letting it go that far."

"Oh. Um, thanks. I'm glad you didn't wait."

"Our pleasure." He sounded like he meant that in a literal sense.

Embry drove past the easternmost house on the highway before turning off onto a narrow dirt road. "Your truck is slow," he noted.

"Sorry."

At the end of the lane was a tiny house that had once been gray. There was only one narrow window beside the weathered blue door, but the window box under it was filled with bright orange and yellow marigolds, giving the whole place a cheerful look.

Embry opened the truck door and inhaled. "Mmm, Emily's cooking."

Jared jumped out of the back of the truck and headed for the door, but Embry stopped him with one hand on his chest. He looked at me meaningfully, and cleared his throat.

"I don't have my wallet on me," Jared said.

"That's okay. I won't forget."

They climbed up the one step and entered the house without knocking. I followed timidly after them.

The front room, like Billy's house, was mostly kitchen. A young woman with satiny copper skin and long, straight, crow-black hair was standing at the counter by the sink, popping big muffins out of a tin and placing them on a paper plate. For one second, I thought the reason Embry had told me not to stare was because the girl was so beautiful.

And then she asked "You guys hungry?" in a melodic voice, and she turned to face us full on, a smile on half of her face.

The right side of her face was scarred from hairline to chin by three thick, red lines, livid in color though they were long healed. One line pulled down the corner of her dark, almond-shaped right eye, another twisted the right side of her mouth into a permanent grimace.

Thankful for Embry's warning, I quickly turned my eyes to the muffins in her hands. They smelled wonderful—like fresh blueberries.

"Oh," Emily said, surprised. "Who's this?"

I looked up, trying to focus on the left half of her face.

"Bella Swan," Jared told her, shrugging. Apparently, I'd been a topic of conversation before. "Who else?"

"Leave it to Jacob to find a way around," Emily murmured. She stared at me, and neither half of her once-beautiful face was friendly. "So, you're the vampire girl."

I stiffened. "Yes. Are you the wolf girl?"

She laughed, as did Embry and Jared. The left half of her face warmed. "I guess I am." She turned to Jared. "Where's Sam?"

"Bella, er, surprised Paul this morning."

Emily rolled her good eye. "Ah, Paul," she sighed. "Do you think they'll be long? I was just about to start the eggs."

"Don't worry," Embry told her. "If they're late, we won't let anything go to waste."

Emily chuckled, and then opened the refrigerator. "No doubt," she agreed. "Bella, are you hungry? Go ahead and help yourself to a muffin."

"Thanks." I took one from the plate and started nibbling around the edges. It was delicious, and it felt good in my tender stomach. Embry picked up his third and shoved it into his mouth whole.

"Save some for your brothers," Emily chastised him, hitting him on the head with a wooden spoon. The word surprised me, but the others thought nothing of it.

"Pig," Jared commented.

I leaned against the counter and watched the three of them banter like a family. Emily's kitchen was a friendly place, bright with white cupboards and pale wooden floorboards. On the little round table, a cracked blue-and-white china pitcher was overflowing with wildflowers. Embry and Jared seemed entirely at ease here.

Emily was mixing a humongous batch of eggs, several dozen, in a big yellow bowl. She had the sleeves of her lavender shirt pushed up, and I could see that the scars extended all the way down her arm to the back of her right hand. Hanging out with werewolves truly did have its risks, just as Embry had said.

The front door opened, and Sam stepped through.

"Emily," he said, and so much love saturated his voice that I felt embarrassed, intrusive, as I watched him cross the room in one stride and take her face in his wide hands. He leaned down and kissed the dark scars on her right cheek before he kissed her lips.

"Hey, none of that," Jared complained. "I'm eating."

"Then shut up and eat," Sam suggested, kissing Emily's ruined mouth again.

"Ugh," Embry groaned.

This was worse than any romantic movie; this was so real that it sang out loud with joy and life and true love. I put my muffin down and folded my arms across my empty chest. I stared at the flowers, trying to ignore the utter peace of their moment, and the wretched throbbing of my wounds.

I was grateful for the distraction when Jacob and Paul

came through the door, and then shocked when I saw that they were laughing. While I watched, Paul punched Jacob on the shoulder and Jacob went for a kidney jab in return. They laughed again. They both appeared to be in one piece.

Jacob scanned the room, his eyes stopping when he found me leaning, awkward and out of place, against the counter in the far corner of the kitchen.

"Hey, Bells," he greeted me cheerfully. He grabbed two muffins as he passed the table and came to stand beside me. "Sorry about before," he muttered under his breath. "How are you holding up?"

"Don't worry, I'm okay. Good muffins." I picked mine back up and started nibbling again. My chest felt better as soon as Jacob was beside me.

"Oh, man!" Jared wailed, interrupting us.

I looked up, and he and Embry were examining a fading pink line on Paul's forearm. Embry was grinning, exultant.

"Fifteen dollars," he crowed.

"Did you do that?" I whispered to Jacob, remembering the bet.

"I barely touched him. He'll be perfect by sundown."

"By sundown?" I looked at the line on Paul's arm. Odd, but it looked weeks old.

"Wolf thing," Jacob whispered.

I nodded, trying to not look weirded out.

"*You* okay?" I asked him under my breath.

"Not a scratch on me." His expression was smug.

"Hey, guys," Sam said in a loud voice, interrupting all

the conversations going on in the small room. Emily was at the stove, scraping the egg mixture around a big skillet, but Sam still had one hand touching the small of her back, an unconscious gesture. "Jacob has information for us."

Paul looked unsurprised. Jacob must have explained this to him and Sam already. Or . . . they'd just heard his thoughts.

"I know what the redhead wants." Jacob directed his words toward Jared and Embry. "That's what I was trying to tell you before." He kicked the leg of the chair Paul had settled into.

"And?" Jared asked.

Jacob's face got serious. "She *is* trying to avenge her mate—only it wasn't the black-haired leech *we* killed. The Cullens got her mate last year, and she's after Bella now."

This wasn't news to me, but I still shivered.

Jared, Embry, and Emily stared at me with open-mouthed surprise.

"She's just a girl," Embry protested.

"I didn't say it made sense. But that's why the bloodsucker's been trying to get past us. She's been heading for Forks."

They continued to stare at me, mouths still hanging open, for a long moment. I ducked my head.

"Excellent," Jared finally said, a smile beginning to pull up the corners of his mouth. "We've got bait."

With stunning speed, Jacob yanked a can opener from the counter and launched it at Jared's head. Jared's hand flicked up faster than I would have thought possible, and he snagged the tool just before it hit his face.

"Bella is *not* bait."

"You know what I mean," Jared said, unabashed.

"So we'll be changing our patterns," Sam said, ignoring their squabble. "We'll try leaving a few holes, and see if she falls for it. We'll have to split up, and I don't like that. But if she's really after Bella, she probably won't try to take advantage of our divided numbers."

"Quil's got to be close to joining us," Embry murmured. "Then we'll be able to split evenly."

Everyone looked down. I glanced at Jacob's face, and it was hopeless, like it had been yesterday afternoon, outside his house. No matter how comfortable they seemed to be with their fate, here in this happy kitchen, none of these werewolves wanted the same fate for their friend.

"Well, we won't count on that," Sam said in a low voice, and then continued at his regular volume. "Paul, Jared, and Embry will take the outer perimeter, and Jacob and I will take the inner. We'll collapse in when we've got her trapped."

I noticed that Emily didn't particularly like that Sam would be in the smaller grouping. Her worry had me glancing up at Jacob, worrying, too.

Sam caught my eye. "Jacob thinks it would be best if you spent as much time as possible here in La Push. She won't know where to find you so easily, just in case."

"What about Charlie?" I demanded.

"March Madness is still going," Jacob said. "I think Billy and Harry can manage to keep Charlie down here when he's not at work."

"Wait," Sam said, holding one hand up. His glance

flickered to Emily and then back to me. "That's what Jacob thinks is best, but you need to decide for yourself. You should weigh the risks of both options very seriously. You saw this morning how easily things can get dangerous here, how quickly they get out of hand. If you choose to stay with us, I can't make any guarantees about your safety."

"I won't hurt her," Jacob mumbled, looking down.

Sam acted as if he hadn't heard him speak. "If there was somewhere else you felt safe . . ."

I bit my lip. Where could I go that wouldn't put some-one else in danger? I recoiled again from the idea of bring-ing Renée into this—pulling her into the circle of the target I wore. . . . "I don't want to lead Victoria anywhere else," I whispered.

Sam nodded. "That's true. It's better to have her here, where we can end this."

I flinched. I didn't want Jacob or any of the rest of them trying to *end* Victoria. I glanced at Jake's face; it was re-laxed, almost the same as I remembered it from before the onset of the wolf thing, and utterly unconcerned by the idea of hunting vampires.

"You'll be careful, right?" I asked, an audible lump in my throat.

The boys burst into loud hoots of amusement. Everyone laughed at me—except Emily. She met my eyes, and I could suddenly see the symmetry underlying her defor-mity. Her face was still beautiful, and alive with a concern even more fierce than mine. I had to look away, before the love behind that concern could start me aching again.

"Food's ready," she announced then, and the strategic conversation was history. The guys hurried to surround the table—which looked tiny and in danger of being crushed by them—and devoured the buffet-sized pan of eggs Emily placed in their midst in record time. Emily ate leaning against the counter like me—avoiding the bedlam at the table—and watched them with affectionate eyes. Her expression clearly stated that this was her family.

All in all, it wasn't exactly what I'd been expecting from a pack of werewolves.

I spent the day in La Push, the majority of it in Billy's house. He left a message on Charlie's phone and at the station, and Charlie showed up around dinnertime with two pizzas. It was good he brought two larges; Jacob ate one all by himself.

I saw Charlie eyeing the two of us suspiciously all night, especially the much-changed Jacob. He asked about the hair; Jacob shrugged and told him it was just more convenient.

I knew that as soon as Charlie and I were headed home, Jacob would take off—off to run around as a wolf, as he had done intermittently through the entire day. He and his brothers of sorts kept up a constant watch, looking for some sign of Victoria's return. But since they'd chased her away from the hot springs last night—chased her halfway to Canada, according to Jacob—she'd yet to make another foray.

I had no hope at all that she might just give up. I didn't have that kind of luck.

Jacob walked me to my truck after dinner and lingered by the window, waiting for Charlie to drive away first.

"Don't be afraid tonight," Jacob said, while Charlie pretended to be having trouble with his seat belt. "We'll be out there, watching."

"I won't worry about myself," I promised.

"You're silly. Hunting vampires is fun. It's the best part of this whole mess."

I shook my head. "If I'm silly, then you're dangerously unbalanced."

He chuckled. "Get some rest, Bella, honey. You look exhausted."

"I'll try."

Charlie honked his horn impatiently.

"See you tomorrow," Jacob said. "Come down first thing."

"I will."

Charlie followed me home. I paid scant attention to the lights in my rearview mirror. Instead, I wondered where Sam and Jared and Embry and Paul were, out running in the night. I wondered if Jacob had joined them yet.

When we got home, I hurried for the stairs, but Charlie was right behind me.

"What's going on, Bella?" he demanded before I could escape. "I thought Jacob was part of a gang and you two were fighting."

"We made up."

"And the gang?"

"I don't know—who can understand teenage boys? They're a mystery. But I met Sam Uley and his fiancée, Emily. The seemed pretty nice to me." I shrugged. "Must have all been a misunderstanding."

His face changed. "I hadn't heard that he and Emily had made it official. That's nice. Poor girl."

"Do you know what happened to her?"

"Mauled by a bear, up north, during salmon spawning season—horrible accident. It was more than a year ago now. I heard Sam was really messed up over it."

"That's horrible," I echoed. More than a year ago. I'd bet that meant it had happened when there was just one werewolf in La Push. I shuddered at the thought of how Sam must have felt every time he looked at Emily's face.

That night, I lay awake for a long time trying to sort through the day. I worked my way backward through dinner with Billy, Jacob, and Charlie, to the long afternoon in the Blacks' house, waiting anxiously to hear something from Jacob, to Emily's kitchen, to the horror of the werewolf fight, to talking with Jacob on the beach.

I thought about what Jacob had said early this morning, about hypocrisy. I thought about that for a long time. I didn't like to think that I was a hypocrite, only what was the point of lying to myself?

I curled into a tight ball. No, Edward wasn't a killer. Even in his darker past, he'd never been a murderer of innocents, at least.

But what if he *had* been? What if, during the time that I'd known him, he'd been just like any other vampire? What if people had been disappearing from the woods, just like now? Would that have kept me away from him?

I shook my head sadly. Love is irrational, I reminded myself. The more you loved someone, the less sense anything made.

I rolled over and tried to think of something else—and I thought of Jacob and his brothers, out running in the darkness. I fell asleep imagining the wolves, invisible in the night, guarding me from danger. When I dreamed, I stood in the forest again, but I didn't wander. I was holding Emily's scarred hand as we faced into the shadows and waited anxiously for our werewolves to come home.

15. PRESSURE

IT WAS SPRING BREAK IN FORKS AGAIN. WHEN I WOKE up
on Monday morning, I lay in bed for a few seconds absorb-
ing that. Last spring break, I'd been hunted by a vampire,
too. I hoped this wasn't some kind of tradition forming.

Already I was falling into the pattern of things in La
Push. I'd spent Sunday mostly on the beach, while Charlie
hung out with Billy at the Blacks' house. I was supposed
to be with Jacob, but Jacob had other things to do, so I
wandered alone, keeping the secret from Charlie.

When Jacob dropped in to check on me, he apologized
for ditching me so much. He told me his schedule wasn't
always this crazy, but until Victoria was stopped, the
wolves were on red alert.

When we walked along the beach now, he always held my hand.

This made me brood over what Jared had said, about Jacob involving his "girlfriend." I supposed that that was exactly what it looked like from the outside. As long as Jake and I knew how it really was, I shouldn't let those kinds of assumptions bother me. And maybe they wouldn't, if I hadn't known that Jacob would have loved for things to be what they appeared. But his hand felt nice as it warmed mine, and I didn't protest.

I worked Tuesday afternoon—Jacob followed me on his bike to make sure I arrived safely—and Mike noticed.

"Are you dating that kid from La Push? The sophomore?" He asked, poorly disguising the resentment in his tone.

I shrugged. "Not in the technical sense of the word. I do spent most of my time with Jacob, though. He's my best friend."

Mike's eyes narrowed shrewdly. "Don't kid yourself, Bella. The guy's head over heels for you."

"I know," I sighed. "Life is complicated."

"And girls are cruel," Mike said under his breath.

I supposed that was an easy assumption to make, too.

That night, Sam and Emily joined Charlie and me for dessert at Billy's house. Emily brought a cake that would have won over a harder man than Charlie. I could see, as the conversation flowed naturally through a range of casual subjects, that any worries Charlie might have harbored about gangs in La Push were being dissolved.

Jake and I skipped out early, to get some privacy. We

went out to his garage and sat in the Rabbit. Jacob leaned his head back, his face drawn with exhaustion.

"You need some sleep, Jake."

"I'll get around to it."

He reached over and took my hand. His skin was blazing on mine.

"Is that one of those wolf things?" I asked him. "The heat, I mean."

"Yeah. We run a little warmer than the normal people. About one-oh-eight, one-oh-nine. I never get cold anymore. I could stand like this"— he gestured to his bare torso—"in a snowstorm and it wouldn't bother me. The flakes would turn to rain where I stood."

"And you all heal fast—that's a wolf thing, too?"

"Yeah, wanna see? It's pretty cool." His eyes flipped open and he grinned. He reached around me to the glove compartment and dug around for a minute. His hand came out with a pocketknife.

"No, I do not want to see!" I shouted as soon as I realized what he was thinking. "Put that away!"

Jacob chuckled, but shoved the knife back where it belonged. "Fine. It's a good thing we heal, though. You can't go see just any doctor when you're running a temperature that should mean you're dead."

"No, I guess not." I thought about that for a minute. ". . . And being so big—that's part of it? Is that why you're all worried about Quil?"

"That and the fact that Quil's grandfather says the kid could fry an egg on his forehead." Jacob's face turned hopeless. "It won't be long now. There's no exact age . . . it just builds and builds and then suddenly—" He broke off, and it was a moment before he could speak again. "Sometimes, if you get really upset or something, that can trigger it early. But I wasn't upset about anything—I was *happy*." He laughed bitterly. "Because of you, mostly. That's why it didn't happen to me sooner. Instead it just kept on building up inside me—I was like a time bomb. You know what set me off? I got back from that movie and Billy said I looked weird. That was all, but I just snapped. And then I—I exploded. I almost ripped his face off—my own father!" He shuddered, and his face paled.

"Is it really bad, Jake?" I asked anxiously, wishing I had some way to help him. "Are you miserable?"

"No, I'm not miserable," he told me. "Not anymore. Not now that you know. That was hard, before." He leaned over so that his cheek was resting on top of my head.

He was quiet for a moment, and I wondered what he was thinking about. Maybe I didn't want to know.

"What's the hardest part?" I whispered, still wishing I could help.

"The hardest part is feeling . . . out of control," he said slowly. "Feeling like I can't be sure of myself—like maybe you *shouldn't* be around me, like maybe nobody should. Like I'm a monster who might hurt somebody. You've seen Emily. Sam lost control of his temper for just one second . . . and she was standing too close. And now there's nothing he can ever do to put it right again. I hear his thoughts—I know what that feels like. . . .

"Who wants to be a nightmare, a monster?

"And then, the way it comes so easily to me, the way I'm better at it than the rest of them—does that make me even less human than Embry or Sam? Sometimes I'm afraid that I'm losing myself."

"Is it hard? To find yourself again?"

"At first," he said. "It takes some practice to phase back and forth. But it's easier for me."

"Why?" I wondered.

"Because Ephraim Black was my father's grandfather, and Quil Ateara was my mother's grandfather."

"Quil?" I asked in confusion.

"His great-grandfather," Jacob clarified. "The Quil you know is my second cousin."

"But why does it matter who your great-grandfathers are?"

"Because Ephraim and Quil were in the last pack. Levi Uley was the third. It's in my blood on both sides. I never had a chance. Like Quil doesn't have a chance."

His expression was bleak.

"What's the very best part?" I asked, hoping to cheer him up.

"The best part," he said, suddenly smiling again, "is the *speed*."

"Better than the motorcycles?"

He nodded, enthusiastic. "There's no comparison."

"How fast can you . . . ?"

"Run?" he finished my question. "Fast enough. What can I measure it by? We caught . . . what was his name? Laurent? I imagine that means more to you than it would to someone else."

It did mean something to me. I couldn't imagine that—the wolves running faster than a vampire. When the Cullens ran, they all but turned invisible with speed.

"So, tell me something *I* don't know," he said. "Something about vampires. How did you stand it, being around them? Didn't it creep you out?"

"No," I said curtly.

My tone made him thoughtful for a moment.

"Say, why'd your bloodsucker kill that James, anyway?" he asked suddenly.

"James was trying to kill me—it was like a game for him. He lost. Do you remember last spring when I was in the hospital down in Phoenix?"

Jacob sucked in a breath. "He got that close?"

"He got very, very close." I stroked my scar. Jacob noticed, because he held the hand I moved.

"What's that?" He traded hands, examining my right. "This is your funny scar, the cold one." He looked at it closer, with new eyes, and gasped.

"Yes, it's what you think it is," I said. "James bit me."

His eyes bulged, and his face turned a strange, sallow color under the russet surface. He looked like he was about to be sick.

"But if he bit you . . . ? Shouldn't you be . . . ?" He choked.

"Edward saved me twice," I whispered. "He sucked the venom out—you know, like with a rattlesnake." I twitched as the pain lashed around the edges of the hole.

But I wasn't the only one twitching. I could feel Jacob's whole body trembling next to mine. Even the car shook.

"Careful, Jake. Easy. Calm down."

"Yeah," he panted. "Calm." He shook his head back and forth quickly. After a moment, only his hands were shaking.

"You okay?"

"Yeah, almost. Tell me something else. Give me something else to think about."

"What do you want to know?"

"I don't know." He had his eyes closed, concentrating. "The extra stuff I guess. Did any of the other Cullens have . . . extra talents? Like the mind reading?"

I hesitated a second. This felt like a question he would ask of his spy, not his friend. But what was the point of hiding what I knew? It didn't matter now, and it would help him control himself.

So I spoke quickly, the image of Emily's ruined face in my mind, and the hair rising on my arms. I couldn't imagine how the russet wolf would fit inside the Rabbit—Jacob would tear the whole garage apart if he changed now.

"Jasper could . . . sort of control the emotions of the people around him. Not in a bad way, just to calm someone down, that kind of thing. It would probably help Paul a lot," I added, teasing weakly. "And then Alice could see things that were going to happen. The future, you know, but not absolutely. The things she saw would change when someone changed the path they were on. . . ."

Like how she'd seen me dying . . . and she'd seen me becoming one of them. Two things that had not happened. And one that never would. My head started to spin—I couldn't seem to pull in enough oxygen from the air. No lungs.

Jacob was entirely in control now, very still beside me.

"Why do you do that?" he asked. He tugged lightly at one of my arms, which was bound around my chest, and then gave up when it wouldn't come loose easily. I hadn't even realized I'd moved them. "You do that when you're upset. Why?"

"It hurts to think about them," I whispered. "It's like I can't breathe . . . like I'm breaking into pieces. . . ." It was bizarre how much I could tell Jacob now. We had no more secrets.

He smoothed my hair. "It's okay, Bella, it's okay. I won't bring it up again. I'm sorry."

"I'm fine." I gasped. "Happens all the time. Not your fault."

"We're a pretty messed-up pair, aren't we?" Jacob said. "Neither one of us can hold our shape together right."

"Pathetic," I agreed, still breathless.

"At least we have each other," he said, clearly comforted by the thought.

I was comforted, too. "At least there's that," I agreed.

And when we were together, it was fine. But Jacob had a horrible, dangerous job he felt compelled to do, and so I was often alone, stuck in La Push for safety, with nothing to do to keep my mind off any of my worries.

I felt awkward, always taking up space at Billy's. I did some studying for another Calculus test that was coming up next week, but I could only look at math for so long. When I didn't have something obvious to do in my hands,

I felt like I ought to be making conversation with Billy—the pressure of normal societal rules. But Billy wasn't one for filling up the long silences, and so the awkwardness continued.

I tried hanging out at Emily's place Wednesday afternoon, for a change. At first it was kind of nice. Emily was a cheerful person who never sat still. I drifted behind her while she flitted around her little house and yard, scrubbing at the spotless floor, pulling a tiny weed, fixing a broken hinge, tugging a string of wool through an ancient loom, and always cooking, too. She complained lightly about the increase in the boys' appetites from all their extra running, but it was easy to see she didn't mind taking care of them. It wasn't hard to be with her—after all, we were both wolf girls now.

But Sam checked in after I'd been there for a few hours. I only stayed long enough to ascertain that Jacob was fine and there was no news, and then I had to escape. The aura of love and contentment that surrounded them was harder to take in concentrated doses, with no one else around to dilute it.

So that left me wandering the beach, pacing the length of the rocky crescent back and forth, again and again.

Alone time wasn't good for me. Thanks to the new honesty with Jacob, I'd been talking and thinking about the Cullens way too much. No matter how I tried to distract myself—and I had plenty to think of: I was honestly and desperately worried about Jacob and his wolf-brothers, I was terrified for Charlie and the others who thought they were hunting animals, I was getting in deeper and deeper with Jacob without ever having consciously decided to progress in that direction and I didn't know what to do about it—none of these very real, very deserving of thought, very pressing concerns could take my mind off the pain in my chest for long. Eventually, I couldn't even walk anymore, because I couldn't breathe. I sat down on a patch of semidry rocks and curled up in a ball.

Jacob found me like that, and I could tell from his expression that he understood.

"Sorry," he said right away. He pulled me up from the ground and wrapped both arms around my shoulders. I hadn't realized that I was cold until then. His warmth made me shudder, but at least I could breathe with him there.

"I'm ruining your spring break," Jacob accused himself as we walked back up the beach.

"No, you're not. I didn't have any plans. I don't think I like spring breaks, anyway."

"I'll take tomorrow morning off. The others can run without me. We'll do something fun."

The word seemed out of place in my life right now, barely comprehensible, bizarre. "Fun?"

"Fun is exactly what you need. Hmm . . ." he gazed out across the heaving gray waves, deliberating. As his eyes scanned the horizon, he had a flash of inspiration.

"Got it!" he crowed. "Another promise to keep."

"What are you talking about?"

He let go of my hand and pointed toward the southern edge of the beach, where the flat, rocky half-moon

dead-ended against the sheer sea cliffs. I stared, uncomprehending.

"Didn't I promise to take you cliff diving?"

I shivered.

"Yeah, it'll be pretty cold—not as cold as it is today.
Can you feel the weather changing? The pressure? It will
be warmer tomorrow. You up for it?"

The dark water did not look inviting, and, from this
angle, the cliffs looked even higher than before.

But it had been days since I'd heard Edward's voice.
That was probably part of the problem. I was addicted to
the sound of my delusions. It made things worse if I went
too long without them. Jumping off a cliff was certain to
remedy that situation.

"Sure, I'm up for it. Fun."

"It's a date," he said, and draped his arm around my
shoulders.

"Okay—now let's go get you some sleep." I didn't like
the way the circles under his eyes were beginning to look
permanently etched onto his skin.

I woke early the next morning and snuck a change of
clothes out to the truck. I had a feeling that Charlie would
approve of today's plan just about as much as he would approve of the motorcycle.

The idea of a distraction from all my worries had me almost excited. Maybe it *would* be fun. A date with Jacob, a
date with Edward . . . I laughed darkly to myself. Jake
could say what he wanted about us being a messed-up

pair—I was the one who was truly messed up. I made the werewolf seem downright normal.

I expected Jacob to meet me out front, the way he usually did when my noisy truck announced my arrival. When he didn't, I guessed that he might still be sleeping. I would wait—let him get as much rest as he could. He needed his sleep, and that would give the day time to warm a bit more. Jake had been right about the weather, though; it had changed in the night. A thick layer of clouds pressed heavily on the atmosphere now, making it almost sultry; it was warm and close under the gray blanket. I left my sweater in the truck.

I knocked quietly on the door.

"C'mon in, Bella," Billy said.

He was at the kitchen table, eating cold cereal.

"Jake sleeping?"

"Er, no." He set his spoon down, and his eyebrows pulled together.

"What happened?" I demanded. I could tell from his expression that *something* had.

"Embry, Jared, and Paul crossed a fresh trail early this morning. Sam and Jake took off to help. Sam was hopeful—she's hedged herself in beside the mountains. He thinks they have a good chance to finish this."

"Oh, no, Billy," I whispered. "Oh, no."

He chuckled, deep and low. "Do you really like La Push so well that you want to extend your sentence here?"

"Don't make jokes, Billy. This is too scary for that."

"You're right," he agreed, still complacent. His ancient eyes were impossible to read. "This one's tricky."

I bit my lip.

"It's not as dangerous for them as you think it is. Sam knows what he's doing. You're the one that you should worry about. The vampire doesn't want to fight them. She's just trying to find a way around them . . . to you."

"How does Sam know what he's doing?" I demanded, brushing aside his concern for me. "They've only killed just the one vampire—that could have been luck."

"We take what we do very seriously, Bella. Nothing's been forgotten. Everything they need to know has been passed down from father to son for generations."

That didn't comfort me the way he probably intended it to. The memory of Victoria, wild, catlike, lethal, was too strong in my head. If she couldn't get around the wolves, she *would* eventually try to go through them.

Billy went back to his breakfast; I sat down on the sofa and flipped aimlessly though the TV channels. That didn't last long. I started to feel closed in by the small room, claustrophobic, upset by the fact that I couldn't see out the curtained windows.

"I'll be at the beach," I told Billy abruptly, and hurried out the door.

Being outside didn't help as much as I'd hoped. The clouds pushed down with an invisible weight that kept the claustrophobia from easing. The forest seemed strangely vacant as I walked toward the beach. I didn't see any animals—no birds, no squirrels. I couldn't hear any birds, either. The silence was eerie; there wasn't even the sound of wind in the trees.

I knew it was all just a product of the weather, but it still made me edgy. The heavy, warm pressure of the atmosphere was perceptible even to my weak human senses, and it hinted at something major in the storm department. A glance at the sky backed this up; the clouds were churning sluggishly despite the lack of breeze on the ground. The closest clouds were a smoky gray, but between the cracks I could see another layer that was a gruesome purple color. The skies had a ferocious plan in store for today. The animals must be bunkering down.

As soon as I reached the beach, I wished I hadn't come—I'd already had enough of this place. I'd been here almost every day, wandering alone. Was it so much different from my nightmares? But where else to go? I trudged down to the driftwood tree, and sat at the end so that I could lean against the tangled roots. I stared up at the angry sky broodingly, waiting for the first drops to break the stillness.

I tried not to think about the danger Jacob and his friends were in. Because nothing could happen to Jacob. The thought was unendurable. I'd lost too much already—would fate take the last few shreds of peace left behind? That seemed unfair, out of balance. But maybe I'd violated some unknown rule, crossed some line that had condemned me. Maybe it was wrong to be so involved with myths and legends, to turn my back on the human world. Maybe . . .

No. Nothing would happen to Jacob. I had to believe that or I wouldn't be able to function.

"Argh!" I groaned, and jumped off the log. I couldn't sit still; it was worse than pacing.

I'd really been counting on hearing Edward this morning. It seemed like that was the one thing that might make it bearable to live through this day. The hole had been festering lately, like it was getting revenge for the times that Jacob's presence had tamed it. The edges burned.

The waves picked up as I paced, beginning to crash against the rocks, but there was still no wind. I felt pinned down by the pressure of the storm. Everything swirled around me, but it was perfectly still where I stood. The air had a faint electric charge—I could feel the static in my hair.

Farther out, the waves were angrier than they were along the shore. I could see them battering against the line of the cliffs, spraying big white clouds of sea foam into the sky. There was still no movement in the air, though the clouds roiled more quickly now. It was eerie looking—like the clouds were moving by their own will. I shivered, though I knew it was just a trick of the pressure.

The cliffs were a black knife edge against the livid sky. Staring at them, I remembered the day Jacob had told me about Sam and his "gang." I thought of the boys—the werewolves—throwing themselves into the empty air. The image of the falling, spiraling figures was still vivid in my mind. I imagined the utter freedom of the fall. . . . I imagined the way Edward's voice would have sounded in my head—furious, velvet, perfect. . . . The burning in my chest flared agonizingly.

There had to be some way to quench it. The pain was

growing more and more intolerable by the second. I glared at the cliffs and the crashing waves.

Well, why not? Why not quench it right now?

Jacob had promised me cliff diving, hadn't he? Just because he was unavailable, should I have to give up the distraction I needed so badly—needed even worse *because* Jacob was out risking his life? Risking it, in essence, for me. If it weren't for me, Victoria would not be killing people here . . . just somewhere else, far away. If anything happened to Jacob, it would be my fault. That realization stabbed deep and had me jogging back up to the road toward Billy's house, where my truck waited.

I knew my way to the lane that passed closest to the cliffs, but I had to hunt for the little path that would take me out to the ledge. As I followed it, I looked for turns or forks, knowing that Jake had planned to take me off the lower outcropping rather than the top, but the path wound in a thin single line toward the brink with no options. I didn't have time to find another way down—the storm was moving in quickly now. The wind was finally beginning to touch me, the clouds pressing closer to the ground. Just as I reached the place where the dirt path fanned out into the stone precipice, the first drops broke through and splattered on my face.

It was not hard to convince myself that I didn't have time to search for another way—I *wanted* to jump from the top. This was the image that had lingered in my head. I wanted the long fall that would feel like flying.

I knew that this was the stupidest, most reckless thing I had done yet. The thought made me smile. The pain was already easing, as if my body knew that Edward's voice was just seconds away. . . .

The ocean sounded very far away, somehow farther than before, when I was on the path in the trees. I grimaced when I thought of the probable temperature of the water. But I wasn't going to let that stop me.

The wind blew stronger now, whipping the rain into eddies around me.

I stepped out to the edge, keeping my eyes on the empty space in front of me. My toes felt ahead blindly, caressing the edge of the rock when they encountered it. I drew in a deep breath and held it . . . waiting.

"Bella."

I smiled and exhaled.

Yes? I didn't answer out loud, for fear that the sound of my voice would shatter the beautiful illusion. He sounded so real, so close. It was only when he was disapproving like this that I could hear the true memory of his voice—the velvet texture and the musical intonation that made up the most perfect of all voices.

"Don't do this," he pleaded.

You wanted me to be human, I reminded him. *Well, watch me.*

"Please. For me."

But you won't stay with me any other way.

"Please." It was just a whisper in the blowing rain that tossed my hair and drenched my clothes—making me as wet as if this were my second jump of the day.

I rolled up onto the balls of my feet.

"No, Bella!" He was angry now, and the anger was so lovely.

I smiled and raised my arms straight out, as if I were going to dive, lifting my face into the rain. But it was too ingrained from years of swimming at the public pool—feet first, first time. I leaned forward, crouching to get more spring . . .

And I flung myself off the cliff.

I screamed as I dropped through the open air like a meteor, but it was a scream of exhilaration and not fear. The wind resisted, trying vainly to fight the unconquerable gravity, pushing against me and twirling me in spirals like a rocket crashing to the earth.

Yes! The word echoed through my head as I sliced through the surface of the water. It was icy, colder than I'd feared, and yet the chill only added to the high.

I was proud of myself as I plunged deeper into the freezing black water. I hadn't had one moment of terror—just pure adrenaline. Really, the fall wasn't scary at all. Where was the challenge?

That was when the current caught me.

I'd been so preoccupied by the size of the cliffs, by the obvious danger of their high, sheer faces, that I hadn't worried at all about the dark water waiting. I never dreamed that the true menace was lurking far below me, under the heaving surf.

It felt like the waves were fighting over me, jerking me back and forth between them as if determined to share by pulling me into halves. I knew the right way to avoid a riptide: swim parallel to the beach rather than struggling for the shore. But the knowledge did me little good when I didn't know which way the shore was.

I couldn't even tell which way the surface was.

The angry water was black in every direction; there was no brightness to direct me upward. Gravity was all-powerful when it competed with the air, but it had nothing on the waves—I couldn't feel a downward pull, a sinking in any direction. Just the battering of the current that flung me round and round like a rag doll.

I fought to keep my breath in, to keep my lips locked around my last store of oxygen.

It didn't surprise me that my delusion of Edward was there. He owed me that much, considering that I was dying. I *was* surprised by how sure that knowledge was. I was going to drown. I was drowning.

"Keep swimming!" Edward begged urgently in my head.

Where? There was nothing but the darkness. There was no place to swim to.

"Stop that!" he ordered. "Don't you dare give up!"

The cold of the water was numbing my arms and legs. I didn't feel the buffeting so much as before. It was more of just a dizziness now, a helpless spinning in the water.

But I listened to him. I forced my arms to continue reaching, my legs to kick harder, though every second I was facing a new direction. It couldn't be doing any good. What was the point?

"Fight!" he yelled. "Damn it, Bella, keep fighting."

Why?

I didn't want to fight anymore. And it wasn't the light-headedness, or the cold, or the failure of my arms as the muscles gave out in exhaustion, that made me content to stay where I was. I was almost happy that it was over. This was an easier death than others I'd faced. Oddly peaceful.

I thought briefly of the clichés, about how you were suppose to see your life flash before your eyes. I was so much luckier. Who wanted to see a rerun, anyway?

I saw *him*, and I had no will to fight. It was so clear, so much more defined than any memory. My subconscious had stored Edward away in flawless detail, saving him for this final moment. I could see his perfect face as if he were really there; the exact shade of his icy skin, the shape of his lips, the line of his jaw, the gold glinting in his furious eyes. He was angry, naturally, that I was giving up. His teeth were clenched and his nostrils flared with rage.

"No! Bella, no!"

My ears were flooded with the freezing water, but his voice was clearer than ever. I ignored his words and concentrated on the sound of his voice. Why would I fight when I was so happy where I was? Even as my lungs burned for more air and my legs cramped in the icy cold, I was content. I'd forgotten what real happiness felt like.

Happiness. It made the whole dying thing pretty bearable.

The current won at that moment, shoving me abruptly

against something hard, a rock invisible in the gloom. It hit me solidly across the chest, slamming into me like an iron bar, and the breath whooshed out of my lungs, escaping in a thick cloud of silver bubbles. Water flooded down my throat, choking and burning. The iron bar seemed to be dragging me, pulling me away from Edward, deeper into the dark, to the ocean floor.

Goodbye, I love you, was my last thought.

16. PARIS

At that moment, my head broke the surface.

How disorienting. I'd been sure I was sinking.

The current wouldn't let up. It was slamming me against more rocks; they beat against the center of my back sharply, rhythmically, pushing the water from my lungs. It gushed out in amazing volume, absolute torrents pouring from my mouth and nose. The salt burned and my lungs burned and my throat was too full of water to catch a breath and the rocks were hurting my back. Somehow I stayed in one place, though the waves still heaved around me. I couldn't see anything but water everywhere, reaching for my face.

"Breathe!" a voice, wild with anxiety, ordered, and I

felt a cruel stab of pain when I recognized the voice—because it wasn't Edward's.

I could not obey. The waterfall pouring from my mouth didn't stop long enough for me to catch a breath. The black, icy water filled my chest, burning.

The rock smacked into my back again, right between my shoulder blades, and another volley of water choked its way out of my lungs.

"Breathe, Bella! C'mon!" Jacob begged.

Black spots bloomed across my vision, getting wider and wider, blocking out the light.

The rock struck me again.

The rock wasn't cold like the water; it was hot on my skin. I realized it was Jacob's hand, trying to beat the water from my lungs. The iron bar that had dragged me from the sea was also . . . warm . . . My head whirled, the black spots covered everything. . . .

Was I dying again, then? I didn't like it—this wasn't as good as the last time. It was only dark now, nothing worth looking at here. The sound of the crashing waves faded into the black and became a quiet, even *whoosh* that sounded like it was coming from the inside of my ears. . . .

"Bella?" Jacob asked, his voice still tense, but not as wild as before. "Bells, honey, can you hear me?"

The contents of my head swished and rolled sickeningly, like they'd joined the rough water. . . .

"How long has she been unconscious?" someone else asked.

The voice that was not Jacob's shocked me, jarred me into a more focused awareness.

I realized that I was still. There was no tug of the current on me—the heaving was inside my head. The surface under me was flat and motionless. It felt grainy against my bare arms.

"I don't know," Jacob reported, still frantic. His voice was very close. Hands—so warm they had to be his—brushed wet hair from my cheeks. "A few minutes? It didn't take long to tow her to the beach."

The quiet *whoosh*ing inside my ears was not the waves—it was the air moving in and out of my lungs again. Each breath burned—the passageways were as raw as if I'd scrubbed them out with steel wool. But I was breathing.

And I was freezing. A thousand sharp, icy beads were striking my face and arms, making the cold worse.

"She's breathing. She'll come around. We should get her out of the cold, though. I don't like the color she's turning. . . ." I recognized Sam's voice this time.

"You think it's okay to move her?"

"She didn't hurt her back or anything when she fell?"

"I don't know."

They hesitated.

I tried to open my eyes. It took me a minute, but then I could see the dark, purple clouds, flinging the freezing rain down at me. "Jake?" I croaked.

Jacob's face blocked out the sky. "Oh!" he gasped, relief washing over his features. His eyes were wet from the rain. "Oh, Bella! Are you okay? Can you hear me? Do you hurt anywhere?"

"J-Just m-my throat," I stuttered, my lips quivering from the cold.

"Let's get you out of here, then," Jacob said. He slid his arms under me and lifted me without effort—like picking up an empty box. His chest was bare and warm; he hunched his shoulders to keep the rain off of me. My head lolled over his arm. I stared vacantly back toward the furious water, beating the sand behind him.

"You got her?" I heard Sam ask.

"Yeah, I'll take it from here. Get back to the hospital. I'll join you later. Thanks, Sam."

My head was still rolling. None of his words sunk in at first. Sam didn't answer. There was no sound, and I wondered if he were already gone.

The water licked and writhed up the sand after us as Jacob carried me away, like it was angry that I'd escaped. As I stared wearily, a spark of color caught my unfocused eyes—a small flash of fire was dancing on the black water, far out in the bay. The image made no sense, and I wondered how conscious I really was. My head swirled with the memory of the black, churning water—of being so lost that I couldn't find up or down. So lost . . . but somehow Jacob . . .

"How did you find me?" I rasped.

"I was searching for you," he told me. He was half-jogging through the rain, up the beach toward the road. "I followed the tire tracks to your truck, and then I heard you scream. . . ." He shuddered. "Why would you jump, Bella? Didn't you notice that it's turning into a hurricane out here? Couldn't you have waited for me?" Anger filled his tone as the relief faded.

"Sorry," I muttered. "It was stupid."

"Yeah, it was *really* stupid," he agreed, drops of rain shaking free of his hair as he nodded. "Look, do you mind saving the stupid stuff for when I'm around? I won't be able to concentrate if I think you're jumping off cliffs behind my back."

"Sure," I agreed. "No problem." I sounded like a chain-smoker. I tried to clear my throat—and then winced; the throat-clearing felt like stabbing a knife down there. "What happened today? Did you . . . find *her*?" It was my turn to shudder, though I wasn't so cold here, right next to his ridiculous body heat.

Jacob shook his head. He was still more running than walking as he headed up the road to his house. "No. She took off into the water—the bloodsuckers have the advantage there. That's why I raced home—I was afraid she was going to double back swimming. You spend so much time on the beach. . . ." He trailed off, a catch in his throat.

"Sam came back with you . . . is everyone else home, too?" I hoped they weren't still out searching for her.

"Yeah. Sort of."

I tried to read his expression, squinting into the hammering rain. His eyes were tight with worry or pain.

The words that hadn't made sense before suddenly did. "You said . . . hospital. Before, to Sam. Is someone hurt? Did she fight you?" My voice jumped up an octave, sounding strange with the hoarseness.

"No, no. When we got back, Em was waiting with the news. It's Harry Clearwater. Harry had a heart attack this morning."

"Harry?" I shook my head, trying to absorb what he was staying. "Oh, no! Does Charlie know?"

"Yeah. He's over there, too, with my dad."

"Is Harry going to be okay?"

Jacob's eyes tightened again. "It doesn't look so great right now."

Abruptly, I felt really sick with guilt—felt truly horrible about the brainless cliff dive. Nobody needed to be worrying about me right now. What a stupid time to be reckless.

"What can I do?" I asked.

At that moment the rain stopped. I hadn't realized we were already back to Jacob's house until he walked through the door. The storm pounded against the roof.

"You can stay *here*," Jacob said as he dumped me on the short couch. "I mean it—right here. I'll get you some dry clothes."

I let my eyes adjust to the dark room while Jacob banged around in his bedroom. The cramped front room seemed so empty without Billy, almost desolate. It was strangely ominous—probably just because I knew where he was.

Jacob was back in seconds. He threw a pile of gray cotton at me. "These will be huge on you, but it's the best I've got. I'll, er, step outside so you can change."

"Don't go anywhere. I'm too tired to move yet. Just stay with me."

Jacob sat on the floor next to me, his back against the couch. I wondered when he'd slept last. He looked as exhausted as I felt.

He leaned his head on the cushion next to mine and yawned. "Guess I could rest for a minute. . . ."

His eyes closed. I let mine slide shut, too.

Poor Harry. Poor Sue. I knew Charlie was going to be beside himself. Harry was one of his best friends. Despite Jake's negative take on things, I hoped fervently that Harry would pull through. For Charlie's sake. For Sue's and Leah's and Seth's . . .

Billy's sofa was right next to the radiator, and I was warm now, despite my soaked clothes. My lungs ached in a way that pushed me toward unconsciousness rather than keeping me awake. I wondered vaguely if it was wrong to sleep . . . or was I getting drowning mixed up with concussions . . . ? Jacob began softly snoring, and the sound of it soothed like a lullaby. I fell asleep quickly.

For the first time in a very long time, my dream was just a normal dream. Just a blurred wandering through old memories—blinding bright visions of the Phoenix sun, my mother's face, a ramshackle tree house, a faded quilt, a wall of mirrors, a flame on the black water . . . I forgot each of them as soon as the picture changed.

The last picture was the only one that stuck in my head. It was meaningless—just a set on a stage. A balcony at night, a painted moon hanging in the sky. I watched the girl in her nightdress lean on the railing and talk to herself.

Meaningless . . . but when I slowly struggled back to consciousness, Juliet was on my mind.

Jacob was still asleep; he'd slumped down to the floor and his breathing was deep and even. The house was darker now than before, it was black outside the window. I was stiff, but warm and almost dry. The inside of my throat burned with every breath I took.

I was going to have to get up—at least to get a drink. But my body just wanted to lie here limp, to never move again.

Instead of moving, I thought about Juliet some more.

I wondered what she would have done if Romeo had left her, not because he was banished, but because he lost interest? What if Rosalind had given him the time of day, and he'd changed his mind? What if, instead of marrying Juliet, he'd just disappeared?

I thought I knew how Juliet would feel.

She wouldn't go back to her old life, not really. She wouldn't ever have moved on, I was sure of that. Even if she'd lived until she was old and gray, every time she closed her eyes, it would have been Romeo's face she saw behind her lids. She would have accepted that, eventually.

I wondered if she would have married Paris in the end, just to please her parents, to keep the peace. No, probably not, I decided. But then, the story didn't say much about Paris. He was just a stick figure—a placeholder, a threat, a deadline to force her hand.

What if there were more to Paris?

What if Paris had been Juliet's friend? Her very best friend? What if he was the only one she could confide in about the whole devastating thing with Romeo? The one person who really understood her and made her feel halfway human again? What if he was patient and kind? What if he took care of her? What if Juliet knew she couldn't survive without him? What if he really loved her, and wanted her to be happy?

And . . . what if she loved Paris? Not like Romeo. Nothing like that, of course. But enough that she wanted him to be happy, too?

Jacob's slow, deep breathing was the only sound in the room—like a lullaby hummed to a child, like the whisper of a rocking chair, like the ticking of an old clock when you had nowhere you needed to go. . . . It was the sound of comfort.

If Romeo was really gone, never coming back, would it have mattered whether or not Juliet had taken Paris up on his offer? Maybe she should have tried to settle into the leftover scraps of life that were left behind. Maybe that would have been as close to happiness as she could get.

I sighed, and then groaned when the sigh scraped my throat. I was reading too much into the story. Romeo wouldn't change his mind. That's why people still remembered his name, always twined with hers: Romeo and Juliet. That's why it was a good story. "Juliet gets dumped and ends up with Paris" would have never been a hit.

I closed my eyes and drifted again, letting my mind wander away from the stupid play I didn't want to think about anymore. I thought about reality instead—about jumping off the cliff and what a brainless mistake that had been. And not just the cliff, but the motorcycles and the whole irresponsible Evel Knievel bit. What if something bad happened to me? What would that do to Charlie? Harry's heart attack had pushed everything suddenly into perspective for me. Perspective that I didn't want to see, because—if I admitted to the truth of it—it would mean that I would have to change my ways. Could I live like that?

Maybe. It wouldn't be easy; in fact, it would be downright miserable to give up my hallucinations and try to be a grown-up. But maybe I should do it. And maybe I could. If I had Jacob.

I couldn't make that decision right now. It hurt too much. I'd think about something else.

Images from my ill-considered afternoon stunt rolled through my head while I tried to come up with something pleasant to think about . . . the feel of the air as I fell, the blackness of the water, the thrashing of the current . . . Edward's face . . . I lingered there for a long time. Jacob's warm hands, trying to beat life back into me . . . the stinging rain flung down by the purple clouds . . . the strange fire on the waves . . .

There was something familiar about that flash of color on top of the water. Of course it couldn't really be fire—

My thoughts were interrupted by the sound of a car squelching through the mud on the road outside. I heard it stop in front of the house, and doors started opening and closing. I thought about sitting up, and then decided against that idea.

Billy's voice was easily identifiable, but he kept it uncharacteristically low, so that it was only a gravelly grumble.

The door opened, and the light flicked on. I blinked, momentarily blind. Jake startled awake, gasping and jumping to his feet.

"Sorry," Billy grunted. "Did we wake you?"

My eyes slowly focused on his face, and then, as I could read his expression, they filled with tears.

"Oh, no, Billy!" I moaned.

He nodded slowly, his expression hard with grief. Jake hurried to his father and took one of his hands. The pain made his face suddenly childlike—it looked odd on top of the man's body.

Sam was right behind Billy, pushing his chair through the door. His normal composure was absent from his agonized face.

"I'm so sorry," I whispered.

Billy nodded. "It's gonna be hard all around."

"Where's Charlie?"

"Your dad is still at the hospital with Sue. There are a lot of . . . arrangements to be made."

I swallowed hard.

"I'd better get back there," Sam mumbled, and he ducked hastily out the door.

Billy pulled his hand away from Jacob, and then he rolled himself through the kitchen toward his room.

Jake stared after him for a minute, then came to sit on the floor beside me again. He put his face in his hands. I rubbed his shoulder, wishing I could think of anything to say.

After a long moment, Jacob caught my hand and held it to his face.

"How are you feeling? Are you okay? I probably should have taken you to a doctor or something." He sighed.

"Don't worry about me," I croaked.

He twisted his head to look at me. His eyes were rimmed in red. "You don't look so good."

"I don't feel so good, either, I guess."

"I'll go get your truck and then take you home—you probably ought to be there when Charlie gets back."

"Right."

I lay listlessly on the sofa while I waited for him. Billy was silent in the other room. I felt like a peeping tom, peering through the cracks at a private sorrow that wasn't mine.

It didn't take Jake long. The roar of my truck's engine broke the silence before I expected it. He helped me up from the couch without speaking, keeping his arm around my shoulder when the cold air outside made me shiver. He took the driver's seat without asking, and then pulled me next to his side to keep his arm tight around me. I leaned my head against his chest.

"How will you get home?" I asked.

"I'm not going home. We still haven't caught the bloodsucker, remember?"

My next shudder had nothing to do with cold.

It was a quiet ride after that. The cold air had woken me up. My mind was alert, and it was working very hard and very fast.

What if? What was the right thing to do?

I couldn't imagine my life without Jacob now—I cringed away from the idea of even trying to imagine that. Somehow, he'd become essential to my survival. But to leave things the way they were . . . was that cruel, as Mike had accused?

I remembered wishing that Jacob were my brother. I realized now that all I really wanted was a claim on him. It didn't feel brotherly when he held me like this. It just felt nice—warm and comforting and familiar. Safe. Jacob was a safe harbor.

I could stake a claim. I had that much within my power.

I'd have to tell him everything, I knew that. It was the only way to be fair. I'd have to explain it right, so that he'd know I wasn't settling, that he was much too good for me. He already knew I was broken, that part wouldn't surprise him, but he'd need to know the extent of it. I'd even have to admit that I was crazy—explain about the voices I heard. He'd need to know everything before he made a decision.

But, even as I recognized that necessity, I knew he would take me in spite of it all. He wouldn't even pause to think it through.

I would have to commit to this—commit as much of me as there was left, every one of the broken pieces. It was the only way to be fair to him. Would I? Could I?

Would it be so wrong to try to make Jacob happy? Even if the love I felt for him was no more than a weak echo of what I was capable of, even if my heart was far away, wandering and grieving after my fickle Romeo, would it be so very wrong?

Jacob stopped the truck in front of my dark house, cutting the engine so it was suddenly silent. Like so many other times, he seemed to be in tune with my thoughts now.

He threw his other arm around me, crushing me against his chest, binding me to him. Again, this felt nice. Almost like being a whole person again.

I thought he would be thinking of Harry, but then he spoke, and his tone was apologetic. "Sorry. I know you don't feel exactly the way I do, Bells. I swear I don't mind. I'm just so glad you're okay that I could sing—and that's something no one wants to hear." He laughed his throaty laugh in my ear.

My breathing kicked up a notch, sanding the walls of my throat.

Wouldn't Edward, indifferent as he might be, want me to be as happy as was possible under the circumstances? Wouldn't enough friendly emotion linger for him to want that much for me? I thought he would. He wouldn't begrudge me this: giving just a small bit of the love he didn't want to my friend Jacob. After all, it wasn't the same love at all.

Jake pressed his warm cheek against the top of my hair.

If I turned my face to the side—if I pressed my lips against his bare shoulder . . . I knew without any doubt exactly what would follow. It would be very easy. There would be no need for explanations tonight.

But could I do it? Could I betray my absent heart to save my pathetic life?

Butterflies assaulted my stomach as I thought about turning my head.

And then, as clearly as if I were in immediate danger, Edward's velvet voice whispered in my ear.

"Be happy," he told me.

I froze.

Jacob felt me stiffen and released me automatically, reaching for the door.

Wait, I wanted to say. *Just a minute.* But I was still locked in place, listening to the echo of Edward's voice in my head.

Storm-cooled air blew through the cab of the truck.

"OH!" The breath whooshed out of Jacob like someone had punched him in the gut. "Holy *crap*!"

He slammed the door and twisted the keys in the ignition in the same moment. His hands were shaking so hard I didn't know how he managed it.

"What's wrong?"

He revved the engine too fast; it sputtered and faltered.

"Vampire," he spit out.

The blood rushed from my head and left me dizzy. "How do you know?"

"Because I can smell it! Dammit!"

Jacob's eyes were wild, raking the dark street. He barely seemed aware of the tremors that were rolling through his body. "Phase or get her out of here?" he hissed at himself.

He looked down at me for a split second, taking in my horror-struck eyes and white face, and then he was scanning the street again. "Right. Get you out."

The engine caught with a roar. The tires squealed as he spun the truck around, turning toward our only escape. The headlights washed across the pavement, lit the front line of the black forest, and finally glinted off a car parked across the street from my house.

"Stop!" I gasped.

It was a black car—a car I knew. I might be the furthest thing from an autophile, but I could tell you everything about that particular car. It was a Mercedes S55 AMG. I knew the horsepower and the color of the interior. I knew the feel of the powerful engine purring through the frame. I knew the rich smell of the leather seats and the way the extra-dark tint made noon look like dusk through those windows.

It was Carlisle's car.

"Stop!" I cried again, louder this time, because Jacob was gunning the truck down the street.

"What?!"

"It's not Victoria. Stop, stop! I want to go back."

He stomped on the brake so hard I had to catch myself against the dashboard.

"What?" he asked again, aghast. He stared at me with horror in his eyes.

"It's Carlisle's car! It's the Cullens. I know it."

He watched dawn break across my face, and a violent tremor rocked his frame.

"Hey, calm down, Jake. It's okay. No danger, see? Relax."

"Yeah, calm," he panted, putting his head down and closing his eyes. While he concentrated on not exploding into a wolf, I stared out the back window at the black car.

It was just Carlisle, I told myself. Don't expect anything more. Maybe Esme . . . *Stop right there*, I told myself. Just Carlisle. That was plenty. More than I'd ever hoped to have again.

"There's a vampire in your house," Jacob hissed. "And you *want* to go back?"

I glanced at him, ripping my unwilling eyes off the Mercedes—terrified that it would disappear the second I looked away.

"Of course," I said, my voice blank with surprise at his question. Of course I wanted to go back.

Jacob's face hardened while I stared at him, congealing into the bitter mask that I'd thought was gone for good. Just before he had the mask in place, I caught the spasm of betrayal that flashed in his eyes. His hands were still shaking. He looked ten years older than me.

He took a deep breath. "You're sure it's not a trick?" he asked in a slow, heavy voice.

"It's not a trick. It's Carlisle. Take me back!"

A shudder rippled through his wide shoulders, but his eyes were flat and emotionless. "No."

"Jake, it's okay—"

"No. Take yourself back, Bella." His voice was a slap— I flinched as the sound of it struck me. His jaw clenched and unclenched.

"Look, Bella," he said in the same hard voice. "I can't go back. Treaty or no treaty, that's my enemy in there."

"It's not like that—"

"I have to tell Sam right away. This changes things. We can't be caught on their territory."

"Jake, it's not a war!"

He didn't listen. He put the truck in neutral and jumped out the door, leaving it running.

"Bye, Bella," he called back over his shoulder. "I really

hope you don't die." He sprinted into the darkness, shaking so hard that his shape seemed blurred; he disappeared before I could open my mouth to call him back.

Remorse pinned me against the seat for one long second. What had I just done to Jacob?

But remorse couldn't hold me very long.

I slid across the seat and put the truck back in drive. My hands were shaking almost as hard as Jake's had been, and this took a minute of concentration. Then I carefully turned the truck around and drove it back to my house.

It was very dark when I turned off the headlights. Charlie had left in such a hurry that he'd forgotten to leave the porch lamp on. I felt a pang of doubt, staring at the house, deep in shadow. What if it *was* a trick?

I looked back at the black car, almost invisible in the night. No. I knew that car.

Still, my hands were shaking even worse than before as I reached for the key above the door. When I grabbed the doorknob to unlock it, it twisted easily under my hand. I let the door fall open. The hallway was black.

I wanted to call out a greeting, but my throat was too dry. I couldn't quite seem to catch my breath.

I took a step inside and fumbled for the light switch. It was so black—like the black water . . . Where was that switch?

Just like the black water, with the orange flame flickering impossibly on top of it. Flame that couldn't be a fire, but what then . . . ? My fingers traced the wall, still searching, still shaking—

Suddenly, something Jacob had told me this afternoon

echoed in my head, finally sinking in. . . . *She took off into the water*, he'd said. *The bloodsuckers have the advantage there. That's why I raced home—I was afraid she was going to double back swimming.*

My hand froze in its searching, my whole body froze into place, as I realized why I recognized the strange orange color on the water.

Victoria's hair, blowing wild in the wind, the color of fire . . .

She'd been right there. Right there in the harbor with me and Jacob. If Sam hadn't been there, if it had been just the two of us . . . ? I couldn't breathe or move.

The light flicked on, though my frozen hand had still not found the switch.

I blinked into the sudden light, and saw that someone was there, waiting for me.

17. VISITOR

UNNATURALLY STILL AND WHITE, WITH HER LARGE BLACK eyes intent on my face, my visitor waited perfectly motionless in the center of the hall, beautiful beyond imagining.

My knees trembled for a second, and I nearly fell. Then I hurled myself at her.

"Alice, oh, Alice!" I cried, as I slammed into her.

I'd forgotten how *hard* she was; it was like running headlong into a wall of cement.

"Bella?" There was a strange mingling of relief and confusion in her voice.

I locked my arms around her, gasping to inhale as much of the scent of her skin as possible. It wasn't like anything else—not floral or spice, citrus or musk. No perfume in the world could compare. My memory hadn't done it justice.

I didn't notice when the gasping turned into something else—I only realized I was sobbing when Alice dragged me to the living room couch and pulled me into her lap. It was like curling up into a cool stone, but a stone that was contoured comfortingly to the shape of my body. She rubbed my back in a gentle rhythm, waiting for me to get control of myself.

"I'm . . . sorry," I blubbered. "I'm just . . . so happy . . . to see you!"

"It's okay, Bella. Everything's okay."

"Yes," I bawled. And, for once, it seemed that way.

Alice sighed. "I'd forgotten how exuberant you are," she said, and her tone was disapproving.

I looked up at her through my streaming eyes. Alice's neck was tight, straining away from me, her lips pressed together firmly. Her eyes were black as pitch.

"Oh," I puffed, as I realized the problem. She was thirsty. And I smelled appetizing. It had been a while since I'd had to think about that kind of thing. "Sorry."

"It's my own fault. It's been too long since I hunted. I shouldn't let myself get so thirsty. But I was in a hurry today." The look she directed at me then was a glare. "Speaking of which, would you like to explain to me how you're alive?"

That brought me up short and stopped the sobs. I realized what must have happened immediately, and why Alice was here.

I swallowed loudly. "You saw me fall."

"No," she disagreed, her eyes narrowing. "I saw you *jump*."

I pursed my lips as I tried to think of an explanation that wouldn't sound nuts.

Alice shook her head. "I told him this would happen, but he didn't believe me. 'Bella promised,'" her voice imitated his so perfectly that I froze in shock while the pain ripped through my torso. "'Don't be looking for her future, either,'" she continued to quote him. "'We've done enough damage.'

"But just because I'm not looking, doesn't mean I don't *see*," she went on. "I wasn't keeping tabs on you, I swear, Bella. It's just that I'm already attuned to you . . . when I saw you jumping, I didn't think, I just got on a plane. I knew I would be too late, but I couldn't do *nothing*. And then I get here, thinking maybe I could help Charlie somehow, and you drive up." She shook her head, this time in confusion. Her voice was strained. "I saw you go into the water and I waited and waited for you to come up, but you didn't. What happened? And how could you do that to Charlie? Did you stop to think what this would do to him? And my brother? Do you have *any* idea what Edward—"

I cut her off then, as soon as she said his name. I'd let her go on, even after I realized the misunderstanding she was under, just to hear the perfect bell tone of her voice. But it was time to interrupt.

"Alice, I wasn't committing suicide."

She eyed me dubiously. "Are you saying you didn't jump off a cliff?"

"No, but . . . " I grimaced. "It was for recreational purposes only."

Her expression hardened.

"I'd seen some of Jacob's friends cliff diving," I insisted. "It looked like . . . fun, and I was bored. . . ."

She waited.

"I didn't think about how the storm would affect the currents. Actually, I didn't think about the water much at all."

Alice didn't buy it. I could see that she still thought I had been trying to kill myself. I decided to redirect. "So if you saw me go in, why didn't you see Jacob?"

She cocked her head to the side, distracted.

I continued. "It's true that I probably would have drowned if Jacob hadn't jumped in after me. Well, okay, there's no probably about it. But he did, and he pulled me out, and I guess he towed me back to shore, though I was kind of out for that part. It couldn't have been more than a minute that I was under before he grabbed me. How come you didn't see that?"

She frowned in perplexity. "Someone pulled you out?"

"Yes. Jacob saved me."

I watched curiously as an enigmatic range of emotions flitted across her face. Something was bothering her—her imperfect vision? But I wasn't sure. Then she deliberately leaned in and sniffed my shoulder.

I froze.

"Don't be ridiculous," she muttered, sniffing at me some more.

"What are you doing?"

She ignored my question. "Who was with you out there just now? It sounded like you were arguing."

"Jacob Black. He's . . . sort of my best friend, I guess. At least, he was . . ." I thought of Jacob's angry, betrayed face, and wondered what he was to me now.

Alice nodded, seeming preoccupied.

"What?"

"I don't know," she said. "I'm not sure what it means."

"Well, I'm not dead, at least."

She rolled her eyes. "He was a fool to think you could survive alone. I've never seen anyone so prone to life-threatening idiocy."

"I survived," I pointed out.

She was thinking of something else. "So, if the currents were too much for you, how did this Jacob manage?"

"Jacob is . . . strong."

She heard the reluctance in my voice, and her eyebrows rose.

I gnawed on my lip for a second. Was this a secret, or not? And if it was, then who was my greatest allegiance to? Jacob, or Alice?

It was too hard to keep secrets, I decided. Jacob knew everything, why not Alice, too?

"See, well, he's . . . sort of a werewolf," I admitted in a rush. "The Quileutes turn into wolves when there are vampires around. They know Carlisle from a long time ago. Were you with Carlisle back then?"

Alice gawked at me for a moment, and then recovered herself, blinking rapidly. "Well, I guess that explains the smell," she muttered. "But does it explain what I didn't see?" She frowned, her porcelain forehead creasing.

"The smell?" I repeated.

"You smell awful," she said absently, still frowning. "A werewolf? Are you sure about that?"

"Very sure," I promised, wincing as I remembered Paul and Jacob fighting in the road. "I guess you weren't with Carlisle the last time there were werewolves here in Forks?"

"No. I hadn't found him yet." Alice was still lost in thought. Suddenly, her eyes widened, and she turned to stare at me with a shocked expression. "Your best friend is a werewolf?"

I nodded sheepishly.

"How long has this been going on?"

"Not long," I said, my voice sounding defensive. "He's only been a werewolf for just a few weeks."

She glowered at me. "A *young* werewolf? Even worse! Edward was right—you're a magnet for danger. Weren't you supposed to be staying out of trouble?"

"There's nothing wrong with werewolves," I grumbled, stung by her critical tone.

"Until they lose their tempers." She shook her head sharply from side to side. "Leave it to you, Bella. Anyone else would be better off when the vampires left town. But you have to start hanging out with the first monsters you can find."

I didn't want to argue with Alice—I was still trembling

with joy that she was really, truly here, that I could touch her marble skin and hear her wind-chime voice—but she had it all wrong.

"No, Alice, the vampires didn't really leave—not all of them, anyway. That's the whole trouble. If it weren't for the werewolves, Victoria would have gotten me by now. Well, if it weren't for Jake and his friends, Laurent would have gotten me before she could, I guess, so—"

"Victoria?" she hissed. "Laurent?"

I nodded, a teensy bit alarmed by the expression in her black eyes. I pointed at my chest. "Danger magnet, remember?"

She shook her head again. "Tell me everything—start at the beginning."

I glossed over the beginning, skipping the motorcycles and the voices, but telling her everything else right up to today's misadventure. Alice didn't like my thin explanation about boredom and the cliffs, so I hurried on to the strange flame I'd seen on the water and what I thought it meant. Her eyes narrowed almost to slits at that part. It was strange to see her look so . . . so dangerous—like a vampire. I swallowed hard and went on with the rest about Harry.

She listened to my story without interrupting. Occasionally, she would shake her head, and the crease in her forehead deepened until it looked like it was carved permanently into the marble of her skin. She didn't speak and, finally, I fell quiet, struck again by the borrowed grief at Harry's passing. I thought of Charlie; he would be home soon. What condition would he be in?

"Our leaving didn't do you any good at all, did it?" Alice murmured.

I laughed once—it was a slightly hysterical sound. "That was never the point, though, was it? It's not like you left for my benefit."

Alice scowled at the floor for a moment. "Well . . . I guess I acted impulsively today. I probably shouldn't have intruded."

I could feel the blood draining from my face. My stomach dropped. "Don't go, Alice," I whispered. My fingers locked around the collar of her white shirt and I began to hyperventilate. "Please don't leave me."

Her eyes opened wider. "All right," she said, enunciating each word with slow precision. "I'm not going anywhere tonight. Take a deep breath."

I tried to obey, though I couldn't quite locate my lungs.

She watched my face while I concentrated on my breathing. She waited till I was calmer to comment.

"You look like hell, Bella."

"I drowned today," I reminded her.

"It goes deeper than that. You're a mess."

I flinched. "Look, I'm doing my best."

"What do you mean?"

"It hasn't been easy. I'm working on it."

She frowned. "I told him," she said to herself.

"Alice," I sighed. "What did you think you were going to find? I mean, besides me dead? Did you expect to find me skipping around and whistling show tunes? You know me better than that."

"I do. But I hoped."

"Then I guess I don't have the corner on the idiocy market."

The phone rang.

"That has to be Charlie," I said, staggering to my feet. I grabbed Alice's stone hand and dragged her with me to the kitchen. I wasn't about to let her out of my sight.

"Charlie?" I answered the phone.

"No, it's me," Jacob said.

"Jake!"

Alice scrutinized my expression.

"Just making sure you were still alive," Jacob said sourly.

"I'm fine. I told you that it wasn't—"

"Yeah. I got it. 'Bye."

Jacob hung up on me.

I sighed and let my head hang back, staring at the ceiling. "That's going to be a problem."

Alice squeezed my hand. "They aren't excited I'm here."

"Not especially. But it's none of their business anyway."

Alice put her arm around me. "So what do we do now?" she mused. She seemed to talk to herself for a moment. "Things to do. Loose ends to tie."

"What things to do?"

Her face was suddenly careful. "I don't know for sure . . . I need to see Carlisle."

Would she leave so soon? My stomach dropped.

"Could you stay?" I begged. "Please? For just a little while. I've missed you so much." My voice broke.

"If you think that's a good idea." Her eyes were unhappy.

"I do. You can stay here—Charlie would love that."

"I have a house, Bella."

I nodded, disappointed but resigned. She hesitated, studying me.

"Well, I need to go get a suitcase of clothes, at the very least."

I threw my arms around her. "Alice, you're the best!"

"And I think I'll need to hunt. Immediately," she added in a strained voice.

"Oops." I took a step back.

"Can you stay out of trouble for one hour?" she asked skeptically. Then, before I could answer, she held up one finger and closed her eyes. Her face went smooth and blank for a few seconds.

And then her eyes opened and she answered her own question. "Yes, you'll be fine. For tonight, anyway." She grimaced. Even making faces, she looked like an angel.

"You'll come back?" I asked in a small voice.

"I promise—one hour."

I glanced at the clock over the kitchen table. She laughed and leaned in quickly to kiss me on the cheek. Then she was gone.

I took a deep breath. Alice would be back. I suddenly felt so much better.

I had plenty to do to keep myself busy while I waited. A shower was definitely first on the agenda. I sniffed my shoulders as I undressed, but I couldn't smell anything but the brine and seaweed scent of the ocean. I wondered what Alice had meant about me smelling bad.

When I was cleaned up, I went back to the kitchen. I couldn't see any signs that Charlie had eaten recently, and he would probably be hungry when he got back. I hummed tunelessly to myself as I moved around the kitchen.

While Thursday's casserole rotated in the microwave, I made up the couch with sheets and an old pillow. Alice wouldn't need it, but Charlie would need to see it. I was careful not to watch the clock. There was no reason to start myself panicking; Alice had promised.

I hurried through my dinner, not tasting it—just feeling the ache as it slid down my raw throat. Mostly I was thirsty; I must have drunk a half gallon of water by the time I was finished. All the salt in my system had dehydrated me.

I went to go try to watch TV while I waited.

Alice was already there, sitting on her improvised bed. Her eyes were a liquid butterscotch. She smiled and patted the pillow. "Thanks."

"You're early," I said, elated.

I sat down next to her and leaned my head on her shoulder. She put her cold arms around me and sighed.

"Bella. What *are* we going to do with you?"

"I don't know," I admitted. "I really have been trying my hardest."

"I believe you."

It was silent.

"Does—does he . . ." I took a deep breath. It was harder

to say his name out loud, even though I was able to think it now. "Does Edward know you're here?" I couldn't help asking. It was my pain, after all. I'd deal with it when she was gone, I promised myself, and felt sick at the thought.

"No."

There was only one way that could be true. "He's not with Carlisle and Esme?"

"He checks in every few months."

"Oh." He must still be out enjoying his distractions. I focused my curiosity on a safer topic. "You said you flew here. . . . Where did you come from?"

"I was in Denali. Visiting Tanya's family."

"Is Jasper here? Did he come with you?"

She shook her head. "He didn't approve of my interfering. We promised. . . ." she trailed off, and then her tone changed. "And you think Charlie won't mind my being here?" she asked, sounding worried.

"Charlie thinks you're wonderful, Alice."

"Well, we're about to find out."

Sure enough, a few seconds later I heard the cruiser pull into the driveway. I jumped up and hurried to open the door.

Charlie trudged slowly up the walk, his eyes on the ground and his shoulders slumped. I walked forward to meet him; he didn't even see me until I hugged him around the waist. He embraced me back fiercely.

"I'm so sorry about Harry, Dad."

"I'm really going to miss him," Charlie mumbled.

"How's Sue doing?"

"She seems dazed, like she hasn't grasped it yet. Sam's

staying with her. . . ." The volume of his voice faded in and out. "Those poor kids. Leah's just a year older than you, and Seth is only fourteen. . . ." He shook his head.

He kept his arms tight around me as he started toward the door again.

"Um, Dad?" I figured I'd better warn him. "You'll never guess who's here."

He looked at me blankly. His head swiveled around, and he spied the Mercedes across the street, the porch light reflecting off the glossy black paint. Before he could react, Alice was in the doorway.

"Hi, Charlie," she said in a subdued voice. "I'm sorry I came at such a bad time."

"Alice Cullen?" he peered at the slight figure in front of him as if he doubted what his eyes were telling him. "Alice, is that you?"

"It's me," she confirmed. "I was in the neighborhood."

"Is Carlisle . . .?"

"No, I'm alone."

Both Alice and I knew he wasn't really asking about Carlisle. His arm tightened over my shoulder.

"She can stay here, can't she?" I pleaded. "I already asked her."

"Of course," Charlie said mechanically. "We'd love to have you, Alice."

"Thank you, Charlie. I know it's horrid timing."

"No, it's fine, really. I'm going to be really busy doing what I can for Harry's family; it will be nice for Bella to have some company."

"There's dinner for you on the table, Dad," I told him.

"Thanks, Bell." He gave me one more squeeze before he shuffled toward the kitchen.

Alice went back to the couch, and I followed her. This time, she was the one to pull me against her shoulder.

"You look tired."

"Yeah," I agreed, and shrugged. "Near-death experiences do that to me. . . . So, what does Carlisle think of you being here?"

"He doesn't know. He and Esme were on a hunting trip. I'll hear from him in a few days, when he gets back."

"You won't tell *him*, though . . . when he checks in again?" I asked. She knew I didn't mean Carlisle now.

"No. He'd bite my head off," Alice said grimly.

I laughed once, and then sighed.

I didn't want to sleep. I wanted to stay up all night talking to Alice. And it didn't make sense for me to be tired, what with crashing on Jacob's couch all day. But drowning really *had* taken a lot out of me, and my eyes wouldn't stay open. I rested my head on her stone shoulder, and drifted into a more peaceful oblivion than I had any hope of.

I woke early, from a deep and dreamless sleep, feeling well-rested, but stiff. I was on the couch tucked under the blankets I'd laid out for Alice, and I could hear her and Charlie talking in the kitchen. It sounded like Charlie was fixing her breakfast.

"How bad was it, Charlie?" Alice asked softly, and at first I thought they were talking about the Clearwaters.

Charlie sighed. "Real bad."

"Tell me about it. I want to know exactly what happened when we left."

There was a pause while a cupboard door was closed and a dial on the stove was clicked off. I waited, cringing.

"I've never felt so helpless," Charlie began slowly. "I didn't know what to do. That first week—I thought I was going to have to hospitalize her. She wouldn't eat or drink, she wouldn't move. Dr. Gerandy was throwing around words like 'catatonic,' but I didn't let him up to see her. I was afraid it would scare her."

"She snapped out of it though?"

"I had Renée come to take her to Florida. I just didn't want to be the one . . . if she had to go to a hospital or something. I hoped being with her mother would help. But when we started packing her clothes, she woke up with a vengeance. I've never seen Bella throw a fit like that. She was never one for the tantrums, but, boy, did she fly into a fury. She threw her clothes everywhere and screamed that we couldn't make her leave—and then she finally started crying. I thought that would be the turning point. I didn't argue when she insisted on staying here . . . and she did seem to get better at first. . . ."

Charlie trailed off. It was hard listening to this, knowing how much pain I'd caused him.

"But?" Alice prompted.

"She went back to school and work, she ate and slept and did her homework. She answered when someone asked her a direct question. But she was . . . empty. Her eyes were blank. There were lots of little things—she wouldn't listen to music anymore; I found a bunch of CDs broken in the trash. She didn't read; she wouldn't be in the same room when the TV was on, not that she watched it so much before. I finally figured it out—she was avoiding everything that might remind her of . . . him.

"We could hardly talk; I was so worried about saying something that would upset her—the littlest things would make her flinch—and she never volunteered anything. She would just answer if I asked her something.

"She was alone all the time. She didn't call her friends back, and after a while, they stopped calling.

"It was night of the living dead around here. I still hear her screaming in her sleep. . . ."

I could almost see him shuddering. I shuddered, too, remembering. And then I sighed. I hadn't fooled him at all, not for one second.

"I'm so sorry, Charlie," Alice said, voice glum.

"It's not *your* fault." The way he said it made it perfectly clear that he was holding someone responsible. "You were always a good friend to her."

"She seems better now, though."

"Yeah. Ever since she started hanging out with Jacob Black, I've noticed a real improvement. She has some color in her cheeks when she comes home, some light in her eyes. She's happier." He paused, and his voice was different when he spoke again. "He's a year or so younger than her, and I know she used to think of him as a friend, but I think maybe it's something more now, or headed that direction, anyway." Charlie said this in a tone that was almost belligerent. It was a warning, not for Alice, but for her to pass along. "Jake's old for his years," he continued, still sounding defensive. "He's taken care of his father physically the way Bella took care of her mother emotionally. It matured him. He's a good-looking kid, too—takes after his mom's side. He's good for Bella, you know," Charlie insisted.

"Then it's good she has him," Alice agreed.

Charlie sighed out a big gust of air, folding quickly to the lack of opposition. "Okay, so I guess that's overstating things. I don't know . . . even with Jacob, now and then I see something in her eyes, and I wonder if I've ever grasped how much pain she's really in. It's not normal, Alice, and it . . . it frightens me. Not normal at all. Not like someone . . . left her, but like someone died." His voice cracked.

It *was* like someone had died—like *I* had died. Because it had been more than just losing the truest of true loves, as if that were not enough to kill anyone. It was also losing a whole future, a whole family—the whole life that I'd chosen. . . .

Charlie went on in a hopeless tone. "I don't know if she's going to get over it—I'm not sure if it's in her nature to heal from something like this. She's always been such a constant little thing. She doesn't get past things, change her mind."

"She's one of a kind," Alice agreed in a dry voice.

"And Alice . . ." Charlie hesitated. "Now, you know how fond I am of you, and I can tell that she's happy to see you, but . . . I'm a little worried about what your visit will do to her."

"So am I, Charlie, so am I. I wouldn't have come if I'd had any idea. I'm sorry."

"Don't apologize, honey. Who knows? Maybe it will be good for her."

"I hope you're right."

There was a long break while forks scraped plates and Charlie chewed. I wondered where Alice was hiding the food.

"Alice, I have to ask you something," Charlie said awkwardly.

Alice was calm. "Go ahead."

"He's not coming back to visit, too, is he?" I could hear the suppressed anger in Charlie's voice.

Alice answered in a soft, reassuring tone. "He doesn't even know I'm here. The last time I spoke with him, he was in South America."

I stiffened as I heard this new information, and listened harder.

"That's something, at least." Charlie snorted. "Well, I hope he's enjoying himself."

For the first time, Alice's voice had a bit of steel in it. "I wouldn't make assumptions, Charlie." I knew how her eyes would flash when she used that tone.

A chair scooted from the table, scraping loudly across the floor. I pictured Charlie getting up; there was no way Alice would make that kind of noise. The faucet ran, splashing against a dish.

It didn't sound like they were going to say anything more about Edward, so I decided it was time to wake up.

I turned over, bouncing against the springs to make them squeak. Then I yawned loudly.

All was quiet in the kitchen.

I stretched and groaned.

"Alice?" I asked innocently; the soreness rasping in my throat added nicely to the charade.

"I'm in the kitchen, Bella," Alice called, no hint in her voice that she suspected my eavesdropping. But she was good at hiding things like that.

Charlie had to leave then—he was helping Sue Clearwater with the funeral arrangements. It would have been a very long day without Alice. She never spoke about leaving, and I didn't ask her. I knew it was inevitable, but I put it out of my mind.

Instead, we talked about her family—all but one.

Carlisle was working nights in Ithaca and teaching part time at Cornell. Esme was restoring a seventeenth century house, a historical monument, in the forest north of the city. Emmett and Rosalie had gone to Europe for a few months on another honeymoon, but they were back now. Jasper was at Cornell, too, studying philosophy this time. And Alice had been doing some personal research, concerning the information I'd accidentally uncovered for her last spring. She'd successfully tracked down the asylum where she'd spent the last years of her human life. The life she had no memory of.

"My name was Mary Alice Brandon," she told me quietly. "I had a little sister named Cynthia. Her daughter—my niece—is still alive in Biloxi."

"Did you find out why they put you in . . . that place?" What would drive parents to that extreme? Even if their daughter saw visions of the future. . . .

She just shook her head, her topaz eyes thoughtful. "I

couldn't find much about them. I went through all the old newspapers on microfiche. My family wasn't mentioned often; they weren't part of the social circle that made the papers. My parents' engagement was there, and Cynthia's." The name fell uncertainly from her tongue. "My birth was announced . . . and my death. I found my grave. I also filched my admissions sheet from the old asylum archives. The date on the admission and the date on my tombstone are the same."

I didn't know what to say, and, after a short pause, Alice moved on to lighter topics.

The Cullens were reassembled now, with the one exception, spending Cornell's spring break in Denali with Tanya and her family. I listened too eagerly to even the most trivial news. She never mentioned the one I was most interested in, and for that I was grateful. It was enough to listen to the stories of the family I'd once dreamed of belonging to.

Charlie didn't get back until after dark, and he looked more worn than he had the night before. He would be headed back to the reservation first thing in the morning for Harry's funeral, so he turned in early. I stayed on the couch with Alice again.

Charlie was almost a stranger when he came down the stairs before the sun was up, wearing an old suit I'd never seen him in before. The jacket hung open; I guessed it was too tight to fasten the buttons. His tie was a bit wide for the current style. He tiptoed to the door, trying not to wake us up. I let him go, pretending to sleep, as Alice did on the recliner.

As soon as he was out the door, Alice sat up. Under the quilt, she was fully dressed.

"So, what are we doing today?" she asked.

"I don't know—do you see anything interesting happening?"

She smiled and shook her head. "But it's still early."

All the time I'd been spending in La Push meant a pile of things I'd been neglecting at home, and I decided to catch up on my chores. I wanted to do something, anything that might make life easier for Charlie—maybe it would make him feel just a little better to come home to a clean, organized house. I started with the bathroom—it showed the most signs of neglect.

While I worked, Alice leaned against the doorjamb and asked nonchalant questions about my, well, *our* high school friends and what they been up to since she'd left. Her face stayed casual and emotionless, but I sensed her disapproval when she realized how little I could tell her. Or maybe I just had a guilty conscience after eavesdropping on her conversation with Charlie yesterday morning.

I was literally up to my elbows in Comet, scrubbing the floor of the bathtub, when the doorbell rang.

I looked to Alice at once, and her expression was perplexed, almost worried, which was strange; Alice was never taken by surprise.

"Hold on!" I shouted in the general direction of the

front door, getting up and hurrying to the sink to rinse my arms off.

"Bella," Alice said with a trace of frustration in her voice, "I have a fairly good guess who that might be, and I think I'd better step out."

"Guess?" I echoed. Since when did Alice have to guess anything?

"If this is a repeat of my egregious lapse in foresight yesterday, then it's most likely Jacob Black or one of his . . . friends."

I stared at her, putting it together. "You can't *see* werewolves?"

She grimaced. "So it would seem." She was obviously annoyed by this fact—*very* annoyed.

The doorbell rang again—buzzing twice quickly and impatiently.

"You don't have go anywhere, Alice. You were here first."

She laughed her silvery little laugh—it had a dark edge. "Trust me—it wouldn't be a good idea to have me and Jacob Black in a room together."

She kissed my cheek swiftly before she vanished through Charlie's door—and out his back window, no doubt.

The doorbell rang again.

18. THE FUNERAL

I sprinted down the stairs and threw the door open.

It was Jacob, of course. Even blind, Alice wasn't slow.

He was standing about six feet back from the door, his nose wrinkled in distaste, but his face otherwise smooth—masklike. He didn't fool me; I could see the faint trembling of his hands.

Hostility rolled off of him in waves. It brought back that awful afternoon when he'd chosen Sam over me, and I felt my chin jerk up defensively in response.

Jacob's Rabbit idled by the curb with Jared behind the wheel and Embry in the passenger seat. I understood what this meant: they were afraid to let him come here alone. It made me sad, and a little annoyed. The Cullens weren't like that.

"Hey," I finally said when he didn't speak.

Jake pursed his lips, still hanging back from the door. His eyes flickered across the front of the house.

I ground my teeth. "She's not here. Do you need something?"

He hesitated. "You're alone?"

"Yes." I sighed.

"Can I talk to you a minute?"

"*Of course* you can, Jacob. Come on in."

Jacob glanced over his shoulder at his friends in the car. I saw Embry shake his head just a tiny bit. For some reason, this bugged me to no end.

My teeth clenched together again. "*Chicken*," I mumbled under my breath.

Jake's eyes flashed back to me, his thick, black brows pushing into a furious angle over his deep-set eyes. His jaw set, and he marched—there was no other way to describe the way he moved—up the sidewalk and shrugged past me into the house.

I locked gazes with first Jared and then Embry—I didn't like the hard way they eyed me; did they really think I would let anything hurt Jacob?—before I shut the door on them.

Jacob was in the hall behind me, staring at the mess of blankets in the living room.

"Slumber party?" he asked, his tone sarcastic.

"Yeah," I answered with the same level of acid. I didn't like Jacob when he acted this way. "What's it to you?"

He wrinkled his nose again like he smelled something unpleasant. "Where's your 'friend'?" I could hear the quotation marks in his tone.

"She had some errands to run. Look, Jacob, what do you want?"

Something about the room seemed to make him edgier—his long arms were quivering. He didn't answer my question. Instead he moved on to the kitchen, his restless eyes darting everywhere.

I followed him. He paced back and forth along the short counter.

"Hey," I said, putting myself in his way. He stopped pacing and stared down at me. "What's your problem?"

"I don't like having to be here."

That stung. I winced, and his eyes tightened.

"Then I'm sorry you had to come," I muttered. "Why don't you tell me what you need so you can leave?"

"I just have to ask you a couple of questions. It shouldn't take long. We have to get back for the funeral."

"Okay. Get it over with then." I was probably overdoing it with the antagonism, but I didn't want him to see how much this hurt. I knew I wasn't being fair. After all, I'd picked the *bloodsucker* over him last night. I'd hurt him first.

He took a deep breath, and his trembling fingers were suddenly still. His face smoothed into a serene mask.

"One of the Cullens is staying here with you," he stated.

"Yes. Alice Cullen."

He nodded thoughtfully. "How long is she here for?"

"As long as she wants to be." The belligerence was still there in my tone. "It's an open invitation."

"Do you think you could . . . please . . . explain to her about the other one—Victoria?"

I paled. "I told her about that."

He nodded. "You should know that we can only watch our own lands with a Cullen here. You'll only be safe in La Push. I can't protect you here anymore."

"Okay," I said in a small voice.

He looked away then, out the back windows. He didn't continue.

"Is that all?"

He kept his eyes on the glass as he answered. "Just one more thing."

I waited, but he didn't continue. "Yes?" I finally prompted.

"Are the rest of them coming back now?" he asked in a cool, quiet voice. It reminded me of Sam's always calm manner. Jacob was becoming more like Sam. . . . I wondered why that bothered me so much.

Now *I* didn't speak. He looked back at my face with probing eyes.

"Well?" he asked. He struggled to conceal the tension behind his serene expression.

"No." I said finally. Grudgingly. "They aren't coming back."

His expression didn't change. "Okay. That's all."

I glared at him, annoyance rekindled. "Well, run along now. Go tell Sam that the scary monsters aren't coming to get you."

"Okay," he repeated, still calm.

That seemed to be it. Jacob walked swiftly from the

kitchen. I waited to hear the front door open, but I heard nothing. I could hear the clock over the stove ticking, and I marveled again at how quiet he'd become.

What a disaster. How could I have alienated him so completely in such a short amount of time?

Would he forgive me when Alice was gone? What if he didn't?

I slumped against the counter and buried my face in my hands. How had I made such a mess of everything? But what could I have done differently? Even in hindsight, I couldn't think of any better way, any perfect course of action.

"Bella . . . ?" Jacob asked in a troubled voice.

I pulled my face out of my hands to see Jacob hesitating in the kitchen doorway; he hadn't left when I'd thought. It was only when I saw the clear drops sparkling in my hands that I realized I was crying.

Jacob's calm expression was gone; his face was anxious and unsure. He walked quickly back to stand in front of me, ducking his head so that his eyes were closer to being on the same level with mine.

"Did it again, didn't I?"

"Did what?" I asked, my voice cracking.

"Broke my promise. Sorry."

"'S'okay," I mumbled. "I started it this time."

His face twisted. "I knew how you felt about them. It shouldn't have taken me by surprise like that."

I could see the revulsion in his eyes. I wanted to explain to him what Alice was really like, to defend her against the judgments he'd made, but something warned me that now was not the time.

So I just said, "Sorry," again.

"Let's not worry about it, okay? She's just visiting, right? She'll leave, and things will go back to normal."

"Can't I be friends with you both at the same time?" I asked, my voice not hiding an ounce of the hurt I felt.

He shook his head slowly. "No, I don't think you can."

I sniffed and stared at his big feet. "But you'll wait, right? You'll still be my friend, even though I love Alice, too?"

I didn't look up, afraid to see what he'd think of that last part. It took him a minute to answer, so I was probably right not to look.

"Yeah, I'll always be your friend," he said gruffly. "No matter what you love."

"Promise?"

"Promise."

I felt his arms wind around me, and I leaned against his chest, still sniffling. "This sucks."

"Yeah." Then he sniffed my hair and said, "Ew."

"*What*!" I demanded. I looked up to see that his nose was wrinkled again. "Why does everyone keep doing that to me? I don't smell!"

He smiled a little. "Yes, you do—you smell like *them*. Blech. Too sweet—sickly sweet. And . . . icy. It burns my nose."

"Really?" That was strange. Alice smelled unbelievably wonderful. To a human, anyway. "But why would Alice think I smelled, too, then?"

That wiped his smile away. "Huh. Maybe I don't smell so good to her, either. Huh."

"Well, you both smell fine to me." I rested my head against him again. I was going to miss him terribly when he walked out my door. It was a nasty catch-22—on the one hand, I wanted Alice to stay forever. I was going to die—metaphorically—when she left me. But how was I supposed to go without seeing Jake for any length of time? *What a mess*, I thought again.

"I'll miss you," Jacob whispered, echoing my thoughts. "Every minute. I hope she leaves soon."

"It really doesn't have to be that way, Jake."

He sighed. "Yes, it really does, Bella. You . . . love her. So I'd better not get anywhere near her. I'm not sure that I'm even-tempered enough to handle that. Sam would be mad if I broke the treaty, and"—his voice turned sarcastic—"you probably wouldn't like it too much if I killed your friend."

I recoiled from him when he said that, but he only tightened his arms, refusing to let me escape. "There's no point in avoiding the truth. That's the way things are, Bells."

"I do *not* like the way things are."

Jacob freed one arm so that he could cup his big brown hand under my chin and make me look at him. "Yeah. It was easier when we were both human, wasn't it?"

I sighed.

We stared at each other for a long moment. His hand smoldered against my skin. In my face, I knew there was nothing but wistful sadness—I didn't want to have to say goodbye now, no matter for how short a time. At first his face reflected mine, but then, as neither of us looked away, his expression changed.

He released me, lifting his other hand to brush his fingertips along my cheek, trailing them down to my jaw. I could feel his fingers tremble—not with anger this time. He pressed his palm against my cheek, so that my face was trapped between his burning hands.

"Bella," he whispered.

I was frozen.

No! I hadn't made this decision yet. I didn't know if I could do this, and now I was out of time to think. But I would have been a fool if I thought rejecting him now would have no consequences.

I stared back at him. He was not *my* Jacob, but he could be. His face was familiar and beloved. In so many real ways, I did love him. He was my comfort, my safe harbor. Right now, I could choose to have him belong to me.

Alice was back for the moment, but that changed nothing. True love was forever lost. The prince was never coming back to kiss me awake from my enchanted sleep. I was not a princess, after all. So what was the fairy-tale protocol for *other* kisses? The mundane kind that didn't break any spells?

Maybe it would be easy—like holding his hand or having his arms around me. Maybe it would feel nice. Maybe it wouldn't feel like a betrayal. Besides, who was I betraying, anyway? Just myself.

Keeping his eyes on mine, Jacob began to bend his face toward me. And I was still absolutely undecided.

The shrill ring of the phone made us both jump, but it did not break his focus. He took his hand from under my chin and reached over me to grab the receiver, but still held my face securely with the hand against my cheek. His dark eyes did not free mine. I was too muddled to react, even to take advantage of the distraction.

"Swan residence," Jacob said, his husky voice low and intense.

Someone answered, and Jacob altered in an instant. He straightened up, and his hand dropped from my face. His eyes went flat, his face blank, and I would have bet the measly remainder of my college fund that it was Alice.

I recovered myself and held out my hand for the phone. Jacob ignored me.

"He's not here," Jacob said, and the words were menacing.

There was some very short reply, a request for more information it seemed, because he added unwillingly, "He's at the funeral."

Then Jacob hung up the phone. "Filthy bloodsucker," he muttered under his breath. The face he turned back to me was the bitter mask again.

"Who did you just hang up on?" I gasped, infuriated. "In *my* house, and on *my* phone?"

"Easy! He hung up on me!"

"He? Who was it?!"

He sneered the title. "*Dr.* Carlisle Cullen."

"Why didn't you let me talk to him?!"

"He didn't ask for you," Jacob said coldly. His face was smooth, expressionless, but his hands shook. "He asked where Charlie was and I told him. I don't think I broke any rules of etiquette."

"You listen to me, Jacob Black—"

But he obviously wasn't listening. He looked quickly over his shoulder, as if someone had called his name from the other room. His eyes went wide and his body stiff, then he started trembling. I listened too, automatically, but heard nothing.

"Bye, Bells," he spit out, and wheeled toward the front door.

I ran after him. "What is it?"

And then I ran into him, as he rocked back on his heels, cussing under his breath. He spun around again, knocking me sideways. I bobbled and fell to the floor, my legs tangled with his.

"Shoot, ow!" I protested as he hurriedly jerked his legs free one at a time.

I struggled to pull myself up as he darted for the back door; he suddenly froze again.

Alice stood motionless at the foot of the stairs.

"Bella," she choked.

I scrambled to my feet and lurched to her side. Her eyes were dazed and far away, her face drawn and whiter than bone. Her slim body trembled to an inner turmoil.

"Alice, what's wrong?" I cried. I put my hands on her face, trying to calm her.

Her eyes focused on mine abruptly, wide with pain.

"Edward," was all she whispered.

My body reacted faster than my mind was able to catch up with the implications of her reply. I didn't at first understand why the room was spinning or where the hollow roar in my ears was coming from. My mind labored, unable to make sense of Alice's bleak face and how it could possibly relate to Edward, while my body was already swaying, seeking the relief of unconsciousness before the reality could hit me.

The stairway tilted at the oddest angle.

Jacob's furious voice was suddenly in my ear, hissing out a stream of profanities. I felt a vague disapproval. His new friends were clearly a bad influence.

I was on the couch without understanding how I got there, and Jacob was still swearing. It felt like there was an earthquake—the couch was shaking under me.

"What did you do to her?" he demanded.

Alice ignored him. "Bella? Bella, snap out of it. We have to hurry."

"Stay back," Jacob warned.

"Calm down, Jacob Black," Alice ordered. "You don't want to do that so close to her."

"I don't think I'll have any problem keeping my focus," he retorted, but his voice sounded a little cooler.

"Alice?" My voice was weak. "What happened?" I asked, even though I didn't want to hear.

"I don't know," she suddenly wailed. "What is he thinking?!"

I labored to pull myself up despite the dizziness. I realized it was Jacob's arm I was gripping for balance. He was the one shaking, not the couch.

Alice was pulling a small silver phone from her bag

when my eyes relocated her. Her fingers dialed the numbers so fast they were a blur.

"Rose, I need to talk to Carlisle *now*." Her voice whipped through the words. "Fine, as soon as he's back. No, I'll be on a plane. Look, have you heard anything from Edward?"

Alice paused now, listening with an expression that grew more appalled every second. Her mouth opened into a little O of horror, and the phone shook in her hand.

"Why?" she gasped. "*Why* would you do that, Rosalie?"

Whatever the answer was, it made her jaw tighten in anger. Her eyes flashed and narrowed.

"Well, you're wrong on both counts, though, Rosalie, so that would be a problem, don't you think?" she asked acidly. "Yes, that's right. She's absolutely fine—I was wrong. . . . It's a long story. . . . But you're wrong about that part, too, that's why I'm calling. . . . Yes, that's exactly what I saw."

Alice's voice was very hard and her lips were pulled back from her teeth. "It's a bit late for that, Rose. Save your remorse for someone who believes it." Alice snapped the phone shut with a sharp twist of her fingers.

Her eyes were tortured as she turned to face me.

"Alice," I blurted out quickly. I couldn't let her speak yet. I needed a few more seconds before she spoke and her words destroyed what was left of my life. "Alice, Carlisle is back, though. He called just before. . . ."

She stared at me blankly. "How long ago?" she asked in a hollow voice.

"Half a minute before you showed up."

"What did he say?" She really focused now, waiting for my answer.

"I didn't talk to him." My eyes flickered to Jacob.

Alice turned her penetrating gaze on him. He flinched, but held his place next to me. He sat awkwardly, almost as if he were trying to shield me with his body.

"He asked for Charlie, and I told him Charlie wasn't here," Jacob muttered resentfully.

"Is that everything?" Alice demanded, her voice like ice.

"Then he hung up on me," Jacob spit back. A tremor rolled down his spine, shaking me with it.

"You told him Charlie was at the funeral," I reminded him.

Alice jerked her head back toward me. "What were his exact words?"

"He said, 'He's not here,' and when Carlisle asked where Charlie was, Jacob said, 'At the funeral.'"

Alice moaned and sank to her knees.

"Tell me Alice," I whispered.

"That wasn't Carlisle on the phone," she said hopelessly.

"Are you calling me a liar?" Jacob snarled from beside me.

Alice ignored him, focusing on my bewildered face.

"It was Edward." The words were just a choked whisper. "He thinks you're dead."

My mind started to work again. These words weren't the ones I'd been afraid of, and the relief cleared my head.

"Rosalie told him I killed myself, didn't she?" I said, sighing as I relaxed.

"Yes," Alice admitted, her eyes flashing hard again.

"In her defense, she did believe it. They rely on my sight far too much for something that works so imperfectly. But for her to track him down to tell him this! Didn't she realize . . . or care . . . ?" Her voice faded away in horror.

"And when Edward called here, he thought Jacob meant *my* funeral," I realized. It stung to know how close I'd been, just inches away from his voice. My nails dug into Jacob's arm, but he didn't flinch.

Alice looked at me strangely. "You're not upset," she whispered.

"Well, it's really rotten timing, but it will all get straightened out. The next time he calls, someone will tell him . . . what . . . really . . ." I trailed off. Her gaze strangled the words in my throat.

Why was she so panicked? Why was her face twisting now with pity and horror? What was it she had said to Rosalie on the phone just now? Something about what she'd seen . . . and Rosalie's remorse; Rosalie would never feel remorse for anything that happened to me. But if she'd hurt her family, hurt her brother . . .

"Bella," Alice whispered. "Edward won't call again. He believed her."

"I. Don't. Understand." My mouth framed each word in silence. I couldn't push the air out to actually say the words that would make her explain what that meant.

"He's going to Italy."

It took the length of one heartbeat for me to comprehend.

When Edward's voice came back to me now, it was not the perfect imitation of my delusions. It was just the weak, flat tone of my memories. But the words alone were enough to shred through my chest and leave it gaping open. Words from a time when I would have bet everything that I owned or could borrow on that fact that he loved me.

Well, I wasn't going to live without you, he'd said as we watched Romeo and Juliet die, here in this very room. *But I wasn't sure how to do it. . . . I knew Emmett and Jasper would never help. . . . so I was thinking maybe I would go to Italy and do something to provoke the Volturi. . . . You don't irritate them. Not unless you want to die.*

Not unless you want to die.

"NO!" The half-shrieked denial was so loud after the whispered words, it made us all jump. I felt the blood rushing to my face as I realized what she'd seen. "No! No, no, no! He can't! He can't do that!"

"He made up his mind as soon as your friend confirmed that it was too late to save you."

"But he . . . he *left*! He didn't want me anymore! What difference does it make now? He knew I would die sometime!"

"I don't think he ever planned to outlive you by long," Alice said quietly.

"How *dare* he!" I screamed. I was on my feet now, and Jacob rose uncertainly to put himself between Alice and me again.

"Oh, get out of the way, Jacob!" I elbowed my way around his trembling body with desperate impatience. "What do we do?" I begged Alice. There had to be something. "Can't we call him? Can Carlisle?"

She was shaking her head. "That was the first thing I

tried. He left his phone in a trash can in Rio—someone answered it . . . ," she whispered.

"You said before we had to hurry. Hurry how? Let's do it, whatever it is!"

"Bella, I—I don't think I can ask you to . . ." She trailed off in indecision.

"Ask me!" I commanded.

She put her hands on my shoulders, holding me in place, her fingers flexing sporadically to emphasize her words. "We may already be too late. I saw him going to the Volturi . . . and asking to die." We both cringed, and my eyes were suddenly blind. I blinked feverishly at the tears. "It all depends on what they choose. I can't see that till they make a decision.

"But if they say no, and they might—Aro is fond of Carlisle, and wouldn't want to offend him—Edward has a backup plan. They're very protective of their city. If Edward does something to upset the peace, he thinks they'll act to stop him. And he's right. They will."

I stared at her with my jaw clenched in frustration. I'd heard nothing yet that would explain why we were still standing here.

"So if they agree to grant his favor, we're too late. If they say no, and he comes up with a plan to offend them quickly enough, we're too late. If he gives into his more theatrical tendencies . . . we might have time."

"Let's go!"

"Listen, Bella! Whether we are in time or not, we will be in the heart of the Volturi city. I will be considered his accomplice if he is successful. You will be a human who not only knows too much, but also smells too good. There's a very good chance that they will eliminate us all—though in your case it won't be punishment so much as dinnertime."

"This is what's keeping us here?" I asked in disbelief. "I'll go alone if you're afraid." I mentally tabulated what money was left in my account, and wondered if Alice would lend me the rest.

"I'm only afraid of getting you killed."

I snorted in disgust. "I almost get myself killed on a daily basis! Tell me what I need to do!"

"You write a note to Charlie. I'll call the airlines."

"Charlie," I gasped.

Not that my presence was protecting him, but could I leave him here alone to face . . .

"I'm not going to let anything happen to Charlie." Jacob's low voice was gruff and angry. "Screw the treaty."

I glanced up at him, and he scowled at my panicked expression.

"Hurry, Bella," Alice interrupted urgently.

I ran to the kitchen, yanking the drawers open and throwing the contents all over the floor as I searched for a pen. A smooth, brown hand held one out to me.

"Thanks," I mumbled, pulling the cap off with my teeth. He silently handed me the pad of paper we wrote phone messages on. I tore off the top sheet and threw it over my shoulder.

Dad, I wrote. *I'm with Alice. Edward's in trouble. You can ground me when I get back. I know it's a bad time. So sorry. Love you so much. Bella.*

"Don't go," Jacob whispered. The anger was all gone now that Alice was out of sight.

I wasn't about to waste time arguing with him. "Please, please, *please* take care of Charlie," I said as I dashed back out to the front room. Alice was waiting in the doorway with a bag over her shoulder.

"Get your wallet—you'll need ID. *Please* tell me you have a passport. I don't have time to forge one."

I nodded and then raced up the stairs, my knees weak with gratitude that my mother had wanted to marry Phil on a beach in Mexico. Of course, like all her plans, it had fallen through. But not before I'd made all the practical arrangements I could for her.

I tore through my room. I stuffed my old wallet, a clean T-shirt, and sweatpants into my backpack, and then threw my toothbrush on top. I hurled myself back down the stairs. The sense of déjà vu was nearly stifling by this point. At least, unlike the last time—when I'd run away from Forks to *escape* thirsty vampires rather than to *find* them—I wouldn't have to say goodbye to Charlie in person.

Jacob and Alice were locked in some kind of confrontation in front of the open door, standing so far apart you wouldn't assume at first that they were having a conversation. Neither one seemed to notice my noisy reappearance.

"You might control yourself on occasion, but these leeches you're taking her to—" Jacob was furiously accusing her.

"Yes. You're right, dog." Alice was snarling, too. "The Volturi are the very essence of our kind—they're the reason your hair stands on end when you smell me. They are the substance of your nightmares, the dread behind your instincts. I'm not unaware of that."

"And you take her to them like a bottle of wine for a party!" he shouted.

"You think she'd be better off if I left her here alone, with Victoria stalking her?"

"We can handle the redhead."

"Then why is she still hunting?"

Jacob growled, and a shudder rippled through his torso.

"Stop that!" I shouted at them both, wild with impatience. "Argue when we get back, let's go!"

Alice turned for the car, disappearing in her haste. I hurried after her, pausing automatically to turn and lock the door.

Jacob caught my arm with a shivering hand. "Please, Bella. I'm begging."

His dark eyes were glistening with tears. A lump filled my throat.

"Jake, I *have* to—"

"You don't, though. You really don't. You could stay here with me. You could stay alive. For Charlie. For me."

The engine of Carlisle's Mercedes purred; the rhythm of the thrumming spiked when Alice revved it impatiently.

I shook my head, tears spattering from my eyes with the sharp motion. I pulled my arm free, and he didn't fight me.

"Don't die, Bella," he choked out. "Don't go. Don't."

What if I never saw him again?

The thought pushed me past the silent tears; a sob broke out from my chest. I threw my arms around his waist and hugged for one too-short moment, burying my tear-wet face against his chest. He put his big hand on the back of my hair, as if to hold me there.

"Bye, Jake." I pulled his hand from my hair, and kissed his palm. I couldn't bear to look at his face. "Sorry," I whispered.

Then I spun and raced for the car. The door on the passenger side was open and waiting. I threw my backpack over the headrest and slid in, slamming the door behind me.

"Take care of Charlie!" I turned to shout out the window, but Jacob was nowhere in sight. As Alice stomped on the gas and—with the tires screeching like human screams—spun us around to face the road, I caught sight of a shred of white near the edge of the trees. A piece of a shoe.

19. RACE

WE MADE OUR FLIGHT WITH SECONDS TO SPARE, AND then the true torture began. The plane sat idle on the tarmac while the flight attendants strolled—so casually—up and down the aisle, patting the bags in the overhead compartments to make sure everything fit. The pilots leaned out of the cockpit, chatting with them as they passed. Alice's hand was hard on my shoulder, holding me in my seat while I bounced anxiously up and down.

"It's faster than running," she reminded me in a low voice.

I just nodded in time with my bouncing.

At last the plane rolled lazily from the gate, building speed with a gradual steadiness that tortured me further. I expected some kind of relief when we achieved liftoff, but my frenzied impatience didn't lessen.

Alice lifted the phone on the back of the seat in front of her before we'd stopped climbing, turning her back on the stewardess who eyed her with disapproval. Something about my expression stopped the stewardess from coming over to protest.

I tried to tune out what Alice was murmuring to Jasper; I didn't want to hear the words again, but some slipped through.

"I can't be sure, I keep seeing him do different things, he keeps changing his mind. . . . A killing spree through the city, attacking the guard, lifting a car over his head in the main square . . . mostly things that would expose them—he knows that's the fastest way to force a reaction. . . .

"No, you can't." Alice's voice dropped till it was nearly inaudible, though I was sitting inches from her. Contrarily, I listened harder. "Tell Emmett no. . . . Well, go after Emmett and Rosalie and bring them back. . . . Think about it, Jasper. If he sees any of us, what do you think he will do?"

She nodded. "Exactly. I think Bella is the only chance—if there is a chance. . . . I'll do everything that can be done, but prepare Carlisle; the odds aren't good."

She laughed then, and there was a catch in her voice. "I've thought of that. . . . Yes, I promise." Her voice became pleading. "Don't follow me. I promise, Jasper. One way or another, I'll get out. . . . And I love you."

She hung up, and leaned back in her seat with her eyes closed. "I hate lying to him."

"Tell me everything, Alice," I begged. "I don't understand. Why did you tell Jasper to stop Emmett, why can't they come help us?"

"Two reasons," she whispered, her eyes still closed. "The first I told him. We *could* try to stop Edward ourselves—if Emmett could get his hands on him, we might be able to stop him long enough to convince him you're alive. But we can't sneak up on Edward. And if he sees us coming for him, he'll just act that much faster. He'll throw a Buick through a wall or something, and the Volturi will take him down.

"That's the second reason of course, the reason I couldn't say to Jasper. Because if they're there and the Volturi kill Edward, they'll fight them. Bella." She opened her eyes and stared at me, beseeching. "If there were any chance we could win . . . if there were a way that the four of us could save my brother by fighting for him, maybe it would be different. But we can't, and, Bella, I can't lose Jasper like that."

I realized why her eyes begged for my understanding. She was protecting Jasper, at our expense, and maybe at Edward's, too. I understood, and I did not think badly of her. I nodded.

"Couldn't Edward hear you, though?" I asked. "Wouldn't he know, as soon as he heard your thoughts, that I was alive, that there was no point to this?"

Not that there was any justification, either way. I still couldn't believe that he was capable of reacting like this. It made no sense! I remembered with painful clarity his words that day on the sofa, while we watched Romeo and

Juliet kill themselves, one after the other. *I wasn't going to live without you*, he'd said, as if it should be such an obvious conclusion. But the words he had spoken in the forest as he'd left me had canceled all that out—forcefully.

"*If* he were listening," she explained. "But believe it or not, it's possible to lie with your thoughts. If you had died, I would still try to stop him. And I would be thinking 'she's alive, she's alive' as hard as I could. He knows that."

I ground my teeth in mute frustration.

"If there were any way to do this without you, Bella, I wouldn't be endangering you like this. It's very wrong of me."

"Don't be stupid. I'm the last thing you should be worrying about." I shook my head impatiently. "Tell me what you meant, about hating to lie to Jasper."

She smiled a grim smile. "I promised him I would get out before they killed me, too. It's not something I can guarantee—not by a long shot." She raised her eyebrows, as if willing me to take the danger more seriously.

"Who are these Volturi?" I demanded in a whisper. "What makes them so much more dangerous than Emmett, Jasper, Rosalie, and you?" It was hard to imagine something scarier than that.

She took a deep breath, and then abruptly leveled a dark glance over my shoulder. I turned in time to see the man in the aisle seat looking away as if he wasn't listening to us. He appeared to be a businessman, in a dark suit with a power tie and a laptop on his knees. While I stared at him with irritation, he opened the computer and very conspicuously put headphones on.

I leaned closer to Alice. Her lips were at my ears as she breathed the story.

"I was surprised that you recognized the name," she said. "That you understood so immediately what it meant—when I said he was going to Italy. I thought I would have to explain. How much did Edward tell you?"

"He just said they were an old, powerful family—like royalty. That you didn't antagonize them unless you wanted to . . . die," I whispered. The last word was hard to choke out.

"You have to understand," she said, her voice slower, more measured now. "We Cullens are unique in more ways than you know. It's . . . *abnormal* for so many of us to live together in peace. It's the same for Tanya's family in the north, and Carlisle speculates that abstaining makes it easier for us to be civilized, to form bonds based on love rather than survival or convenience. Even James's little coven of three was unusually large—and you saw how easily Laurent left them. Our kind travel alone, or in pairs, as a general rule. Carlisle's family is the biggest in existence, as far as I know, with the one exception. The Volturi.

"There were three of them originally, Aro, Caius, and Marcus."

"I've seen them," I mumbled. "In the picture in Carlisle's study."

Alice nodded. "Two females joined them over time, and the five of them make up the family. I'm not sure, but I suspect that their age is what gives them the ability to live peacefully together. They are well over three thousand years old. Or maybe it's their gifts that give them extra tolerance. Like Edward and I, Aro and Marcus are . . . talented."

She continued before I could ask. "Or maybe it's just their love of power that binds them together. Royalty is an apt description."

"But if there are only five——"

"Five that make up the family," she corrected. "That doesn't include their guard."

I took a deep breath. "That sounds . . . serious."

"Oh, it is," she assured me. "There were nine members of the guard that were permanent, the last time we heard. Others are more . . . transitory. It changes. And many of them are gifted as well—with formidable gifts, gifts that make what I can do look like a parlor trick. The Volturi chose them for their abilities, physical or otherwise."

I opened my mouth, and then closed it. I didn't think I wanted to know how bad the odds were.

She nodded again, as if she understood exactly what I was thinking. "They don't get into too many confrontations. No one is stupid enough to mess with them. They stay in their city, leaving only as duty calls."

"Duty?" I wondered.

"Didn't Edward tell you what they do?"

"No," I said, feeling the blank expression on my face.

Alice looked over my head again, toward the business-man, and put her wintry lips back to my ear.

"There's a reason he called them royalty . . . the ruling class. Over the millennia, they have assumed the position of enforcing our rules—which actually translates to punishing transgressors. They fulfill that duty decisively."

My eyes popped wide with shock. "There are *rules*?" I asked in a voice that was too loud.

"Shh!"

"Shouldn't somebody have mentioned this to me earlier?" I whispered angrily. "I mean, I wanted to be a . . . to be one of you! Shouldn't somebody have explained the rules to me?"

Alice chuckled once at my reaction. "It's not that complicated, Bella. There's only one core restriction—and if you think about it, you can probably figure it out for yourself."

I thought about it. "Nope, I have no idea."

She shook her head, disappointed. "Maybe it's too obvious. We just have to keep our existence a secret."

"Oh," I mumbled. It *was* obvious.

"It makes sense, and most of us don't need policing," she continued. "But, after a few centuries, sometimes one of us gets bored. Or crazy. I don't know. And then the Volturi step in before it can compromise them, or the rest of us."

"So Edward . . ."

"Is planning to flout that in their own city—the city they've secretly held for three thousand years, since the time of the Etruscans. They are so protective of their city that they don't allow hunting within its walls. Volterra is probably the safest city in the world—from vampire attack at the very least."

"But you said they didn't leave. How do they eat?"

"They don't leave. They bring in their food from the outside, from quite far away sometimes. It gives their guard something to do when they're not out annihilating mavericks. Or protecting Volterra from exposure . . ."

"From situations like this one, like Edward," I finished her sentence. It was amazingly easy to say his name now. I wasn't sure what the difference was. Maybe because I wasn't really planning on living much longer without seeing him. Or at all, if we were too late. It was comforting to know that I would have an easy out.

"I doubt they've ever had a situation quite like this," she muttered, disgusted. "You don't get a lot of suicidal vampires."

The sound that escaped out of my mouth was very quiet, but Alice seemed to understand that it was a cry of pain. She wrapped her thin, strong arm around my shoulders.

"We'll do what we can, Bella. It's not over yet."

"Not yet." I let her comfort me, though I knew she thought our chances were poor. "And the Volturi will get us if we mess up."

Alice stiffened. "You say that like it's a good thing."

I shrugged.

"Knock it off, Bella, or we're turning around in New York and going back to Forks."

"What?"

"You know what. If we're too late for Edward, I'm going to do my damnedest to get you back to Charlie, and I don't want any trouble from you. Do you understand that?"

"Sure, Alice."

She pulled back slightly so that she could glare at me. "No trouble."

"Scout's honor," I muttered.

She rolled her eyes.

"Let me concentrate, now. I'm trying to see what he's planning."

She left her arm around me, but let her head fall back against the seat and closed her eyes. She pressed her free hand to the side of her face, rubbing her fingertips against her temple.

I watched her in fascination for a long time. Eventually, she became utterly motionless, her face like a stone sculpture. The minutes passed, and if I didn't know better, I would have thought she'd fallen asleep. I didn't dare interrupt her to ask what was going on.

I wished there was something safe for me to think about. I couldn't allow myself to consider the horrors we were headed toward, or, more horrific yet, the chance that we might fail—not if I wanted to keep from screaming aloud.

I couldn't *anticipate* anything, either. Maybe, if I were very, very, *very* lucky, I would somehow be able to save Edward. But I wasn't so stupid as to think that saving him would mean that I could stay with him. I was no different, no more special than I'd been before. There would be no new reason for him to want me now. Seeing him and losing him again . . .

I fought back against the pain. This was the price I had to pay to save his life. I would pay it.

They showed a movie, and my neighbor got head-phones. Sometimes I watched the figures moving across the little screen, but I couldn't even tell if the movie was supposed to be a romance or a horror film.

After an eternity, the plane began to descend toward New York City. Alice remained in her trance. I dithered, reaching out to touch her, only to pull my hand back again. This happened a dozen times before the plane touched town with a jarring impact.

"Alice," I finally said. "Alice, we have to go."

I touched her arm.

Her eyes came open very slowly. She shook her head from side to side for a moment.

"Anything new?" I asked in a low voice, conscious of the man listening on the other side of me.

"Not exactly," she breathed in a voice I could barely catch. "He's getting closer. He's deciding how he's going to ask."

We had to run for our connection, but that was good—better than having to wait. As soon as the plane was in the air, Alice closed her eyes and slid back into the same stupor as before. I waited as patiently as I could. When it was dark again, I opened the window to stare out into the flat black that was no better than the window shade.

I was grateful that I'd had so many months' practice with controlling my thoughts. Instead of dwelling on the terrifying possibilities that, no matter what Alice said, I did not intend to survive, I concentrated on lesser problems. Like, what I was going to say to Charlie if I got back? That was a thorny enough problem to occupy several hours. And Jacob? He'd promised to wait for me, but did that promise still apply? Would I end up home alone in Forks, with no one at all? Maybe I didn't *want* to survive, no matter what happened.

It felt like seconds later when Alice shook my shoulder—I hadn't realized I'd fallen asleep.

"Bella," she hissed, her voice a little too loud in the darkened cabin full of sleeping humans.

I wasn't disoriented—I hadn't been out long enough for that.

"What's wrong?"

Alice's eyes gleamed in the dim light of a reading lamp in the row behind us.

"It's not wrong." She smiled fiercely. "It's right. They're deliberating, but they've decided to tell him no."

"The Volturi?" I muttered, groggy.

"Of course, Bella, keep up. I can see what they're going to say."

"Tell me."

An attendant tiptoed down the aisle to us. "Can I get you ladies a pillow?" His hushed whisper was a rebuke to our comparatively loud conversation.

"No, thank you." Alice beamed at up at him, her smile shockingly lovely. The attendant's expression was dazed as he turned and stumbled his way back.

"Tell me," I breathed almost silently.

She whispered into my ear. "They're interested in him—they think his talent could be useful. They're going to offer him a place with them."

"What will he say?"

"I can't see that yet, but I'll bet it's colorful." She grinned again. "This is the first good news—the first break. They're intrigued; they truly don't want to destroy him—'wasteful,' that's the word Aro will use—and that may be enough to force him to get creative. The longer he spends on his plans, the better for us."

It wasn't enough to make me hopeful, to make me feel the relief she obviously felt. There were still so many ways that we could be too late. And if I didn't get through the walls into the Volturi city, I wouldn't be able to stop Alice from dragging me back home.

"Alice?"

"What?"

"I'm confused. How are you seeing this so clearly? And then other times, you see things far away—things that don't happen?"

Her eyes tightened. I wondered if she guessed what I was thinking of.

"It's clear because it's immediate and close, and I'm really concentrating. The faraway things that come on their own—those are just glimpses, faint maybes. Plus, I see my kind more easily than yours. Edward is even easier because I'm so attuned to him."

"You see me sometimes," I reminded her.

She shook her head. "Not as clearly."

I sighed. "I really wish you could have been right about me. In the beginning, when you first saw things about me, before we even met . . ."

"What do you mean?"

"You saw me become one of you." I barely mouthed the words.

She sighed. "It was a possibility at the time."

"At the time," I repeated.

"Actually, Bella . . ." She hesitated, and then seemed to make a choice. "Honestly, I think it's all gotten beyond ridiculous. I'm debating whether to just change you my-self."

I stared at her, frozen with shock. Instantly, my mind resisted her words. I couldn't afford that kind of hope if she changed her mind.

"Did I scare you?" she wondered. "I thought that's what you wanted."

"I do!" I gasped. "Oh, Alice, do it now! I could help you so much—and I wouldn't slow you down. Bite me!"

"Shh," she cautioned. The attendant was looking in our direction again. "Try to be reasonable," she whispered. "We don't have enough time. We have to get into Volterra tomorrow. You'd be writhing in pain for days." She made a face. "And I don't think the other passengers would react well."

I bit my lip. "If you don't do it now, you'll change your mind."

"No." She frowned, her expression unhappy. "I don't think I will. He'll be furious, but what will he be able to do about it?"

My heart beat faster. "Nothing at all."

She laughed quietly, and then sighed. "You have too

much faith in me, Bella. I'm not sure that I *can*. I'll probably just end up killing you."

"I'll take my chances."

"You are so bizarre, even for a human."

"Thanks."

"Oh well, this is purely hypothetical at this point, anyway. First we have to live through tomorrow."

"Good point." But at least I had something to hope for if we did. If Alice made good on her promise—and if she didn't kill me—then Edward could run after his distractions all he wanted, and I could follow. I wouldn't let him be distracted. Maybe, when I was beautiful and strong, he wouldn't want distractions.

"Go back to sleep," she encouraged me. "I'll wake you up when there's something new."

"Right," I grumbled, certain that sleep was a lost cause now. Alice pulled her legs up on the seat, wrapping her arms around them and leaning her forehead against her knees. She rocked back and forth as she concentrated.

I rested my head against the seat, watching her, and the next thing I knew, she was snapping the shade closed against the faint brightening in the eastern sky.

"What's happening?" I mumbled.

"They've told him no," she said quietly. I noticed at once that her enthusiasm was gone.

My voice choked in my throat with panic. "What's he going to do?"

"It was chaotic at first. I was only getting flickers, he was changing plans so quickly."

"What kinds of plans?" I pressed.

"There was a bad hour," she whispered. "He'd decided to go hunting."

She looked at me, seeing the incomprehension in my face.

"In the city," she explained. "It got very close. He changed his mind at the last minute."

"He wouldn't want to disappoint Carlisle," I mumbled. Not at the end.

"Probably," she agreed.

"Will there be enough time?" As I spoke, there was a shift in the cabin pressure. I could feel the plane angling downward.

"I'm hoping so—if he sticks to his latest decision, maybe."

"What is that?"

"He's going to keep it simple. He's just going to walk out into the sun."

Just walk out into the sun. That was all.

It would be enough. The image of Edward in the meadow—glowing, shimmering like his skin was made of a million diamond facets—was burned into my memory. No human who saw that would ever forget. The Volturi couldn't possibly allow it. Not if they wanted to keep their city inconspicuous.

I looked at the slight gray glow that shone through the opened windows. "We'll be too late," I whispered, my throat closing in panic.

She shook her head. "Right now, he's leaning toward the melodramatic. He wants the biggest audience possible, so he'll choose the main plaza, under the clock tower. The walls are high there. He'll wait till the sun is exactly overhead."

"So we have till noon?"

"If we're lucky. If he sticks with this decision."

The pilot came on over the intercom, announcing, first in French and then in English, our imminent landing. The seat belt lights dinged and flashed.

"How far is it from Florence to Volterra?"

"That depends on how fast you drive. . . . Bella?"

"Yes?"

She eyed me speculatively. "How strongly are you opposed to grand theft auto?"

A bright yellow Porsche screamed to a stop a few feet in front of where I paced, the word TURBO scrawled in silver cursive across its back. Everyone beside me on the crowded airport sidewalk stared.

"Hurry, Bella!" Alice shouted impatiently through the open passenger window.

I ran to the door and threw myself in, feeling as though I might as well be wearing a black stocking over my head.

"Sheesh, Alice," I complained. "Could you pick a *more* conspicuous car to steal?"

The interior was black leather, and the windows were tinted dark. It felt safer inside, like nighttime.

Alice was already weaving, too fast, through the thick airport traffic—sliding through tiny spaces between the cars as I cringed and fumbled for my seat belt.

"The important question," she corrected, "is whether I could have stolen a faster car, and I don't think so. I got lucky."

"I'm sure that will be very comforting at the roadblock."

She trilled a laugh. "Trust me, Bella. If anyone sets up a roadblock, it will be *behind* us." She hit the gas then, as if to prove her point.

I probably should have watched out the window as first the city of Florence and then the Tuscan landscape flashed past with blurring speed. This was my first trip anywhere, and maybe my last, too. But Alice's driving frightened me, despite the fact that I knew I could trust her behind the wheel. And I was too tortured with anxiety to really see the hills or the walled towns that looked like castles in the distance.

"Do you see anything more?"

"There's something going on," Alice muttered. "Some kind of festival. The streets are full of people and red flags. What's the date today?"

I wasn't entirely sure. "The nineteenth, maybe?"

"Well, that's ironic. It's Saint Marcus Day."

"Which means?"

She chuckled darkly. "The city holds a celebration every year. As the legend goes, a Christian missionary, a Father Marcus—Marcus of the Volturi, in fact—drove all the vampires from Volterra fifteen hundred years ago. The story claims he was martyred in Romania, still trying to drive away the vampire scourge. Of course that's nonsense—he's never left the city. But that's where some of the superstitions about things like crosses and garlic come from. *Father* Marcus used them so successfully. And vampires don't trouble Volterra, so they must work." Her smile was sardonic. "It's become more of a celebration of the city, and recognition for the police force—after all, Volterra is an amazingly safe city. The police get the credit."

I was realizing what she meant when she'd said *ironic*. "They're not going to be very happy if Edward messes things up for them on St. Marcus Day, are they?"

She shook her head, her expression grim. "No. They'll act very quickly."

I looked away, fighting against my teeth as they tried to break through the skin of my lower lip. Bleeding was not the best idea right now.

The sun was terrifyingly high in the pale blue sky.

"He's still planning on noon?" I checked.

"Yes. He's decided to wait. And they're waiting for him."

"Tell me what I have to do."

She kept her eyes on the winding road—the needle on the speedometer was touching the far right on the dial.

"You don't have to do anything. He just has to see you before he moves into the light. And he has to see you before he sees me."

"How are we going to work that?"

A small red car seemed to be racing backward as Alice zoomed around it.

"I'm going to get you as close as possible, and then you're going to run in the direction I point you."

I nodded.

"Try not to trip," she added. "We don't have time for a concussion today."

I groaned. That would be just like me—ruin every-thing, destroy the world, in a moment of klutziness.

The sun continued to climb in the sky while Alice raced against it. It was too bright, and that had me pan-icking. Maybe he wouldn't feel the need to wait for noon after all.

"There," Alice said abruptly, pointing to the castle city atop the closest hill.

I stared at it, feeling the very first hint of a new kind of fear. Every minute since yesterday morning—it seemed like a week ago—when Alice had spoken his name at the foot of the stairs, there had been only one fear. And yet, now, as I stared at the ancient sienna walls and towers crowning the peak of the steep hill, I felt another, more selfish kind of dread thrill through me.

I supposed the city was very beautiful. It absolutely terrified me.

"Volterra," Alice announced in a flat, icy voice.

20. VOLTERRA

WE BEGAN THE STEEP CLIMB, AND THE ROAD GREW congested. As we wound higher, the cars became too close together for Alice to weave insanely between them anymore. We slowed to a crawl behind a little tan Peugeot.

"Alice," I moaned. The clock on the dash seemed to be speeding up.

"It's the only way in," she tried soothe me. But her voice was too strained to comfort.

The cars continued to edge forward, one car length at a time. The sun beamed down brilliantly, seeming already overhead.

The cars crept one by one toward the city. As we got closer, I could see cars parked by the side of the road with people getting out to walk the rest of the way. At first I thought it was just impatience—something I could easily understand. But then we came around a switchback, and I could see the filled parking lot outside the city wall, the crowds of people walking through the gates. No one was being allowed to drive through.

"Alice," I whispered urgently.

"I know," she said. Her face was chiseled from ice.

Now that I was looking, and we were crawling slowly enough to see, I could tell that it was very windy. The people crowding toward the gate gripped their hats and tugged their hair out of their faces. Their clothes billowed around them. I also noticed that the color red was everywhere. Red shirts, red hats, red flags dripping like long ribbons beside the gate, whipping in the wind—as I watched, the brilliant crimson scarf one woman had tied around her hair was caught in a sudden gust. It twisted up into the air above her, writhing like it was alive. She reached for it, jumping in the air, but it continued to flutter higher, a patch of bloody color against the dull, ancient walls.

"Bella." Alice spoke quickly in a fierce, low voice. "I can't see what the guard here will decide now—if this doesn't work, you're going to have to go in alone. You're going to have to run. Just keep asking for the Palazzo dei Priori, and running in the direction they tell you. Don't get lost."

"Palazzo dei Priori, Palazzo dei Priori," I repeated the name over and over again, trying to get it down.

"Or 'the clock tower,' if they speak English. I'll go

around and try to find a secluded spot somewhere behind the city where I can go over the wall."

I nodded. "Palazzo dei Priori."

"Edward will be under the clock tower, to the north of the square. There's a narrow alleyway on the right, and he'll be in the shadow there. You have to get his attention before he can move into the sun."

I nodded furiously.

Alice was near the front of the line. A man in a navy blue uniform was directing the flow of traffic, turning the cars away from the full lot. They U-turned and headed back to find a place beside the road. Then it was Alice's turn.

The uniformed man motioned lazily, not paying attention. Alice accelerated, edging around him and heading for the gate. He shouted something at us, but held his ground, waving frantically to keep the next car from following our bad example.

The man at the gate wore a matching uniform. As we approached him, the throngs of tourists passed, crowding the sidewalks, staring curiously at the pushy, flashy Porsche.

The guard stepped into the middle of the street. Alice angled the car carefully before she came to a full stop. The sun beat against my window, and she was in shadow. She swiftly reached behind the seat and grabbed something from her bag.

The guard came around the car with an irritated expression, and tapped on her window angrily.

She rolled the window down halfway, and I watched

him do a double take when he saw the face behind the dark glass.

"I'm sorry, only tour buses allowed in the city today, miss," he said in English, with a heavy accent. He was apologetic, now, as if he wished he had better news for the strikingly beautiful woman.

"It's a private tour," Alice said, flashing an alluring smile. She reached her hand out of the window, into the sunlight. I froze, until I realized she was wearing an elbow-length, tan glove. She took his hand, still raised from tapping her window, and pulled it into the car. She put something into his palm, and folded his fingers around it.

His face was dazed as he retrieved his hand and stared at the thick roll of money he now held. The outside bill was a thousand dollar bill.

"Is this a joke?" he mumbled.

Alice's smile was blinding. "Only if you think it's funny."

He looked at her, his eyes staring wide. I glanced nervously at the clock on the dash. If Edward stuck to his plan, we had only five minutes left.

"I'm in a wee bit of a hurry," she hinted, still smiling.

The guard blinked twice, and then shoved the money inside his vest. He took a step away from the window and waved us on. None of the passing people seemed to notice the quiet exchange. Alice drove into the city, and we both sighed in relief.

The street was very narrow, cobbled with the same color stones as the faded cinnamon brown buildings that darkened the street with their shade. It had the feel of an alleyway. Red flags decorated the walls, spaced only a few yards apart, flapping in the wind that whistled through the narrow lane.

It was crowded, and the foot traffic slowed our progress.

"Just a little farther," Alice encouraged me; I was gripping the door handle, ready to throw myself into the street as soon as she spoke the word.

She drove in quick spurts and sudden stops, and the people in the crowd shook their fists at us and said angry words that I was glad I couldn't understand. She turned onto a little path that couldn't have been meant for cars; shocked people had to squeeze into doorways as we scraped by. We found another street at the end. The buildings were taller here; they leaned together overhead so that no sunlight touched the pavement—the thrashing red flags on either side nearly met. The crowd was thicker here than anywhere else. Alice stopped the car. I had the door open before we were at a standstill.

She pointed to where the street widened into a patch of bright openness. "There—we're at the southern end of the square. Run straight across, to the right of the clock tower. I'll find a way around—"

Her breath caught suddenly, and when she spoke again, her voice was a hiss. "They're *everywhere*!"

I froze in place, but she pushed me out of the car. "Forget about them. You have two minutes. Go, Bella, go!" she shouted, climbing out of the car as she spoke.

I didn't pause to watch Alice melt into the shadows. I didn't stop to close my door behind me. I shoved a heavy woman out of my way and ran flat out, head down, paying little attention to anything but the uneven stones beneath my feet.

Coming out of the dark lane, I was blinded by the brilliant sunlight beating down into the principal plaza. The wind *whoosh*ed into me, flinging my hair into my eyes and blinding me further. It was no wonder that I didn't see the wall of flesh until I'd smacked into it.

There was no pathway, no crevice between the close pressed bodies. I pushed against them furiously, fighting the hands that shoved back. I heard exclamations of irritation and even pain as I battled my way through, but none were in a language I understood. The faces were a blur of anger and surprise, surrounded by the ever-present red. A blond woman scowled at me, and the red scarf coiled around her neck looked like a gruesome wound. A child, lifted on a man's shoulders to see over the crowd, grinned down at me, his lips distended over a set of plastic vampire fangs.

The throng jostled around me, spinning me the wrong direction. I was glad the clock was so visible, or I'd never keep my course straight. But both hands on the clock pointed up toward the pitiless sun, and, though I shoved viciously against the crowd, I knew I was too late. I wasn't halfway across. I wasn't going to make it. I was stupid and slow and human, and we were all going to die because of it.

I hoped Alice would get out. I hoped that she would see me from some dark shadow and know that I had failed, so she could go home to Jasper.

I listened, above the angry exclamations, trying to hear

the sound of discovery: the gasp, maybe the scream, as Edward came into someone's view.

But there was a break in the crowd—I could see a bubble of space ahead. I pushed urgently toward it, not realizing till I bruised my shins against the bricks that there was a wide, square fountain set into the center of the plaza.

I was nearly crying with relief as I flung my leg over the edge and ran through the knee-deep water. It sprayed all around me as I thrashed my way across the pool. Even in the sun, the wind was glacial, and the wet made the cold actually painful. But the fountain was very wide; it let me cross the center of the square and then some in mere seconds. I didn't pause when I hit the far edge—I used the low wall as a springboard, throwing myself into the crowd.

They moved more readily for me now, avoiding the icy water that splattered from my dripping clothes as I ran. I glanced up at the clock again.

A deep, booming chime echoed through the square. It throbbed in the stones under my feet. Children cried, covering their ears. And I started screaming as I ran.

"Edward!" I screamed, knowing it was useless. The crowd was too loud, and my voice was breathless with exertion. But I couldn't stop screaming.

The clock tolled again. I ran past a child in his mother's arms—his hair was almost white in the dazzling sunlight. A circle of tall men, all wearing red blazers, called out warnings as I barreled through them. The clock tolled again.

On the other side of the men in blazers, there was a break in the throng, space between the sightseers who milled aimlessly around me. My eyes searched the dark narrow passage to the right of the wide square edifice under the tower. I couldn't see the street level—there were still too many people in the way. The clock tolled again.

It was hard to see now. Without the crowd to break the wind, it whipped at my face and burned my eyes. I couldn't be sure if that was the reason behind my tears, or if I was crying in defeat as the clock tolled again.

A little family of four stood nearest to the alley's mouth. The two girls wore crimson dresses, with matching ribbons tying their dark hair back. The father wasn't tall. It seemed like I could see something bright in the shadows, just over his shoulder. I hurtled toward them, trying to see past the stinging tears. The clock tolled, and the littlest girl clamped her hands over her ears.

The older girl, just waist high on her mother, hugged her mother's leg and stared into the shadows behind them. As I watched, she tugged on her mother's elbow and pointed toward the darkness. The clock tolled, and I was so close now.

I was close enough to hear her high-pitched voice. Her father stared at me in surprise as I bore down on them, rasping out Edward's name over and over again.

The older girl giggled and said something to her mother, gesturing toward the shadows again impatiently.

I swerved around the father—he clutched the baby out of my way—and sprinted for the gloomy breach behind them as the clock tolled over my head.

"Edward, no!" I screamed, but my voice was lost in the roar of the chime.

I could see him now. And I could see that he could not see me.

It was really him, no hallucination this time. And I realized that my delusions were more flawed than I'd realized; they'd never done him justice.

Edward stood, motionless as a statue, just a few feet from the mouth of the alley. His eyes were closed, the rings underneath them deep purple, his arms relaxed at his sides, his palms turned forward. His expression was very peaceful, like he was dreaming pleasant things. The marble skin of his chest was bare—there was a small pile of white fabric at his feet. The light reflecting from the pavement of the square gleamed dimly from his skin.

I'd never seen anything more beautiful—even as I ran, gasping and screaming, I could appreciate that. And the last seven months meant nothing. And his words in the forest meant nothing. And it did not matter if he did not want me. I would never want anything but him, no matter how long I lived.

The clock tolled, and he took a large stride toward the light.

"No!" I screamed. "Edward, look at me!"

He wasn't listening. He smiled very slightly. He raised his foot to take the step that would put him directly in the path of the sun.

I slammed into him so hard that the force would have hurled me to the ground if his arms hadn't caught me and held me up. It knocked my breath out of me and snapped my head back.

His dark eyes opened slowly as the clock tolled again.

He looked down at me with quiet surprise.

"Amazing," he said, his exquisite voice full of wonder, slightly amused. "Carlisle was right."

"Edward," I tried to gasp, but my voice had no sound. "You've got to get back into the shadows. You have to move!"

He seemed bemused. His hand brushed softly against my cheek. He didn't appear to notice that I was trying to force him back. I could have been pushing against the alley walls for all the progress I was making. The clock tolled, but he didn't react.

It was very strange, for I knew we were both in mortal danger. Still, in that instant, I felt *well*. Whole. I could feel my heart racing in my chest, the blood pulsing hot and fast through my veins again. My lungs filled deep with the sweet scent that came off his skin. It was like there had never been any hole in my chest. I was perfect—not healed, but as if there had been no wound in the first place.

"I can't believe how quick it was. I didn't feel a thing— they're very good," he mused, closing his eyes again and pressing his lips against my hair. His voice was like honey and velvet. "*Death, that hath sucked the honey of thy breath, hath had no power yet upon thy beauty*," he murmured, and I recognized the line spoken by Romeo in the tomb. The clock boomed out its final chime. "You smell just exactly the same as always," he went on. "So maybe this *is* hell. I don't care. I'll take it."

"I'm not dead," I interrupted. "And neither are you! Please Edward, we have to move. They can't be far away!"

I struggled in his arms, and his brow furrowed in confusion.

"What was that?" he asked politely.

"We're not dead, not yet! But we have to get out of here before the Volturi—"

Comprehension flickered on his face as I spoke. Before I could finish, he suddenly yanked me away from the edge of the shadows, spinning me effortlessly so that my back was tight against the brick wall, and his back was to me as he faced away into the alley. His arms spread wide, protectively, in front of me.

I peeked under his arm to see two dark shapes detach themselves from the gloom.

"Greetings, gentlemen," Edward's voice was calm and pleasant, on the surface. "I don't think I'll be requiring your services today. I would appreciate it very much, however, if you would send my thanks to your masters."

"Shall we take this conversation to a more appropriate venue?" a smooth voice whispered menacingly.

"I don't believe that will be necessary." Edward's voice was harder now. "I know your instructions, Felix. I haven't broken any rules."

"Felix merely meant to point out the proximity of the sun," the other shadow said in a soothing tone. They were both concealed within smoky gray cloaks that reached to the ground and undulated in the wind. "Let us seek better cover."

"I'll be right behind you," Edward said dryly. "Bella, why don't you go back to the square and enjoy the festival?"

"No, bring the girl," the first shadow said, somehow injecting a leer into his whisper.

"I don't think so." The pretense of civility disappeared. Edward's voice was flat and icy. His weight shifted infinitesimally, and I could see that he was preparing to fight.

"No." I mouthed the word.

"Shh," he murmured, only for me.

"Felix," the second, more reasonable shadow cautioned. "Not here." He turned to Edward. "Aro would simply like to speak with you again, if you have decided not to force our hand after all."

"Certainly," Edward agreed. "But the girl goes free."

"I'm afraid that's not possible," the polite shadow said regretfully. "We do have rules to obey."

"Then *I'm* afraid that I'll be unable to accept Aro's invitation, Demetri."

"That's just fine," Felix purred. My eyes were adjusting to the deep shade, and I could see that Felix was very big, tall and thick through the shoulders. His size reminded me of Emmett.

"Aro will be disappointed," Demetri sighed.

"I'm sure he'll survive the letdown," Edward replied.

Felix and Demetri stole closer toward the mouth of the alley, spreading out slightly so they could come at Edward from two sides. They meant to force him deeper into the alley, to avoid a scene. No reflected light found access to their skin; they were safe inside their cloaks.

Edward didn't move an inch. He was dooming himself by protecting me.

Abruptly, Edward's head whipped around, toward the darkness of the winding alley, and Demetri and Felix did the same, in response to some sound or movement too subtle for my senses.

"Let's behave ourselves, shall we?" a lilting voice suggested. "There are ladies present."

Alice tripped lightly to Edward's side, her stance casual. There was no hint of any underlying tension. She looked so tiny, so fragile. Her little arms swung like a child's.

Yet Demetri and Felix both straightened up, their cloaks swirling slightly as a gust of wind funneled through the alley. Felix's face soured. Apparently, they didn't like even numbers.

"We're not alone," she reminded them.

Demetri glanced over his shoulder. A few yards into the square, the little family, with the girls in their red dresses, was watching us. The mother was speaking urgently to her husband, her eyes on the five of us. She looked away when Demetri met her gaze. The man walked a few steps farther into the plaza, and tapped one of the red-blazered men on the shoulder.

Demetri shook his head. "Please, Edward, let's be reasonable," he said.

"Let's," Edward agreed. "And we'll leave quietly now, with no one the wiser."

Demetri sighed in frustration. "At least let us discuss this more privately."

Six men in red now joined the family as they watched us with anxious expressions. I was very conscious of Edward's protective stance in front of me—sure that this was what caused their alarm. I wanted to scream to them to run.

Edward's teeth came together audibly. "No."

Felix smiled.

"Enough."

The voice was high, reedy, and it came from behind us.

I peeked under Edward's other arm to see a small, dark shape coming toward us. By the way the edges billowed, I knew it would be another one of them. Who else?

At first I thought it was a young boy. The newcomer was as tiny as Alice, with lank, pale brown hair trimmed short. The body under the cloak—which was darker, almost black—was slim and androgynous. But the face was too pretty for a boy. The wide-eyed, full-lipped face would make a Botticelli angel look like a gargoyle. Even allowing for the dull crimson irises.

Her size was so insignificant that the reaction to her appearance confused me. Felix and Demetri relaxed immediately, stepping back from their offensive positions to blend again with the shadows of the overhanging walls.

Edward dropped his arms and relaxed his position as well—but in defeat.

"Jane," he sighed in recognition and resignation.

Alice folded her arms across her chest, her expression impassive.

"Follow me," Jane spoke again, her childish voice a monotone. She turned her back on us and drifted silently into the dark.

Felix gestured for us to go first, smirking.

Alice walked after the little Jane at once. Edward wrapped his arm around my waist and pulled me along beside her. The alley angled slightly downward as it narrowed. I looked up at him with frantic questions in my eyes, but he just shook his head. Though I couldn't hear the others behind us, I was sure they were there.

"Well, Alice," Edward said conversationally as we walked. "I suppose I shouldn't be surprised to see you here."

"It was my mistake," Alice answered in the same tone. "It was my job to set it right."

"What happened?" His voice was polite, as if he were barely interested. I imagined this was due to the listening ears behind us.

"It's a long story." Alice's eyes flickered toward me and away. "In summary, she did jump off a cliff, but she wasn't trying to kill herself. Bella's all about the extreme sports these days."

I flushed and turned my eyes straight ahead, looking after the dark shadow that I could no longer see. I could imagine what he was hearing in Alice's thoughts now. Near-drownings, stalking vampires, werewolf friends . . .

"Hm," Edward said curtly, and the casual tone of his voice was gone.

There was a loose curve to the alley, still slanting downward, so I didn't see the squared-off dead end coming until we reached the flat, windowless, brick face. The little one called Jane was nowhere to be seen.

Alice didn't hesitate, didn't break pace as she strode

toward the wall. Then, with easy grace, she slid down an open hole in the street.

It looked like a drain, sunk into the lowest point of the paving. I hadn't noticed it until Alice disappeared, but the grate was halfway pushed aside. The hole was small, and black.

I balked.

"It's all right, Bella," Edward said in a low voice. "Alice will catch you."

I eyed the hole doubtfully. I imagine he would have gone first, if Demetri and Felix hadn't been waiting, smug and silent, behind us.

I crouched down, swinging my legs into the narrow gap.

"Alice?" I whispered, voice trembling.

"I'm right here, Bella," she reassured me. Her voice came from too far below to make me feel better.

Edward took my wrists—his hands felt like stones in winter—and lowered me into the blackness.

"Ready?" he asked.

"Drop her," Alice called.

I closed my eyes so I couldn't see the darkness, scrunching them together in terror, clamping my mouth shut so I wouldn't scream. Edward let me fall.

It was silent and short. The air whipped past me for just half a second, and then, with a huff as I exhaled, Alice's waiting arms caught me.

I was going to have bruises; her arms were very hard. She stood me upright.

It was dim, but not black at the bottom. The light from the hole above provided a faint glow, reflecting wetly from the stones under my feet. The light vanished for a second, and then Edward was a faint, white radiance beside me. He put his arm around me, holding me close to his side, and began to tow me swiftly forward. I wrapped both arms around his cold waist, and tripped and stumbled my way across the uneven stone surface. The sound of the heavy grate sliding over the drain hole behind us rang with metallic finality.

The dim light from the street was quickly lost in the gloom. The sound of my staggering footsteps echoed through the black space; it sounded very wide, but I couldn't be sure. There were no sounds other than my frantic heartbeat and my feet on the wet stones—except for once, when an impatient sigh whispered from behind me.

Edward held me tightly. He reached his free hand across his body to hold my face, too, his smooth thumb tracing across my lips. Now and then, I felt his face press into my hair. I realized that this was the only reunion we would get, and I clutched myself closer to him.

For now, it felt like he wanted me, and that was enough to offset the horror of the subterranean tunnel and the prowling vampires behind us. It was probably no more than guilt—the same guilt that compelled him to come here to die when he'd believed that it was his fault that I'd killed myself. But I felt his lips press silently against my forehead, and I didn't care what the motivation was. At least I could be with him again before I died. That was better than a long life.

I wished I could ask him exactly what was going to happen now. I wanted desperately to know how we were going to die—as if that would somehow make it better, knowing in advance. But I couldn't speak, even in a whisper, surrounded as we were. The others could hear everything—my every breath, my every heartbeat.

The path beneath our feet continued to slant downward, taking us deeper into the ground, and it made me claustrophobic. Only Edward's hand, soothing against my face, kept me from screaming out loud.

I couldn't tell where the light was coming from, but it slowly turned dark gray instead of black. We were in a low, arched tunnel. Long trails of ebony moisture seeped down the gray stones, like they were bleeding ink.

I was shaking, and I thought it was from fear. It wasn't until my teeth started to chatter together that I realized I was cold. My clothes were still wet, and the temperature underneath the city was wintry. As was Edward's skin.

He realized this at the same time I did, and let go of me, keeping only my hand.

"N-n-no," I chattered, throwing my arms around him. I didn't care if I froze. Who knew how long we had left?

His cold hand chafed against my arm, trying to warm me with the friction.

We hurried through the tunnel, or it felt like hurrying to me. My slow progress irritated someone—I guessed Felix—and I heard him heave a sigh now and then.

At the end of the tunnel was a grate—the iron bars were rusting, but thick as my arm. A small door made of thinner, interlaced bars was standing open. Edward ducked through and hurried on to a larger, brighter stone room. The grille slammed shut with a *clang*, followed by the snap of a lock. I was too afraid to look behind me.

On the other side of the long room was a low, heavy wooden door. It was very thick—as I could tell because it, too, stood open.

We stepped through the door, and I glanced around me in surprise, relaxing automatically. Beside me, Edward tensed, his jaw clenched tight.

21. VERDICT

WE WERE IN A BRIGHTLY LIT, UNREMARKABLE HALLWAY. The walls were off-white, the floor carpeted in industrial gray. Common rectangular fluorescent lights were spaced evenly along the ceiling. It was warmer here, for which I was grateful. This hall seemed very benign after the gloom of the ghoulish stone sewers.

Edward didn't seem to agree with my assessment. He glowered darkly down the long hallway, toward the slight, black shrouded figure at the end, standing by an elevator.

He pulled me along, and Alice walked on my other side. The heavy door creaked shut behind us, and then there was the thud of a bolt sliding home.

Jane waited by the elevator, one hand holding the doors open for us. Her expression was apathetic.

Once inside the elevator, the three vampires that belonged to the Volturi relaxed further. They threw back their cloaks, letting the hoods fall back on their shoulders. Felix and Demetri were both of a slightly olive complexion—it looked odd combined with their chalky pallor. Felix's black hair was cropped short, but Demetri's waved to his shoulders. Their irises were deep crimson around the edges, darkening until they were black around the pupil. Under the shrouds, their clothes were modern, pale, and nondescript. I cowered in the corner, cringing against Edward. His hand still rubbed against my arm. He never took his eyes off Jane.

The elevator ride was short; we stepped out into what looked like a posh office reception area. The walls were paneled in wood, the floors carpeted in thick, deep green. There were no windows, but large, brightly lit paintings of the Tuscan countryside hung everywhere as replacements. Pale leather couches were arranged in cozy groupings, and the glossy tables held crystal vases full of vibrantly colored bouquets. The flowers' smell reminded me of a funeral home.

In the middle of the room was a high, polished mahogany counter. I gawked in astonishment at the woman behind it.

She was tall, with dark skin and green eyes. She would have been very pretty in any other company—but not here. Because she was every bit as human as I was. I couldn't comprehend what this human woman was doing here, totally at ease, surrounded by vampires.

She smiled politely in welcome. "Good afternoon, Jane," she said. There was no surprise in her face as she glanced at Jane's company. Not Edward, his bare chest glinting dimly in the white lights, or even me, disheveled and comparatively hideous.

Jane nodded. "Gianna." She continued toward a set of double doors in the back of the room, and we followed.

As Felix passed the desk, he winked at Gianna, and she giggled.

On the other side of the wooden doors was a different kind of reception. The pale boy in the pearl gray suit could have been Jane's twin. His hair was darker, and his lips were not as full, but he was just as lovely. He came forward to meet us. He smiled, reaching for her. "Jane."

"Alec," she responded, embracing the boy. They kissed each other's cheeks on both sides. Then he looked at us.

"They send you out for one and you come back with two . . . and a half," he noted, looking at me. "Nice work."

She laughed—the sound sparkled with delight like a baby's cooing.

"Welcome back, Edward," Alec greeted him. "You seem in a better mood."

"Marginally," Edward agreed in a flat voice. I glanced at Edward's hard face, and wondered how his mood could have been darker before.

Alec chuckled, and examined me as I clung to Edward's side. "And this is the cause of all the trouble?" he asked, skeptical.

Edward only smiled, his expression contemptuous. Then he froze.

"Dibs," Felix called casually from behind.

Edward turned, a low snarl building deep in his chest. Felix smiled—his hand was raised, palm up; he curled his fingers twice, inviting Edward forward.

Alice touched Edward's arm. "Patience," she cautioned him.

They exchanged a long glance, and I wished I could hear what she was telling him. I figured that it was something to do with not attacking Felix, because Edward took a deep breath and turned back to Alec.

"Aro will be so pleased to see you again," Alec said, as if nothing had passed.

"Let's not keep him waiting," Jane suggested.

Edward nodded once.

Alec and Jane, holding hands, led the way down yet another wide, ornate hall—would there ever be an end?

They ignored the doors at the end of the hall—doors entirely sheathed in gold—stopping halfway down the hall and sliding aside a piece of the paneling to expose a plain wooden door. It wasn't locked. Alec held it open for Jane.

I wanted to groan when Edward pulled me through to the other side of the door. It was the same ancient stone as the square, the alley, and the sewers. And it was dark and cold again.

The stone antechamber was not large. It opened quickly into a brighter, cavernous room, perfectly round like a huge castle turret . . . which was probably exactly what it was.

Two stories up, long window slits threw thin rectangles of bright sunlight onto the stone floor below. There were no artificial lights. The only furniture in the room were several massive wooden chairs, like thrones, that were spaced unevenly, flush with the curving stone walls. In the very center of the circle, in a slight depression, was another drain. I wondered if they used it as an exit, like the hole in the street.

The room was not empty. A handful of people were convened in seemingly relaxed conversation. The murmur of low, smooth voices was a gentle hum in the air. As I watched, a pair of pale women in summer dresses paused in a patch of light, and, like prisms, their skin threw the light in rainbow sparkles against the sienna walls.

The exquisite faces all turned toward our party as we entered the room. Most of the immortals were dressed in inconspicuous pants and shirts—things that wouldn't stick out at all on the streets below. But the man who spoke first wore one of the long robes. It was pitch-black, and brushed against the floor. For a moment, I thought his long, jet-black hair was the hood of his cloak.

"Jane, dear one, you've returned!" he cried in evident delight. His voice was just a soft sighing.

He drifted forward, and the movement flowed with such surreal grace that I gawked, my mouth hanging open. Even Alice, whose every motion looked like dancing, could not compare.

I was only more astonished as he floated closer and I could see his face. It was not like the unnaturally attractive faces that surrounded him (for he did not approach us alone; the entire group converged around him, some following, and some walking ahead of him with the alert manner of bodyguards). I couldn't decide if his face was beautiful or not. I suppose the features were perfect. But he was as different from the vampires beside him as they were from me. His skin was translucently white, like onionskin, and it looked just as delicate—it stood in shocking contrast to the long black hair that framed his face. I felt a strange, horrifying urge to touch his cheek, to see if it was softer than Edward's or Alice's, or if it was powdery, like chalk. His eyes were red, the same as the others around him, but the color was clouded, milky; I wondered if his vision was affected by the haze.

He glided to Jane, took her face in his papery hands, kissed her lightly on her full lips, and then floated back a step.

"Yes, Master." Jane smiled; the expression made her look like an angelic child. "I brought him back alive, just as you wished."

"Ah, Jane." He smiled, too. "You are such a comfort to me."

He turned his misty eyes toward us, and the smile brightened—became ecstatic.

"And Alice and Bella, too!" he rejoiced, clapping his thin hands together. "This *is* a happy surprise! Wonderful!"

I stared in shock as he called our names informally, as if we were old friends dropping in for an unexpected visit.

He turned to our hulking escort. "Felix, be a dear and

tell my brothers about our company. I'm sure they wouldn't want to miss this."

"Yes, Master." Felix nodded and disappeared back the way we had come.

"You see, Edward?" The strange vampire turned and smiled at Edward like a fond but scolding grandfather. "What did I tell you? Aren't you glad that I didn't give you what you wanted yesterday?"

"Yes, Aro, I am," he agreed, tightening his arm around my waist.

"I love a happy ending." Aro sighed. "They are so rare. But I want the whole story. How did this happen? Alice?" He turned to gaze at Alice with curious, misty eyes. "Your brother seemed to think you infallible, but apparently there was some mistake."

"Oh, I'm far from infallible." She flashed a dazzling smile. She looked perfectly at ease, except that her hands were balled into tight little fists. "As you can see today, I cause problems as often as I cure them."

"You're too modest," Aro chided. "I've seen some of your more amazing exploits, and I must admit I've never observed anything like your talent. Wonderful!"

Alice flickered a glance at Edward. Aro did not miss it.

"I'm sorry, we haven't been introduced properly at all, have we? It's just that I feel like I know you already, and I tend get ahead of myself. Your brother introduced us yesterday, in a peculiar way. You see, I share some of your brother's talent, only I am limited in a way that he is not." Aro shook his head; his tone was envious.

"And also exponentially more powerful," Edward added dryly. He looked at Alice as he swiftly explained. "Aro needs physical contact to hear your thoughts, but he hears much more than I do. You know I can only hear what's passing through your head in the moment. Aro hears every thought your mind has ever had."

Alice raised her delicate eyebrows, and Edward inclined his head.

Aro didn't miss that either.

"But to be able to hear from a distance . . ." Aro sighed, gesturing toward the two of them, and the exchange that had just taken place. "That would be so *convenient*."

Aro looked over our shoulders. All the other heads turned in the same direction, including Jane, Alec, and Demetri, who stood silently beside us.

I was the slowest to turn. Felix was back, and behind him floated two more black-robed men. Both looked very much like Aro, one even had the same flowing black hair. The other had a shock of snow-white hair—the same shade as his face—that brushed against his shoulders. Their faces had identical, paper-thin skin.

The trio from Carlisle's painting was complete, unchanged by the last three hundred years since it was painted.

"Marcus, Caius, look!" Aro crooned. "Bella is alive after all, and Alice is here with her! Isn't that wonderful?"

Neither of the other two looked as if *wonderful* would be their first choice of words. The dark-haired man seemed utterly bored, like he'd seen too many millennia of Aro's enthusiasm. The other's face was sour under the snowy hair.

Their lack of interest did not curb Aro's enjoyment.

"Let us have the story," Aro almost sang in his feathery voice.

The white-haired ancient vampire drifted away, gliding toward one of the wooden thrones. The other paused beside Aro, and he reached his hand out, at first I thought to take Aro's hand. But he just touched Aro's palm briefly and then dropped his hand to his side. Aro raised one black brow. I wondered how his papery skin did not crumple in the effort.

Edward snorted very quietly, and Alice looked at him, curious.

"Thank you, Marcus," Aro said. "That's quite interesting."

I realized, a second late, that Marcus was letting Aro know his thoughts.

Marcus didn't *look* interested. He glided away from Aro to join the one who must be Caius, seated against the wall. Two of the attending vampires followed silently behind him—bodyguards, like I'd thought before. I could see that the two women in the sundresses had gone to stand beside Caius in the same manner. The idea of any vampire needing a guard was faintly ridiculous to me, but maybe the ancient ones were as frail as their skin suggested.

Aro was shaking his head. "Amazing," he said. "Absolutely amazing."

Alice's expression was frustrated. Edward turned to her

and explained again in a swift, low voice. "Marcus sees relationships. He's surprised by the intensity of ours."

Aro smiled. "So convenient," he repeated to himself. Then he spoke to us. "It takes quite a bit to surprise Marcus, I can assure you."

I looked at Marcus's dead face, and I believed that.

"It's just so difficult to understand, even now," Aro mused, staring at Edward's arm wrapped around me. It was hard for me to follow Aro's chaotic train of thought. I struggled to keep up. "How can you stand so close to her like that?"

"It's not without effort," Edward answered calmly.

"But still—*la tua cantante*! What a waste!"

Edward chuckled once without humor. "I look at it more as a price."

Aro was skeptical. "A very high price."

"Opportunity cost."

Aro laughed. "If I hadn't smelled her through your memories, I wouldn't have believed the call of anyone's blood could be so strong. I've never felt anything like it myself. Most of us would trade much for such a gift, and yet you. . . ."

"Waste it," Edward finished, his voice sarcastic now.

Aro laughed again. "Ah, how I miss my friend Carlisle! You remind me of him—only he was not so angry."

"Carlisle outshines me in many other ways as well."

"I certainly never thought to see Carlisle bested for self-control of all things, but you put him to shame."

"Hardly." Edward sounded impatient. As if he were

tired of the preliminaries. It made me more afraid; I couldn't help but try to imagine what he expected would follow.

"I am gratified by his success," Aro mused. "Your memories of him are quite a gift for me, though they astonish me exceedingly. I am surprised by how it . . . *pleases* me, his success in this unorthodox path he's chosen. I expected that he would waste, weaken with time. I'd scoffed at his plan to find others who would share his peculiar vision. Yet, somehow, I'm happy to be wrong."

Edward didn't reply.

"But *your* restraint!" Aro sighed. "I did not know such strength was possible. To inure yourself against such a siren call, not just once but again and again—if I had not felt it myself, I would not have believed."

Edward gazed back at Aro's admiration with no expression. I knew his face well enough—time had not changed that—to guess at something seething beneath the surface. I fought to keep my breathing even.

"Just remembering how she appeals to you . . ." Aro chuckled. "It makes me thirsty."

Edward tensed.

"Don't be disturbed," Aro reassured him. "I mean her no harm. But I am *so* curious, about one thing in particular." He eyed me with bright interest. "May I?" he asked eagerly, lifting one hand.

"Ask *her*," Edward suggested in a flat voice.

"Of course, how rude of me!" Aro exclaimed. "Bella," he addressed me directly now. "I'm fascinated that you are the one exception to Edward's impressive talent—so very interesting that such a thing should occur! And I was wondering, since our talents are similar in many ways, if you would be so kind as to allow me to try—to see if you are an exception for *me*, as well?"

My eyes flashed up to Edward's face in terror. Despite Aro's overt politeness, I didn't believe I really had a choice. I was horrified at the thought of allowing him to touch me, and yet also perversely intrigued by the chance to feel his strange skin.

Edward nodded in encouragement—whether because he was sure Aro would not hurt me, or because there was no choice, I couldn't tell.

I turned back to Aro and raised my hand slowly in front of me. It was trembling.

He glided closer, and I believe he meant his expression to be reassuring. But his papery features were too strange, too alien and frightening, to reassure. The look on his face was more confident than his words had been.

Aro reached out, as if to shake my hand, and pressed his insubstantial-looking skin against mine. It was hard, but felt brittle—shale rather than granite—and even colder than I expected.

His filmy eyes smiled down at mine, and it was impossible to look away. They were mesmerizing in an odd, unpleasant way.

Aro's face altered as I watched. The confidence wavered and became first doubt, then incredulity before he calmed it into a friendly mask.

"So very interesting," he said as he released my hand and drifted back.

My eyes flickered to Edward, and, though his face was composed, I thought he seemed a little smug.

Aro continued to drift with a thoughtful expression. He was quiet for a moment, his eyes flickering between the three of us. Then, abruptly, he shook his head.

"A first," he said to himself. "I wonder if she is immune to our other talents. . . . Jane, dear?"

"No!" Edward snarled the word. Alice grabbed his arm with a restraining hand. He shook her off.

Little Jane smiled up happily at Aro. "Yes, Master?"

Edward was truly snarling now, the sound ripping and tearing from him, glaring at Aro with baleful eyes. The room had gone still, everyone watching him with amazed disbelief, as if he were committing some embarrassing social faux pas. I saw Felix grin hopefully and move a step forward. Aro glanced at him once, and he froze in place, his grin turning to a sulky expression.

Then he spoke to Jane. "I was wondering, my dear one, if Bella is immune to *you*."

I could barely hear Aro over Edward's furious growls. He let go of me, moving to hide me from their view. Caius ghosted in our direction, with his entourage, to watch.

Jane turned toward us with a beatific smile.

"Don't!" Alice cried as Edward launched himself at the little girl.

Before I could react, before anyone could jump between them, before Aro's bodyguards could tense, Edward was on the ground.

No one had touched him, but he was on the stone floor writhing in obvious agony, while I stared in horror.

Jane was smiling only at him now, and it all clicked together. What Alice had said about *formidable gifts*, why everyone treated Jane with such deference, and why Edward had thrown himself in her path before she could do that to me.

"Stop!" I shrieked, my voice echoing in the silence, jumping forward to put myself between them. But Alice threw her arms around me in an unbreakable grasp and ignored my struggles. No sound escaped Edward's lips as he cringed against the stones. It felt like my head would explode from the pain of watching this.

"Jane," Aro recalled her in a tranquil voice. She looked up quickly, still smiling with pleasure, her eyes questioning. As soon as Jane looked away, Edward was still.

Aro inclined his head toward me.

Jane turned her smile in my direction.

I didn't even meet her gaze. I watched Edward from the prison of Alice's arms, still struggling pointlessly.

"He's fine," Alice whispered in a tight voice. As she spoke, he sat up, and then sprang lightly to his feet. His eyes met mine, and they were horror-struck. At first I thought the horror was for what he had just suffered. But then he looked quickly at Jane, and back to me—and his face relaxed into relief.

I looked at Jane, too, and she no longer smiled. She glared at me, her jaw clenched with the intensity of her focus. I shrank back, waiting for the pain.

Nothing happened.

Edward was by my side again. He touched Alice's arm, and she surrendered me to him.

Aro started to laugh. "Ha, ha, ha," he chuckled. "This is wonderful!"

Jane hissed in frustration, leaning forward like she was preparing to spring.

"Don't be put out, dear one," Aro said in a comforting tone, placing a powder-light hand on her shoulder. "She confounds us all."

Jane's upper lip curled back over her teeth as she continued to glare at me.

"Ha, ha, ha," Aro chortled again. "You're very brave, Edward, to endure in silence. I asked Jane to do that to me once—just out of curiosity." He shook his head in admiration.

Edward glared, disgusted.

"So what do we do with you now?" Aro sighed.

Edward and Alice stiffened. This was the part they'd been waiting for. I began to tremble.

"I don't suppose there's any chance that you've changed your mind?" Aro asked Edward hopefully. "Your talent would be an excellent addition to our little company."

Edward hesitated. From the corner of my eye, I saw both Felix and Jane grimace.

Edward seemed to weigh each word before he spoke it. "I'd . . . rather . . . not."

"Alice?" Aro asked, still hopeful. "Would you perhaps be interested in joining with us?"

"No, thank you," Alice said.

"And you, Bella?" Aro raised his eyebrows.

Edward hissed, low in my ears. I stared at Aro blankly. Was he joking? Or was he really asking me if I wanted to stay for dinner?

It was the white-haired Caius who broke the silence.

"What?" he demanded of Aro; his voice, though no more than a whisper, was flat.

"Caius, surely you see the potential," Aro chided him affectionately. "I haven't seen a prospective talent so promising since we found Jane and Alec. Can you imagine the possibilities when she is one of us?"

Caius looked away with a caustic expression. Jane's eyes sparked with indignation at the comparison.

Edward fumed beside me. I could hear a rumble in his chest, building toward a growl. I couldn't let his temper get him hurt.

"No, thank you," I spoke up in barely more than a whisper, my voice breaking in fright.

Aro sighed. "That's unfortunate. Such a waste."

Edward hissed. "Join or die, is that it? I suspected as much when we were brought to *this* room. So much for your laws."

The tone of his voice surprised me. He sounded irate, but there was something deliberate about his delivery—as if he'd chosen his words with great care.

"Of course not." Aro blinked, astonished. "We were already convened here, Edward, awaiting Heidi's return. Not for you."

"Aro," Caius hissed. "The law claims them."

Edward glared at Caius. "How so?" he demanded. He

must have known what Caius was thinking, but he seemed determined to make him speak it aloud.

Caius pointed a skeletal finger at me. "She knows too much. You have exposed our secrets." His voice was papery thin, just like his skin.

"There are a few humans in on your charade here, as well," Edward reminded him, and I thought of the pretty receptionist below.

Caius's face twisted into a new expression. Was it supposed to be a smile?

"Yes," he agreed. "But when they are no longer useful to us, they will serve to sustain us. That is not your plan for this one. If she betrays our secrets, are you prepared to destroy her? I think not," he scoffed.

"I wouldn't—," I began, still whispering. Caius silenced me with an icy look.

"Nor do you intend to make her one of us," Caius continued. "Therefore, she is a vulnerability. Though it is true, for this, only *her* life is forfeit. You may leave if you wish."

Edward bared his teeth.

"That's what I thought," Caius said, with something akin to pleasure. Felix leaned forward, eager.

"Unless . . . ," Aro interrupted. He looked unhappy with the way the conversation had gone. "Unless you do intend to give her immortality?"

Edward pursed his lips, hesitating for a moment before he answered. "And if I do?"

Aro smiled, happy again. "Why, then you would be free to go home and give my regards to my friend Carlisle." His expression turned more hesitant. "But I'm afraid you would have to mean it."

Aro raised his hand in front of him.

Caius, who had begun to scowl furiously, relaxed.

Edward's lips tightened into a fierce line. He stared into my eyes, and I stared back.

"Mean it," I whispered. "Please."

Was it really such a loathsome idea? Would he rather *die* than change me? I felt like I'd been kicked in the stomach.

Edward stared down at me with a tortured expression.

And then Alice stepped away from us, forward toward Aro. We turned to watch her. Her hand was raised like his.

She didn't say anything, and Aro waved off his anxious guard as they moved to block her approach. Aro met her halfway, and took her hand with an eager, acquisitive glint in his eyes.

He bent his head over their touching hands, his eyes closing as he concentrated. Alice was motionless, her face blank. I heard Edward's teeth snap together.

No one moved. Aro seemed frozen over Alice's hand. The seconds passed and I grew more and more stressed, wondering how much time would pass before it was *too* much time. Before it meant something was wrong—more wrong than it already was.

Another agonizing moment passed, and then Aro's voice broke the silence.

"Ha, ha, ha," he laughed, his head still bent forward. He looked up slowly, his eyes bright with excitement. "That was *fascinating*!"

Alice smiled dryly. "I'm glad you enjoyed it."

"To see the things you've seen—especially the ones that haven't happened yet!" He shook his head in wonder.

"But that will," she reminded him, voice calm.

"Yes, yes, it's quite determined. Certainly there's no problem."

Caius looked bitterly disappointed—a feeling he seemed to share with Felix and Jane.

"Aro," Caius complained.

"Dear Caius," Aro smiled. "Do not fret. Think of the possibilities! They do not join us today, but we can always hope for the future. Imagine the joy young Alice alone would bring to our little household. . . . Besides, I'm so terribly curious to see how Bella turns out!"

Aro seemed convinced. Did he not realize how subjective Alice's visions were? That she could make up her mind to transform me today, and then change it tomorrow? A million tiny decisions, her decisions and so many others', too—Edward's—could alter her path, and with that, the future.

And would it really matter that Alice was willing, would it make any difference if I *did* become a vampire, when the idea was so repulsive to Edward? If death was, to him, a better alternative than having me around forever, an immortal annoyance? Terrified as I was, I felt myself sinking down into depression, drowning in it. . . .

"Then we are free to go now?" Edward asked in an even voice.

"Yes, yes," Aro said pleasantly. "But please visit again. It's been absolutely enthralling!"

"And we will visit you as well," Caius promised, his eyes suddenly half-closed like the heavy-lidded gaze of a lizard. "To be sure that you follow through on your side. Were I you, I would not delay too long. We do not offer second chances."

Edward's jaw clenched tight, but he nodded once.

Caius smirked and drifted back to where Marcus still sat, unmoving and uninterested.

Felix groaned.

"Ah, Felix." Aro smiled, amused. "Heidi will be here at any moment. Patience."

"Hmm." Edward's voice had a new edge to it. "In that case, perhaps we'd better leave sooner rather than later."

"Yes," Aro agreed. "That's a good idea. Accidents *do* happen. Please wait below until after dark, though, if you don't mind."

"Of course," Edward agreed, while I cringed at the thought of waiting out the day before we could escape.

"And here," Aro added, motioning to Felix with one finger. Felix came forward at once, and Aro unfastened the gray cloak the huge vampire wore, pulling from his shoulders. He tossed it to Edward. "Take this. You're a little conspicuous."

Edward put the long cloak on, leaving the hood down.

Aro sighed. "It suits you."

Edward chuckled, but broke off suddenly, glancing over his shoulder. "Thank you, Aro. We'll wait below."

"Goodbye, young friends," Aro said, his eyes bright as he stared in the same direction.

"Let's go," Edward said, urgent now.

Demetri gestured that we should follow, and then set off the way we'd come in, the only exit by the look of things.

Edward pulled me swiftly along beside him. Alice was close by my other side, her face hard.

"Not fast enough," she muttered.

I stared up at her, frightened, but she only seemed chagrined. It was then that I first heard the babble of voices—loud, rough voices—coming from the antechamber.

"Well this is unusual," a man's coarse voice boomed.

"So medieval," an unpleasantly shrill, female voice gushed back.

A large crowd was coming through the little door, filling the smaller stone chamber. Demetri motioned for us to make room. We pressed back against the cold wall to let them pass.

The couple in front, Americans from the sound of them, glanced around themselves with appraising eyes.

"Welcome, guests! Welcome to Volterra!" I could hear Aro sing from the big turret room.

The rest of them, maybe forty or more, filed in after the couple. Some studied the setting like tourists. A few even snapped pictures. Others looked confused, as if the story that had led them to this room was not making sense anymore. I noticed one small, dark woman in particular. Around her neck was a rosary, and she gripped the cross tightly in one hand. She walked more slowly than the others, touching someone now and then and asking a question in an unfamiliar language. No one seemed to understand her, and her voice grew more panicked.

Edward pulled my face against his chest, but it was too late. I already understood.

As soon as the smallest break appeared, Edward pushed me quickly toward the door. I could feel the horrified expression on my face, and the tears beginning to pool in my eyes.

The ornate golden hallway was quiet, empty except for one gorgeous, statuesque woman. She stared at us curiously, me in particular.

"Welcome home, Heidi," Demetri greeted her from behind us.

Heidi smiled absently. She reminded me of Rosalie, though they looked nothing alike—it was just that her beauty, too, was exceptional, unforgettable. I couldn't seem to look away.

She was dressed to emphasize that beauty. Her amazingly long legs, darkened with tights, were exposed by the shortest of miniskirts. Her top was long-sleeved and high-necked, but extremely close-fitting, and constructed of red vinyl. Her long mahogany hair was lustrous, and her eyes were the strangest shade of violet—a color that might result from blue-tinted contacts over red irises.

"Demetri," she responded in a silky voice, her eyes flickering between my face and Edward's gray cloak.

"Nice fishing," Demetri complimented her, and I suddenly understood the attention-grabbing outfit she wore . . . she was not only the fisherman, but also the bait.

"Thanks." She flashed a stunning smile. "Aren't you coming?"

"In a minute. Save a few for me."

Heidi nodded and ducked through the door with one last curious look at me.

Edward set a pace that had me running to keep up. But we still couldn't get through the ornate door at the end of the hallway before the screaming started.

22. FLIGHT

DEMETRI LEFT US IN THE CHEERFULLY OPULENT RECEP-
tion area, where the woman Gianna was still at her post behind the polished counter. Bright, harmless music tinkled
from hidden speakers.

"Do not leave until dark," he warned us.

Edward nodded, and Demetri hurried away.

Gianna did not seem at all surprised by the exchange,
though she did eye Edward's borrowed cloak with shrewd
speculation.

"Are you all right?" Edward asked under his breath, to
low for the human woman to hear. His voice was rough—
if velvet can be rough—with anxiety. Still stressed by our
situation, I imagined.

"You'd better make her sit before she falls," Alice said. "She's going to pieces."

It was only then that I realize I was shaking, shaking hard, my entire frame vibrating until my teeth chattered and the room around me seemed to wobble and blur in my eyes. For one wild second, I wondered if this was how Jacob felt just before exploding into a werewolf.

I heard a sound that didn't make sense, a strange, ripping counterpart to the otherwise cheery background music. Distracted by the shaking, I couldn't tell where it was coming from.

"Shh, Bella, shh," Edward said as he pulled me to the sofa farthest away from the curious human at the desk.

"I think she's having hysterics. Maybe you should slap her," Alice suggested.

Edward threw a frantic glance at her.

Then I understood. Oh. The noise was me. The ripping sound was the sobs coming from my chest. That's what was shaking me.

"It's all right, you're safe, it's all right," he chanted again and again. He pulled me onto his lap and tucked the thick wool cloak around me, protecting me from his cold skin.

I knew it was stupid to react like this. Who knew how much time I had to look at his face? He was saved, and I was saved, and he could leave me as soon as we were free. To have my eyes so filled with tears that I could not see his features clearly was wasteful—insanity.

But, behind my eyes where the tears could not wash

the image away, I could still see the panicked face of the tiny woman with the rosary.

"All those people," I sobbed.

"I know," he whispered.

"It's so horrible."

"Yes, it is. I wish you hadn't had to see that."

I rested my head against his cold chest, using the thick cloak to wipe my eyes. I took a few deep breaths, trying to calm myself.

"Is there anything I can get you?" a voice asked politely. It was Gianna, leaning over Edward's shoulder with a look that was both concerned and yet still professional and detached at the same time. It didn't seem to bother her that her face was inches from a hostile vampire. She was either totally oblivious, or very good at her job.

"No," Edward answered coldly.

She nodded, smiled at me, and then disappeared.

I waited until she was out of hearing range. "Does she know what's going on here?" I demanded, my voice low and hoarse. I was getting control of myself, my breathing evening out.

"Yes. She knows everything," Edward told me.

"Does she know they're going to kill her someday?"

"She's knows it's a possibility," he said.

That surprised me.

Edward's face was hard to read. "She's hoping they'll decide to keep her."

I felt the blood leave my face. "She wants to be one of them?"

He nodded once, his eyes sharp on my face, watching my reaction.

I shuddered. "How can she want that?" I whispered, more to myself than really looking for an answer. "How can she watch those people file through to that hideous room and want to be a part of *that*?"

Edward didn't answer. His expression twisted in response to something I'd said.

As I stared at his too beautiful face, trying to understand the change, it suddenly struck me that I was really here, in Edward's arms, however fleetingly, and that we were not—at this exact moment—about to be killed.

"Oh, Edward," I cried, and I was sobbing again. It was such a stupid reaction. The tears were too thick for me to see his face again, and that was inexcusable. I only had until sunset for sure. Like a fairy tale again, with deadlines that ended the magic.

"What's wrong?" he asked, still anxious, rubbing my back with gentle pats.

I wrapped my arms around his neck—what was the worst he could do? Just push me away—and hugged myself closer to him. "Is it really sick for me to be happy right now?" I asked. My voice broke twice.

He didn't push me away. He pulled me tight against his ice-hard chest, so tight it was hard to breathe, even with my lungs securely intact. "I know exactly what you mean," he whispered. "But we have lots of reasons to be happy. For one, we're alive."

"Yes," I agreed. "That's a good one."

"And together," he breathed. His breath was so sweet it made my head swim.

I just nodded, sure that he did not place the same weight on that consideration as I did.

"And, with any luck, we'll still be alive tomorrow."

"Hopefully," I said uneasily.

"The outlook is quite good," Alice assured me. She'd been so quiet, I'd almost forgotten her presence. "I'll see Jasper in less than twenty-four hours," she added in a satisfied tone.

Lucky Alice. She could trust her future.

I couldn't keep my eyes off of Edward's face for long. I stared at him, wishing more than anything that the future would never happen. That this moment would last forever, or, if it couldn't, that I would stop existing when it did.

Edward stared right back at me, his dark eyes soft, and it was easy to pretend that he felt the same way. So that's what I did. I pretended, to make the moment sweeter.

His fingertips traced the circles under my eyes. "You look so tired."

"And you look thirsty," I whispered back, studying the purple bruises under his black irises.

He shrugged. "It's nothing."

"Are you sure? I could sit with Alice," I offered, unwilling; I'd rather he killed me now than move one inch from where I was.

"Don't be ridiculous." He sighed; his sweet breath caressed my face. "I've never been in better control of *that* side of my nature than right now."

I had a million questions for him. One of them bubbled to my lips now, but I held my tongue. I didn't want to ruin the moment, as imperfect as it was, here in this room that made me sick, under the eyes of the would-be monster.

Here in his arms, it was so easy to fantasize that he wanted me. I didn't want to think about his motivations now—about whether he acted this way to keep me calm while we were still in danger, or if he just felt guilty for where we were and relieved that he wasn't responsible for my death. Maybe the time apart had been enough that I didn't bore him for the moment. But it didn't matter. I was so much happier pretending.

I lay quiet in his arms, re-memorizing his face, pretending. . . .

He stared at my face like he was doing the same, while he and Alice discussed how to get home. Their voices were so quick and low that I knew Gianna couldn't understand. I missed half of it myself. It sounded like more theft would be involved, though. I wondered idly if the yellow Porsche had made it back to its owner yet.

"What was all that talk about *singers?*" Alice asked at one point.

"*La tua cantante*," Edward said. His voice made the words into music.

"Yes, that," Alice said, and I concentrated for a moment. I'd wondered about that, too, at the time.

I felt Edward shrug around me. "They have a name for someone who smells the way Bella does to me. They call her my *singer*—because her blood sings for me."

Alice laughed.

I was tired enough to sleep, but I fought against the weariness. I wasn't going to miss a second of the time I had with him. Now and then, as he talked with Alice, he would lean down suddenly and kiss me—his glass-smooth lips brushing against my hair, my forehead, the tip of my nose. Each time it was like an electric shock to my long dormant heart. The sound of its beating seemed to fill the entire room.

It was heaven—right smack in the middle of hell.

I lost track of the time completely. So when Edward's arms tightened around me, and both he and Alice looked to the back of the room with wary eyes, I panicked. I cringed into Edward's chest as Alec—his eyes now a vivid ruby, but still spotless in his light gray suit despite the afternoon meal—walked through the double doors.

It was good news.

"You're free to leave now," Alec told us, his tone so warm you'd think we were all lifelong friends. "We ask that you don't linger in the city."

Edward made no answering pretense; his voice was ice cold. "That won't be a problem."

Alec smiled, nodded, and disappeared again.

"Follow the right hallway around the corner to the first set of elevators," Gianna told us as Edward helped me to my feet. "The lobby is two floors down, and exits to the street. Goodbye, now," she added pleasantly. I wondered if her competence would be enough to save her.

Alice shot her a dark look.

I was relieved there was another way out; I wasn't sure if I could handle another tour through the underground.

We left through a tastefully luxurious lobby. I was the only one who glanced back at the medieval castle that housed the elaborate business façade. I couldn't see the turret from here, for which I was grateful.

The party was still in full swing in the streets. The street lamps were just coming on as we walked swiftly through the narrow, cobbled lanes. The sky was a dull, fading gray overhead, but the buildings crowded the streets so closely that it felt darker.

The party was darker, too. Edward's long, trailing cloak did not stand out in the way it might have on a normal evening in Volterra. There were others in black satin cloaks now, and the plastic fangs I'd seen on the child in the square today seemed to be very popular with the adults.

"Ridiculous," Edward muttered once.

I didn't notice when Alice disappeared from beside me. I looked over to ask her a question, and she was gone.

"Where's Alice?" I whispered in a panic.

"She went to retrieve your bags from where she stashed them this morning."

I'd forgotten that I had access to a toothbrush. It brightened my outlook considerably.

"She's stealing a car, too, isn't she?" I guessed.

He grinned. "Not till we're outside."

It seemed like a very long way to the entryway. Edward could see that I was spent; he wound his arm around my waist and supported most of my weight as we walked.

I shuddered as he pulled me through the dark stone archway. The huge, ancient portcullis above was like a cage door, threatening to drop on us, to lock us in.

He led me toward a dark car, waiting in a pool of shadow to the right of the gate with the engine running. To my surprise, he slid into the backseat with me, instead of insisting on driving.

Alice was apologetic. "I'm sorry." She gestured vaguely toward the dashboard. "There wasn't much to choose from."

"It's fine, Alice." He grinned. "They can't all be 911 Turbos."

She sighed. "I may have to acquire one of those legally. It was fabulous."

"I'll get you one for Christmas," Edward promised.

Alice turned to beam at him, which worried me, as she was already speeding down the dark and curvy hillside at the same time.

"Yellow," she told him.

Edward kept me tight in his arms. Inside the gray cloak, I was warm and comfortable. More than comfortable.

"You can sleep now, Bella," he murmured. "It's over."

I knew he meant the danger, the nightmare in the ancient city, but I still had to swallow hard before I could answer.

"I don't want to sleep. I'm not tired." Just the second part was a lie. I wasn't about to close my eyes. The car was only dimly lit by the dashboard controls, but it was enough that I could see his face.

He pressed his lips to the hollow under my ear. "Try," he encouraged.

I shook my head.

He sighed. "You're still just as stubborn."

I *was* stubborn; I fought with my heavy lids, and I won.

The dark road was the hardest part; the bright lights at the airport in Florence made it easier, as did the chance to brush my teeth and change into clean clothes; Alice bought Edward new clothes, too, and he left the dark cloak on a pile of trash in an alley. The plane trip to Rome was so short that there wasn't really a chance for the fatigue to drag me under. I knew the flight from Rome to Atlanta would be another matter entirely, so I asked the flight attendant if she could bring me a Coke.

"Bella," Edward said disapprovingly. He knew my low tolerance for caffeine.

Alice was behind us. I could hear her murmuring to Jasper on the phone.

"I don't want to sleep," I reminded him. I gave him an excuse that was believable because it was true. "If I close my eyes now, I'll see things I don't want to see. I'll have nightmares."

He didn't argue with me after that.

It would have been a very good time to talk, to get the answers I needed—needed but not really wanted; I was already despairing at the thought of what I might hear. We had an uninterrupted block of time ahead of us, and he couldn't escape me on an airplane—well, not easily, at least. No one would hear us except Alice; it was late, and most of the passengers were turning off lights and asking for pillows in muted voices. Talk would help me fight off the exhaustion.

But, perversely, I bit my tongue against the flood of questions. My reasoning was probably flawed by exhaustion, but I hoped that by postponing the discussion, I could buy a few more hours with him at some later time—spin this out for another night, Scheherazade-style.

So I kept drinking soda, and resisting even the urge to blink. Edward seemed perfectly content to hold me in his arms, his fingers tracing my face again and again. I touched his face, too. I couldn't stop myself, though I was afraid it would hurt me later, when I was alone again. He continued to kiss my hair, my forehead, my wrists . . . but never my lips, and that was good. After all, how many ways can one heart be mangled and still be expected to keep beating? I'd lived through a lot that should have finished me in the last few days, but it didn't make me feel strong. Instead, I felt horribly fragile, like one word could shatter me.

Edward didn't speak. Maybe he was hoping I would sleep. Maybe he had nothing to say.

I won the fight against my heavy lids. I was awake when we reached the airport in Atlanta, and I even watched the sun beginning to rise over Seattle's cloud cover before Edward slid the window shut. I was proud of myself. I hadn't missed one minute.

Neither Alice nor Edward was surprised by the reception that waited for us at Sea-Tac airport, but it caught me off guard. Jasper was the first one I saw—he didn't seem to see me at all. His eyes were only for Alice. She went quickly to his side; they didn't embrace like other couples meeting there. They only stared into each other's faces, yet, somehow, the moment was so private that I still felt the need to look away.

Carlisle and Esme waited in a quiet corner far from the

line for the metal detectors, in the shadow of a wide pillar. Esme reached for me, hugging me fiercely, yet awkwardly, because Edward kept his arms around me, too.

"Thank you so much," she said in my ear.

Then she threw her arms around Edward, and she looked like she would be crying if that were possible.

"You will *never* put me through that again," she nearly growled.

Edward grinned, repentant. "Sorry, Mom."

"Thank you, Bella," Carlisle said. "We owe you."

"Hardly," I mumbled. The sleepless night was suddenly overpowering. My head felt disconnected from my body.

"She's dead on her feet," Esme scolded Edward. "Let's get her home."

Not sure if home was what I wanted at this point, I stumbled, half-blind, through the airport, Edward dragging me on one side and Esme on the other. I didn't know if Alice and Jasper were behind us or not, and I was too exhausted to look.

I think I was mostly asleep, though I was still walking, when we reached their car. The surprise of seeing Emmett and Rosalie leaning against the black sedan under the dim lights of the parking garage revived me some. Edward stiffened.

"Don't," Esme whispered. "She feels awful."

"She should," Edward said, making no attempt to keep his voice down.

"It's not her fault," I said, my words garbled with exhaustion.

"Let her make amends," Esme pleaded. "We'll ride with Alice and Jasper."

Edward glowered at the absurdly lovely blond vampire waiting for us.

"Please, Edward," I said. I didn't want to ride with Rosalie any more than he seemed to, but I'd caused more than enough discord in his family.

He sighed, and towed me toward the car.

Emmett and Rosalie got in the front seat without speaking, while Edward pulled me in the back again. I knew I wasn't going to be able to fight my eyelids anymore, and I laid my head against his chest in defeat, letting them close. I felt the car purr to life.

"Edward," Rosalie began.

"I know." Edward's brusque tone was not generous.

"Bella?" Rosalie asked softly.

My eyelids fluttered open in shock. It was the first time she'd ever spoken directly to me.

"Yes, Rosalie?" I asked, hesitant.

"I'm so very sorry, Bella. I feel wretched about every part of this, and so grateful that you were brave enough to go save my brother after what I did. Please say you'll forgive me."

The words were awkward, stilted because of her embarrassment, but they seemed sincere.

"Of course, Rosalie," I mumbled, grasping at any chance to make her hate me a little less. "It's not your fault at all. I'm the one who jumped off the damn cliff. Of course I forgive you."

The words came out like mush.

"It doesn't count until she's conscious, Rose," Emmett chuckled.

"I'm conscious," I said; it just sounded like a garbled sigh.

"Let her sleep," Edward insisted, but his voice was a little warmer.

It was quiet then, except for the gentle thrum of the engine. I must have fallen asleep, because it seemed like seconds later when the door opened and Edward was carrying me from the car. My eyes wouldn't open. At first I thought we were still at the airport.

And then I heard Charlie.

"Bella!" he shouted from some distance.

"Charlie," I mumbled, trying to shake off the stupor.

"Shh," Edward whispered. "It's okay; you're home and safe. Just sleep."

"I can't believe you have the nerve to show your face here." Charlie bellowed at Edward, his voice much closer now.

"Stop it, Dad," I groaned. He didn't hear me.

"What's wrong with her?" Charlie demanded.

"She's just very tired, Charlie," Edward assured him quietly. "Please let her rest."

"Don't tell me what to do!" Charlie yelled. "Give her to me. Get your hands off her!"

Edward tried to pass me to Charlie, but I clung to him with locked, tenacious fingers. I could feel my dad yanking on my arm.

"Cut it out, Dad," I said with more volume. I managed

to drag my lids back to stare at Charlie with bleary eyes. "Be mad at *me*."

We were in front of my house. The front door was standing open. The cloud cover overhead was too thick to guess at a time of day.

"You bet I will be," Charlie promised. "Get inside."

"'Kay. Let me down," I sighed.

Edward set me on my feet. I could see that I was upright, but I couldn't feel my legs. I trudged forward anyway, until the sidewalk swirled up toward my face. Edward's arms caught me before I hit the concrete.

"Just let me get her upstairs," Edward said. "Then I'll leave."

"No," I cried, panicking. I hadn't got my answers yet. He had to stay for at least that much, didn't he?

"I won't be far," Edward promised, whispering so low in my ear that Charlie didn't have a hope of hearing.

I didn't hear Charlie answer, but Edward headed into the house. My open eyes only made it till the stairs. The last thing I felt was Edward's cool hands prying my fingers loose from his shirt.

23. THE TRUTH

I HAD THE SENSE THAT I'D BEEN ASLEEP FOR A VERY long time—my body was stiff, like I hadn't moved once through all that time, either. My mind was dazed and slow; strange, colorful dreams—dreams and nightmares—swirled dizzily around the inside of my head. They were so vivid. The horrible and the heavenly, all mixed together into a bizarre jumble. There was sharp impatience and fear, both part of that frustrating dream where your feet can't move fast enough. . . . And there were plenty of monsters, red-eyed fiends that were all the more ghastly for their genteel civility. The dream was still strong—I could even remember the names. But the strongest, clearest part of the dream was not the horror. It was the angel that was *most* clear.

It was hard to let him go and wake up. This dream did not want to be shoved away into the vault of dreams I refused to revisit. I struggled with it as my mind became more alert, focusing on reality. I couldn't remember what day of the week it was, but I was sure Jacob or school or work or something was waiting for me. I inhaled deeply, wondering how to face another day.

Something cold touched my forehead with the softest pressure.

I squeezed my eyes more tightly shut. I was still dreaming, it seemed, and it felt abnormally real. I was so close to waking . . . any second now, and it would be gone.

But I realized that it felt too real, too real to be good for me. The stone arms I imagined wrapped around me were far too substantial. If I let this go any further, I'd be sorry for it later. With a resigned sigh, I wrenched back my eyelids to dispel the illusion.

"Oh!" I gasped, and threw my fists over my eyes.

Well, clearly, I'd gone too far; it must have been a mistake to let my imagination get so out of hand. Okay, so "let" was the wrong word. I'd *forced* it to get out of hand—pretty much stalked my hallucinations—and now my mind had snapped.

It took less than half a second for me to realize that, as long as I was truly insane now, I might as well enjoy the delusions while they were pleasant.

I opened my eyes again—and Edward was still there, his perfect face just inches away from mine.

"Did I frighten you?" His low voice was anxious.

This was very good, as delusions went. The face, the

voice, the scent, everything—it was so much better than drowning. The beautiful figment of my imagination watched my changing expressions with alarm. His irises were pitch-black, with bruise-like shadows under them. This surprised me; my hallucinatory Edwards were usually better fed.

I blinked twice, desperately trying to remember the last thing that I was sure was real. Alice was part of my dream, and I wondered if she had really come back at all, or if that was just the preamble. I *thought* she'd returned the day I'd nearly drowned. . . .

"Oh, *crap*," I croaked. My throat was thick with sleeping.

"What's wrong, Bella?"

I frowned at him unhappily. His face was even more anxious than before.

"I'm dead, right?" I moaned. "I *did* drown. Crap, crap, crap! This is gonna kill Charlie."

Edward frowned, too. "You're not dead."

"Then why am I not waking up?" I challenged, raising my eyebrows.

"You *are* awake, Bella."

I shook my head. "Sure, sure. That's what you want me to think. And then it will be worse when I do wake up. *If* I wake up, which I won't, because I'm dead. This is awful. Poor Charlie. And Renée and Jake . . ." I trailed off in horror at what I had done.

"I can see where you might confuse me with a nightmare." His short-lived smile was grim. "But I can't imagine what you could have done to wind up in hell. Did you commit many murders while I was away?"

I grimaced. "Obviously not. If I was in hell, you wouldn't be with me."

He sighed.

My head was getting clearer. My eyes flickered away from his face—unwillingly—for one second, to the dark, open window, and then back to him. I started to remember details . . . and I felt a faint, unfamiliar blush warm the skin over my cheekbones as I slowly realized that Edward was really, truly here with me, and I was wasting time being an idiot.

"Did all of that really happen, then?" It was almost impossible to reassign my dream as reality. I couldn't wrap my head around the concept.

"That depends." Edward's smile was still hard. "If you're referring to us nearly being massacred in Italy, then, yes."

"How strange," I mused. "I really went to Italy. Did you know I'd never been farther east than Albuquerque?"

He rolled his eyes. "Maybe you should go back to sleep. You're not coherent."

"I'm not tired anymore." It was all coming clear now. "What time is it? How long have I been sleeping?"

"It's just after one in the morning. So, about fourteen hours."

I stretched as he spoke. I was so stiff.

"Charlie?" I asked.

Edward frowned. "Sleeping. You should probably know that I'm breaking the rules right now. Well, not technically, since he said I was never to walk through his door again, and I came in the window. . . . But, still, the intent was clear."

"Charlie banned you from the house?" I asked, disbelief quickly melting into fury.

His eyes were sad. "Did you expect anything else?"

My eyes were mad. I was going to have a few words with my father—perhaps it would be a good time to remind him that I was over the legal age of adulthood. It didn't matter so much, of course, except in principle. All too soon there would be no reason for the prohibition. I turned my thoughts to less painful avenues.

"What's the story?" I asked, genuinely curious, but also trying desperately to keep the conversation casual, to keep a firm grip on myself, so I wouldn't scare him away with the frantic, gnawing craving that was raging inside me.

"What do you mean?"

"What am I telling Charlie? What's my excuse for disappearing for . . . how long was I gone, anyway?" I tried to count the hours in my head.

"Just three days." His eyes tightened, but he smiled more naturally this time. "Actually, I was hoping you might have a good explanation. I've got nothing."

I groaned. "Fabulous."

"Well, maybe Alice will come up with something," he offered, trying to comfort me.

And I was comforted. Who cared what I had to deal with later? Every second that he was here—so close, his flawless face glowing in the dim light from the numbers on my alarm clock—was precious and not to be wasted.

"So," I began, picking the least important—though still vitally interesting—question to start with. I was safely delivered home, and he might decide to leave at any moment. I had to keep him talking. Besides, this temporary heaven wasn't entirely complete without the sound of his voice. "What have you been doing, up until three days ago?"

His face turned wary in an instant. "Nothing terribly exciting."

"Of course not," I mumbled.

"Why are you making that face?"

"Well . . ." I pursed my lips, considering. "If you were, after all, just a dream, that's exactly the kind of thing you would say. My imagination must be used up."

He sighed. "If I tell you, will you finally believe that you're not having a nightmare?"

"Nightmare!" I repeated scornfully. He waited for my answer. "Maybe," I said after a second of thought. "If you tell me."

"I was . . . hunting."

"Is that the best you can do?" I criticized. "That definitely doesn't prove I'm awake."

He hesitated, and then spoke slowly, choosing his words with care. "I wasn't hunting for food . . . I was actually trying my hand at . . . tracking. I'm not very good at it."

"What were you tracking?" I asked, intrigued.

"Nothing of consequence." His words didn't match his expression; he looked upset, uncomfortable.

"I don't understand."

He hesitated; his face, shining with an odd green cast from the light of the clock, was torn.

"I—" He took a deep breath. "I owe you an apology. No, of course I owe you much, much more than that. But you have to know"—the words began to flow so fast, the way I remembered he spoke sometimes when he was agitated, that I really had to concentrate to catch them all—"that I had no idea. I didn't realize the mess I was leaving behind. I thought it was safe for you here. So safe. I had no idea that Victoria"—his lips curled back when he said the name—"would come back. I'll admit, when I saw her that one time, I was paying much more attention to James's thoughts. But I just didn't see that she had this kind of response in her. That she even had such a tie to him. I think I realize why now—she was so sure of him, the thought of him failing never occurred to her. It was her overconfidence that clouded her feelings about him—that kept me from seeing the depth of them, the bond there.

"Not that there's any excuse for what I left you to face. When I heard what you told Alice—what she saw herself—when I realized that you had to put your life in the hands of *werewolves*, immature, volatile, the worst thing out there besides Victoria herself"—he shuddered and the gush of words halted for a short second. "Please know that I had no idea of any of this. I feel sick, sick to my core, even now, when I can see and feel you safe in my arms. I am the most miserable excuse for—"

"Stop," I interrupted him. He stared at me with agonized eyes, and I tried to find the right words—the words that would free him from this imagined obligation that caused him so much pain. They were very hard words to say. I didn't know if I could get them out without breaking down. But I had to *try* to do it right. I didn't want to be a source of guilt and anguish in his life. He should be happy, no matter what it cost me.

I'd really been hoping to put off this part of our last conversation. It was going to bring things to an end so much sooner.

Drawing on all my months of practice with trying to be normal for Charlie, I kept my face smooth.

"Edward," I said. His name burned my throat a little on the way out. I could feel the ghost of the hole, waiting to rip itself wide again as soon as he disappeared. I didn't quite see how I was going to survive it this time. "This has to stop now. You can't think about things that way. You can't let this . . . this *guilt* . . . rule your life. You can't take responsibility for the things that happen to me here. None of it is your fault, it's just part of how life *is* for me. So, if I trip in front of a bus or whatever it is next time, you have to realize that it's not your job to take the blame. You can't just go running off to Italy because you feel bad that you didn't save me. Even if I had jumped off that cliff to die, that would have been my choice, and *not your fault*. I know it's your . . . your nature to shoulder the blame for everything, but you really can't let that make you go to such extremes! It's very irresponsible—think of Esme and Carlisle and—"

I was on the edge of losing it. I stopped to take a deep breath, hoping to calm myself. I had to set him free. I had to make sure this never happened again.

"Isabella Marie Swan," he whispered, the strangest expression crossing his face. He almost looked mad. "Do you believe that I asked the Volturi to kill me *because I felt guilty?*"

I could feel the blank incomprehension on my face. "Didn't you?"

"Feel guilty? Intensely so. More than you can comprehend."

"Then . . . what are you saying? I don't understand."

"Bella, I went to the Volturi because I thought you were dead," he said, voice soft, eyes fierce. "Even if I'd had no hand in your death"—he shuddered as he whispered the last word—"even if it *wasn't* my fault, I would have gone to Italy. Obviously, I should have been more careful—I should have spoken to Alice directly, rather than accepting it secondhand from Rosalie. But, really, what was I supposed to think when the boy said Charlie was at the funeral? What are the odds?

"The odds . . . ," he muttered then, distracted. His voice was so low I wasn't sure I heard it right. "The odds are always stacked against us. Mistake after mistake. I'll never criticize Romeo again."

"But I still don't understand," I said. "That's my whole point. So what?"

"Excuse me?"

"So what if I *was* dead?"

He stared at me dubiously for a long moment before answering. "Don't you remember anything I told you before?"

"I remember *everything* that you told me." Including the words that had negated all the rest.

He brushed the tip of his cool finger against my lower

lip. "Bella, you seem to be under a misapprehension." He closed his eyes, shaking his head back and forth with half a smile on his beautiful face. It wasn't a happy smile. "I thought I'd explained it clearly before. Bella, I can't live in a world where you don't exist."

"I am . . ." My head swam as I looked for the appropriate word. "Confused." That worked. I couldn't make sense of what he was saying.

He stared deep into my eyes with his sincere, earnest gaze. "I'm a good liar, Bella, I have to be."

I froze, my muscles locking down as if for impact. The fault line in my chest rippled; the pain of it took my breath away.

He shook my shoulder, trying to loosen my rigid pose. "Let me finish! I'm a good liar, but still, for you to believe me so quickly." He winced. "That was . . . excruciating."

I waited, still frozen.

"When we were in the forest, when I was telling you goodbye—"

I didn't allow myself to remember. I fought to keep myself in the present second only.

"You weren't going to let go," he whispered. "I could see that. I didn't want to do it—it felt like it would kill me to do it—but I knew that if I couldn't convince you that I didn't love you anymore, it would just take you that much longer to get on with your life. I hoped that, if you thought I'd moved on, so would you."

"A clean break," I whispered through unmoving lips.

"Exactly. But I never imagined it would be so easy to do! I thought it would be next to impossible—that you would be so sure of the truth that I would have to lie through my teeth for hours to even plant the seed of doubt in your head. I lied, and I'm so sorry—sorry because I hurt you, sorry because it was a worthless effort. Sorry that I couldn't protect you from what I am. I lied to save you, and it didn't work. I'm sorry.

"But how could you believe me? After all the thousand times I've told you I love you, how could you let one word break your faith in me?"

I didn't answer. I was too shocked to form a rational response.

"I could see it in your eyes, that you honestly *believed* that I didn't want you anymore. The most absurd, ridiculous concept—as if there were any way that *I* could exist without needing *you*!"

I was still frozen. His words were incomprehensible, because they were impossible.

He shook my shoulder again, not hard, but enough that my teeth rattled a little.

"Bella," he sighed. "Really, what were you thinking!"

And so I started to cry. The tears welled up and then gushed miserably down my cheeks.

"I knew it," I sobbed. "I *knew* I was dreaming."

"You're impossible," he said, and he laughed once—a hard laugh, frustrated. "How can I put this so that you'll believe me? You're not asleep, and you're not dead. I'm here, and I love you. I *have* always loved you, and I *will* always love you. I was thinking of you, seeing your face in my mind, every second that I was away. When I told you that I didn't want you, it was the very blackest kind of blasphemy."

I shook my head while the tears continued to ooze from the corners of my eyes.

"You don't believe me, do you?" he whispered, his face paler than his usual pale—I could see that even in the dim light. "Why can you believe the lie, but not the truth?"

"It never made sense for you to love me," I explained, my voice breaking twice. "I always knew that."

His eyes narrowed, his jaw tightened.

"I'll prove you're awake," he promised.

He caught my face securely between his iron hands, ignoring my struggles when I tried to turn my head away.

"Please don't," I whispered.

He stopped, his lips just half an inch from mine.

"Why not?" he demanded. His breath blew into my face, making my head whirl.

"When I wake up"—He opened his mouth to protest, so I revised—"okay, forget that one—when you leave again, it's going to be hard enough without this, too."

He pulled back an inch, to stare at my face.

"Yesterday, when I would touch you, you were so . . . hesitant, so careful, and yet still the same. I need to know why. Is it because I'm too late? Because I've hurt you too much? Because you *have* moved on, as I meant for you to? That would be . . . quite fair. I won't contest your decision. So don't try to spare my feelings, please—just tell me now whether or not you can still love me, after everything I've done to you. Can you?" he whispered.

"What kind of an idiotic question is that?"

"Just answer it. Please."

I stared at him darkly for a long moment. "The way I

feel about you will never change. Of course I love you—and there's nothing you can do about it!"

"That's all I needed to hear."

His mouth was on mine then, and I couldn't fight him. Not because he was so many thousand times stronger than me, but because my will crumbled into dust the second our lips met. This kiss was not quite as careful as others I remembered, which suited me just fine. If I was going to rip myself up further, I might as well get as much in trade as possible.

So I kissed him back, my heart pounding out a jagged, disjointed rhythm while my breathing turned to panting and my fingers moved greedily to his face. I could feel his marble body against every line of mine, and I was so glad he hadn't listened to me—there was no pain in the world that would have justified missing this. His hands memorized my face, the same way mine were tracing his, and, in the brief seconds when his lips were free, he whispered my name.

When I was starting to get dizzy, he pulled away, only to lay his ear against my heart.

I lay there, dazed, waiting for my gasping to slow and quiet.

"By the way," he said in a casual tone. "I'm not leaving you."

I didn't say anything, and he seemed to hear skepticism in my silence.

He lifted his face to lock my gaze in his. "I'm not going anywhere. Not without you," he added more seriously. "I only left you in the first place because I wanted you to have a chance at a normal, happy, human life. I could see what I was doing to you—keeping you constantly on the edge of danger, taking you away from the world you belonged in, risking your life every moment I was with you. So I had to try. I had to do *something*, and it seemed like leaving was the only way. If I hadn't thought you would be better off, I could have never made myself leave. I'm much too selfish. Only *you* could be more important than what I wanted . . . what I needed. What I want and need is to be with you, and I know I'll never be strong enough to leave again. I have too many excuses to stay—thank heaven for that! It seems you *can't* be safe, no matter how many miles I put between us."

"Don't promise me anything," I whispered. If I let myself hope, and it came to nothing . . . that would kill me. Where all those merciless vampires had not been able to finish me off, hope would do the job.

Anger glinted metallic in his black eyes. "You think I'm lying to you now?"

"No—not lying." I shook my head, trying to think it through coherently. To examine the hypothesis that he *did* love me, while staying objective, clinical, so I wouldn't fall into the trap of hoping. "You could mean it . . . now. But what about tomorrow, when you think about all the reasons you left in the first place? Or next month, when Jasper takes a snap at me?"

He flinched.

I thought back over those last days of my life before he left me, tried to see them through the filter of what he was telling me now. From that perspective, imagining that he'd left me while loving me, left me *for* me, his brooding and cold silences took on a different meaning. "It isn't as if you hadn't thought the first decision through, is it?" I guessed. "You'll end up doing what you think is right."

"I'm not as strong as you give me credit for," he said. "Right and wrong have ceased to mean much to me; I was coming back anyway. Before Rosalie told me the news, I was already past trying to live through one week at a time, or even one day. I was fighting to make it through a single hour. It was only a matter of time—and not much of it—before I showed up at your window and begged you to take me back. I'd be happy to beg now, if you'd like that."

I grimaced. "Be serious, please."

"Oh, I am," he insisted, glaring now. "Will you please try to hear what I'm telling you? Will you let me attempt to explain what you mean to me?"

He waited, studying my face as he spoke to make sure I was really listening.

"Before you, Bella, my life was like a moonless night. Very dark, but there were stars—points of light and reason. . . . And then you shot across my sky like a meteor. Suddenly everything was on fire; there was brilliancy, there was beauty. When you were gone, when the meteor had fallen over the horizon, everything went black. Nothing had changed, but my eyes were blinded by the light. I couldn't see the stars anymore. And there was no more reason for anything."

I wanted to believe him. But this was *my* life without *him* that he was describing, not the other way around.

"Your eyes will adjust," I mumbled.

"That's just the problem—they can't."

"What about your distractions?"

He laughed without a trace of humor. "Just part of the lie, love. There was no distraction from the . . . the *agony*. My heart hasn't beat in almost ninety years, but this was different. It was like my heart was gone—like I was hollow. Like I'd left everything that was inside me here with you."

"That's funny," I muttered.

He arched one perfect eyebrow. "Funny?"

"I meant strange—I thought it was just me. Lots of pieces of me went missing, too. I haven't been able to really breathe in so long." I filled my lungs, luxuriating in the sensation. "And my heart. That was definitely lost."

He closed his eyes and laid his ear over my heart again. I let my cheek press against his hair, felt the texture of it on my skin, smelled the delicious scent of him.

"Tracking wasn't a distraction then?" I asked, curious, and also needing to distract *myself*. I was very much in danger of hoping. I wouldn't be able to stop myself for long. My heart throbbed, singing in my chest.

"No." He sighed. "That was never a distraction. It was an obligation."

"What does that mean?"

"It means that, even though I never expected any danger from Victoria, I wasn't going to let her get away with . . . Well, like I said, I was horrible at it. I traced her as far as Texas, but then I followed a false lead down to Brazil—and really she came here." He groaned. "I wasn't even on the right continent! And all the while, worse than my worst fears—"

"You were hunting *Victoria*?" I half-shrieked as soon as I could find my voice, shooting through two octaves.

Charlie's distant snores stuttered, and then picked up a regular rhythm again.

"Not well," Edward answered, studying my outraged expression with a confused look. "But I'll do better this time. She won't be tainting perfectly good air by breathing in and out for much longer."

"That is . . . out of the question," I managed to choke out. Insanity. Even if he had Emmett or Jasper help him. Even if he had Emmett *and* Jasper help. It was worse than my other imaginings: Jacob Black standing across a small space from Victoria's vicious and feline figure. I couldn't bear to picture Edward there, even though he was so much more durable than my half-human best friend.

"It's too late for her. I might have let the other time slide, but not now, not after—"

I interrupted him again, trying to sound calm. "Didn't you just promise that you weren't going to leave?" I asked, fighting the words as I said them, not letting them plant themselves in my heart. "That isn't exactly compatible with an extended tracking expedition, is it?"

He frowned. A snarl began to build low in his chest. "I will keep my promise, Bella. But Victoria"—the snarl became more pronounced—"is going to die. Soon."

"Let's not be hasty," I said, trying to hide my panic. "Maybe she's not coming back. Jake's pack probably scared her off. There's really no reason to go looking for her. Besides, I've got bigger problems than Victoria."

Edward's eyes narrowed, but he nodded. "It's true. The werewolves are a problem."

I snorted. "I wasn't talking about *Jacob*. My problems are a lot worse that a handful of adolescent wolves getting themselves into trouble."

Edward looked as if he were about to say something, and then thought better of it. His teeth clicked together, and he spoke through them. "Really?" he asked. "Then what would be your greatest problem? That would make Victoria's returning for you seem like such an inconsequential matter in comparison?"

"How about the second greatest?" I hedged.

"All right," he agreed, suspicious.

I paused. I wasn't sure I could say the name. "There are others who are coming to look for me," I reminded him in a subdued whisper.

He sighed, but the reaction was not as strong as I would have imagined after his response to Victoria.

"The Volturi are only the *second* greatest?"

"You don't seem that upset about it," I noted.

"Well, we have plenty of time to think it through. Time means something very different to them than it does to you, or even me. They count years the way you count days. I wouldn't be surprised if you were thirty before you crossed their minds again," he added lightly.

Horror washed through me.

Thirty.

So his promises meant nothing, in the end. If I were going to turn thirty someday, then he couldn't be planning on staying long. The harsh pain of this knowledge made me realize that I'd already begun to hope, without giving myself permission to do so.

"You don't have to be afraid," he said, anxious as he watched the tears dew up again on the rims of my eyes. "I won't let them hurt you."

"While you're here." Not that I cared what happened to me when he left.

He took my face between his two stone hands, holding it tightly while his midnight eyes glared into mine with the gravitational force of a black hole. "I will never leave you again."

"But you said *thirty*," I whispered. The tears leaked over the edge. "What? You're going to stay, but let me get all old anyway? Right."

His eyes softened, while his mouth went hard. "That's exactly what I'm going to do. What choice have I? I cannot be without you, but I will not destroy your soul."

"Is this really . . ." I tried to keep my voice even, but this question was too hard. I remembered his face when Aro had almost begged him to consider making me immortal. The sick look there. Was this fixation with keeping me human really about my soul, or was it because he wasn't sure that he wanted me around that long?

"Yes?" he asked, waiting for my question.

I asked a different one. Almost—but not quite—as hard.

"But what about when I get so old that people think

I'm your mother? Your *grandmother?*" My voice was pale with revulsion—I could see Gran's face again in the dream mirror.

His whole face was soft now. He brushed the tears from my cheek with his lips. "That doesn't mean anything to me," he breathed against my skin. "You will always be the most beautiful thing in my world. Of course . . ." He hesitated, flinching slightly. "If you outgrew *me*—if you wanted something more—I would understand that, Bella. I promise I wouldn't stand in your way if you wanted to leave me."

His eyes were liquid onyx and utterly sincere. He spoke as if he'd put endless amounts of thought into this asinine plan.

"You do realize that I'll die eventually, right?" I demanded.

He'd thought about this part, too. "I'll follow after as soon as I can."

"That is seriously . . ." I looked for the right word. "Sick."

"Bella, it's the only right way left—"

"Let's just back up for a minute," I said; feeling angry made it so much easier to be clear, decisive. "You do remember the Volturi, right? I can't stay human forever. They'll kill me. Even if they don't think of me till I'm *thirty*"—I hissed the word—"do you really think they'll forget?"

"No," he answered slowly, shaking his head. "They won't forget. But . . ."

"But?"

He grinned while I stared at him warily. Maybe I wasn't the only crazy one.

"I have a few plans."

"And these plans," I said, my voice getting more acidic with each word. "These plans all center around me staying *human*."

My attitude hardened his expression. "Naturally." His tone was brusque, his divine face arrogant.

We glowered at each other for a long minute.

Then I took a deep breath, squared my shoulders, I pushed his arms away so that I could sit up.

"Do you want me to leave?" he asked, and it made my heart flutter to see that this idea hurt him, though he tried not to show it.

"No," I told him. "*I'm* leaving."

He watched me suspiciously as I climbed out of the bed and fumbled around in the dark room, looking for my shoes.

"May I ask where you are going?" he asked.

"I'm going to your house," I told him, still feeling around blindly.

He got up and came to my side. "Here are your shoes. How did you plan to get there?"

"My truck."

"That will probably wake Charlie," he offered as a deterrent.

I sighed. "I know. But honestly, I'll be grounded for weeks as it is. How much more trouble can I really get in?"

"None. He'll blame me, not you."

"If you have a better idea, I'm all ears."

"Stay here," he suggested, but his expression wasn't hopeful.

"No dice. But you go ahead and make yourself at home," I encouraged, surprised at how natural my teasing sounded, and headed for the door.

He was there before me, blocking my way.

I frowned, and turned for the window. It wasn't really that far to the ground, and it was mostly grass beneath. . . .

"Okay," he sighed. "I'll give you a ride."

I shrugged. "Either way. But you probably *should* be there, too."

"And why is that?"

"Because you're extraordinarily opinionated, and I'm sure you'll want a chance to air your views."

"My views on which subject?" He asked through his teeth.

"This isn't just about you anymore. You're not the center of the universe, you know." My own personal universe was, of course, a different story. "If you're going to bring the Volturi down on us over something as stupid as leaving me human, then your family ought to have a say."

"A say in what?" he asked, each word distinct.

"My mortality. I'm putting it to a vote."

24. VOTE

HE WAS NOT PLEASED, THAT MUCH WAS EASY TO READ IN his face. But, without further argument, he took me in his arms and sprang lithely from my window, landing without the slightest jolt, like a cat. It *was* a little bit farther down than I'd imagined.

"All right then," he said, his voice seething with disapproval. "Up you go."

He helped me onto his back, and took off running. Even after all this time, it felt routine. Easy. Evidently this was something you never forgot, like riding a bicycle.

It was so very quiet and dark as he ran through the forest, his breathing slow and even—dark enough that the trees flying past us were nearly invisible, and only the rush of air in my face truly gave away our speed. The air was damp; it didn't burn my eyes the way the wind in the big plaza had, and that was comforting. As was the night, too, after that terrifying brightness. Like the thick quilt I'd played under as a child, the dark felt familiar and protecting.

I remembered that running through the forest like this used to frighten me, that I used to have to close my eyes. It seemed a silly reaction to me now. I kept my eyes wide, my chin resting on his shoulder, my cheek against his neck. The speed was exhilarating. A hundred times better than the motorcycle.

I turned my face toward him and pressed my lips into the cold stone skin of his neck.

"Thank you," he said, as the vague, black shapes of trees raced past us. "Does that mean you've decided you're awake?"

I laughed. The sound was easy, natural, effortless. It sounded *right*. "Not really. More that, either way, I'm not trying to wake up. Not tonight."

"I'll earn your trust back somehow," he murmured, mostly to himself. "If it's my final act."

"I trust *you*," I assured him. "It's me I don't trust."

"Explain that, please."

He'd slowed to a walk—I could only tell because the wind ceased—and I guessed that we weren't far from the house. In fact, I thought I could make out the sound of the river rushing somewhere close by in the darkness.

"Well—" I struggled to find the right way to phrase it. "I don't trust myself to be . . . enough. To deserve you. There's nothing about me that could *hold* you."

He stopped and reached around to pull me from his back. His gentle hands did not release me; after he'd set me on my feet again, he wrapped his arms tightly around me, hugging me to his chest.

"Your hold is permanent and unbreakable," he whispered. "Never doubt that."

But how could I not?

"You never did tell me . . . ," he murmured.

"What?"

"What your greatest problem is."

"I'll give you one guess." I sighed, and reached up to touch the tip of his nose with my index finger.

He nodded. "I'm worse than the Volturi," he said grimly. "I guess I've earned that."

I rolled my eyes. "The worst the Volturi can do is kill me."

He waited with tense eyes.

"You can leave me," I explained. "The Volturi, Victoria . . . they're nothing compared to that."

Even in the darkness, I could see the anguish twist his face—it reminded me of his expression under Jane's torturing gaze; I felt sick, and regretted speaking the truth.

"Don't," I whispered, touching his face. "Don't be sad."

He pulled one corner of his mouth up halfheartedly, but the expression didn't touch his eyes. "If there was only some way to make you see that I *can't* leave you," he whispered. "Time, I suppose, will be the way to convince you."

I liked the idea of time. "Okay," I agreed.

His face was still tormented. I tried to distract him with inconsequentials.

"So—since you're staying. Can I have my stuff back?" I asked, making my tone as light as I could manage.

My attempt worked, to an extent: he laughed. But his eyes retained the misery. "Your things were never gone," he told me. "I knew it was wrong, since I promised you peace without reminders. It was stupid and childish, but I wanted to leave something of myself with you. The CD, the pictures, the tickets—they're all under your floorboards."

"*Really?*"

He nodded, seeming slightly cheered by my obvious pleasure in this trivial fact. It wasn't enough to heal the pain in his face completely.

"I think," I said slowly, "I'm not sure, but I wonder . . . I think maybe I knew it the whole time."

"What did you know?"

I only wanted to take away the agony in his eyes, but as I spoke the words, they sounded truer than I expected they would.

"Some part of me, my subconscious maybe, never stopped believing that you still cared whether I lived or died. That's probably why I was hearing the voices."

There was a very deep silence for a moment. "Voices?" he asked flatly.

"Well, just one voice. Yours. It's a long story." The wary look on his face made me wish that I hadn't brought that up. Would he think I was crazy, like everyone else? Was everyone else right about that? But at least that expression—the one that made him look like something was burning him—faded.

"I've got time." His voice was unnaturally even.

"It's pretty pathetic."

He waited.

I wasn't sure how to explain. "Do you remember what Alice said about extreme sports?"

He spoke the words without inflection or emphasis. "You jumped off a cliff for fun."

"Er, right. And before that, with the motorcycle—"

"Motorcycle?" he asked. I knew his voice well enough to hear something brewing behind the calm.

"I guess I didn't tell Alice about that part."

"No."

"Well, about that . . . See, I found that . . . when I was doing something dangerous or stupid . . . I could remember you more clearly," I confessed, feeling completely mental. "I could remember how your voice sounded when you were angry. I could hear it, like you were standing right there next to me. Mostly I tried not to think about you, but this didn't hurt so much—it was like you were protecting me again. Like you didn't want me to be hurt.

"And, well, I wonder if the reason I could hear you so clearly was because, underneath it all, I always knew that you hadn't stopped loving me."

Again, as I spoke, the words brought with them a sense of conviction. Of rightness. Some deep place inside me recognized truth.

His words came out half-strangled. "You . . . were . . . risking your life . . . to hear—"

"Shh," I interrupted him. "Hold on a second. I think I'm having an epiphany here."

I thought of that night in Port Angeles when I'd had

my first delusion. I'd come up with two options. Insanity or wish fulfillment. I'd seen no third option.

But what if . . .

What if you sincerely believed something was true, but you were dead wrong? What if you were so stubbornly sure that you were right, that you wouldn't even consider the truth? Would the truth be silenced, or would it try to break through?

Option three: Edward loved me. The bond forged between us was not one that could be broken by absence, distance, or time. And no matter how much more special or beautiful or brilliant or perfect than me he might be, he was as irreversibly altered as I was. As I would always belong to him, so would he always be mine.

Was that what I'd been trying to tell myself?

"Oh!"

"Bella?"

"Oh. Okay. I see."

"Your epiphany?" he asked, his voice uneven and strained.

"You love me," I marveled. The sense of conviction and rightness washed through me again.

Though his eyes were still anxious, the crooked smile I loved best flashed across his face. "Truly, I do."

My heart inflated like it was going to crack right through my ribs. It filled my chest and blocked my throat so that I could not speak.

He really did want me the way I wanted him—forever. It *was* only fear for my soul, for the human things he didn't want to take from me, that made him so desperate to leave me mortal. Compared to the fear that he didn't want me, this hurdle—my soul—seemed almost insignificant.

He took my face tightly between his cool hands and kissed me until I was so dizzy the forest was spinning. Then he leaned his forehead against mine, and I was not the only one breathing harder than usual.

"You were better at it than I was, you know," he told me.

"Better at what?"

"Surviving. You, at least, made an effort. You got up in the morning, tried to be normal for Charlie, followed the pattern of your life. When I wasn't actively tracking, I was . . . totally useless. I couldn't be around my family— I couldn't be around anyone. I'm embarrassed to admit that I more or less curled up into a ball and let the misery have me." He grinned, sheepish. "It was much more pathetic than hearing voices. And, of course, you know I do that, too."

I was deeply relieved that he really seemed to understand—comforted that this all made sense to him. At any rate, he wasn't looking at me like I was crazy. He was looking at me like . . . he loved me.

"I only heard one voice," I corrected him.

He laughed and then pulled me tight against his right side and started to lead me forward.

"I'm just humoring you with this." He motioned broadly with his hand toward the darkness in front of us as we walked. There was something pale and immense there—the house, I realized. "It doesn't matter in the slightest what they say."

"This affects them now, too."

He shrugged indifferently.

He led me through the open front door into the dark house and flipped the lights on. The room was just as I'd remembered it—the piano and the white couches and the pale, massive staircase. No dust, no white sheets.

Edward called out the names with no more volume than I'd use in regular conversation. "Carlisle? Esme? Rosalie? Emmett? Jasper? Alice?" They would hear.

Carlisle was suddenly standing beside me, as if he'd been there all along. "Welcome back, Bella." He smiled. "What can we do for you this morning? I imagine, due to the hour, that this is not a purely social visit?"

I nodded. "I'd like to talk to everyone at once, if that's okay. About something important."

I couldn't help glancing up at Edward's face as I spoke. His expression was critical, but resigned. When I looked back to Carlisle, he was looking at Edward, too.

"Of course," Carlisle said. "Why don't we talk in the other room?"

Carlisle led the way through the bright living room, around the corner to the dining room, turning on lights as he went. The walls were white, the ceilings high, like the living room. In the center of the room, under the iow-hanging chandelier, was a large, polished oval table surrounded by eight chairs. Carlisle held out a chair for me at the head.

I'd never seen the Cullens use the dining room table before—it was just a prop. They didn't eat in the house.

As soon as I turned to sit in the chair, I saw that we were not alone. Esme had followed Edward, and behind her the rest of the family filed in.

Carlisle sat down on my right, and Edward on my left. Everyone else took their seats in silence. Alice was grinning at me, already in on the plot. Emmett and Jasper looked curious, and Rosalie smiled at me tentatively. My answering smile was just as timid. That was going to take some getting used to.

Carlisle nodded toward me. "The floor is yours."

I swallowed. Their gazing eyes made me nervous. Edward took my hand under the table. I peeked at him, but he was watching the others, his face suddenly fierce.

"Well," I paused. "I'm hoping Alice has already told you everything that happened in Volterra?"

"Everything," Alice assured me.

I threw her a meaningful look. "And on the way?"

"That, too," she nodded.

"Good," I sighed with relief. "Then we're all on the same page."

They waited patiently while I tried to order my thoughts.

"So, I have a problem," I began. "Alice promised the Volturi that I would become one of you. They're going to send someone to check, and I'm sure that's a bad thing— something to avoid.

"And so, now, this involves you all. I'm sorry about that." I looked at each one of their beautiful faces, saving the most beautiful for last. Edward's mouth was turned down into a grimace. "But, if you don't want me, then I'm not going to force myself on you, whether Alice is willing or not."

Esme opened her mouth to speak, but I held up one finger to stop her.

"Please, let me finish. You all know what I want. And I'm sure you know what Edward thinks, too. I think the only fair way to decide is for everyone to have a vote. If you decide you don't want me, then . . . I guess I'll go back to Italy alone. I can't have *them* coming *here*." My forehead creased as I considered that.

There was the faint rumble of a growl in Edward's chest. I ignored him.

"Taking into account, then, that I won't put any of you in danger either way, I want you to vote yes or no on the issue of me becoming a vampire."

I half-smiled on the last word, and gestured toward Carlisle to begin.

"Just a minute," Edward interrupted.

I glared at him through narrowed eyes. He raised his eyebrows at me, squeezing my hand.

"I have something to add before we vote."

I sighed.

"About the danger Bella's referring to," he continued. "I don't think we need to be overly anxious."

His expression became more animated. He put his free hand on the shining table and leaned forward.

"You see," he explained, looking around the table while he spoke, "there was more than one reason why I didn't want to shake Aro's hand there at the end. There's something they didn't think of, and I didn't want to clue them in." He grinned.

"Which was?" Alice prodded. I was sure my expression was just as skeptical as hers.

"The Volturi are overconfident, and with good reason. When they decide to find someone, it's not really a problem. Do you remember Demetri?" He glanced down at me.

I shuddered. He took that as a yes.

"He finds people—that's his talent, why they keep him.

"Now, the whole time we were with any of them, I was picking their brains for anything that might save us, getting as much information as possible. So I saw how Demetri's talent works. He's a tracker—a tracker a thousand times more gifted than James was. His ability is loosely related to what I do, or what Aro does. He catches the . . . flavor? I don't know how to describe it . . . the tenor . . . of someone's mind, and then he follows that. It works over immense distances.

"But after Aro's little experiments, well . . ." Edward shrugged.

"You think he won't be able to find me," I said flatly.

He was smug. "I'm sure of it. He relies totally on that other sense. When it doesn't work with you, they'll all be blind."

"And how does that solve anything?"

"Quite obviously, Alice will be able to tell when they're planning a visit, and I'll hide you. They'll be helpless," he said with fierce enjoyment. "It will be like looking for a piece of straw in a haystack!"

He and Emmett exchanged a glance and a smirk.

This made no sense. "But they can find you," I reminded him.

"And I can take care of myself."

Emmett laughed, and reached across the table toward his brother, extending a fist.

"Excellent plan, my brother," he said with enthusiasm. Edward stretched out his arm to smack Emmett's fist with his own.

"No," Rosalie hissed.

"Absolutely not," I agreed.

"Nice." Jasper's voice was appreciative.

"Idiots," Alice muttered.

Esme just glared at Edward.

I straightened up in my chair, focusing. This was *my* meeting.

"All right, then. Edward has offered an alternative for you to consider," I said coolly. "Let's vote."

I looked toward Edward this time; it would be better to get his opinion out of the way. "Do you want me to join your family?"

His eyes were hard and black as flint. "Not that way. You're staying human."

I nodded once, keeping my face businesslike, and then moved on.

"Alice?"

"Yes."

"Jasper?"

"Yes," he said, voice grave. I was a little surprised—I hadn't been at all sure of his vote—but I suppressed my reaction and moved on.

"Rosalie?"

She hesitated, biting down on her full, perfect bottom lip. "No."

I kept my face blank and turned my head slightly to move on, but she held up both her hands, palms forward.

"Let me explain," she pleaded. "I don't mean that I have any aversion to you as a sister. It's just that . . . this is not the life I would have chosen for myself. I wish there had been someone there to vote no for me."

I nodded slowly, and then turned to Emmett.

"Hell, yes!" He grinned. "We can find some other way to pick a fight with this Demetri."

I was still grimacing at that when I looked at Esme.

"Yes, of course, Bella. I already think of you as part of my family."

"Thank you, Esme," I murmured as I turned toward Carlisle.

I was suddenly nervous, wishing I had asked for his vote first. I was sure that this was the vote that mattered most, the vote that counted more than any majority.

Carlisle wasn't looking at me.

"Edward," he said.

"No," Edward growled. His jaw was strained tight, his lips curled back from his teeth.

"It's the only way that makes sense," Carlisle insisted. "You've chosen not to live without her, and that doesn't leave me a choice."

Edward dropped my hand, shoving away from the table. He stalked out of the room, snarling under his breath.

"I guess you know my vote." Carlisle sighed.

I was still staring after Edward. "Thanks," I mumbled.

An earsplitting crash echoed from the other room.

I flinched, and spoke quickly. "That's all I needed. Thank you. For wanting to keep me. I feel exactly the same way about all of you, too." My voice was jagged with emotion by the end.

Esme was at my side in a flash, her cold arms around me.

"Dearest Bella," she breathed.

I hugged her back. Out of the corner of my eye, I noticed Rosalie looking down at the table, and I realized that my words could be construed in two ways.

"Well, Alice," I said when Esme released me. "Where do you want to do this?"

Alice stared at me, her eyes widening with terror.

"No! *No!* NO!" Edward roared, charging back into the room. He was in my face before I had time to blink, bending over me, his expression twisted in rage. "Are you insane?" he shouted. "Have you utterly lost your mind?"

I cringed away, my hands over my ears.

"Um, Bella," Alice interjected in an anxious voice. "I don't think I'm *ready* for that. I'll need to prepare. . . ."

"You promised," I reminded her, glaring under Edward's arm.

"I know, but . . . Seriously, Bella! I don't have any idea how to *not* kill you."

"You can do it," I encouraged. "I trust you."

Edward snarled in fury.

Alice shook her head quickly, looking panicked.

"Carlisle?" I turned to look at him.

Edward grabbed my face in his hand, forcing me to look at him. His other hand was out, palm toward Carlisle.

Carlisle ignored that. "I'm able to do it," he answered my question. I wished I could see his expression. "You would be in no danger of me losing control."

"Sounds good." I hoped he could understand; it was hard to talk clearly the way Edward held my jaw.

"Hold on," Edward said between his teeth. "It doesn't have to be now."

"There's no reason for it not to be now," I said, the words coming out distorted.

"I can think of a few."

"Of course you can," I said sourly. "Now let go of me."

He freed my face, and folded his arms across his chest. "In about two hours, Charlie will be here looking for you. I wouldn't put it past him to involve the police."

"All three of them." But I frowned.

This was always the hardest part. Charlie, Renée. Now Jacob, too. The people I would lose, the people I would hurt. I wished there was some way that I could be the only one to suffer, but I knew that was impossible.

At the same time, I was hurting them more by staying human. Putting Charlie in constant danger through my proximity. Putting Jake in worse danger still by drawing his enemies across the land he felt bound to protect. And Renée—I couldn't even risk a visit to see my own mother for fear of bringing my deadly problems along with me!

I was a danger magnet; I'd accepted that about myself. Accepting this, I knew I needed to be able to take care of myself and protect the ones I loved, even if that meant that I couldn't be *with* them. I needed to be strong.

"In the interest of remaining *inconspicuous*," Edward said, still talking through his gritted teeth, but looking at Carlisle now, "I suggest that we put this conversation off, at the very least until Bella finishes high school, and moves out of Charlie's house."

"That's a reasonable request, Bella," Carlisle pointed out.

I thought about Charlie's reaction when he woke up this morning, if—after all that life had put him through in the last week with Harry's loss, and then *I* had put him through with my unexplained disappearance—he were to find my bed empty. Charlie deserved better than that. It was just a little more time; graduation wasn't so far away . . .

I pursed my lips. "I'll consider it."

Edward relaxed. His jaw unclenched.

"I should probably take you home," he said, more calm now, but clearly in a hurry to get me out of here. "Just in case Charlie wakes up early."

I looked at Carlisle. "After graduation?"

"You have my word."

I took a deep breath, smiled, and turned back to Edward. "Okay. You can take me home."

Edward rushed me out of the house before Carlisle could promise me anything else. He took me out the back, so I didn't get to see what was broken in the living room.

It was a quiet trip home. I was feeling triumphant, and a little smug. Scared stiff, too, of course, but I tried not to think about that part. It did me no good to worry about the pain—the physical or the emotional—so I wouldn't. Not until I absolutely had to.

When we got to my house, Edward didn't pause. He dashed up the wall and through my window in half a second. Then he pulled my arms from around his neck and set me on the bed.

I thought I had a pretty good idea of what he was thinking, but his expression surprised me. Instead of furious, it was calculating. He paced silently back and forth across my dark room while I watched with growing suspicion.

"Whatever you're planning, it's not going to work," I told him.

"Shh. I'm thinking."

"Ugh," I groaned, throwing myself back on the bed and pulling the quilt over my head.

There was no sound, but suddenly he was there. He flipped the cover back so he could see me. He was lying next to me. His hand reached up to brush my hair from my cheek.

"If you don't mind, I'd much rather you didn't hide your face. I've lived without it for as long as I can stand. Now . . . tell me something."

"What?" I asked, unwilling.

"If you could have anything in the world, anything at all, what would it be?"

I could feel the skepticism in my eyes. "You."

He shook his head impatiently. "Something you don't already have."

I wasn't sure where he was trying to lead me, so I thought

carefully before I answered. I came up with something that was both true, and also probably impossible.

"I would want . . . Carlisle not to have to do it. I would want *you* to change me."

I watched his reaction warily, expecting more of the fury I'd seen at his house. I was surprised that his expression didn't change. It was still calculating, thoughtful.

"What would you be willing to trade for that?"

I couldn't believe my ears. I gawked at his composed face and blurted out the answer before I could think about it.

"Anything."

He smiled faintly, and then pursed his lips. "Five years?"

My face twisted into an expression somewhere between chagrin and horror.

"You said anything," he reminded me.

"Yes, but . . . you'll use the time to find a way out of it. I have to strike while the iron is hot. Besides, it's just too dangerous to be human—for me, at least. So, anything but *that*."

He frowned. "Three years?"

"No!"

"Isn't it worth anything to you at all?"

I thought about how much I wanted this. Better to keep a poker face, I decided, and not let him know how *very* much that was. It would give me more leverage. "Six months?"

He rolled his eyes. "Not good enough."

"One year, then," I said. "That's my limit."

"At least give me two."

"No way. Nineteen I'll do. But I'm not going anywhere *near* twenty. If you're staying in your teens forever, then so am I."

He thought for a minute. "All right. Forget time limits. If you want me to be the one—then you'll just have to meet one condition."

"Condition?" My voice went flat. "What condition?"

His eyes were cautious—he spoke slowly. "Marry me first."

I stared at him, waiting. . . . "Okay. What's the punch line?"

He sighed. "You're wounding my ego, Bella. I just proposed to you, and you think it's a joke."

"Edward, please be serious."

"I am one hundred percent serious." He gazed at me with no hint of humor in his face.

"Oh, c'mon," I said, an edge of hysteria in my voice. "I'm only eighteen."

"Well, I'm nearly a hundred and ten. It's time I settled down."

I looked away, out the dark window, trying to control the panic before it gave me away.

"Look, marriage isn't exactly that high on my list of priorities, you know? It was sort of the kiss of death for Renée and Charlie."

"Interesting choice of words."

"You know what I mean."

He inhaled deeply. "Please don't tell me that you're afraid of the commitment," his voice was disbelieving, and I understood what he meant.

"That's not it exactly," I hedged. "I'm . . . afraid of Renée. She has some really intense opinions on getting married before you're thirty."

"Because she'd rather you became one of the eternal damned than get married." He laughed darkly.

"You think you're joking."

"Bella, if you compare the level of commitment between a marital union as opposed to bartering your soul in exchange for an eternity as a vampire . . ." He shook his head. "If you're not brave enough to marry me, then—"

"Well," I interrupted. "What if I did? What if I told you to take me to Vegas now? Would I be a vampire in three days?"

He smiled, his teeth flashing in the dark. "Sure," he said, calling my bluff. "I'll get my car."

"Dammit." I muttered. "I'll give you eighteen months."

"No deal," he said, grinning. "I like *this* condition."

"Fine. I'll have Carlisle do it when I graduate."

"If that's what you really want." He shrugged, and his smile became absolutely angelic.

"You're impossible," I groaned. "A monster."

He chuckled. "Is that why you won't marry me?"

I groaned again.

He leaned toward me; his night-dark eyes melted and smoldered and shattered my concentration. "*Please*, Bella?" he breathed.

I forgot how to breathe for a moment. When I recovered, I shook my head quickly, trying to clear my suddenly clouded mind.

"Would this have gone better if I'd had time to get a ring?"

"No! No rings!" I very nearly shouted.

"Now you've done it," he whispered.

"Oops."

"Charlie's getting up; I'd better leave," Edward said with resignation.

My heart stopped beating.

He gauged my expression for a second. "Would it be childish of me to hide in your closet, then?"

"No," I whispered eagerly. "Stay. Please."

Edward smiled and disappeared.

I seethed in the darkness as I waited for Charlie to check on me. Edward knew exactly what he was doing, and I was willing to bet that all the injured surprise was part of the ploy. Of course, I still had the Carlisle option, but now that I knew there was a chance that Edward would change me himself, I wanted it bad. He was such a cheater.

My door cracked open.

"Morning, Dad."

"Oh, hey, Bella." He sounded embarrassed at getting caught. "I didn't know you were awake."

"Yeah. I've just been waiting for you to wake up so I could take a shower." I started to get up.

"Hold on," Charlie said, flipping the light on. I blinked in the sudden brightness, and carefully kept my eyes away from the closet. "Let's talk for a minute first."

I couldn't control my grimace. I'd forgotten to ask Alice for a good excuse.

"You know you're in trouble."

"Yeah, I know."

"I just about went crazy these last three days. I come home from Harry's *funeral*, and you're gone. Jacob could only tell me that you'd run off with Alice Cullen, and that he thought you were in trouble. You didn't leave me a number, and you didn't call. I didn't know where you were or when—or if—you were coming back. Do you have any idea how . . . how . . ." He couldn't finish the sentence. He sucked in a sharp breath and moved on. "Can you give me one reason why I shouldn't ship you off to Jacksonville this second?"

My eyes narrowed. So it was going to be threats, was it? Two could play at that game. I sat up, pulling the quilt around me. "Because I won't go."

"Now just one minute, young lady—"

"Look, Dad, I accept complete responsibility for my actions, and you have the right to ground me for as long as you want. I will also do all the chores and laundry and dishes until you think I've learned my lesson. And I guess you're within your rights if you want to kick me out, too— but that won't make me to go to Florida."

His face turned bright red. He took a few deep breaths before he answered.

"Would you like to explain where you've been?"

Oh, crap. "There was . . . an emergency."

He raised his eyebrows in expectation of my brilliant explanation.

I filled my cheeks with air and then blew it out noisily. "I don't know what to tell you, Dad. It was mostly a misunderstanding. He said, she said. It got out of hand."

He waited with a distrustful expression.

"See, Alice told Rosalie about me jumping off the cliff. . . ." I was scrambling frantically to make this work, to keep it as close to the truth as possible so that my inability to lie convincingly would not undermine the excuse, but before I could go on, Charlie's expression reminded me that he didn't know anything about the cliff.

Major oops. As if I wasn't already toast.

"I guess I didn't tell you about that," I choked out. "It was nothing. Just messing around, swimming with Jake. Anyway, Rosalie told Edward, and he was upset. She sort of accidentally made it sound like I was trying to kill myself or something. He wouldn't answer his phone, so Alice dragged me to . . . L.A., to explain in person." I shrugged, desperately hoping that he would not be so distracted by my slip that he'd miss the brilliant explanation I'd provided.

Charlie's face was frozen. "*Were* you trying to kill yourself, Bella?"

"No, of course not. Just having fun with Jake. Cliff diving. The La Push kids do it all the time. Like I said, nothing."

Charlie's face heated up—from frozen to hot with fury. "What's it to Edward Cullen anyway?" he barked. "All this time, he's just left you dangling without a word—"

I interrupted him. "Another misunderstanding."

His face flushed again. "So is he back then?"

"I'm not sure what the exact plan is. I *think* they all are."

He shook his head, the vein in his forehead pulsing. "I want you to stay away from him, Bella. I don't trust him.

He's rotten for you. I won't let him mess you up like that again."

"Fine," I said curtly.

Charlie rocked back onto his heels. "Oh." He scrambled for a second, exhaling loudly in surprise. "I thought you were going to be difficult."

"I am." I stared straight into his eyes. "I meant, 'Fine, I'll move out.'"

His eyes bulged; his face turned puce. My resolve wavered as I started to worry about his health. He was no younger than Harry. . . .

"Dad, I don't *want* to move out," I said in a softer tone. "I love you. I know you're worried, but you need to trust me on this. And you're going to have to ease up on Edward if you want me to stay. Do you want me to live here or not?"

"That's not fair, Bella. You know I want you to stay."

"Then be nice to Edward, because he's going to be where I am." I said it with confidence. The conviction of my epiphany was still strong.

"Not under my roof," Charlie stormed.

I sighed a heavy sigh. "Look, I'm not going to give you any more ultimatums tonight—or I guess it's this morning. Just think about it for a few days, okay? But keep in mind that Edward and I are sort of a package deal."

"Bella—"

"Think it over," I insisted. "And while you're doing that, could you give me some privacy? I *really* need a shower."

Charlie's face was a strange shade of purple, but he left,

slamming the door behind him. I heard him stomp furiously down the stairs.

I threw off my quilt, and Edward was already there, sitting in the rocking chair as if he'd been present through the whole conversation.

"Sorry about that," I whispered.

"It's not as if I don't deserve far worse," he murmured. "Don't start anything with Charlie over me, please."

"Don't worry about it," I breathed as I gathered up my bathroom things and a set of clean clothes. "I will start exactly as much as is necessary, and no more than that. Or are you trying to tell me I have nowhere to go?" I widened my eyes with false alarm.

"You'd move in with a house full of vampires?"

"That's probably the safest place for someone like me. Besides . . ." I grinned. "If Charlie kicks me out, then there's no need for a graduation deadline, is there?"

His jaw tightened. "So eager for eternal damnation," he muttered.

"You know you don't really believe that."

"Oh, don't I?" he fumed.

"No. You don't."

He glowered at me and started to speak, but I cut him off.

"If you really believed that you'd lost your soul, then when I found you in Volterra, you would have realized immediately what was happening, instead of thinking we were both dead together. But you didn't—you said '*Amazing. Carlisle was right*,'" I reminded him, triumphant. "There's hope in you, after all."

For once, Edward was speechless.

"So let's both just be hopeful, all right?" I suggested. "Not that it matters. If you stay, I don't need heaven."

He got up slowly, and came to put his hands on either side of my face as he stared into my eyes. "Forever," he vowed, still a little staggered.

"That's all I'm asking for," I said, and stretched up on my toes so that I could press my lips to his.

EPILOGUE—TREATY

ALMOST EVERYTHING WAS BACK TO NORMAL—THE GOOD, pre-zombie normal—in less time than I would have believed possible. The hospital welcomed Carlisle back with eager arms, not even bothering to conceal their delight that Esme had found life in L.A. so little to her liking. Thanks to the Calculus test I'd missed while abroad, Alice and Edward were in better to shape to graduate than I was at the moment. Suddenly, college was a priority (college was still plan B, on the off chance that Edward's offer swayed me from the post-graduation Carlisle option). Many deadlines had passed me by, but Edward had a new stack of applications for me to fill out every day. He'd already done the Harvard route, so it didn't bother him that, thanks to my procrastination, we might both end up at Peninsula Community College next year.

Charlie was not happy with me, or speaking to Edward. But at least Edward was allowed—during my designated visiting hours—inside the house again. I just wasn't allowed *out* of it.

School and work were the only exceptions, and the dreary, dull yellow walls of my classrooms had become oddly inviting to me of late. That had a lot to do with the person who sat in the desk beside me.

Edward had resumed his schedule from the beginning of the year, which put him in most of my classes again. My behavior had been such last fall, after the Cullens' supposed move to L.A., that the seat beside me had never been filled. Even Mike, always eager to take any advantage, had kept a safe distance. With Edward back in place, it was almost as if the last eight months were just a disturbing nightmare.

Almost, but not quite. There was the house arrest situation, for one thing. And for another, before the fall, I hadn't been best friends with Jacob Black. So, of course, I hadn't missed him then.

I wasn't at liberty to go to La Push, and Jacob wasn't coming to see me. He wouldn't even answer my phone calls.

I made these calls mostly at night, after Edward had been kicked out—promptly at nine by a grimly gleeful Charlie—and before Edward snuck back through my window when Charlie was asleep. I chose that time to make my fruitless calls because I'd noticed that Edward made a certain face every time I mentioned Jacob's name. Sort of disapproving and wary . . . maybe even angry. I guessed that he had some reciprocal prejudice against the were-wolves, though he wasn't as vocal as Jacob had been about the "bloodsuckers."

So, I didn't mention Jacob much.

With Edward near me, it was hard to think about un-happy things—even my former best friend, who was prob-ably very unhappy right now, due to me. When I did think of Jake, I always felt guilty for not thinking of him more.

The fairy tale was back on. Prince returned, bad spell broken. I wasn't sure exactly what to do about the leftover, unresolved character. Where was *his* happily ever after?

Weeks passed, and Jacob still wouldn't answer my calls. It started to become a constant worry. Like a dripping faucet in the back of my head that I couldn't shut off or ignore. Drip, drip, drip. Jacob, Jacob, Jacob.

So, though I didn't mention Jacob *much*, sometimes my frustration and anxiety boiled over.

"It's just plain rude!" I vented one Saturday afternoon when Edward picked me up from work. Being angry about things was easier than feeling guilty. "Downright insulting!"

I'd varied my pattern, in hopes of a different response. I'd called Jake from work this time, only to get an unhelp-ful Billy. Again.

"Billy said he didn't *want* to talk to me," I fumed, glaring at the rain oozing down the passenger window.

"That he was there, and wouldn't walk three steps to get to the phone! Usually Billy just says he's out or busy or sleeping or something. I mean, it's not like I didn't know he was lying to me, but at least it was a polite way to handle it. I guess Billy hates me now, too. It's not fair!"

"It's not you, Bella," Edward said quietly. "Nobody hates you."

"Feels that way," I muttered, folding my arms across my chest. It was no more than a stubborn gesture. There was no hole there now—I could barely remember the empty feeling anymore.

"Jacob knows we're back, and I'm sure that he's ascertained that I'm with you," Edward said. "He won't come anywhere near me. The enmity is rooted too deeply."

"That's stupid. He knows you're not . . . like other vampires."

"There's still good reason to keep a safe distance."

I glared blindly out the windshield, seeing only Jacob's face, set in the bitter mask I hated.

"Bella, we are what we are," Edward said quietly. "I can control myself, but I doubt he can. He's very young. It would most likely turn into a fight, and I don't know if I could stop it before I k—" he broke off, and then quickly continued. "Before I hurt him. You would be unhappy. I don't want that to happen."

I remembered what Jacob had said in the kitchen, hearing the words with perfect recall in his husky voice. *I'm not sure that I'm even-tempered enough to handle that. . . . You probably wouldn't like it so much if I killed your friend.* But he'd been able to handle it, that time. . . .

"Edward Cullen," I whispered. "Were you about to say '*killed* him'? Were you?"

He looked away from me, staring into the rain. In front of us, the red light I hadn't noticed turned green and he started forward again, driving very slowly. Not his usual way of driving.

"I would try . . . very hard . . . not to do that," Edward finally said.

I stared at him with my mouth hanging open, but he continued to look straight ahead. We were paused at the corner stop sign.

Abruptly, I remembered what had happened to Paris when Romeo came back. The stage directions were simple: *They fight. Paris falls.*

But that was ridiculous. Impossible.

"Well," I said, and took a deep breath, shaking my head to dispel the words in my head. "Nothing like that is ever going to happen, so there's no reason to worry about it. And you know Charlie's staring at the clock right now. You'd better get me home before I get in more trouble for being late."

I turned my face up toward him, to smile halfheartedly.

Every time I looked at his face, that impossibly perfect face, my heart pounded strong and healthy and very *there* in my chest. This time, the pounding raced ahead of its usual besotted pace. I recognized the expression on his statue-still face.

"You're already in more trouble, Bella," he whispered through unmoving lips.

I slid closer, clutching his arm as I followed his gaze to see what he was seeing. I don't know what I expected—maybe Victoria standing in the middle of the street, her flaming red hair blowing in the wind, or a line of tall black cloaks . . . or a pack of angry werewolves. But I didn't see anything at all.

"What? What is it?"

He took a deep breath. "Charlie . . ."

"My dad?" I screeched.

He looked down at me then, and his expression was calm enough to ease some of my panic.

"Charlie . . . is probably *not* going to kill you, but he's thinking about it," he told me. He started to drive forward again, down my street, but he passed the house and parked by the edge of the trees.

"What did I do?" I gasped.

Edward glanced back at Charlie's house. I followed his gaze, and noticed for the first time what was parked in the driveway next to the cruiser. Shiny, bright red, impossible to miss. My motorcycle, flaunting itself in the driveway.

Edward had said that Charlie was ready to kill me, so he must know that—that it was *mine*. There was only one person who could be behind this treachery.

"No!" I gasped. "*Why?* Why would Jacob do this to me?" The sting of betrayal washed through me. I had trusted Jacob implicitly—trusted him with every single secret I had. He was supposed to be my safe harbor—the person I could always rely on. Of course things were strained right now, but I didn't think any of the underlying foundation had changed. I didn't think that was *changeable*!

What had I done to deserve this? Charlie was going to be so mad—and worse than that, he was going to be hurt and worried. Didn't he have enough to deal with already? I would have never imagined that Jake could be so petty and just plain *mean*. Tears sprang, smarting, into my eyes, but they were not tears of sadness. I had been betrayed. I was suddenly so angry that my head throbbed like it was going to explode.

"Is he still here?" I hissed.

"Yes. He's waiting for us there." Edward told me, nodding toward the slender path that divided the dark fringe of the forest in two.

I jumped out of the car, launching myself toward the trees with my hands already balled into fists for the first punch.

Why did Edward have to be so much faster than me?

He caught me around the waist before I made the path.

"Let me go! I'm going to murder him! *Traitor*!" I shouted the epithet toward the trees.

"Charlie will hear you," Edward warned me. "And once he gets you inside, he may brick over the doorway."

I glanced back at the house instinctively, and it seemed like the glossy red bike was all I could see. I was seeing red. My head throbbed again.

"Just give me one round with Jacob, and then I'll deal with Charlie." I struggled futilely to break free.

"Jacob Black wants to see *me*. That's why he's still here."

That stopped me cold—took the fight right out of me. My hands went limp. *They fight; Paris falls.*

I was furious, but not *that* furious.

"Talk?" I asked.

"More or less."

"How much more?" My voice shook.

Edward smoothed my hair back from my face. "Don't worry, he's not here to fight me. He's acting as . . . spokesperson for the pack."

"Oh."

Edward looked at the house again, then tightened his arm around my waist and pulled me toward the woods. "We should hurry. Charlie's getting impatient."

We didn't have to go far; Jacob waited just a short ways up the path. He lounged against a mossy tree trunk as he waited, his face hard and bitter, exactly the way I knew it would be. He looked at me, and then at Edward. Jacob's mouth stretched into a humorless sneer, and he shrugged away from the tree. He stood on the balls of his bare feet, leaning slightly forward, with his trembling hands clenched into fists. He looked bigger than the last time I'd seen him. Somehow, impossibly, he was still growing. He would tower over Edward, if they stood next to each other.

But Edward stopped as soon as we saw him, leaving a wide space between us and Jacob. Edward turned his body, shifting me so that I was behind him. I leaned around him to stare at Jacob—to accuse him with my eyes.

I would have thought that seeing his resentful, cynical

expression would only make me angrier. Instead, it re-minded me of the last time I'd seen him, with tears in his eyes. My fury weakened, faltered, as I stared at Jacob. It had been so long since I'd seen him—I hated that our reunion had to be like *this*.

"Bella," Jacob said as a greeting, nodding once toward me without looking away from Edward.

"Why?" I whispered, trying to hide the sound of the lump in my throat. "How could you do this to me, Jacob?"

The sneer vanished, but his face stayed hard and rigid. "It's for the best."

"What is *that* supposed to mean? Do you want Charlie to *strangle* me? Or did you want him to have a heart attack, like Harry? No matter how mad you are at me, how could you do this to *him*?"

Jacob winced, and his eyebrows pulled together, but he didn't answer.

"He didn't want to hurt anyone—he just wanted to get you grounded, so that you wouldn't be allowed to spend time with me," Edward murmured, explaining the thoughts Jacob wouldn't say.

Jacob's eyes sparked with hate as he glowered at Edward again.

"Aw, Jake!" I groaned. "I'm *already* grounded! Why do you think I haven't been down to La Push to kick your butt for avoiding my phone calls?"

Jacob's eyes flashed back to me, confused for the first time. "That's why?" he asked, and then locked his jaw, like he was sorry he'd said anything.

"He thought *I* wouldn't let you, not Charlie," Edward explained again.

"Stop that," Jacob snapped.

Edward didn't answer.

Jacob shuddered once, and then gritted his teeth as hard as his fists. "Bella wasn't exaggerating about your . . . abilities," he said through his teeth. "So you must already know why I'm here."

"Yes," Edward agreed in a soft voice. "But, before you begin, I need to say something."

Jacob waited, clenching and unclenching his hands as he tried to control the shivers rolling down his arms.

"Thank you," Edward said, and his voice throbbed with the depth of his sincerity. "I will never be able to tell you how grateful I am. I will owe you for the rest of my . . . existence."

Jacob stared at him blankly, his shudders stilled by surprise. He exchanged a quick glance with me, but my face was just as mystified.

"For keeping Bella alive," Edward clarified, his voice rough and fervent. "When I . . . didn't."

"Edward—," I started to say, but he held one hand up, his eyes on Jacob.

Understanding washed over Jacob's face before the hard mask returned. "I didn't do it for your benefit."

"I know. But that doesn't erase the gratitude I feel. I thought you should know. If there's ever anything in my power to do for you . . ."

Jacob raised one black brow.

Edward shook his head. "That's not in my power."

"Whose, then?" Jacob growled.

Edward looked down at me. "Hers. I'm a quick learner, Jacob Black, and I don't make the same mistake twice. I'm here until she orders me away."

I was immersed momentarily in his golden gaze. It wasn't hard to understand what I'd missed in the conversation. The only thing that Jacob would want from Edward would be his absence.

"Never," I whispered, still locked in Edward's eyes.

Jacob made a gagging sound.

I unwillingly broke free from Edward's gaze to frown at Jacob. "Was there something else you needed, Jacob? You wanted me in trouble—mission accomplished. Charlie might just send me to military school. But that won't keep me away from Edward. There's nothing that can do *that*. What more do you want?"

Jacob kept his eyes on Edward. "I just needed to remind your bloodsucking friends of a few key points in the treaty they agreed to. The treaty that is the only thing stopping me from ripping his throat out right this minute."

"We haven't forgotten," Edward said at the same time that I demanded, "What key points?"

Jacob still glowered at Edward, but he answered me. "The treaty is quite specific. If any of them bite a human, the truce is over. *Bite*, not kill," he emphasized. Finally, he looked at me. His eyes were cold.

It only took me a second to grasp the distinction, and then my face was as cold as his.

"That's none of your business."

"The hell it—" was all he managed to choke out.

I didn't expect my hasty words to bring on such a strong response. Despite the warning he'd come to give, he must not have known. He must have thought the warning was just a precaution. He hadn't realized—or didn't want to believe—that I had already made my choice. That I was really intending to become a member of the Cullen family.

My answer sent Jacob into near convulsions. He pressed his fists hard against his temples, closing his eyes tight and curling in on himself as he tried to control the spasms. His face turned sallow green under the russet skin.

"Jake? You okay?" I asked anxiously.

I took a half-step toward him, then Edward caught me and yanked me back behind his own body. "Careful! He's not under control," he warned me.

But Jacob was already somewhat himself again; only his arms were shaking now. He scowled at Edward with pure hate. "Ugh. *I* would never hurt her."

Neither Edward or I missed the inflection, or the accusation it contained. A low hiss escaped Edward's lips. Jacob clenched his fists reflexively.

"BELLA!" Charlie's roar echoed from the direction of the house. "YOU GET IN THIS HOUSE THIS INSTANT!"

All of us froze, listening to the silence that followed.

I was the first to speak; my voice trembled. "Crap."

Jacob's furious expression faltered. "I *am* sorry about that," he muttered. "I had to do what I could—I had to try. . . ."

"Thanks." The tremor in my voice ruined the sarcasm. I stared up the path, half-expecting Charlie to come barreling through the wet ferns like an enraged bull. I would be the red flag in that scenario.

"Just one more thing," Edward said to me, and then he looked at Jacob. "We've found no trace of Victoria on our side of the line—have you?"

He knew the answer as soon as Jacob thought it, but Jacob spoke the answer anyway. "The last time was while Bella was . . . away. We let her think she was slipping through—we were tightening the circle, getting ready to ambush her—"

Ice shot down my spine.

"But then she took off like a bat out of hell. Near as we can tell, she caught your little female's scent and bailed. She hasn't come near our lands since."

Edward nodded. "When she comes back, she's not your problem anymore. We'll—"

"She killed on our turf," Jacob hissed. "She's ours!"

"No—," I began to protest both declarations.

"*BELLA*! I *SEE* HIS CAR AND I *KNOW* YOU'RE OUT THERE! IF YOU AREN'T *INSIDE* THIS HOUSE IN *ONE* MINUTE . . . !" Charlie didn't bother to finish his threat.

"Let's go," Edward said.

I looked back at Jacob, torn. Would I see him again?

"Sorry," he whispered so low that I had to read his lips to understand. "'Bye, Bells."

"You promised," I reminded him desperately. "Still friends, right?"

Jacob shook his head slowly, and the lump in my throat nearly strangled me.

"You know how hard I've tried to keep that promise, but . . . I can't see how to keep trying. Not now . . ." He struggled to keep his hard mask in place, but it wavered, and then disappeared. "Miss you," he mouthed. One of his hands reached toward me, his fingers outstretched, like he wished they were long enough to cross the distance between us.

"Me, too," I choked out. My hand reached toward his across the wide space.

Like we were connected, the echo of his pain twisted inside me. His pain, my pain.

"Jake . . ." I took a step toward him. I wanted to wrap my arms around his waist and erase the expression of misery on his face.

Edward pulled me back again, his arms restraining instead of defending.

"It's okay," I promised him, looking up to read his face with trust in my eyes. He would understand.

His eyes were unreadable, his face expressionless. Cold. "No, it's not."

"Let her go," Jacob snarled, furious again. "She *wants* to!" He took two long strides forward. A glint of anticipation flashed in his eyes. His chest seemed to swell as it shuddered.

Edward pushed me behind himself, wheeling to face Jacob.

"No! Edward—!"

"ISABELLA *SWAN*!"

"Come on! Charlie's mad!" My voice was panicked, but not because of Charlie now. "Hurry!"

I tugged on him and he relaxed a little. He pulled me back slowly, always keeping his eyes on Jacob as we retreated.

Jacob watched us with a dark scowl on his bitter face. The anticipation drained from his eyes, and then, just before the forest came between us, his face suddenly crumpled in pain.

I knew that last glimpse of his face would haunt me until I saw him smile again.

And right there I vowed that I *would* see him smile, and soon. I would find a way to keep my friend.

Edward kept his arm tight around my waist, holding me close. That was the only thing that held the tears inside my eyes.

I had some serious problems.

My best friend counted me with his enemies.

Victoria was still on the loose, putting everyone I loved in danger.

If I didn't become a vampire soon, the Volturi would kill me.

And now it seemed that if I *did*, the Quileute were-wolves would try to do the job themselves—along with trying to kill my future family. I didn't think they had any chance really, but would my best friend get himself killed in the attempt?

Very serious problems. So why did they all suddenly seem insignificant when we broke through the last of the trees and I caught sight of the expression on Charlie's purple face?

Edward squeezed me gently. "I'm here."

I drew in a deep breath.

That was true. Edward was here, with his arms around me.

I could face anything as long as that was true.

I squared my shoulders and walked forward to meet my fate, with my destiny solidly at my side.

Acknowledgments

⤙ ⤚

So much love and thanks to my husband and sons
for their continuing understanding and sacrifice in support of my writing.
At least I'm not the only one to benefit—I'm sure many local restaurants
are grateful that I don't cook anymore.

Thank you, Mom, for being my best friend and letting me talk your ear off
through all the rough spots. Thanks, also, for being so insanely creative and
intelligent, and bequeathing a small portion of both into my genetic makeup.

Thanks to all my siblings, Emily, Heidi, Paul, Seth, and Jacob,
for letting me borrow your names. I hope I didn't do anything with them
that makes you wish you hadn't.

A special thanks to my brother Paul for the motorcycle riding lesson—
you have a true gift for teaching.

I can't thank my brother Seth enough for all the hard work and genius
he put into the creation of www.stepheniemeyer.com. I'm so grateful for the
effort he continues to expend as my Webmaster. Check's in the mail, kid.
This time, I mean it.

Thanks *again* to my brother Jacob for his ongoing expert advice
on all my automotive choices.

A big thank you to my agent, Jodi Reamer, for her continued guidance
and assistance in my career. And also for enduring my craziness with a smile
when I know she'd like to use some of her ninja moves on me instead.

Love, kisses, and gratitude to my publicist, the beautiful Elizabeth Eulberg,
for making my touring experience less a chore and more a pajama party,
for aiding and abetting my cyber-stalkery, for convincing those exclusive snobs
in the EEC (Elizabeth Eulberg Club) to let me in, and, oh yeah,
also for getting me on the *New York Times* bestseller's list.

A huge vat of thanks to everyone at Little, Brown and Company
for their support and their belief in the potential of my stories.

And, finally, thank you to the talented musicians who inspire me,
particularly the band Muse—there are emotions, scenes, and plot threads in this
novel that were born from Muse songs and would not exist without their genius.
Also Linkin Park, Travis, Elbow, Coldplay, Marjorie Fair, My Chemical Romance,
Brand New, The Strokes, Armor for Sleep, The Arcade Fire, and The Fray
have all been instrumental in staving off the writer's block.

Turn the page for an
Exclusive Preview
of the much-anticipated sequel
to *New Moon*. . . .

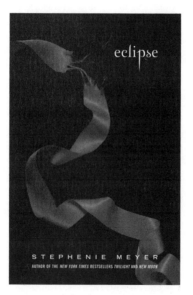

COMING AUGUST 2007

1. ULTIMATUM

Bella,

~~I don't know why you're making~~
~~charlie carry notes to Billy like~~
~~we're in second grade — if I wanted~~
~~to talk to you I would answer the~~

~~You made the choice here, okay?~~
~~You can't have it both ways when~~

~~What part of 'mortal enemies' is too~~
~~complicated for you to~~

~~Look, I know I'm being a jerk, but
there's just no way around~~

~~We can't be friends when you're
spending all your time with a bunch of~~

~~It just makes it worse when I
think about you too much, so don't
write anymore~~

Yeah, I miss you, too. A lot.
Doesn't change anything. Sorry.

Jacob

I ran my fingers across the page, feeling the dents where he had pressed the pen to the paper so hard that it had nearly broken through. I could picture him writing this — scrawling the angry letters in his rough handwriting, slashing through line after line when the words came out wrong, maybe even snapping the pen in his too-big hand; that would explain the ink splatters. I could imagine the frustration pulling his black eyebrows together and crumpling his forehead. If I'd been there, I might have laughed. *Don't give yourself a brain hemorrhage, Jacob,* I would have told him. *Just spit it out.*

Laughing was the last thing I felt like doing now as I reread the words I'd already memorized. His answer to my pleading note — passed from Charlie to Billy to him, just like second grade, as he'd pointed out — was no surprise.

I'd known the essence of what it would say before I'd opened it.

What was surprising was how much each crossed-out line wounded me — as if the points of the letters had cutting edges. More than that, behind each angry beginning lurked a vast pool of hurt; Jacob's pain cut me deeper than my own.

While I was pondering this, I caught the unmistakable scent of a smoking burner rising from the kitchen. In another house, the fact that someone besides myself was cooking might not be a cause for panicking.

I shoved the wrinkled paper into my back pocket and ran. I made it downstairs in the nick of time.

The jar of spaghetti sauce Charlie'd stuck in the microwave was only on its first revolution when I yanked the door open and pulled it out.

"What did I do wrong?" Charlie demanded.

"You're supposed to take the lid off first, Dad. Metal's bad for microwaves." I swiftly removed the lid as I spoke, poured half the sauce into a bowl, and then put the bowl inside the microwave and the jar back in the fridge; I fixed the time and pressed start.

Charlie watched my adjustments with pursed lips. "Did I get the noodles right?"

I looked in the pan on the stove — the source of the smell that had alerted me. "Stirring helps," I said mildly. I found a spoon and tried to de-clump the mushy hunk that was scalded to the bottom.

Charlie sighed.

"So what's all this about?" I asked him.

He folded his arms across his chest and glared out the back windows into the sheeting rain. "Don't know what you're talking about," he grumbled.

I was mystified. Charlie cooking? And what was with the surly attitude? Edward wasn't here yet; usually my dad reserved this kind of behavior for my boyfriend's benefit, doing his best to illustrate the theme of "unwelcome" with every word and posture. Charlie's efforts were unnecessary — Edward knew exactly what my dad was thinking without the show.

The word *boyfriend* had me chewing on the inside of my cheek with a familiar tension while I stirred. It wasn't the right word, not at all. I needed something more expressive of eternal commitment. . . . But words like *destiny* and *fate* sounded hokey when you used them in casual conversation.

Edward had another word in mind, and that word was the source of the tension I felt. It put my teeth on edge just to think it to myself.

Fiancée. Ugh. I shuddered away from the thought.

"Did I miss something? Since when do you make dinner?" I asked Charlie. The pasta lump bobbed in the boiling water as I poked it. "Or *try* to make dinner, I should say."

Charlie shrugged. "There's no law that says I can't cook in my own house."

"You would know," I replied, grinning as I eyed the badge pinned to his leather jacket.

"Ha. Good one." He shrugged out of the jacket as if my glance had reminded him he still had it on, and hung it on the peg reserved for his gear. His gun belt was already slung in place — he hadn't felt the need to wear that to the station for a few weeks. There had been no more disturbing disappearances to trouble the small town of Forks, Washington, no more sightings of the giant, mysterious wolves in the ever-rainy woods. . . .

I prodded the noodles in silence, guessing that Charlie would get around to talking about whatever was bothering him in his own time. My dad was not a man of many words, and the effort he had put into trying to orchestrate a sit-down dinner with me made it clear there were an uncharacteristic number of words on his mind.

I glanced at the clock routinely — something I did every few minutes around this time. Less than a half hour to go now.

Afternoons were the hardest part of my day. Ever since my former best friend (and werewolf), Jacob Black, had informed on me about the motorcycle I'd been riding on the sly — a betrayal he had devised in order to get me grounded so that I couldn't spend time with my boyfriend (and vampire), Edward Cullen — Edward had been allowed to see me only from seven till nine-thirty p.m., always inside the confines of my home and under the supervision of my dad's unfailingly crabby glare.

This was an escalation from the previous, slightly less stringent grounding that I'd earned for an unexplained three-day disappearance and one episode of cliff diving.

Of course, I still saw Edward at school, because there wasn't anything Charlie could do about that. And then, Edward spent almost every night in my room, too, but Charlie wasn't precisely aware of that. Edward's ability to climb easily and silently through my second-story window was almost as useful as his ability to read Charlie's mind.

Though the afternoon was the only time I spent away from Edward, it was enough to make me restless, and the hours always dragged. Still, I endured my punishment without complaining because — for one thing — I knew I'd earned it, and — for another — because I couldn't bear to hurt my dad by moving out now, when a much more permanent separation hovered, invisible to Charlie, so close on my horizon.

My dad sat down at the table with a grunt and unfolded the damp newspaper there; within seconds he was clucking his tongue in disapproval.

"I don't know why you read the paper, Dad. It only ticks you off."

He ignored me, grumbling at the paper in his hands. "This is why everyone wants to live in a small town! Ridiculous."

"What have big cities done wrong now?"

"Seattle's making a run for murder capitol of the country. Five unsolved homicides in the last two weeks. Can you imagine living like that?"

"I think Phoenix is actually higher up the homicide list, Dad. I *have* lived like that." And I'd never come close to being a murder victim until after I moved to his safe little town. In fact, I was still on several hit lists. . . . The spoon shook in my hands, making the water tremble.

"Well, you couldn't pay me enough," Charlie said.

I gave up on saving dinner and settled for serving it; I had to use a steak knife to cut a portion of spaghetti for

Charlie and then myself, while he watched with a sheepish expression. Charlie coated his helping with sauce and dug in. I disguised my own clump as well as I could and followed his example without much enthusiasm. We ate in silence for a moment. Charlie was still scanning the news, so I picked up my much-abused copy of *Wuthering Heights* from where I'd left it this morning at breakfast, and tried to lose myself in turn-of-the-century England while I waited for him to start talking.

I was just to the part where Heathcliff returns when Charlie cleared his throat and threw the paper to the floor.

"You're right," Charlie said. "I did have a reason for doing this." He waved his fork at the gluey spread. "I wanted to talk to you."

I laid the book aside; the binding was so destroyed that it slumped flat to the table. "You could have just asked."

He nodded, his eyebrows pulling together. "Yeah. I'll remember that next time. I thought taking dinner off your hands would soften you up."

I laughed. "It worked — your cooking skills have me soft as a marshmallow. What do you need, Dad?"

"Well, it's about Jacob."

I felt my face harden. "What about him?" I asked through stiff lips.

"Easy, Bells. I know you're still upset that he told on you, but it was the right thing. He was being responsible."

"Responsible," I repeated scathingly, rolling my eyes. "Right. So, what about Jacob?"

The careless question repeated inside my head, anything but trivial. *What about Jacob?* What *was* I going to do about him? My former best friend who was now . . . what? My enemy? I cringed.

Charlie's face was suddenly wary. "Don't get mad at me, okay?"

"Mad?"

"Well, it's about Edward, too."

My eyes narrowed.

Charlie's voice got gruffer. "I let him in the house, don't I?"

"You do," I admitted. "For brief periods of time. Of course, you might let me *out* of the house for brief periods now and then, too," I continued — only jokingly; I knew I was on lockdown for the duration of the school year. "I've been pretty good lately."

"Well, that's kind of where I was heading with this. . . ." And then Charlie's face stretched into an unexpected eye-crinkling grin; for a second he looked twenty years younger.

I saw a dim glimmer of possibility in that smile, but I proceeded slowly. "I'm confused, Dad. Are we talking about Jacob, or Edward, or me being grounded?"

The grin flashed again. "Sort of all three."

"And how do they relate?" I asked, cautious.

"Okay." He sighed, raising his hands as if in surrender. "So I'm thinking maybe you deserve a parole for good behavior. For a teenager, you're amazingly non-whiney."

My voice and eyebrows shot up. "Seriously? I'm free?"

Where was this coming from? I'd been positive I would be under house arrest until I actually moved out, and Edward hadn't picked up any wavering in Charlie's thoughts. . . .

Charlie held up one finger. "Conditionally."

The enthusiasm vanished. "Fantastic," I groaned.

"Bella, this is more of a request than a demand, okay? You're free. But I'm hoping you'll use that freedom . . . judiciously."

"What does that mean?"

He sighed again. "I know you're satisfied to spend all of your time with Edward —"

"I spend time with Alice, too," I interjected. Edward's sister had no hours of visitation; she came and went as she pleased. Charlie was putty in her capable hands.

"That's true," he said. "But you have other friends besides the Cullens, Bella. Or you *used* to."

We stared at each other for a long moment.

"When was the last time you spoke to Angela Weber?" he threw at me.

"Friday at lunch," I answered immediately.

Before Edward's return, my school friends had polarized into two groups. I liked to think of those groups as *good* vs. *evil*. *Us* and *them* worked, too. The good guys were Angela, her steady boyfriend Ben Cheney, and Mike Newton; these three had all very generously forgiven me for going crazy when Edward left. Lauren Mallory was the evil core of the *them* side, and almost everyone else, including my first friend in Forks, Jessica Stanley, seemed content to go along with her anti-Bella agenda.

With Edward back at school, the dividing line had

become even more distinct. Edward's return had taken its toll on Mike's friendship, but Angela was unswervingly loyal, and Ben followed her lead. Despite the natural aversion most humans felt toward the Cullens, Angela sat dutifully beside Alice every day at lunch. After a few weeks, Angela even looked comfortable there. It was difficult not to be charmed by the Cullens — once one gave them the chance to be charming.

"Outside of school?" Charlie asked, calling my attention back.

"I haven't seen *anyone* outside of school, Dad. Grounded, remember? And Angela has a boyfriend, too. She's always with Ben. *If* I'm really free," I added, heavy on the skepticism, "maybe we could double."

"Okay. But then . . ." He hesitated. "You and Jake used to be joined at the hip, and now —"

I cut him off. "Can you get to the point, Dad? What's your condition — exactly?"

"I don't think you should dump all your other friends for your boyfriend, Bella," he said in a stern voice. "It's not nice, and I think your life would be better balanced if you kept some other people in it. What happened last September . . ."

I flinched.

"Well," he said defensively. "If you'd had more of a life outside of Edward Cullen, it might not have been like that."

"It would have been exactly like that," I muttered.

"Maybe, maybe not."

"The point?" I reminded him.

"Use your new freedom to see your other friends, too. Keep it balanced."

I nodded slowly. "Balance is good. Do I have specific time quotas to fill, though?"

He made a face, but shook his head. "I don't want to make this complicated. Just don't forget your friends — particularly Jacob."

It took me a moment to find the right words. "Jacob might be . . . difficult."

"The Blacks are practically family, Bella," he said, stern and fatherly again. "And Jacob has been a very, *very* good friend to you."

"I know that."

"Don't you miss him at all?" Charlie asked, frustrated.

My throat suddenly felt swollen; I had to clear it twice before I answered. "Yes, I do miss him," I admitted, still looking down. "I miss him a lot."

"Then why is it difficult?"

It wasn't something I was at liberty to explain. It was against the rules for normal people — *human* people like me and Charlie — to know about the clandestine world full of myths and monsters that existed secretly around us. I knew all about that world — and I was in no small amount of trouble as a result. I wasn't about to get Charlie in the same trouble.

"With Jacob there is a . . . conflict," I said slowly. "A conflict about the friendship thing, I mean. Friendship doesn't always seem to be enough for Jake." I wound my excuse out of details that were true but insignificant, hardly crucial compared to the fact that Jacob's werewolf pack bitterly hated Edward's vampire family — and therefore me, too, as I fully intended to join that family. It just wasn't something I could work out with him in a note, and he wouldn't answer my calls. But my plan to deal with the werewolf in person had definitely not gone over well with the vampires.

"Isn't Edward up for a little healthy competition?" Charlie's voice was sarcastic now.

I leveled a dark look at him. "There's no competition."

"You're hurting Jake's feelings, avoiding him like this. He'd rather be just friends than nothing."

Oh, now *I* was avoiding *him*?

"I'm pretty sure Jake doesn't want to be friends at all." The words burned in my mouth. "Where'd you get that idea, anyway?"

Charlie looked embarrassed now. "The subject might have come up today with Billy. . . ."

"You and Billy gossip like old women," I complained, stabbing my fork viciously into the congealed spaghetti on my plate.

"Billy's worried about Jacob," Charlie said. "Jake's having a hard time right now. . . . He's depressed."

I winced, but kept my eyes on the blob.

"And then you were always so happy after spending the day with Jake." Charlie sighed.

"I'm happy *now*," I growled fiercely through my teeth.

The contrast between my words and tone broke through the tension. Charlie burst into laughter, and I had to join in.

"Okay, okay," I agreed. "Balance."

"And Jacob," he insisted.

"I'll try."

"Good. Find that balance, Bella. And, oh, yeah, you've got some mail," Charlie said, closing the subject with no attempt at subtlety. "It's by the stove."

I didn't move, my thoughts twisting into snarls around Jacob's name. It was most likely junk mail; I'd just gotten a package from my mom yesterday and I wasn't expecting anything else.

Charlie shoved his chair away from the table and stretched as he got to his feet. He took his plate to the sink, but before he turned the water on to rinse it, he paused to toss a thick envelope at me. The letter skidded across the table and *thunk*ed into my elbow.

"Er, thanks," I muttered, puzzled by his pushiness. Then I saw the return address — the letter was from the University of Alaska Southeast. "That was quick. I guess I missed the deadline on that one, too."

Charlie chuckled.

I flipped the envelope over and then glared up at him. "It's open."

"I was curious."

"I'm shocked, Sheriff. That's a federal crime."

"Oh, just read it."

I pulled out the letter, and a folded schedule of courses.

"Congratulations," he said before I could read anything. "Your first acceptance."

"Thanks, Dad."

"We should talk about tuition. I've got some money saved up —"

"Hey, hey, none of that. I'm not touching your retirement, Dad. I've got my college fund." What was left of it — and there hadn't been much to begin with.

Charlie frowned. "Some of these places are pretty pricey, Bells. I want to help. You don't have to go all the way to Alaska just because it's cheaper."

It wasn't cheaper, not at all. But it *was* far away, and Juneau had an average of three hundred twenty-one overcast days per year. The first was my prerequisite, the second was Edward's.

"I've got it covered. Besides, there's lots of financial aid out there. It's easy to get loans." I hoped my bluff wasn't too obvious. I hadn't actually done a lot of research on the subject.

"So . . . ," Charlie began, and then he pursed his lips and looked away.

"So what?"

"Nothing. I was just . . ." He frowned. "Just wondering what . . . Edward's plans are for next year?"

"Oh."

"Well?"

Three quick raps on the door saved me. Charlie rolled his eyes and I jumped up.

"Coming!" I called while Charlie mumbled something that sounded like, "Go away." I ignored him and went to let Edward in.

I wrenched the door out of my way — ridiculously eager — and there he was, my personal miracle.

Time had not made me immune to the perfection of his face, and I was sure that I would never take any aspect of him for granted. My eyes traced over his pale white features: the hard square of his jaw, the softer curve of his full lips — twisted up into a smile now, the straight line of his nose, the sharp angle of his cheekbones, the smooth marble span of his forehead — partially obscured by a tangle of rain-darkened bronze hair. . . .

I saved his eyes for last, knowing that when I looked into them I was likely to lose my train of thought. They were wide, warm with liquid gold, and framed by a thick fringe of black lashes. Staring into his eyes always made me feel extraordinary — sort of like my bones were turning spongy. I was also a little lightheaded, but that could have been because I'd forgotten to keep breathing. Again.

It was a face any male model in the world would trade his soul for. Of course, that might be exactly the asking price: one soul.

No. I didn't believe that. I felt guilty for even thinking it, and was glad — as I was often glad — that I was the one person whose thoughts were a mystery to Edward.

I reached for his hand, and sighed when his cold fingers found mine. His touch brought with it the strangest sense of relief — as if I'd been in pain and that pain had suddenly ceased.

"Hey." I smiled a little at my anticlimactic greeting.

He raised our interlaced fingers to brush my cheek with the back of his hand. "How was your afternoon?"

"Slow."

"For me, as well."

He pulled my wrist up to his face, our hands still twisted together. His eyes closed as his nose skimmed along the skin there, and he smiled gently without opening them. Enjoying the bouquet while resisting the wine, as he'd once put it.

I knew that the scent of my blood — so much sweeter to him than any other person's blood, truly like wine beside water to an alcoholic — caused him actual pain from the burning thirst it engendered. But he didn't seem to shy away from it as much as he once had. I could only dimly imagine the Herculean effort behind this simple gesture.

It made me sad that he had to try so hard. I comforted myself with the knowledge that I wouldn't be causing him pain much longer.

I heard Charlie approaching then, stamping his feet on the way to express his customary displeasure with our guest. Edward's eyes snapped open and he let our hands fall, keeping them twined.

"Good evening, Charlie." Edward was always flawlessly polite, though Charlie didn't deserve it.

Charlie grunted at him, and then stood there with his arms crossed over his chest. He was taking the idea of parental supervision to extremes lately.

"I brought another set of applications," Edward told me then, holding up a stuffed manila envelope. He was wearing a roll of stamps like a ring around his littlest finger.

I groaned. How were there any colleges left that he hadn't forced me to apply to already? And how did he keep finding these loophole openings? It was so late in the year.

He smiled as if he *could* read my thoughts; they must

have been very obvious on my face. "There are still a few open deadlines. And a few places willing to make exceptions."

I could just imagine the motivations behind such exceptions. And the dollar amounts involved.

Edward laughed at my expression.

"Shall we?" he asked, towing me toward the kitchen table.

Charlie huffed and followed behind, though he could hardly complain about the activity on tonight's agenda. He'd been pestering me to make a decision about college on a daily basis.

I cleared the table quickly while Edward organized an intimidating stack of forms. When I moved *Wuthering Heights* to the counter, Edward raised one eyebrow. I knew what he was thinking, but Charlie interrupted before Edward could comment.

"Speaking of college applications, Edward," Charlie said, his tone even more sullen — he tried to avoid addressing Edward directly, and when he had to, it exacerbated his bad mood. "Bella and I were just talking about next year. Have you decided where you're going to school?"

Edward smiled up at Charlie and his voice was friendly. "Not yet. I've received a few acceptance letters, but I'm still weighing my options."

"Where have you been accepted?" Charlie pressed.

"Syracuse . . . Harvard . . . Dartmouth . . . and I just got accepted to the University of Alaska Southeast today." Edward turned his face slightly to the side so that he could wink at me. I stifled a giggle.

"Harvard? Dartmouth?" Charlie mumbled, unable to conceal his awe. "Well that's pretty . . . that's something. Yeah, but the University of Alaska . . . you wouldn't really consider that when you could go Ivy League. I mean, your father would want you to . . . ."

"Carlisle's always fine with whatever I choose to do," Edward told him serenely.

"Hmph."

"Guess what, Edward?" I asked in a bright voice, playing along.

"What, Bella?"

I pointed to the thick envelope on the counter. "I just got *my* acceptance to the University of Alaska!"

"Congratulations!" He grinned. "What a coincidence."

Charlie's eyes narrowed and he glared back and forth between the two of us. "Fine," he muttered after a minute. "I'm going to go watch the game, Bella. Nine-thirty."

That was his usual parting command.

"Er, Dad? Remember the very recent discussion about my freedom . . . ?"

He sighed. "Right. Okay, *ten*-thirty. You still have a curfew on school nights."

"Bella's no longer grounded?" Edward asked. Though I knew he wasn't really surprised, I couldn't detect any false note to the sudden excitement in his voice.

"Conditionally," Charlie corrected through his teeth. "What's it to you?"

I frowned at my dad, but he didn't see.

"It's just good to know," Edward said. "Alice has been

itching for a shopping partner, and I'm sure Bella would love to see some city lights." He smiled at me.

But Charlie growled, "No!" and his face flushed purple.

"Dad! What's the problem?"

He made an effort to unclench his teeth. "I don't want you going to Seattle right now."

"Huh?"

"I told you about that story in the paper — there's some kind of gang on a killing spree in Seattle and I want you to steer clear, okay?"

I rolled my eyes. "Dad, there's a better chance that I'll get struck by lightning than that the one day I'm in Seattle —"

"No, that's fine, Charlie," Edward said, interrupting me. "I didn't mean Seattle. I was thinking Portland, actually. I wouldn't have Bella in Seattle, either. Of course not."

I looked at him in disbelief, but he had Charlie's newspaper in his hands and he was reading the front page intently.

He must have been trying to placate my dad. The idea of being in danger from even the most deadly of humans while I was with Alice or Edward was downright hilarious.

It worked. Charlie stared at Edward for one second more, and then shrugged. "Fine." He stalked off toward the living room, in a bit of a hurry now — maybe he didn't want to miss tip-off.

I waited till the TV was on, so that Charlie wouldn't be able to hear me.

"What — ," I started to ask.

"Hold on," Edward said without looking up from the paper. His eyes stayed focused on the page as he pushed the first application toward me across the table. "I think you can recycle your essays for this one. Same questions."

Charlie must still be listening. I sighed and started to fill out the repetitive information: name, address, social. . . . After a few minutes I glanced up, but Edward was now staring pensively out the window. As I bent my head back to my work, I noticed for the first time the name of the school.

I snorted and shoved the papers aside.

"Bella?"

"Be serious, Edward. *Dartmouth?*"

Edward lifted the discarded application and laid it gently in front of me again. "I think you'd like New Hampshire," he said. "There's a full complement of night courses for me, and the forests are very conveniently located for the avid hiker. Plentiful wildlife." He pulled out the crooked smile he knew I couldn't resist.

I took a deep breath through my nose.

"I'll let you pay me back, if that makes you happy," he promised. "If you want, I can charge you interest."

"Like I could even get in without some enormous bribe. Or was that part of the loan? The new Cullen wing of the library? Ugh. Why are we having this discussion again?"

"Will you just fill out the application, please, Bella? It won't hurt you to apply."

My jaw flexed. "You know what? I don't think I will."

I reached for the papers, planning to crumple them

into a suitable shape for lobbing at the trashcan, but they were already gone. I stared at the empty table for a moment, and then at Edward. He didn't appear to have moved, but the application was probably already tucked away in his jacket.

"What are you doing?" I demanded.

"I sign your name better than you do yourself. You've already written the essays."

"You're going way overboard with this, you know." I whispered on the off chance that Charlie wasn't completely lost in his game. "I really don't need to apply anywhere else. I've been accepted in Alaska. I can almost afford the first semester's tuition. It's as good an alibi as any. There's no need to throw away a bunch of money, no matter whose it is."

A pained looked tightened his face. "Bella —"

"Don't start. I agree that I need to go through the motions for Charlie's sake, but we both know I'm not going to be in any condition to go to school next fall. To be anywhere near people."

My knowledge of those first few years as a new vampire was sketchy. Edward had never gone into details — it wasn't his favorite subject — but I knew it wasn't pretty. Self-control was apparently an acquired skill. Anything more than correspondence school was out of the question.

"I thought the timing was still undecided," Edward reminded me softly. "You might enjoy a semester or two of college. There are a lot of human experiences you've never had."

"I'll get to those afterward."

"They won't be *human* experiences afterward. You don't get a second chance at humanity, Bella."

I sighed. "You've got to be reasonable about the timing, Edward. It's just too dangerous to mess around with."

"There's no danger yet," he insisted.

I glared at him. No danger? Sure. I only had a sadistic vampire trying to avenge her mate's death with my own, preferably through some slow and torturous method. Who was worried about Victoria? And, oh yeah, the Volturi — the vampire royal family with their small army of vampire warriors — who insisted that my heart stop beating one way or another in the near future, because humans weren't allowed to know they existed. Right. No reason at all to panic.

Even with Alice keeping watch — Edward was relying on her uncannily accurate visions of the future to give us advance warning — it was insane to take chances.

Besides, I'd already won this argument. The date for my transformation was tentatively set for shortly after my graduation from high school, only a handful of weeks away.

A sharp jolt of unease pierced my stomach as I realized how short the time really was. Of course this change was necessary — and the key to what I wanted more than everything else in the world put together — but I was deeply conscious of Charlie sitting in the other room enjoying his game, just like every other night. And my mother, Renée, far away in sunny Florida, still pleading with me to spend the summer on the beach with her and her new husband. And Jacob, who, unlike my parents, would know exactly what was going on when I disappeared to some distant school. Even if my parents didn't grow suspicious for a long time, even if I could put off visits with excuses about travel expenses or study loads or illnesses, Jacob would know the truth.

For a moment, the idea of Jacob's certain revulsion overshadowed every other pain.

"Bella," Edward murmured, his face twisting when he read the distress in mine. "There's no hurry. I won't let anyone hurt you. You can take all the time you need."

"I want to hurry," I whispered, smiling weakly, trying to make a joke of it. "I want to be a monster, too."

His teeth clenched; he spoke through them. "You have no idea what you're saying." Abruptly, he flung the damp newspaper onto the table in between us. His finger stabbed the headline on the front page:

DEATH TOLL ON THE RISE, POLICE FEAR GANG ACTIVITY

"What does that have to do with anything?"

"Monsters are not a joke, Bella."

I stared at the headline again, and then up to his hard expression. "A . . . a *vampire* is doing this?" I whispered.

He smiled without humor. His voice was low and cold. "You'd be surprised, Bella, at how often my kind are the source behind the horrors in your human news. It's easy to recognize, when you know what to look for. The information here indicates a newborn vampire is loose in Seattle. Bloodthirsty, wild, out of control. The way we all were."

I let my gaze drop to the paper again, avoiding his eyes.

"We've been monitoring the situation for a few weeks. All the signs are there — the unlikely disappearances, always in the night, the poorly disposed-of corpses, the lack of other evidence. . . . Yes, someone brand-new. And no one seems to be taking responsibility for the neophyte. . . ." He took a deep breath. "Well, it's not our problem. We wouldn't even pay attention to the situation if wasn't going on so close to home. Like I said, this happens all the time. The existence of monsters results in monstrous consequences."

I tried not to see the names on the page, but they jumped out from the rest of the print like they were in bold. The five people whose lives were over, whose families were mourning now. It was different from considering murder in the abstract, reading those names. Maureen Gardiner, Geoffrey Campbell, Grace Razi, Michelle O'Connell, Ronald Albrook. People who'd had parents and children and friends and pets and jobs and hopes and plans and memories and futures. . . .

"It won't be the same for me," I whispered, half to myself. "You won't let me be like that. We'll live in Antarctica."

Edward snorted, breaking the tension. "Penguins. Lovely."

I laughed a shaky laugh and knocked the paper off the table so I wouldn't have to see those names; it hit the linoleum with a thud. Of course Edward would consider the hunting possibilities. He and his "vegetarian" family — all committed to protecting human life — preferred the flavor of large predators for satisfying their dietary needs. "Alaska, then, as planned. Only somewhere much more remote than Juneau — somewhere with grizzlies galore."

"Better," he allowed. "There are polar bears, too. Very fierce. And the wolves get quite large."

My mouth fell open and my breath blew out in a sharp gust.

"What's wrong?" he asked. Before I could recover, the confusion vanished and his whole body seemed to harden. "Oh. Never mind the wolves, then, if the idea is offensive to you." His voice was stiff, formal, his shoulders rigid.

"He was my best friend, Edward," I muttered. It stung to use the past tense. "Of course the idea offends me."

"Please forgive my thoughtlessness," he said, still very formal. "I shouldn't have suggested that."

"Don't worry about it." I stared at my hands, clenched into a double fist on the table.

We were both silent for a moment, and then his cool finger was under my chin, coaxing my face up. His expression was much softer now.

"Sorry. Really."

"I know. I know it's not the same thing. I shouldn't have reacted that way. It's just that . . . well, I was already thinking about Jacob before you came over." I hesitated. His tawny eyes seemed to get a little bit darker whenever I said Jacob's name. My voice turned pleading in response. "Charlie says Jake is having a hard time. He's hurting right now, and . . . it's my fault."

"You've done nothing wrong, Bella."

I took a deep breath. "I need to make it better, Edward. I owe him that. And it's one of Charlie's conditions, anyway —"

His face changed while I spoke, turning hard again, statue-like.

"You know it's out of the question for you to be around a werewolf unprotected, Bella. And it would break the treaty if any of us cross over onto their land. Do you want us to start a war?"

"Of course not!"

"Then there's really no point in discussing the matter further." He dropped his hand and looked away, searching for a subject change. His eyes paused on something behind me, and he smiled, though his eyes stayed wary.

"I'm glad Charlie has decided to let you out — you're sadly in need of a visit to the bookstore. I can't believe you're reading *Wuthering Heights* again. Don't you know it by heart yet?"

"Not all of us have photographic memories," I said curtly.

"Photographic memory or not, I don't understand why you like it. The characters are ghastly people who ruin each others' lives. I don't know how Heathcliff and Cathy ended up being ranked with couples like Romeo and Juliet or Elizabeth Bennet and Mr. Darcy. It isn't a love story, it's a hate story."

"You have some serious issues with the classics," I snapped.

"Perhaps it's because I'm not impressed by antiquity." He smiled, evidently satisfied that he'd distracted me.

"Honestly, though, why *do* you read it over and over?" His eyes were vivid with real interest now, trying — again — to unravel the convoluted workings of my mind. He reached across the table to cradle my face in his hand. "What is it that appeals to you?"

His sincere curiosity disarmed me. "I'm not sure," I said, scrambling for coherency while his gaze unintentionally scattered my thoughts. "I think it's something about the inevitability. How nothing can keep them apart — not her selfishness, or his evil, or even death, in the end. . . ."

His face was thoughtful as he considered my words. After a moment he smiled a teasing smile. "I still think it would be a better story if either of them had one redeeming quality."

"I think that may be the point," I disagreed. "Their love *is* their only redeeming quality."

"I hope you have better sense than that — to fall in love with someone so . . . malignant."

"It's a bit late for me to worry about who I fall in love with," I pointed out. "But even without the warning, I seem to have managed fairly well."

He laughed quietly. "I'm glad *you* think so."

"Well, I hope you're smart enough to stay away from someone so selfish. Catherine is really the source of all the trouble, not Heathcliff."

"I'll be on my guard," he promised.

I sighed. He was so good at distractions.

I put my hand over his to hold it to my face. "I need to see Jacob."

His eyes closed. "No."

"It's truly not dangerous at all," I said, pleading again. "I used to spend all day in La Push with the whole lot of them, and nothing ever happened."

But I made a slip; my voice faltered at the end because I realized as I was saying the words that they were a lie. It was not true that *nothing* had ever happened. A brief flash of memory — an enormous gray wolf crouched to spring, baring his dagger-like teeth at me — had my palms sweating with an echo of remembered panic.

Edward heard my heart accelerate and nodded as if I'd acknowledged the lie aloud. "Werewolves are unstable. Sometimes the people near them get hurt. Sometimes, they get killed."

I wanted to deny it, but another image slowed my rebuttal. I saw in my head the once beautiful face of Emily Young, now marred by a trio of dark scars that dragged down the corner of her right eye and left her mouth warped forever into a lopsided scowl.

He waited, grimly triumphant, for me to find my voice.

"You don't know them," I whispered.

"I know them better than you think, Bella. I was here the last time."

"The last time?"

"We started crossing paths with the wolves about seventy years ago. . . . We had just settled near Hoquiam. That was before Alice and Jasper were with us. We outnumbered them, but that wouldn't have stopped it from turning into a fight if not for Carlisle. He managed to convince Ephraim Black that coexisting was possible, and eventually we made the truce."

Jacob's great-grandfather's name startled me.

"We thought the line had died out with Ephraim," Edward muttered; it sounded like he was talking to himself now. "That the genetic quirk which allowed the transmutation had been lost. . . ." He broke off and stared at me accusingly. "Your bad luck seems to get more potent every day. Do you realize that your insatiable pull for all things deadly was strong enough to recover a pack of mutant canines from extinction? If we could bottle your luck, we'd have a weapon of mass destruction on our hands."

I ignored the ribbing, my attention caught by his assumption — was he serious? "But *I* didn't bring them back. Don't you know?"

"Know what?"

"My bad luck had nothing to do with it. The werewolves came back because the vampires did."

Edward stared at me, his body motionless with surprise.

"Jacob told me that your family being here set things in motion. I thought you would already know. . . ."

His eyes narrowed. "Is that what they think?"

"Edward, look at the facts. Seventy years ago, you came here, and the werewolves showed up. You come back now, and the werewolves show up again. Do you think that's a coincidence?"

He blinked and his glare relaxed. "Carlisle will be interested in that theory."

"Theory," I scoffed.

He was silent for a moment, staring out the window into the rain; I imagined he was contemplating the fact that his family's presence was turning the locals into giant dogs.

"Interesting, but not exactly relevant," he murmured after a moment. "The situation remains the same."

I could translate that easily enough: no werewolf friends.

I knew I must be patient with Edward. It wasn't that he was unreasonable, it was just that he didn't *understand.* He had no idea how very much I owed Jacob Black — my life many times over, and possibly my sanity, too.

I didn't like to talk about that barren time with anyone, and especially not Edward. He had only been trying to save me when he'd left, trying to save my soul. I didn't hold him responsible for all the stupid things I'd done in his absence, or the pain I had suffered.

He did.

So I would have to word my explanation very carefully.

I got up and walked around the table. He opened his arms for me and I sat on his lap, nestling into his cool stone embrace. I looked at his hands while I spoke.

"Please just listen for a minute. This is so much more important than some whim to drop in on an old friend. Jacob is in *pain.*" My voice distorted around the word. "I can't *not* try to help him — I can't give up on him now, when he needs me. Just because he's not human all the time. . . . Well, he was there for me when I was . . . not so human myself. You don't know what it was like. . . ." I hesitated. Edward's arms were rigid around me; his hands were in fists now, the tendons standing out. "If Jacob hadn't helped me . . . I'm not sure what you would have come home to. I have to try to make it better. I owe him better than this, Edward."

I looked up at his face warily. His eyes were closed, and his jaw was strained.

"I'll never forgive myself for leaving you," he whispered. "Not if I live a hundred thousand years."

I put my hand against his cold face and waited until he sighed and opened his eyes.

"You were just trying to do the right thing. And I'm sure it would have worked with anyone less mental than me. Besides, you're here now. That's the part that matters."

"If I'd never left, you wouldn't feel the need to go risk your life to comfort a *dog*."

I flinched. I was used to Jacob and all his derogatory slurs — *bloodsucker, leech, parasite*. . . . Somehow it sounded harsher in Edward's velvet voice.

"I don't know how to phrase this properly," Edward said, and his tone was bleak. "It's going to sound cruel, I suppose. But I've come too close to losing you in the past. I know what it feels like to think I have. I am *not* going to tolerate anything dangerous."

"You have to trust me on this. I'll be fine."

His face was pained again. "Please, Bella," he whispered.

I stared into his suddenly burning golden eyes. "Please what?"

"Please, for me. Please make a conscious effort to keep

yourself safe. I'll do everything I can, but I would appreciate a little help."

"I'll work on it," I murmured.

"Do you really have any idea how important you are to me? Any concept at all of how much I love you?" He pulled me tighter against his hard chest, tucking my head under his chin.

I pressed my lips against his snow-cold neck. "I know how much *I* love *you*," I answered.

"You compare one small tree to the entire forest."

I rolled my eyes, but he couldn't see. "Impossible."

He kissed the top of my head and sighed.

"No werewolves."

"I'm not going along with that. I have to see Jacob."

"Then I'll have to stop you."

He sounded utterly confident that this wouldn't be a problem.

I was sure he was right.

"We'll see about that," I bluffed anyway. "He's still my friend."

I could feel Jacob's note in my pocket, like it suddenly weighed ten pounds. I could hear the words in his voice, and he seemed to be agreeing with Edward — something that would never happen in reality.

Doesn't change anything. Sorry.